Praise for *Song of Slaves in the Desert*

"Cheuse passionately evokes a vanished world of master and slave, Jew and Gentile, all hurtling toward the tumult and destruction of war. The novel is full of the loss and longing that come with a world divided forever, people from their people and from their past. Fascinating."

—Lynn Freed, author of *The Servants' Quarters*

"Cheuse shows that in one way or another, we all experience slavery, and that freedom is never given but must be taken at all cost. Using a mix of myth, history, and superb imagination, Cheuse takes us back to Africa, the middle passage, and the slave-owning South to illustrate where and when 'this national horror and the deep bloodstain upon our nation first began.' The book's epic vision is deeply human and humane…its central message is as relevant now as it was in the days of slavery: that slavery, and indeed all forms of oppression and human subjugation, and how it 'bent bodies to the pleasure and finances of the owners was nothing, nothing, compared to the way it bent souls.'"

—Helon Habila, author of
Waiting for an Angel and *Measuring Time*

"Alan Cheuse, one of our most respected men of letters, has written a daring, provocative novel. Some readers will be captivated by his depiction of the horrors of slavery and Jewish involvement in the peculiar institution, and others will be troubled and perhaps even offended, for the subject of race in America is always controversial, but no one who reads *Song of Slaves in the Desert* will emerge from its pages unaffected."

—Charles Johnson, author of the
National Book Award winner *Middle Passage*

"A novelist's dream is to conjure up a whole world, one the reader can tumble right into and inhabit. I fell into Alan Cheuse's *Song of Slaves in the Desert* like that. I confess I felt a twinge of envy at Cheuse's success, his fully imagined song and its people. But the envy immediately gave way to gratitude for having had the chance to enter and treasure the world he's made here."

—Josephine Humphreys, author of *Dreams of Sleep*

For my dear Jeanne —

this copy of

SONG

of

SLAVES

in the

DESERT

With much love & affection —

Alan

Santa Cruz
July, 2011

SONG

of

SLAVES

in the

DESERT

Alan Cheuse

ALAN CHEUSE

sourcebooks
landmark

Published by Sourcebooks Landmark, an imprint of Sourcebooks, Inc.
P.O. Box 4410, Naperville, Illinois 60567-4410
(630) 961-3900
Fax: (630) 961-2168
www.sourcebooks.com

Library of Congress Cataloging-in-Publication Data

Cheuse, Alan.
  Song of slaves in the desert / by Alan Cheuse.
    p. cm.
  1. Slavery--Africa--History--Fiction. 2. Slavery--Southern States--History-
-Fiction. 3. Plantations--Southern States--History--Fiction. 4. Jews--Southern
States--History--Fiction. 5. Jewish fiction. I. Title.
  PS3553.H436S66 2011
  813'.54--dc22
                              2010048514

                Printed and bound in the United States of America.
                    BG 10 9 8 7 6 5 4 3 2 1

Other Books by Alan Cheuse

Fiction
Candace & Other Stories
The Bohemians
The Grandmothers' Club
The Tennessee Waltz
The Light Possessed
Lost and Old Rivers
The Fires
To Catch the Lightning

Nonfiction
Fall Out of Heaven
Listening to the Page: Adventures in Reading and Writing
A Trance After Breakfast

Books Edited
The Sound of Writing (with Caroline Marshall)
Listening to Ourselves (with Caroline Marshall)
Talking Horse: Bernard Malamud on Life and Work (with Nicholas Delbanco)
*Writers Workshop in a Book: The Squaw Valley Community of Writers on
The Art of Fiction* (with Lisa Alvarez)
Seeing Ourselves: Great Early American Short Fiction
Literature: Craft & Voice (with Nicholas Delbanco)

For Minalu

"Sebah, Oasis of Fezzan, 10th March, 1846.—This evening the female slaves were unusually excited in singing, and I had the curiosity to ask my negro servant, Said, what they were singing about. As many of them were natives of his own country, he had no difficulty in translating the Mandara or Bornou language. I had often asked the Moors to translate their songs for me, but got no satisfactory account from them. Said at first said, 'Oh, they sing of Rubee' (God). 'What do you mean?' I replied, impatiently. 'Oh, don't you know?' he continued, 'they asked God to give them their Atka?' (certificate of freedom). I inquired, 'Is that all?' Said: 'No; they say, "Where are we going? The world is large. O God! Where are we going? O God!"'"

Richardson's Journal in Africa

WHERE are we going? where are we going,
Where are we going, Rubee?
Lord of peoples, lord of lands,
Look across these shining sands,
Through the furnace of the noon,
Through the white light of the moon.
Strong the Ghiblee wind is blowing,
Strange and large the world is growing!
Speak and tell us where we are going,
Where are we going, Rubee?...

John Greenleaf Whittier, "Song of Slaves in the Desert"

In the first year of his reign I Daniel understood by books the number of the years, whereof the word of the Lord came to Jeremiah the prophet, that he would accomplish seventy years in the desolations of Jerusalem.

Daniel 9:2

My mother bore me in the southern wild...

William Blake, "The Little Black Boy," *Songs of Innocence & Experience*

An Eruption, the Stone

The shock wave jarred them from sleep and sent them stumbling to their feet. Next came the roar of exploding earth and a sky in flames. From that maelstrom in the heavens did a voice call out to them? Go! Hurry! The three of them, the man first, the woman following slightly behind, the child trailing off to one side, hurried away across the steaming plain, making their first marks, footprints, in the yielding layer of ash.

Light shifted behind the veil of smoky sky. The rumbling went on and on. The man shouted at the gathering mist, coughing as he breathed. The girl slowed up, listed toward the plain, reached down and plucked at the ash. They walked, they walked. Light turned over, revealing a blue sky streaked with a long tail of smoke and ash. The girl pulled away from her mother, clutching something in her hand.

This stone, relatively cool to the touch, born of an earlier eruption…this small, egg-shaped stone—black bluish purple mahogany cocoa dark fire within, three horizontal lines, one vertical, the same pattern carved into your high cheeks—take it and hold it to your lips. Taste earth and sky, the inside of a mouth, the lining of a birth canal, the faintest fleck of something darker even than the blackness through which it has passed. You have now kissed wherever this stone has been, and it has traveled far.

She said this to her child, as her mother had said to her, and her mother's mother before that, and mothers and mothers and mothers, a line stretching all the way back to the first darkness and the first light, from where the stone had spurted up from the heart of the rift, in fire and smoke and steam, blurring the line where light of earth met light of sun, though at night the line showed starkly again.

Who first carved those lines on its face, three horizontal, one vertical? Three horizontal—the trek across the land. The one vertical—the ascent into the heavens. What hand and eye had kept them straight, in both directions, across and up and down? What hands had passed it along from time through time, until it lay in the palm of a man sprawled on his back on the desert floor between the town and the river?

Chapter One

To the West!

A single bright star glowed steadily like a stone fixed in the firmament of ocean blue sky above the red mosque, years and years back, when her grandparents were children. *Their* children? The jar-maker and his wife, he was the potter, she the weaver who made the cloth that held the jars with the distinctive design—three horizontal lines, one vertical—and supplied the household wares to the sheik who paid for the mosque. The father of the jar-maker had put him out to service with the sheik in exchange for the guarantee of an annual supply of grain for the family. In the seventh year of his service, when his father had died and the grain had rotted, the young artisan met the woman who would become his wife—because he noticed the cloth she had woven hanging in the market and imagined his jars wrapped in her weaving—a sign of lightning, a splash of rain, a distinctive design.

This turned out to be either a very good thing or a very bad thing. Her father would not give her up without a large payment, and the young jar-maker had to pledge another ten years to the sheik in order to buy this woman as his wife. As the story went, after the sheik, or, to be specific, his bookkeeper, agreed, the young jar-maker walked away, out to the edge of the town, where the river turned south—it flowed east from near the coast before bending around the city in its southerly way—and looked up into the clear sky and saw a river stork pinned by the light against the pale blue screen of air. He allowed his mind to soar up with the bird, wondering what the future might be like, and if he would ever become a free man, when in the distance the muezzin sang the call to prayer. The potter returned to the town having decided that he would give up one thing in his life, in this case, ten more years, in order to obtain another.

In a crowd of men dark-haired and white, he bent far forward and touched his forehead to the cool tiles of the floor, breathing in breath and sweat, sweet-wretched body-gas and tantalizing anise, and when he drew himself upright again he saw in his mind the weaver, the years ahead, and he knew that he had chosen the right path.

Who knows how to tell of the passing of ten years in happiness and some struggle in just a few words, so that the listener has a sense of how quickly time passes and yet still captures the bittersweet density of all that time together? Bodies entangled at night, hands working together at their craft, cooking, washing, bathing, cleaning, praying, and now and then stealing the time to wander along the river and do nothing but watch for the rising of that same stork he had seen on that day that now seemed so long past.

The weaver gave birth to their first child, a boy. And then another, a girl. And then, another girl.

(And oh, my dear, she said, try to tell you this about birth and you discover how far short of real life words fall, and yet how else to make any of these events known? Words! Words, words, words! The weight, the aches, the fears, the stirring, the shifting bleeding tearing pain and struggle! And the cries of mother, and child! But what do we have but memories, and these translated into words?)

And then there arose a situation on which everything else turned.

It had been the custom, as you may already have wondered about, that artisans such as the jar-maker and weaver might live outside the sheik's compound, even as in other cities the situation might be the reverse. The jar-maker found this to be a good arrangement. It gave him all of the seeming liberty of a free man, at least in that he could move about the city, and when it came time to deliver his goods to the sheik's compound he faced the bookkeeper almost as though he were an equal.

"Six large water jars," he said one morning in the cool season when the river in the distance had become carpeted with migrating birds.

"Six large water jars," the bookkeeper took notice. He recorded the transaction and with a wave of his stylus seemed ready to dismiss the jar-maker.

So it had gone with every delivery of every variety of container the jar-maker had created for his master, many times a year for a long number of years. Six water jars? Six water jars. Twenty cups? Twenty cups. Ten bowls? Ten bowls. He created them and delivered them. And dishes—yes, now and then the jar-maker turned dish-maker, using what he regarded as his wife's family design—three lines horizontal, one vertical—for the plates from which the sheik and his guests would eat. Today, as was more often than not the case, it was diminutive jars. People drank from them often, which meant some got broken, always. Jars. The bookkeeper counted. And raised his hand to dismiss him.

Year in, year out.

All in the name of God.

The artisan in his soul felt as though his supposedly temporary arrangement with the sheik would last forever. His family was growing. And still he found himself, as if in a dream of continuous repetition sometimes talked about by street-shop philosophers in the town, arriving at the compound, ordering the assistant, a blue-black slave from the South given to him by the sheik, to carry the pottery, standing before the bookkeeper, and waiting to be dismissed.

A free life seems so simple, filled with small pleasures! All he desired in those moments was the right to turn and walk away without having to wait for the signal that he was dismissed. As discourteous as that would have been, he contemplated the delicious possibility of it.

But did that moment ever arrive?

Here in the shade of the courtyard, cool shadows drifting down on them and sheltering them from the direct rays of the sun and buffering the heat reflected off the red walls of the main house, he enjoyed feeling liberated within the confines of his indentured state, so that, it seemed to him in his momentary fantasy, if he stood still the moment would never pass and he could live within it, even push against its limits and enlarge them, until old age overtook him and he withered and died free.

A man never knew how free he might be until he became a captive, for a decade or a lifetime, and a free man never knew just how enslaved he was until he found himself behaving as though invisible ropes tethered him to a routine of years and months and days. And so the artisan stood there, deeply immersed in the moment, poised to turn at the lowering of the bookkeeper's hand, fretting about the freedom he might never possess.

The bookkeeper cleared his throat, and the jar-maker shifted in his space, already turning.

"Before you go…" the sheik's man said. "There is something…"

The jar-maker froze in place, fixed like one of the designs on his pots when the heat rose high enough to fix it forever. Freezing, heating—oh, he knew, he felt it in his blood, he was somehow done, done for this world.

The bookkeeper again cleared his throat in such a formal way that the jar-maker believed in that instant that he might be about to announce the sheik's pleasure over the special designs.

"I should not be telling you this."

"Yes, sir?"

The jar-maker, a man old enough so that if he were free others would address him with similar respect, gave the bookkeeper his best attention.

"You must pack your bags. You and your family must pack your bags."

The jar-maker felt the chill and thrill of surprise running in his veins.

"Why do you say this, sir?"

The bookkeeper narrowed his eyes and leaned ever so slightly closer to the jar-maker.

"I should not be saying this at all. But—"

Again, a world in an instant! We're free! the jar-maker told himself, free before our time! The sheik in his wisdom—

"My master—"

"Yes, sir?" The jar-maker interrupted, and then cursed himself for interrupting.

The bookkeeper did not appear insulted.

"My master, who is your master, has, in his wisdom, arranged…"

"Yes, sir?"

The bookkeeper retreated a step and turned his shoulder to the jar-maker.

"As I said, I should not be speaking of this matter with you. You will hear tomorrow, and you will obey."

"Hear what, sir?"

The bookkeeper spoke again, and that bubble of the moment in which the jar-maker had stood collapsed suddenly around him, and he listened to the awful news the man delivered, though he was already, in his sudden desperation, backing away from the man, walking out into the outer courtyard, and hurrying along in the direction of the market.

The muezzin called out over the rooftops.

"Time for prayer. Sluggards, hurry along! Time for prayer!"

"Time to pray," a rough-faced warder told him, standing at a corner, directing men to the mosque with a wave of a pointed stick.

"I am going," the jar-maker said. His blood felt as though it had turned to water, a precious commodity on a summer day but for now a chilling reminder of what the bookkeeper had told him.

"Go now," the warder said.

The jar-maker stepped past him, and just as the warder turned away to chastise another soul the jar-maker began to run.

"What a good man," someone who saw him might have observed. "He cannot wait too soon to pray."

He ran to his house where he hastily collected some belongings in a small bag and without any explanation ordered his wife to gather up a few necessities of clothing and get the children ready to depart.

"Where are we—?"

"Do not inquire," he said, through clenched teeth.

He told her that she had only a few minutes and hurried out the door. When he returned with a donkey (for which he had traded the house and all their belongings!) he got the family mounted—one child on her lap, another behind her (the smallest in his own arms)—and riding toward the limits of the town, with him shuffling alongside even as prayers were ending and men began to move about the streets.

For the jar-maker, the trip to the marshes beyond the limits of the city took an eternity, and always at their heels he could hear—did he imagine it?—the approach of mobs of worshipers calling for his head. What was he doing but sundering the holy bond made between his late father and the sheik? Did it matter what condition this bond led him to? No, it did not matter. All important was the meshing of the words of these two men. His life, and the life of his wife and children, took second, third, fourth, fifth place to this pact. What kind of a world was this where such bonds tied people together, in fact, bound them hand and feet with invisible ropes?

They answered the question by the urgency of their flight. Never in his life had he rushed so headlong into a plan, or, perhaps we ought to say, retreated so vigorously from the life he knew. When the family reached the river it was time to stop a moment, and make a decision.

East or west?

To head east would take them deeper into the heart of the old world from which they were fleeing. Even though the river eventually turned south—or so the jar-maker had heard—and led back toward the ocean near which it originally formed, they would meet too much danger, from other sheiks and rulers large and small, in towns and encampments, in that direction. To the west lay the sources of the river, in highlands where few people lived, though before those hills and green-draped rises, another city—he knew, he had once heard directly from some travelers who originated there—sat on the river's edge, and, because of its slightly more forgiving climate with respect to rains, a growing city at that.

Very well. He set the child down for a moment, pulled himself up to his full height, and then bowed in the direction of the red turrets they had just put behind them.

Then turned to the west.

To the west!

The day grew hotter as they traveled with the sun, though the animal moved so slowly that the sun eventually left them behind in a growing ocean of shadows of scattered river-shore plants and trees. Where did the sun go? The jar-maker knew there was an ocean some great distance in that direction, he had heard of it, yes, this vast body of water filled with a life of its own that led to other mysterious bodies of land. And his mind wandered toward it as they plodded along, and he wondered if he would ever see it. For the moment he gave his best attention to the river. The jar-maker, more and more aware of his wife's fatigue and the children's bewilderment, wanted desperately to make a crossing, but the water ran too deep in this season, and though they came to a ferry he decided it would be unwise to call attention to themselves by making the trip.

Red mud, dark water, now and then a flight of white birds that broke across the face of the fleeing sun, leaving, or so it seemed from the point from which they watched, a blanket of red clouds resting just beneath the still fiery light. As much as he would have liked for them to have kept moving, the jar-maker understood that it was time to stop. He helped the family from the animal's back and took the bag of food as well before weighing down the beast's rope with rocks he found at the waterside.

"I'll bathe the children," the weaver said, and she took them to the river while the jar-maker gathered wood for a small fire. Once the sky faded into the growing shadows of the night out here in the flatlands near the water the air would turn cooler by the hour. However dangerous it was, and just how dangerous he did not really know, no father wanted his children to catch a chill and fall sick. He watched them play in the water, enjoyed listening to their laughter. Here was the difference between animal and man—the small fire he built, daring the odds of discovery, so that the

children might stay warm in their sleep. Immediately upon considering
this thought he sank into a deep pit of gloom.

"I could smell the fire," the weaver upon returning with the children.
"I wonder if it is safe?"

He told her what he believed, and she acquiesced.

In a moment she was serving the figs and flatbread she had snatched
from the larder during their last moments in the house. Not long after the
food disappeared, the children lay down near the fire. It was good that they
settled themselves, because long before sunrise they all must be awake and
traveling again. However his daughter Zainab, a pale-skinned girl, tall for
her sex, and prone to upset, could not find the handle of sleep. The weaver
tried to soothe her, without success. In desperation her mother asked the
jar-maker to tell the girl a story.

"I can make shapes and designs," her father said, "but I am not good at
telling stories."

"I want a tale," the restless girl said, speaking in a voice her father found
slightly intimidating because of its new impersonal tone. "And I want a story."

"Is there a difference?" her father said.

"Yes," the girl said.

"What is it?" said her father.

"I don't know," the girl said.

Zainab pulled herself upright and sat waiting for her father to speak.

"A tale, perhaps," her father said, "tells about people you do not know.
A story tells you about people you do."

"I want both," the girl said.

The jar-maker cleared his throat, trying to rise above his awful feelings
of despair and desperation at the thought of their plight. To be sold to a
stranger to fill a temporary gap in the sheik's finances? He felt suddenly
a deep sense of pity for his master, that the man should find himself so
desperate that he would break the bond between the two of them that the
jar-maker had always fulfilled.

The air grew restless. Somewhere out in the star-lit dark a bird called
and in the farther dark another bird answered. Suddenly the breeze rose,
rustling the reeds and grass around them.

"Tell me," Zainab said.

With her urging he began to speak, telling a story he had heard from his
own father, who once told him that he had heard it from his father, who

had heard it from his father, about a young man who scratched at rocks with a piece of metal, inscribing three horizontal lines and one vertical on the side of a large boulder near the great rift in the earth near where he was born. The boy had a good life, beloved of his parents, his father who was a farmer, his mother who gathered herbs, and—

"Why do you stop?" his daughter asked.

The jar-maker was listening. Beyond the farther dark, where the last birds called, something made a sharp barking noise.

"What?" said the weaver, who also had been giving her attention to the story, and now listened along with him for something else in the night.

The weaver stood up and reconnoitered their little campground.

"The animal is gone," he said. "I did not tie it well enough. In fact, I did not tie it at all."

"Do not worry," his wife said. "Now we have one less mouth to feed."

In the distance more barking.

"Is that the donkey?" his wife said.

"A jackal," the jar-maker said.

"Will the fire be enough to keep it away?"

"It will have to be," the jar-maker said.

"Papa?" Zainab said from where she lay.

"Yes, the story, I know." Again, he cleared his throat. And he knelt back down near her, and talked on, until the girl had fallen asleep, his wife sagged against his shoulder, and the fire had dwindled to a few swirls of sparks that whirled about now and then in the light breeze.

He eased his wife onto the ground and lay down next to her, settling into an old and familiar comfort, despite the roughness of their bed and the fear in his mind. Here, where the late stars gradually asserted themselves in the sky, burning brighter and brighter as the fire diminished, he saw patterns he had not noticed before while living in the city, shapes and forms, also, though the law of God forbade such things as these. An animal head. A hunter's arm, holding a bow. A belt holding at the waist of a figure so large it stretched across a quarter of the night sky. But, oh, God was so strong, all-powerful, it was blasphemy to make any figure because figures suggested the possibility of grasping an awareness of God's face and being. And he grew ashamed, and then worried, and then repentant, and then disturbed, and then angry, and then calmed himself by taking out from his bag the small stone with the old markings and turning it over and over in his hands as he recited a prayer he knew, calming and calming himself with its repetition until he fell asleep.

He awoke at the bark of a jackal. The fire had died. Stars flickered brightly high above but gave no heat. An insect made a chirring noise nearby. In the marsh waters a fish, or snake, splashed like a stone hitting the water. Did fish sleep at night? The jar-maker wondered at the thought. His wife and children lay as quietly as creatures in the grave. Ay! Who wants thoughts such as that? They were merely sleeping, and, with God's help, he would save them. Perhaps he did not pray as often as he should, putting so much time and care into his work as he did. But he never did anything against God. No, no, no. And if he was not free, why, then how could any man say he was truly free, because all men belonged to God? The sheik, for whom he had labored, also belonged to a Master, as did all the citizens, free and slave, in the town. Each of us has his own degree of enslavement, and all of us ultimately call ourselves the creatures of God.

His wife sat up.

"What is it?" she said.

The jar-maker listened attentively to the faint sounds in the dark.

"Nothing. Jackals, wild dogs. They won't come near. Go back to sleep."

He leaned to his left, feeling around for a stick large enough to club any invading beasts. He stood, and ranged out from the fireside, his eyes on the dark ground. Oh, if only there was wood! But then he remembered a small knife that he used as a tool and kept in his sack of essential belongings. He was bent over, on his knees, feeling around in the sack when they heard the camels.

Chapter Two

A Hebrew of New York

$\mathscr{S}$ome time ago, before our nation split in two and the opposing territories, north and south, initiated a great war over the question of freedom, yours truly, Nathaniel Pereira, climbed the plank on a Manhattan winter morning to board a south-bound yawl called the *Godbolt*. My father had charged me with a mission of some family business of the import-export variety. Earnest young man that I was, sandy-haired, blue-eyed, with a handsomely bent nose (which Marzy, our family servant, often joked with me about when I was a child) and just the beginnings of a beard on my pink cheeks, I could then little imagine how much such a journey would change my life and the lives of others in the family.

I awoke that special morning, before dawn, somewhat divided within myself and feeling my nerves. It had been a night of odd dreams about an army of Jews on horseback racing across a windy desert—yes, Jews, Jews, Jews, though I have never been a terribly observant member of my faith—and next came a dream-visitation, not uncommon to me in those days, by my dear late mother, who whispered imperatively about wearing a hat to keep away the cold and the importance of living as a Jew. After saying to the air the elemental prayer we Hebrews make each morning—"Hear, O Israel, the Lord our God, the Lord is One"—and, as was my wont, reading a psalm aloud—for the poetry, as my dear old mop-haired fish-eyed master of a teacher George Washington Halevi always suggested (this one being Psalm 32, which I chose, as I usually did, at random, and begins "Blessed is he whose transgression is forgiven, whose sin is covered...")—I lay abed a while despite the urgency of the day.

Sluggard, arise! I heard Halevi's voice in my mind.

To further prepare me for my inheritance—the care of the family business—my father had hired him as a tutor who worked with me on mathematics and history, philosophy, and Scripture. George Washington Halevi, whose own grandfather had been one of the few Jews who had fought in the Revolutionary War. His grandmother had been a farm girl from a Bronx estate, who attended to a soldier wounded in the Battle of New York. They produced his hybrid father, and his father had wed a Jewess from Rhode Island who produced him. Instead of going to Europe to study for the rabbinate, Halevi had attended Harvard College and was given the only divinity degree our people had received in the New World. Neither a full Hebrew in his own mind nor a Protestant of any standing, Halevi was a curious mixture of Old World and New, Jew and Gentile. A smart fellow then, with only a few difficulties, he was, first, so shy that he could scarcely talk to me about my subjects without trying to withdraw into the woodwork. Second, his breath smelled like manure. And, third, he sometimes stuttered in a terrible way.

Though his manner of speaking in public was less than pleasing, when he settled into himself and found the reassurance to speak, his voice dropped to a whisper and listening to him was like riding a winter sled down a nicely sloped snow-covered hill.

"Master Nathaniel," he would say in that hoarse rasping way of his (and I laughed to myself as I lay abed recalling it), "to-to-today we will consider the P-P-Principia of Sir Isaac Newton." Or, "My question for you to consider is the origin of the stars." Or, "F-free will, Nathaniel, d-d-does it exist?" On this latter topic, we would talk for hours, because in my childish stubbornness I could never agree with his position.

"If God wants us to do something, we do it," I said, hearing myself speak as though I were some wise sage instead of a slender boy with freckles, one slightly drooping eye, and legs so full of life that they would not stop quaking the more excited I became in our discussions.

"The pagan philosophers say that we have a choice."

"Do I have a choice this moment to speak or not speak?"

"You do."

"But if I don't, you will tell my father and he will be quite angry with me."

"The choice remains."

"Bad student or dutiful student?"

"Bad or good."

"Our Hebrew God says what?"

"Nothing on the subject of free will. Obey and please Him, d-d-disobey and he will be quite angry."

"Angry, but will He punish me?"

"Sometimes He does, sometimes He doesn't."

"An odd master," I said, wise before my time—or by mere momentary accident.

"Y-yes," my tutor said. "A quixotic plight we have, we Jews. Only the Christians have it worse."

"They do?"

"Many of them believe their wills are bound to either evil or good. With no choice for them."

"Like slaves to their God?"

"They bend their wills to His."

"And we don't?"

"We don't bend. We choose."

"Choose to give up our will? And is that freedom?"

My tutor shook his head.

"Let me consider this."

But I pursued it further just then.

"When our republic broke from the British Crown, we chose to do so. And gained our freedom. Therefore freedom was not bending our wills to the throne but breaking away from it."

"Bravo, young Nathaniel," my tutor said. "You have made a good point, sir. A good point."

The day I asked him about whether or not he thought my pretty talking parrot Jacobus had a soul, he was also quite pleased. We spoke a little while of that, and then swerved back to his favorite topic, leaving me to ponder the question of the bird soul in my private thoughts.

"We have no literature here in this country of ours," he said. "The ground is seeded, but it has not yet bloomed. We have no time, as in history. And how can you have a story without history for it to blossom in? Read Shakespeare. We have not yet spawned our own."

"This doesn't sound good," I said.

"It is neither good nor bad," he said. "Think of it in this manner. We Jews do not yet have our savior, but one day the savior will come."

Though there was one American book he put forward. Which is how eventually I came into possession of a volume that I took to like a fish to water—the autobiography of our great Benjamin Franklin. Some boys worship their fathers, some worship themselves. I gave all my admiration to young Ben and hoped to live a life like his and emulate his rise from nothing to something.

Such thoughts inspired me that fateful early morning some time after my formal tutoring had ended, and I threw myself out of the bed, dressed, and descended, carrying my bags, to the street level kitchen as quietly as I could for fear of waking my Aunt Isabelle, my late mother's sister, who had become as much of a mother to me as any woman not my mother could.

Red-head Marzy, our gimpy Old New York Dutch maid from a penniless family, was, of course, already awake and greeted me in the kitchen with the porridge.

"I hope you have a good journey, sir," she said, her narrow eyes downcast. I thought it was perhaps because of her feeling some illness, or some guilt at having missed a chore. Lord knows how little she was paid, but I knew how much she had to do!

"Thank you, Marzy," I said.

"Oh, sir!" she said, and burst into a thunderstorm of tears and nose-blowing.

"Oh, sir! Oh, sir!"

This screech of a voice belonged to Jacobus, whom my father had brought home to me from the Indies in the time after my mother died. (My immediate progenitor had been born there, to parents who had emigrated from Holland to make a fortune on the island of Curaçao, and when he reached his majority, after marrying my mother, another Antilles Jew, had emigrated to New York City. His half-brother, of whom much more in a moment or so, had felt a similar inclination to settle in our Promised Land but sailed up only as far north as Charleston, which was and still is, despite its wanton rebelliousness, at this writing, part of our South. How sad, and at the same time provident, that he could not make the other few days' journey north, because where he disembarked changed everything.)

A louder noise up above, and I understood by the sound on the steps that it was my father coming down to meet me.

"Good morning, sir," I said.

"Good morning to you, Nathaniel."

He was a trim, bent-shouldered man, about an inch shorter than my own height of six feet, with shaggy gray hair and eyes just then still red with sleep that made me wonder if some brass band in his dreams might have serenaded him as he mused about sending me off to do his business in the world, which I was about to do on this out-of-the-ordinary day.

"Quite a morning," he said as if reading my thoughts, while Marzy set his coffee on the table.

"Yes, sir."

"Yes, sir, yes sir!"

He blinked into the light streaming in from the east side of our back kitchen.

"Hush, Jacobus." And then to me: "A good day to travel, it appears."

I nodded, and tried to put aside my anger. The week before, the two of us had sat in his study and quarreled, and this morning I was still bitter, for after having concluded my tutorials a month ago I was ready to set out on my grand tour before settling in as a junior partner in the family business of import-export. Instead my father informed me that first I must undertake a voyage to Charleston to make some inquiries into the affairs of his half-brother, who owned a plantation there.

"A good fellow he is," my father had said, his accent, the product of his childhood in the Caribbean (and the faintest hint of his father's Dutch) set ever so slightly at an angle to our New York speech. "Though I have not seen him these many decades since we were boys together in Antigua. He writes to tell me that aside from now weighing as much as two Hebrew men of normal size he is in good health. And awaiting your arrival."

"Awaiting my arrival, father?" I had said.

"Yes, he is."

"And so you have been corresponding with him about this for some weeks now?"

"This happens to be so."

I shook my head. "I wish I had known, Father. I am terribly disappointed. What matter could be so important that I have to travel down to Charleston instead of sailing off on my tour?"

"Your tour, Nathaniel, will come. But family comes first, however distant they may have been in earlier relations. My brother needs some looking to. I do not mean to set your mind against him but he fears that his only son may not be entirely capable of taking over the plantation. There is some question of the boy's—now man's—temperament. I had hopes that I might resolve this matter by letter and so have not spoken about it with you until now. Alas, my dear boy, things have not resolved. My brother has appealed to my familial responsibility. Which is why you must make the voyage to Charleston before the voyage to Europe. I need some advice about this matter. Should we or should we not invest in his enterprise so that we might offer both support and direction? That is the question."

"Are we going to become tobacco merchants, or sell whatever it is he grows down there?"

"No, Nathaniel, not tobacco. Rice. Southern rice to feed the belly of the northern nation. A thousand acres of fields and rice-growing ponds." He paused and blinked into the sunlight as though he had only just discovered it had dawned. "And a hundred slaves."

"Slaves? Father, I know nothing about rice. And less about slaves." At this moment I cleared my throat and tried to assume a vocal posture of certainty. "I certainly do not want to learn about either."

"You will learn. You are old enough now to learn some things about business."

"And young enough to know nothing, Father," I said.

"I like humility in a man," Father said. He smiled, which produced in me a feeling of warm good will. "You will know what to tell me soon enough about whether or not we should invest in my half-brother's enterprise. He is a large man in many ways, this fellow of our blood. I do not know him very well, though am sure he would help me if I needed help. He has asked us for assistance that we cannot give without some investigation. It is my impression that we are his last resort. And you, young man, are mine. Will you help me?"

"Of course, Father," I said. "But after this, Europe?" I said. "My tour?"

"Son, I promise you, assist us first in this matter and I will send you immediately thereafter. Remember, your mother was always a kind person. For her, family came first…"

"Yes, Father."

"There is one more thing."

"Yes, Father?"

He pulled open the bottom drawer of his desk, took out a small pistol, and offered it to me.

"Father?"

"Remember, the world is not always kind. A man needs protection while traveling," he said. "The weapon is at the moment unloaded. Tomorrow

I will buy you bullets. You are a man now, going about your father's business. Carry this weapon always on your person. You may see some things down there in the South…well, never mind." For a moment I stared at it and then took it from him.

He next reached into his pocket and took out his gold timepiece, as if to establish that it was time for one thing and now it was time for another.

"Your grandfather's watch," he said. "Which he consulted often while sitting in his office and looking out at the Carib palms. And which was next mine, and now yours. It is your watch, son, and from now on you will have to wind it."

Chapter Three

In My Margins

What Are the Origins of Man?

Where had they come from? Out of the earth? Fire? Water? Water!

When the mountains sprung up out of the sea, and the cleft of water sprung into the light—

Because it does come first—

Yes, tell me the first part, first—

The mountains arose, and the water poured down their slopes back into the cleft left behind by the rising land, and fire seized the surface of the sea, and the rains came and the fire turned to smoke and the smoke rose to cover the face of the sun. Where once large animals wandered the land when it was hilly and covered with trees, and cleaved to another great mass of land that no one had a name for because no one had yet been born to give things names—

And after another great rain the sea remained burning, the smoke and steam rising higher and higher, and all the animals and trees went up in flame.

Pillars of fire and burning bush…?

Mountains melting and ice arising…and the seas in tumult…?

Do we know, do we know when and where it all began except to say that the oldest rocks came out of Africa and somewhere on those shores some fishy creature probably pushed its snout for the first time up from the sea into the air? This in a long life of reading and speculation is what we have come to believe. But the preachers say otherwise. What do the imams and the rabbis say?

Chapter Four

Boarding the *Godbolt*

*O*n this important morning, the first day of a new turn in my life that would change forever the direction I would take, I could feel the weight of that timepiece, wound and working, in my pocket—and the pistol—as I took a moment now to study my father's face, and tried to imagine someone who looked nearly alike but weighed twice as much as he. I had some questions. But I gave up the thoughts as my Aunt Isabelle, looking, because swaddled in bed-clothes, twice her own normal size, came tottering down the steps from her room.

"Dear boy," she said, "dear, dear boy…"

Her eyes were still dull from sleep, but nothing diminished the effervescent nature of her soul.

"I shall miss you!"

She glided up to me and touched a long extended finger to my collarbone.

"Oh, how I shall miss you!"

"He's not going that far away," my father said. "Imagine if he were going off on his tour how long he'd be gone."

"I wish I were," I said.

"Don't be ungrateful," Father said. "You accomplish this mission, and I'll send you on your travels for two years rather than one."

"Truly, Father? Thank you, sir, thank you."

"That would make me sadder still," said my Aunt Isabelle, turning away as if to mourn in solitude and reaching out a hand so that Marzy might offer her a cup of steaming coffee.

"And make me happier," I said, but immediately, upon seeing the hurt I made in her—she glanced at me over her shoulder and rolled her eyes—tried to jolly my remark away as a joke and a laugh. "Yes, sir," I said to the parrot.

"Yes, sir," Jacobus said to me.

Marzy, weeping quietly, signaled to us that our cab was waiting.

And so Father and I went into the streets of early morning to the clatter of horses' hooves and the cries of vendors and the shouts cast from one building to another as we crossed our narrow island on the way to the river.

I still had many questions for him about the business I was taking up, and about the specific nature of my journey. But he sat back against the seat, his eyes closed in thought, or as I saw him sometimes in synagogue, deep in prayer, and so I did not feel as though I might interrupt him just then. For, truth to say, I felt a confusion of things. I was a bit afraid and also quite honored and somewhat annoyed and a trifle curious as to what would happen on this journey. In all my twenty-some years I was a perfect Manhattan lad and had never wandered further from this rocky island than to the Bronx farm to the north and the Jersey cliffs to the west, and to that Perth Amboy harbor to the southwest, where my mother and I had disembarked when I was a boy of seven to quarantine ourselves against the illness that had swept across the lower part of our borough—to no avail, since she sickened and died soon after our arrival.

Oh, family! Oh, dear mother! As sweet as she was, that old Aunt Isabelle of mine, my late mother's sister, could not take her place.

But hark! Music in the distance, to distract us from our thoughts of woe!

> *Yankee Doodle went to town*
> *Riding on a pony*

Here was a brass band greeting us as our carriage drew up to the pier, with flag-wavers standing behind them, and such bright music pouring out of horns and pipes that the musicians might have been performing at an election rally instead of a harbor farewell for the passengers, soon to include me, of this large yawl bobbing serenely in the rising river tide at pier-side. "It's all a merriment, is it not, son?" My father peered out from his side of the cab.

"I'm feeling rather that way, Father," I said. "I believe I heard them play before when they were in favor of the mayor. Now they are just Yankee Doodles doodling our farewell."

"The music changes with the mood of things," he said. "Has not Halevi taught you your Plato?" He called to the driver and within moments we were standing at the pier-side with my few bags at my feet. Not more than a moment or two went by before a crewman snatched up my luggage and went scurrying up the gangplank to the ship itself.

"'The *Godbolt*,'" I read from the bow.

"A good name, do not you think?" My father raised his eyes to the strong early morning sun while the band played on.

"Any name will do," I said. "It's the journey that matters."

"Well-said, sir!" He clapped me on the back. "When I hear you speak like that, it gives me heart. The money I paid for your education was well-spent. I know that you will stand well for our enterprise. The family is depending on you."

"I am going to try, Father," I said, though in my heart I could not have said that I was sure I would succeed.

"You will keep your eye on the star that guides us," he said.

"I will, sir."

My father then, in an act most uncharacteristic of a man who usually kept his distance, took me by the hand and pulled me so close to him that were he not usually so gentle I could almost imagine he might do me harm.

"I know this will not be easy for you," he said.

"I will do my best, Father."

"The weather will be warm. You will appreciate that."

"I will," I said.

He cleared his throat, a noise he often emitted, though not at such immediate proximity that it sounded in my ear like an animal's roar.

"You will do this for the family," he then said.

"Yes, sir," I responded.

"You will do the family honor in what may be a difficult situation. To invest or not invest? That is the question. Young Hamlet Pereira, do you understand? Down there in that Carolina plantation you will be my eyes."

"Yes, sir," I said, smiling at his jest.

"As far as the matter of the slaves," he said...

"Yes?"

"We do not own such property, but your uncle and older cousin do. You must respect their views on such matters. The question has to do with finance. Do we invest or not? Put your mind to work on this question, not your heart."

"Yes, sir," I said, without much thought to it.

I wanted to say something more, but the ship's bell clanged, and sailors whistled to sailors, and so Father gave me a little push and started me toward the gangplank.

"Father," I said, "is there anything I—?"

"Your uncle will explain," he said, "as he did to me in his letter."

I did not know what to say or what to ask. I felt suddenly orphaned and uneasy, with the pier beneath my feet giving me the impression I was already subject to the cycles of the tides.

"I will write to you, sir!" I spoke up in a burst of emotion.

"As you like." Father gave me one last blink of assent. "*Bon voyage,*" he said as I turned to climb the gangway.

"Thank you," I said over my shoulder, feeling the presence of the watch in one pocket and that of the pistol in another.

As the band played on I mounted higher and higher, and despite my ignorance and my uncertainty, felt in my soul as I gained the deck as though I were growing taller and taller.

"Welcome aboard, sir," said an officer, in smart blue uniform and braids and gold stars, as he snapped me a salute.

Immediately I went to the rail and looked down, seeing my father appearing considerably smaller now that I towered above him on the deck, and I waved, and passed along the salute from the sailor. A carriage raced up to the dock and a small, dark, curly-haired figure emerged from the cab, my childhood sweetheart, Miriam (I should have mentioned her earlier, but truly in the emotional departure from New York I had forgotten her), she whom I walked home with from synagogue on holidays and sat with cheerfully in the parlor of her father's house, nearly tripping as she ran, with her eyes fixed up here where we stood on the deck. True to what I took at that time to be the nature of woman, she appeared always to be late to appointments.

"Hello!" I called to her, feeling my heart sink at the sight of her.

"Nathaniel, Nathaniel, *bon voyage!* I'll wait for you!"

"I'll return soon!" I called, caught up in the romance of the moment, stirring as it was, with the cries of seabirds and the noise of the crowd and the music of the band. Though my father's plan, of which I was the instrument, called for a stay on the plantation of only a month or so, I suffered suddenly the premonition that I would never see her again—shipwreck or drowning or murder would come between us, I feared, rather foolishly I have to say.

Although for an instant it seemed as though the pier began to move, it was us, our ship, which shifted away from the land. Even while I was suffering my outrageous fear of loss, we had loosed ourselves from the mooring, and that sensation of floating free of land stayed with me from then on. One moment land-bound, another and the pier and my father and Miriam and my past life receded swiftly into the distance. Being no sailor I cannot explain what the crew did as they worked the sails, though their shouts sounded smartly from the hold and we moved smoothly down river and then headed east into the Kill van Kull—the purser came alongside me and explained our route—to put old Manhattan behind us. With the New Jersey shore to starboard we sailed down the Kill toward Perth Amboy— this same trip I had made so long ago with my dear mother—where we were to pick up more passengers and some mail. The water was calm, the sun warm, the few other people on deck, older than I was (which meant less hair and more belly) speaking quietly of their various business ventures. The hiss of our prow cutting the water and the low singing of the wind in the sails gave me a false sense of what the rest of our voyage would be like.

But first, Perth Amboy—the original capital of our emerging union of states—a green curtain beyond the waterside as we first caught sight of it. Egrets flew up at our approach and gulls soared and squawked, laughed and squealed, as if to mock my recollections of traveling here when my mother and Marzy and I sought to escape the plague—yes, some escape, when, as I have previously disclosed, Mother had already been infected.

Small boats carrying fishermen drifted in the outgoing tide from the Kill and the late afternoon sun lay limp on the southern horizon, a green line above the line of green water of the river that flowed into this bay from the west. I buried my sorrowful memories in thoughts of the national past. We New York school boys who had studied our history and news of the current day knew that Ben Franklin's son, William, when he was governor here, had built himself a large brick edifice on a hill not far from the waterside. But the trees grew so thickly together that I could not see beyond them, and just when I was thinking that we might have an hour or two to explore this seemingly virgin place we threw down our anchor a quarter mile short of the lone pier jutting out into the water, where the only person in sight was a brown-skinned fellow, an Indian or a servant, who sat with his legs dangling over the edge, sending up large swirls of smoke from a long pipe. Whatever mail or people we might be taking on would be rowed out to us rather than have us come in to shore.

Just as well, I said to myself, so that I would never have to step foot again on that soil where my mother had perished.

I had no sooner turned my head away to look again at the sandy beach across the Kill where the borough of Richmond pointed toward the bay, when a packet boat came rushing toward us. The sailors made to hold her close and a tall man with long, flowing, silver hair, in a dark cloak and tall hat, also black, stepped from the boat onto the rope ladder dangling from our starboard bow and deftly climbed aboard, followed by a young tarry-skinned boy who dangled two bags in one hand while he followed the man up the rope ladder.

A few minutes later a second boat—bearing the mail, apparently—came alongside us, and soon after that the captain shouted his orders and we were underway once more, leaving green Amboy behind.

Medium swells met us at the confluence of river, bay, and ocean, making us mount and fall, mount and fall, like some giant horse running over a series of hurdles. With each heave my stomach climbed into my throat and then receded, climbed up and then receded.

"All the way from the Azorias," said a voice behind me. I turned to see the tall man in the black cloak and hat, though now he held the hat in his hand because of the strong breeze blowing off the ocean that would have easily swept it into the waves. Up close his shoulder-length hair seemed so white it matched the spume of the wave-tops.

"What, sir?" I said.

"The swells," he said. "They begin to roll nearly at the Gates of Hercules and gather strength as they move westward across the ocean. Hard to believe they do not tear apart a state such as New Jersey, but by the time they strike the beach they lose their will."

His breath smelled foul.

"I have never been out on the ocean before," I said, stepping back from him. "It is…a stronger sensation than I imagined."

"But how ever did you get here," the man said, his voice deepening, "if not over the ocean?"

I shook my head, confused slightly, at his question.

"I sailed from New York, sir," I said.

"Not my question," the man said. "Not how did you get to Perth Amboy, but how did you come to these shores first of all if not by ship?"

"Sir," I said, "I was born in New York."

"Remarkable," the man said. "Not in the alleys and shadows of Jerusalem or old Napoli or Lisbon but in New York?"

"I told you the answer, sir, and so I am not sure of your point."

"My point, young man," he said, "is a blunt one. I couldn't help but think you were foreign-born. The shape of the head, the nose—"

"Excuse me, sir," I said, "but I must go below."

I turned abruptly and left the man standing on the deck. It took all of my sense of balance to negotiate the way to the hatch and then the stairs below, but I managed this without falling or banging any part of myself against the wood of the deck. The purser had had one of the crew take my bag below so that it was waiting for me on the bed in the small cabin reserved for my passage. I set it on the floor and removed my coat and stretched out on the bed, closing my eyes and giving myself over to the roll and pitch of the ship. As old as I was—or as young—I had never heard anyone speak of me in that way before, and I felt a bit light-headed, confused, as though I might have had too much wine.

I awoke in the dark to the sound of creaking wood and rushing swells. It took me a moment to recall where I was, and in that moment a spout of terror rose up in me but immediately subsided as I heard the call of one sailor to another over the noise of the slap and drum of the waves.

I had left New York behind; I was on my way to Charleston.

I had no sooner figured this out when there came a knock at my cabin door.

"Señor Pereira?" came the creaky voice of an old sailor.

"Yes?"

"The captain requests that you come to his cabin for supper just now, sir."

"Why does the captain wish to meet me?"

"Why, sir, he enjoys knowing the persons who travel under his care and command."

I withdrew my new pocket watch and studied it, and then got to my feet and immediately lurched with the roll of the ship so that I clanged my shoulder

against one of the timbers in the cabin. When I opened the door the old salt
was still standing there, holding a bowl of water in one hand and a candle in
the other, as though no balancing act were required despite the roll of the ship.

"May I, sir?" and at my nod he entered the cabin and set down the water
bowl, leaving me to wash before supper. Before too long he was leading
me up a set of steps and down another to the entrance of the captain's cabin
at the stern of the ship. This turned out to be more like a real room than
a cabin, with candles everywhere, two trim young sailors assisting in the
service of several passengers, and the mustachioed cook flitting here and
there with pans and pots and spoons at the ready. The scene was not all
that different from home, except for the constant roll and slap of the ocean
waves—and the cook with the mustache.

"Mr. Pereira?" The captain, a burly man with thick side-chops and
spectacles stuck on the tip of his near-spy-glass length nose, bade me enter
and take a seat at the elbow of one of the gentlemen who had boarded with
me in New York. The other sat across from me. The one man I didn't care
to see, the white-haired man in black who had boarded at Perth Amboy,
was blessedly absent.

Midway through our meal and accompanying small talk about business
and politics—there was a question concerning Carolina, our destination,
and its relation to the federal government that came up in conversation,
something that I could not quite understand, since politics had not figured
large in my tutorials with Halevi—my nemesis, for that is how I thought of
him (as you would anyone whose presence immediately chills your blood)
appeared in the doorway.

"Ah," he said, addressing all of us but keeping his eyes on the captain,
"I am, as I have always been in my life, too late."

"No, no, sir," the captain said. "The food is plentiful, and even more
so the wine."

He directed the stewards to fill the man's glass, bade him sit at his left
hand, and then made introductions.

"Young Master Pereira I know," he said, staring me in the eye.

I nodded, and watched the candle flames dance in their wicks.

"Because of business?" the captain asked.

"We met only today," I said. "I assume we are both traveling on business."

"Yes," said the man in black, "the business of Charleston. Always an
interesting business."

One of the other men spoke up.

"It is not *my* business," he said. "I trade in cloth and clothing, nothing more."

"Nor I," said the second man. "I have come to study the agriculture."

"Methinks you protest too much," said the man in black. "Agriculture there means rice, and rice means what you know it means. What do you make of this, young Pereira?"

"It is unclear to me, sir, but then it could just be the light in this room."

"This cabin," the captain corrected me. "Or cabinet. Or, as I sometimes think of it, my womb and my tomb."

Fortified by many glasses of wine, he sailed into a disquisition on the life of a captain and the nature of the sea, which pleased me, because it did not give the man in black any room for his own speech.

Alas, that creature caught up with me on deck after the meal.

"Well, well, my young fellow," he said, speaking to my back while I held onto the rail at starboard, watching the dark gap in the low stars in the west where I knew the land must be only a few miles or so across the hissing water. "I never knew, and I watched you, and I listened to you, and I discovered you have manners, you employ utensils with a certain grace, and who taught you this, what keeper? From a parent? Or your owner?"

Standing this close to him I was forced to breathe in the foul odor that surged past his lips and the last thing I wanted was to stay by. However, instead of moving away, something happened that I never could have supposed I had within me and I turned slowly and giving in to a deep impulse that rose up out of the depths of my feelings surprised myself by taking him by the collar—twisting as I spoke.

"Have you ever studied physics, sir?" I heard myself say. "This cloak of yours that wraps you all in darkness, do you know that soaked with sea water it would quickly drag you down to the bottom, and your body would not float to the surface for some days? All it would need is for me to take you like this—" and I grabbed him with my other hand—"and hurl you overboard like a sack of ash..."

"Easy, my beauty," he said, and I could hear him breathing carefully while still in my grasp. The stench of it I found enormous. "While we are quite different creatures, I am going to make a surmise. And that is that you and I are traveling to Charleston for the same reasons."

"And what might those be?" I said, tightening my hold on him.

"To study nature," he said.

"What kind of nature?"

"The nature of the beast," he said, twisting out of my hold and coming right back to take me by the wrist.

"Away with you!" I gave him a shove and he stumbled back along the planking.

I don't know what might have happened if a sailor, dressed all in white, had not appeared like a blur out of the shadows and inquired as to our business.

"Arm wrestling," the man in black said, "mere arm wrestling."

And with that he faded away into the darkness of the deck.

I stayed there a while, nearly out of breath, wondering what had come over me—and watching the emptiness of the dark, as if in hope some message might flare up that I could read. I saw no lights, and then fatigue and the sea air dragged me below.

For a short while I read by the light of the flickering candle at my bedside, finding a story of Nathaniel Hawthorne that had, when my teacher Halevi had first introduced me to it, pleased me no end. "My Kinsman, Major Molineux," the tale of a young New England boy who starts out one day in one world, the old time of the Tories who reigned in our country less than a hundred years ago, and by nighttime has his view of life turned around.

But I could read no further than the scene where the boy first arrives in town…oh, yes, sleep then pressed me onto my bunk where I lay quietly for a few moments, thinking of tardy Miriam and my father and even crooked-eyed Marzy and darling Aunt Isabelle, before sinking into the place of sea-borne dreams. If I had known it was the last time I would ever find this sort of peaceful slumber, I would have slept even deeper than deep.

Chapter Five

Passages

That stone—the gray face of it, with its three horizontal lines, one vertical—of all the memories of Zainab's childhood, and of all the shuddering recollections she had of that night on the river plain, when, just as the first light broke, the traders riding huge beasts came thundering down on them—that stone, lying pristine in her father's hand even as he gave up his last breath telling her to take it—that stone she plucked from his palm and carried with her, hidden on her body.

"Lie still," her mother said. And she obeyed, while listening to the stomping and snorting of the camels and the harsh voices of the men.

"They hurt Papa," Zainab said.

"Hush," said her mother. "They will take us back to the city. They will care for us."

"Will they make him better?"

"Hush…" Her mother reached over to her and touched her on the arm. "They will not harm us. They will take us back to the sheik."

"I don't want to go," Zainab said in a whisper.

"We have no choice."

The other children made low mewling noises, like hungry animals. Mother crawled toward them.

"Get up," said one of the traders, a lean man wrapped in a gray djellabah, his bald head catching the reflection of the early rising light.

"My children," her mother said.

"They are my children now," the trader said.

"We belong to the sheik," mother said. "If you harm us he will be angry."

"You belong to us now," the trader said. "Do you think the sheik will be happy to see you return after you have run from him? You are safer with us than with him. Is that not right, brothers?"

How many were there? Five, six? Most of them muttered their assent.

The sun lifted up from the eastern rim of the desert, splashing all of them in glorious red first light. The men sat her on a camel, with her siblings behind her. Her mother rode behind one of the traders, her hands bound, and somewhat off balance as they trotted away from the broad beaming rays of the newly risen sun. They rode west along the river. Zainab could hear her mother weep into her scarf as they moved slowly along.

"Where is Papa?" asked one of her sisters.

Zainab herself began to weep.

"You cannot do this to us," she heard her mother say in protest to one of the traders. "We belong to—"

Rough rude sound of flesh meeting flesh.

"We do what we must do," the trader said, moving on his beast up in rank, so that he led the little troop further west along the north bank of the river. The air grew thick with dust as the wind sailed down from the north, and the traders turned their faces away from it, one of them motioning for Zainab to cover her nose and mouth in her scarf. The children began weeping again and she tried to quiet them. It was hot. They were frightened. It was difficult to breathe. A coughing spell overtook her, to the point where one of the traders trotted up to her on his beast and handed her a vessel of water.

"Drink," he said.

She refused.

"Drink, Zainab," her mother called from where she rode along.

As she often would over the years, she felt beneath her clothing for the stone, and rubbed her fingers on it, rubbing, rubbing. Rubbing helped pass the minutes, it helped pass the hours.

One of her siblings coughed, and Zainab looked around and saw that the sun had slid across the southern sky, pointing them now to the west. That much geography she knew—this river ran from west to east, at least up to the near-gates of the city she had just left behind—and the sun rose in the east and set just ahead, in the mountains from whence the river sprang—she had heard the traders talking about the source of the river—and...and...and...Well, she did not know much more than that about the land and water, but she knew that God lived in the sky and watched over those who obeyed his laws.

Did she obey his laws?

"She's just a child," she remembered her mother saying once, when she and the jar-maker talked about the future of their older daughter. Their voices in her mind seemed so real to her, even though she knew her father lay sprawled on the stones back at that rough encampment they had left behind so many hours ago. Now the sun settled itself toward the western horizon. Fingers of light reached past it toward a few straggling clouds, turning them orange and then pink and then a certain variety of blue for which she had no name. These soon faded into the darkening sky behind them. She appeared to be riding toward the end of the earth, and after the short while it took for the darkness to fall on them like a large curtain from above she felt as though she were descending into her own body.

That night as the fire crackled and whistled she listened to the traders talking about their work. It quickly became clear to her that they were traveling toward a city some great long distance away. She stared at the black, star-flushed sky, and at dawn she was still gazing up, up, up, as all the stars paled except one bright point near the west, a crescent moon hovering near it.

Their trail hugged the river, passed over sand and salt-flats, as it turned out, with only low vegetation to break the horizon line, and now and then, after days of travel, they came upon a village and a well. Her mother seemed scarcely able to catch her breath, growing weaker by the day and eventually lying across the saddle like an animal brought down in a hunt, and so Zainab attended to the care of her younger siblings. It became important to her that their hair be neat. And that they stop their quiet weeping.

"Do you miss Father?" she said. "He will meet us where we're going. He will, he told me so."

After a while her lies calmed them, and she began to believe them herself. Yes, Father would be there. He had returned to their house in order to pack more tools, and he would hire another animal and catch up with them. No, he had traveled without stopping—how much faster men can travel without women or children to slow them down! He had passed them on one of the nights when they had camped and built a fire and passed around a jug of fresh water and roasted a lamb and torn away pieces of meat.

But why was it that the traders took so long to make this journey?

She had not wondered, until worried, in her fantasy, that father would pass them by altogether, she dared to ask one of them.

"What?" he said with a laugh. "What?" And he went lurching away into the night, laughing still, saying the word over and over.

A few days later she received an answer. They had been following the sun, and at one point it crossed over the river, or so it seemed, as the river meandered slightly to the north, and then back again, and when she again noticed, the sun had returned to the same place in the sky, only farther away, if that made sense. She felt soaked with sweat, which was unusual for a child her age. Everything was bright with the high sun and yet deeply carved with shadows, as if both the inside of her life—the thoughts she thought, the fears she held clenched in her mind like a fist—and the outside had appeared at the same time, one aspect pressed atop the other into a palimpsest of distress.

As if to ease this, she allowed her heart to take flight!

A small cloud of dust appeared on the horizon to the north, and the leader of the traders said something to the others, and they slowed down.

Father? she said to herself. Oh, Father, hurry, hurry to meet us!

As the animals moved forward along the river she kept peering to the north and watching the small cloud of dust become larger and larger.

At a certain point the traders began to talk among themselves.

It was her father! Yes! It had to be!

"Mother!" she called out. And then she called to her siblings to watch the horizon.

One of the traders turned his beast back toward her and came trotting up.

"Do not make trouble," he said, baring his teeth at her.

"My father, my father is coming!" she said.

He shook his head, and clicked at his mount and turned away.

"Crazy child," he said. "Worth nothing." He rode toward the head of the column as Zainab closed her eyes and prayed to the rhythm of the ambling camel. When next she looked at the horizon to the north the dust cloud had settled, and her heart sank, as she feared all had been an illusion, something even girls her age knew about, at least girls with active minds who sometimes dreamed while awake about things in life they desired.

It was not until they had stopped to pray and make camp for the night that her hopes rose again. The traders talked rapidly among themselves, and the one who had declared she was crazy kept stepping to the edge of their encampment and staring at the northern sky. There the fading light made way for the advent of a few glistering stars, and more and more of them appeared as she watched that dark part of the world return after a day away on the other side of the desert, or wherever the darkness went.

Something happened that night, and it wasn't until a while later that she fully understood. After a series of calm evenings, when only the cool wind that blew after the sun went down gave her any cause for worry, she was awakened by an animal crying, and it took her a few minutes of listening to it before she understood that it was her mother, weeping, as silently as she could but still loud enough to wake her.

Mother, no, Zainab urged her. Please quiet down or the traders will awake.

I will not, her mother said in protest, squirming and squealing like a child.

Mother!

I will not!

At which point Zainab picked up a rather large stone—three horizontal lines across it, she noticed, one vertical—and smashed it into her mother's face.

And sat up awake, crying out, breathing hard. She looked around and saw one of the traders sitting up with a rifle on his lap and keeping watch on the night.

"You have bad dreams? I can give you good dreams." He smiled at her, and she looked away in fear, but he came no closer and finally she slept again.

The next morning came their rendezvous with five traders leading a long line of nearly naked dark men connected by chains attached to iron collars. Some of the men walked upright, others stooped, others had to be dragged by those just in front or pushed along by those just behind them. Their misery sounded on the air like the buzzing of a plague of locusts.

At the end of that day's journey, Zainab stayed close to her mother and the other children. At sundown, a terrible chill overtook her and she shivered through the night. Now and then a strange voice, and then another, broke through the darkness and she heard the sound of the dark men shifting in their chains. At one point she awoke to find one of the new traders hovering over her, smiling, with filed teeth. Or was that a dream again, like the vision of her mother the night before? All through her childhood it had taken her a while to sort out the differences between dreams and actual events, and now she was fast slipping back again into that realm of confusion. She shivered at sunrise, shivered through the long day's ride.

Her mother hovered near her all the while as they moved along the river bank, where they found women bathing and washing clothes, small children clinging to their backs. The traders kept their cargo moving, though the one with filed teeth whistled at the women and his chief gave him a nasty look.

Damp, nearly liquid, heat rose all through what turned out to be the last day of their journey. People began to fill the paths and the traders now and then had to shoo away curious children who poked at the captives with fingers and sticks. Voices of chanting women shimmered through the air, and on the horizon low brown buildings appeared, as if painted into the pale lower half of the sky. Only slightly higher than the rest stood a mosque, also red-brown against the pearl-like scrim of the world.

Zainab, following on her mount the animal of the trader before her, raised her head at the sound of the call to prayer. She was astonished at the noise that followed, the rattle of sticks on drums rising somewhere in the town ahead. And then a great trumpeting, and lurching into view near-stumbled a long-nosed creature, rough, gray, ridged, and monstrous, red lines streaked across its serrated back and enormous plumes tied to its long tusks, and a long line of dancers following behind.

One of the traders turned and grabbed the reins of her beast, and the long line of men chained together at the neck crumpled, one by one, as if pierced by arrows or spears—or bullets.

Who wouldn't have been afraid? Zainab had never seen anything like it, this huge rough animal bedecked with feathers and paint. It gave her a thrill she never knew as a child and made her wonder, as she breathed deeply at the approach of a line of dark-limbed women dressed in gaudy clothes and feathery headdresses, just what kind of a world she was entering here, where the desert ended and hills rose to the west and where, as her own daughters would one day discover, the river struck out from its source. Clouds lurked above the hills, threatening to burst open and drench everything below.

Chapter Six

A Line in the Water

*I*n the first light of the new morning at sea I awoke, sat up, and said my prayers, feeling the very change in the weather, as though a line had been drawn in the water which we had crossed sometime in the night. From where we had sailed, New York, Perth Amboy, the Virginia coast, it had been winter, and now we moved through spring and the air itself sang a different tune in the spreading sails overhead.

"…yawlfancyforatoinpashatteras…"

A voice from above—God? No, a sailor climbing the highest point of the deck.

"What, sir?" I called up to him.

"…past Hatteras," he said, pointing to the coast line, a burnished high yellow green in the first light of morning.

"The Cape Hatteras?"

"Yes, sir," he called down to me. "Turning past it just now…"

I went to the rail and took a deep, deep breath, feeling the salt air rise in my lungs as if I were inhaling the chemic broth of the South. I felt like the boy in the Hawthorne story, a kinship not merely formed by the likeness of the author's name and mine, but because of the sense of having put one world behind me as I faced the new one just coming over the horizon. The paternal old God of my father and his father before him had drawn a line in my life, and I had crossed it already, on my way to the new parts.

Sails and hulls littered the green waters near shore the closer we got to our destination. Past Cape Lookout—another sailor kindly informed me of our location—by lunch (which, not caring much to speak again with the other passengers, I took in my cabin), and after dinner, as the last of the sun quickened toward the western horizon, we sailed past Cape Fear. The winds changed yet again, becoming less intermittent and undependable, as if the gods whose breath they were—I'm joking, of course, in a metaphorical way here, as only old tutor Halevi has taught me to do—were working more in tandem with our fates. Dolphins swooped up out of the depths and skimmed the waves and dove again. Their beautiful swimming gave me such a sign of hope as I can hardly describe!

One more night at sea. Though the ocean was calm my heart and mind were not, no matter how intensely I tried to concentrate on my reading by lamplight. Alas, I felt so suddenly sorry for myself, sailing south as I was instead of across the heaving Atlantic on my way to England and my tour. In disgust at myself and the world, I turned down the lamp. As I lay in the rolling dark, I was not only traveling south over the water in this ship but traveling in my mind back north into the past, to the morning in Perth Amboy when I awoke to my dear mother's last outcries, the morning I watched her slip away into another country. Oh, sleep, I cried out on the stage in my imagination where all this played out. Sleep, come soon and blot all this into blackness!

A bell clanged me awake. Shouts and cries, the shrill pitch of seabird calls, the roar of barrels rolling and sails flapping, announcing Charleston in the morning. If in New York the air was thin and drenched with sun, here it was thick, syrupy and wet with light that seemed to rise up from within the shallow turbulent waters rather than settle upon us from the sun above. And that thick air carried a different sort of sound, not so much music as the essence of birdsong—calls from the seabirds skimming above us, calls from birds ashore—and that thick air bore a certain perfume, the scent you imagined emanating from the gardens of Paradise, a whiff of fruit and tart flower, and sweet fire and the flow of melted sugar and chocolate and coffee and tea. And if in New York there had been a black face or two in the larger crowd, here it was all reversed, with the majority of faces black— from the longshoremen who caught the ropes cast to them from the bow by the *Godbolt*'s crew to the men who lounged in place behind large carts and wheelbarrows heaped high with packets and bales to the children who skidded about underfoot almost as if in a dare to the larger human creatures to step on them if they could—all were black.

The color of things, not just the faces of the slaves (and I was assuming that here, unlike New York, all black people were slaves) but the air and the noise and the light, made me feel as though I had arrived in another country, a place that I might have imagined if I had read about it in one of the history books that Halevi and I had studied together, somewhere that I could not have constructed in my mind without great prompting. It wasn't that I didn't appreciate the sight of the harbor, the ships, the piers, the warehouses, and the city beyond. It was just that I never would have imagined it in this way, perhaps never would have, never could have, imagined it at all.

Was it the kind of mind I had? Or was I just too young and—peace be unto you, Halevi—too unschooled to appreciate or understand these matters? Who knows what I might have decided then and there if I wasn't rudely jarred from my musings by the silver-haired man in black cape and suit brushing past me, followed by his young black servant with the baggage.

As he briskly descended the gangplank he turned and hurled these words up at me:

"Pereira, we'll meet again, I'm sure!"

And then he cut a brusque passage through the crowd, followed by the boy with the bags.

I would have kept my eye on him, except I was immediately distracted by a young woman, sweet of face, who waved a handkerchief at me. Yes, I was sure she was waving to me.

A sailor came up alongside me and picked up my bag. But I took it from him and made my way down the gangplank, pleased that I needed neither slave nor free man to help me carry my baggage. A smile spread across my face—I could feel it stretching the skin of my cheeks—and I advanced toward the waving woman.

"Cousin Nathaniel?"

Her voice, a cooling slow-turned series of noises, wrapped around my name in the oddest way I'd ever heard. She had dark blue eyes and wore her brown hair parted in the middle with curls dangling at either side of her face like twirling vines.

"Sir!"

A man alongside her, a paunchy fellow, much older than me, with a flat nose and a fierce green-eyed gaze, thrust out his hand.

"Hello," I said.

"I am your cousin Jonathan," he said, "and this is my wife Rebecca."

"I'm pleased to meet you," I said, and turning to Rebecca said, "And touched that you waved so heartily at a complete stranger like me."

Rebecca laughed, and pressed herself against my cousin's arm.

"He is just like you," she said to Jonathan. "Why, it runs in the family, doesn't it?"

"What does, darling?" Jonathan said. He spoke to her using sweet words but his tone seemed born of distraction and perhaps more paternal than avuncular.

I could not help but stare at this man, whether because of my own curiosity at meeting someone with my own family blood or because I had been sent to investigate the means of his livelihood or even for some even deeper reason I could not say. Certainly I saw a passionate intensity in his eyes, though mixed with some other extremes that I could not find the words to describe. He certainly looked back to me with great fervor. And he spoke with deep feeling.

"Welcome to Charleston, Nathaniel, we are hoping you are going to stay with us a while."

"Why, yes," I began, "since our fathers—"

At which point I felt a tug at my hand and a slender hard-jawed dark man a year or two younger than myself tugged at my bag.

My first response was to keep holding on to it.

"Allow Isaac to help you," my cousin said, noticing, almost before I did, that I was not about to hand over my possessions.

"Of course," I said, nodding to the young man, who meandered away with the bag toward the edge of the crowd.

We followed slowly along, with my cousin pointing this way and that at various buildings and alleys and streets, saying names I did not catch. I was feeling a bit disoriented, walking on land after my days on the ocean, and the sun lay like a thick cap upon my head and like a heavy cape upon my shoulders. I blinked against its brightness, and felt suddenly rather sleepy and struggled to catch my breath.

"This weather…" I said.

My cousin laughed, and Rebecca reached for my arm.

"You will become accustomed to our weather," she said. "After a few years…"

"I am not—" I said. And then laughed at her joke, enjoying the sweet and appealing way that she laughed in response.

"Are you hungry, sir?" my cousin said. "Because if you are we can take food here or begin our drive to the plantation."

"My head says drive, my stomach says stay here a while."

"Good man," my cousin said, clapping a heavy arm tightly around me. "Rebecca, let us treat him to our best."

Rebecca shook her curls and took me by the other arm.

"I am so happy you are here!"

We ate beneath the shade of a large umbrella at an open-air market near the docks, served by African waiters who carried plates of fried fish and vegetables galore to our long table. After my days and nights on the water I found that I had developed a huge appetite and concentrated on meeting it when I became distracted by shouts and cries from the market building nearby, as though some athletic competition were transpiring. It wasn't until I remarked on it that my cousin mentioned the auction.

"Auction? What kind of auction?" I said.

"Come, I will show you," my cousin said, a thin smile curling at his lip.

Rebecca shook her curly head.

"I was afraid of this. Please, no."

"He should see it, Rebecca, don't you think? He will sooner or later, so why not sooner? It is one of the major attractions of our fair city."

The noises grew louder, and I set down my utensils, my appetite piqued for another variety of hunger.

"No, please, sir," I said. "We are here now. I want to see it, whatever it is you speak of."

"I will not," Rebecca said, with a shake of her curls. "These poor Africans...take him without me."

"Africans?" I said.

"Today there are no Africans," my cousin said. "The federal government allows us no more Africans at our ports, you know."

"You know what I meant," Rebecca said. "You will go alone. Show your cousin, if you dare. Show him what life is really like down here." She gave a toss of her head and turned from him. "I will wait for you at the carriage."

My cousin pretended that his wife had not shown any scorn toward him in public.

"If you will excuse us, my darling," he said. And motioned for me to rise and follow him.

"Women are the frailer kind, are they not?" he said to me.

And so it was only an hour or so after my arrival here on a delightful morning, in bright sunlight, in lovely warm air, with the perfume of flowers on the breeze mingling with the fresh odors of sea salt, that I, a descendent of slaves from Egypt and Babylon, witnessed my first trading in human flesh.

Chapter Seven

In My Margins

What Are the Origins of the Body?

Life and freedom, inextricably bound, can we ever know which came first? I have read the Bible, I have read the Qur'an, I have read Darwin, I have read the commentators, and what do I know for all of that? That I don't know, no, I don't, not unless I say I don't know and I'll let some bearded who-dah in a collar or skull-cap or turban tell me that he has the word of God and will now tell me what I am supposed to know.

But I hold certain ideas over others. Sometimes I walk along the cliffs and stare out at the rushing ocean, the power there nearly convincing me that we began as ocean soup and divided, cell from cell, until we grew more complicated and complex than the early cells could ever imagine—because isn't that like our growing up ourselves, the way we know nothing and then learn as much as we can before the wind snuffs us out like a candle? One cell from another cell, and both are equal, no man cell first and, after you, my dear, then the woman cell.

When the tide recedes and I climb down to walk among the sea-wrack and detritus, the delicious stink of life freshly delivered up by the waves, salt and sun and ammoniac air all mixed together, oh, I know I know, at least I think I know, that the miracle of God making man from clay and then woman from man's clay might be a wonderful metaphor for our creation from the slightly moist and highly compacted earth and sand left behind when the tide went out for a million years. And the spark of lightning, like some old mining prospector's last match, or first, breaks into fire, and heats up life's dinner, first and foremost, once and for all.

Some say the world began in fire, some say in water. Why such opposites? Unless we need to embrace both and all the elements when we think of the extraordinary event that is life?

The bits and parts of living things came together in the oceans to make the fish.

One fish crawled on its stubby legs up onto the beach, and returned again and again. And then another and another.

Did the fish become clay?

The gods molded out of wet clay a man, and then a woman. Or a woman, and then a man. And breathed breath into them.

A complicated story made simple or a simple story made complicated? All these variations, leading back to mystery.

Out of water, out of clay our mother was born.

These meanderings I offer as I try to tell the story.

Chapter Eight

The Auction

Fear, hope, love, hate, illusion, dismay boiled up in the Charleston market, known as the center for slave auctions in the region. Buyers and sellers came from far and wide to attend. And sell and buy. A large crowd wrestled about in the interior of one of the low brick market buildings, and my cousin feigned surprise. There were no longer any fresh shipments of Africans, as he explained, so this was only local chattel, slaves from farms in this county, neighboring counties, and other southern states, some of them—he tried to make a joke—from almost as far away as Africa itself.

"I myself," he said, "have not come here for a rather long while, since we have most of our needs taken care of by our own slave families. That is, breeding and such for new hands. The boy, Isaac, who carries your bag, he was bred on our property. But now and then we do need to come here, and the prices, I have to say, have risen quite sharply since the African trade ended." He paused and stood in quiet thought amidst the din. "Now, do not worry if you feel struck almost by a physical blow as you watch. I recall the first time I came here, Father had me accompany him when I was a boy, and it struck me that way." He then fixed me with a stare, as though he were a scientific investigator of some sort, straining to detect my response.

I did respond. I felt myself becoming overtaken by the noise, by the sight of the bare-backed blacks, men and women, standing in chains, some of them muttering to themselves, a few of them praying aloud, one or two of them even singing, as if no one else could hear. It reeked in here something together like a sick room and a back street after a hot rain in summer. Given the sweat pouring out of me, I had to imagine the other men milling about here were effusing doubt and worry as much as the slaves were sweating in fear. I had a mad impulse to rush up to the manager and grab the keys that dangled from the belt at his waist, and unlock each and every lock on every chain and set these people free. Especially the women. It seemed so cruel to keep these females in chains, as if unchained they might do someone harm. And it was quite astonishing to me that most of the slave men and women remained so calm, and that the free people in the room were acting in such a frenzy.

The white men, some of them of a company arranging the sales, shouted the blacks down, while other whites milling about, studying the wares, or poking and pinching Africans here or there so that black flesh suddenly turned white before the mark faded, kept their silence.

I looked over at my cousin, the sweat running down my forehead into my eyes and stinging, stinging.

"Is it always so hot in here?" I asked.

"The heat aside," my cousin said, "what do you think of this?"

I shook my head, my entire body feeling inflamed by all that went on around us, blacks led around in their chains, white men shouting.

"I can see," he said, "that you have not prepared yourself for this. Here." My cousin reached into his coat pocket and came up with a silver flask, proffering it to me.

"No, thank you," I said.

"Have a sip, sir, a sip only, and that will restore you."

"Very well," I said, and took a sip from the flask, feeling even greater heat and the heady moment afforded by the fine brandy contained therein.

I handed the flask back to my cousin, and he took a long swallow from the container, and, just before returning it to his coat, another.

"Tell me," I said, over the din, "How much does it cost to buy a slave?" From another pocket he took out a piece of coarse paper on which some printing had been made and handed it to me.

OFFER OF SALE

OFFERED BY CHARLES TRISTMAN THE FOLLOWING SIX SLAVES:

MAREE, BLACK GIRL 16 YEARS OLD AT $1250.00

MARYAN, BLACK GIRL 16 YEARS OLD AT $1250.00

LUCY, GRIF GIRL 14 YEARS OLD AT $1150.00

BETTE, GRIF GIRL 14 YEARS OLD AT $1150.00

JANE, BLACK GIRL 12 YEARS OLD AT $1000.00

JAMES, BLACK BOY 14 YEARS OLD AT $1200.00
ALL OF SAID SLAVES ARE WARRANT SOUND AND HEALTHY IN BODY
AND IN MIND AND SLAVES FOR LIFE...

"What is a 'grif girl'?" I asked.

"A slave of mixed blood," my cousin said. "That is, white and African. A mixture that always improves the stock."

My stomach turned at his words. While my cousin talked to me of high prices, of dollars, and the cost of a hardy male and the cost of a breeding female, I felt my temperature rise. After a few moments I thought I might, like some fragile female, fall to the ground in a faint.

"I am afraid I am feeling somewhat ill."

"You are here to learn about our business," he said, "and this is the first part of the first lesson." Once more he offered me a drink from the flask. I hesitated, and he thrust the container at me, refusing to bend until I took another sip.

"Now," he said, after taking another drink for himself and giving me a bullying stare, "New Yorkers are famous for being bold, are they not? Stand tall, Cousin. Look and listen."

Thus, despite my fear that I might succumb to my growing misery, we stayed. With my mind abuzz from the powerful brandy I watched and groaned as the noise grew louder and the bosses urged first one and then another and another black in chains up onto the platform in the center of the building, shouting out names and prices and qualities. Vile sweat and fearful breath drenched the air and as bodies glistened in the heat men moved forward to press and study the flesh and bones of the darker people—some with mouths open in silent prayer, others muttering curses, most of them silent, mouths clenched.

One man bid a slave to raise his arms, one at a time, over his head. Another asked a woman to turn and turn as he gazed at her breasts (and I gazed at him gazing and then gazed back at her, feeling myself become aroused, and scolding myself for that). And there in the middle of it I saw an unwanted if familiar figure, the man from New Jersey, still cloaked all in black, moving in a studious manner from slave to slave, the young black boy tagging along behind him. As if he felt my eyes on him he turned and stared directly at me.

"Young New Yorker!" he called out. "We have some things to discuss!"

"Do you know that man?" my cousin said.

"From the voyage here," I said.

"I have seen him before," my cousin said.

The din grew louder as my cousin appeared to study the man for a few moments, and then turned to me. I felt even more unsteady on my feet and motioned to my cousin, himself with eyes downturned, that I did truly wish to retreat.

"Perhaps it was a mistake to come here first," he said when at last we left the market for the sweeter, fresher air of the pier-side. "But do not judge what we do by what you just witnessed. If you went into a hospital surgery and saw the surgeons sawing off limbs you might be disturbed but you would not think all surgeons did such things to all people they knew."

"I am not here to judge anyone," I said, remembering the business of my purpose. "I am here to learn about the workings of the plantation."

"Of course," said my cousin, leading me, flask in hand, from the place of misery.

"Was it awful?" Rebecca said as we approached.

I nodded.

"It makes me want to run away from here," she said. "Nathaniel, they do not do things like this up north, do they?"

"No, no, they don't," I said. "Up north everyone's free."

"Jews are free, I know."

"Of course," I said. "Everyone is free. Or most everyone."

"Then I cannot wait to visit the North."

"Yes," I said, "you two must come and visit us in New York."

Lapsing into polite chatter, punctuated by further sips from my cousin's flask, I bathed copiously in my own sweat, and soon we made our way to the carriage. I confess that the memory of the auction crowd, bathed in brandy, quickly faded from my mind.

Chapter Nine

Koulikoro

*I*n the land of cloud and rain, first, they separated Zainab from her mother—she, as it turned out, was put into service as one of the caretakers in a nursery—leading her into a large compound where a fountain flowed in a central courtyard and many servants, some jet black, some as brown as the desert and herself, moved languidly to and fro as they carried out various tasks. Two tall dark women led her into a room off this courtyard where they undressed her and bathed her in warm water and rubbed her with oils. They gave her sweet food and something to drink.

"I want my mother," was the last thing she remembered saying before waking up under a carpeted canopy, with moonlight spilling down onto a small central pool. A huge man with a smooth face who smelled of animals held her in his flabby arms.

"From this moment on, I am your mother, and I am your father," the man said, and raised her face to his to give her a wet animal kiss. He reached down toward his waist, as if he were groping for lice or a hidden bag of gold, and before she knew it he had her lying on the carpet, her silks tossed aside, jabbing at her with a large purple-tipped growth from his groin. In he shoved and she screamed in fear that he would rip her apart.

Two-thirds of a year later she felt the same way as she gave birth to her first child, a plump brown girl. Motherhood gave her pleasure. Not so for her own mother, not so when she caught a glimpse of her son carried off in chains to some unknown destination, not so when she heard that one of her sisters had died in child-birth and other, who after producing two children, ran off with one of the other slaves and died somewhere in the forests to the south.

The news of the first death sent her mother into a despair from which she never recovered. She lasted a year, and then came a morning when she never awoke. Ten years after that first morning when the family fled from Timbuktu, Zainab had given birth to four children (one of whom, her second boy, had died within days of being born), and acquired a wealth of silk clothing, and still possessed that stone with the markings. She carried the object with her wherever she went, and at night she kneaded it in her palm, trying to recall the fading details of her father, the jar-maker, her last images of his smiling face and the work of his hands, those plates and pots and jars, but mostly what came to mind was his outstretched hand, the small marked stone resting in his still palm.

Zainab's children grew around her, and she grew complacent in her silks, happy to have her health despite all the births, and happy with the attentions of the Master, the big man, the head of a large clan whose political branch ruled the empire of Koulikoro, who came to her a few months after each child had been born and wedded her again.

How many wives there were altogether, Zainab wasn't sure. The number waxed and waned, and then waxed again. She knew at least half a dozen others here in this compound, and she learned about other harems in other places where he lived, in the city, and in clan villages to the west and south. The women in the compound whispered about his power and reach, from the capital here all the way into the southern forests. His rivals, and he had some in outlying parts of the kingdom, acted feebly, as weak as ants. His powers, if not infinite, for only God had infinite powers, were many. He was big, and grew bigger, in his body and in reputation, and his wives felt big, as though their lives meant something more than what they seemed to be, because they belonged to the big man. But it wasn't until the day of their fateful boat trip that she had any idea of the politics and intrigue that surrounded him.

Heavy rains that winter had made for a large spring flow, and the river swelled beyond its usual borders, a perfect time for an excursion toward the mountains. Five large rafts, each with a tent and a surplus of slaves, who were cooks and tenders and body servants, one or two of whom she thought she recognized as the survivors of that long chain of captives who had accompanied her on her initial journey along the river all those years ago, and there were nurse-maids and young boys whose job was to do everything that none of the others did. The last raft transported the body-guards and warrior-slaves, a mean-looking dozen or so of them.

The sky, a light blue dome above them. The air, warm, a gentle wind rippling the pennants toward the east even as the boatmen poled the rafts westward.

Zainab and her children—just imagine, because she could never have thought of this before she had given birth the first time, a clutch of children—sat on cushions on the lead raft, with the big man, and the others trailing behind her on another of the boats. Women at the shoreline working at their wash waved limp palms at the passing spectacle. From the second boat came intermittent sounds of flutes and drums as the wind carried the noise here and there along the brown swathe of water.

All of this put a big smile on the face of the Master.

"You are happy, Master," Zainab said, addressing him, but averting her eyes, as always.

"The kingdom is quiet, we float on the river, we take our food and drink…What could be better in life? May, God willing, in the years we have left, such calm always descend on us." With a hand the span of which could encompass the heads of two of his small children, he gestured upriver. "As with those fishermen—" a group of men stood and sat in a boat with wings like those of a butterfly, with another boat just like it drifting a few yards behind—"may we find simple fare beneath the slow-flowing waters…"

The Niger current lapped gently at the prow of their barge. A few minutes later and they turned toward the shore, where the chefs would make a feast and the musicians and dancers would perform into the night.

As darkness set in around them and the drumming subsided Zainab, her belly full and her head a bit woozy from the heat of the day-long trip in the sun, felt herself sinking slowly into a familiar state, the dreamy false freedom of the lifelong captive whose only escape from her condition was sleep. And yes, she did dream, dreamed she was dreaming, and listening to a voice from the river.

"Oh, dear girl, I have fallen as rain to meet you here, to assure you that whatever happens all will in the end be well. Lean toward me." Zainab bent her head toward the stream. Out of the flowing current a hand arose and painted her forehead with water from the current. This made her feel so calm she said to herself as she slept that if life always felt like this—a gentle palm upon her forehead—she could live it all the way through.

At which point she was torn from her sleep by shouts and high screams.

Tall figures stood at the fire, waving sticks of flame.

A gunshot rang out across the star-diffused sky, and other screams rose into the shadowy dark.

"Mama!" Her youngest child, a boy as plump as the big man, shouted in her ear. "The fishermen! They killed my father!"

Her daughters came screaming, and nightmares rode into the camp on camels higher than the tallest among the slaves, dark bodies of the beasts and dark bodies of the men blocking out the stars.

These were indeed fishermen, fishers of men.

And women.

Chapter Ten

This Charming City

*F*ree of the stink of the auction house, this charming city overtook me with its delightful houses, narrow structures that faced onto side gardens and stretched back further into gardens behind. There was as much foot traffic as in New York, and the edges of the streets were filled mostly with these walkers, almost exclusively black-faced, women with children slung over their backs in little bundles, and men with garden tools and others hauling crates and packages. But though all of these folk appeared to be working, there was much less of a hurry and hustle about the streets than in my native town, mainly because the heat was such that everyone, slave or free, had to carry about the extra burden of the temperature and its humid essence.

"Here is the courthouse," my cousin said, as we approached an impressively erected building, though of a miniature size compared to our New York structures. And the Episcopal church. And another church. And a meeting hall. At the corner a crowd of men on horseback, in rough country garb, jittered and huddled, their horses covered with dust. A short man with wiry hair sat high upon a tall stallion in the center of them, the horse so white it glowed almost blue.

"What's this?" I asked.

My cousin shook his head.

"It is a man named Langerhans," Rebecca said. "If man he is. He is more like something carved out of the mud…"

As if he had heard her say his name—though over the noise of the horses and at this distance it seemed doubtful—the mud-man turned his head, following us as we moved by

"Halloo!" he called in our direction, touching a finger to his right eyebrow in a sort of salute.

"Ignore him," my cousin said to Rebecca as the white horse stepped closer.

"Saw your nigger girl just now, carrying some basket or other," the man said as his horse danced sidewise toward and yet away from us.

"Thank you, Langerhans," my cousin said, "as you are paid to keep watch, it's good to know you're on the lookout."

"You are welcome, sir," Langerhans said, a shy grin spreading across his face. He showed dark teeth and it was not a pretty sight, and yet, overall, his visage was not unappealing.

"But you are supposed to keep watch outside of town, not here," Jonathan said.

"We are just leaving, sir," the man said.

"Good, then good, just do your job."

With that, my cousin gave a snap of his buggy-whip and we moved along, putting those others behind us.

"Who are they?" I said.

"Patrollers. Poor nasty wretches," my cousin said. "They make a living out of the misery of others."

"That's how many of us up north think of you plantation owners," I said. I no sooner spoke when I felt the heat of deep embarrassment spreading up my chest, neck, and face. "I am sorry."

"No need to apologize," Rebecca said. "No need. We're just going to have to show you a new side of things then," Rebecca said. "Some of us are working to improve the African souls. Jonathan?"

"Yes, although we have a lot of obstacles to overcome," my cousin said, the look he gave me scarcely matching the restrained tone of his voice. Clearly the brandy had soothed whatever troubled him, but not enough. "Now here is our place."

We slowed up and took in the trim stone building on our left, the synagogue called Beth Elohim on Coming Street.

"Where we have recently had quite a revolution," my cousin said. "For there were those who objected to the use of an organ in the service, and they seceded and met just across the way."

"I'm sorry I missed the war," I said.

"Oh, there will be more of it, I am sure," said Rebecca, with a laugh. "A hundred Jews, and each has his own opinion about God."

"Our family remained with the majority," my cousin said. "Rebecca's family left with the secessionists."

"I hope that has not made trouble for you," I said.

"Oh, yes," my cousin said, "but pleasant trouble. Rebecca, would you say it has spiced things up a bit between us?"

"Yes, it is very romantic," she said, "to meet across the line of dispute. Like Juliet and Romeo." She looked at me in a way both shy and inquisitive. "Do you have a Juliet at home?"

"I have a Miriam," I said, and the words struck me like pellets from a gun. Yes, I did, did I not? My Juliet? I had never thought of her that way before.

"That is sweet," Rebecca said. "Do you miss her?"

"I have not been away that long," I said. "But I am sure I will."

By this time in our journey my coat was soaked through, as was the handkerchief I used to dab the rivulets of sweat from my face.

"The weather here," I remarked, happy to change the subject, "it takes some getting used to."

My cousin laughed deep in his throat, but, I was noticing, however deep his merriment seemed somehow forced.

"We are born into it here," he said. "The amusing part is that the Africans themselves have some trouble with the heat."

Rebecca leaned across my cousin's chest and touched me on the arm.

"The worst is not the heat but the sickness. The fevers and agues that abound in this part of the country, they sometimes grow ferocious. With the swamps to the north and west and south and the ocean to our east, it is as though we live on an island, and now and then we find we have an unwanted visitation in the fever. A torrent of it swept through the county last year and took half a dozen of our people. The Africans, in fact, call it 'The Visitor.'"

"So," I said, taking a deep breath and hoping to lift us out of the momentary slough we'd fallen into, "you are comparing me to a disease? I am, after all, just a visitor."

The two of them laughed.

"And quite welcome," my cousin said. "That is true, is it not, Rebecca?"

She reached across my cousin and touched me again, giving me cause to think how fortunate any child of hers would be, to know a mother's touch so gentle.

"Yes, yes, absolutely. Why, we have had no guests in a long while and we're all looking forward to getting to know you."

"Yes, yes," my cousin said, "though with all this talk about disease,

you will be quite sick of all of us long before the time comes for you
to depart."

"I doubt that," I said, but then what did I know at the time?

It was growing late, but there remained a part of the city my cousins
wanted me to see, the lovely turns of road where the town met the ocean,
and we had one more errand to run, so we headed to what he called The
Battery. There we stopped the carriage and admired the pretty houses (with
their white columns and plentiful flowering trees and vines, quite different
from our staid northern brick facades) and gazed awhile at the ocean. Fort
Sumter lay a mile or two offshore, like a man-made shoal, and the sun
showed silver off the placid sea. Few creatures moved around us, and the
heat lay heavy on everything, settling in our lungs. I could imagine that
even the ocean had stopped for a while beneath this weight of sun, the
ceaseless waverings of its surface and perhaps even its deeper current flows.
I could imagine that standing here over and again, time itself might seem
to have a stop.

"But we must go now," my cousin said, speaking as if to contradict me
and rousing me from my overheated reverie. "Liza is waiting."

And so we headed away from the sea, rolling back to the pier where
in the small enclosed market I had first seen the auction of dark human
beings. There a woman emerged to meet us, carrying baskets in each
hand, a bright turban atop her head, her face a splendor of mahogany
cheek bones and bright green eyes and a straight nose that made her look
more Hebraic than African.

The sight of her made me shiver in the heat.

Rebecca smiled as the slave girl approached. "Cousin, she is my prize."

I shut my eyes tight and then opened them to watch the woman climb
aboard the carriage onto the driver's bench, on which sat the lean young
dark man who had taken my bag.

At such close quarters, the sight of her shut my throat.

Chapter Eleven

Tambacounda

The further west they traveled, the worse things became. Unlike most of the Arab men, these slavers, mostly dark-skinned ruffians, some with decorative scars on faces and foreheads and some with filed teeth, treated them roughly and without respect. They touched, they pinched, they pulled, and then laughed and spat. Brutes, infidels who never stopped to pray, they worried her. They harried everyone to move along during the day, and at night around the fires, as if picking a piece of roasted meat from a tray, they would pluck a woman from the group and carry her off into the dark.

Twice they took Zainab, and each time she prayed and resisted, but to no avail. The pain settled into her as if an exquisite punishment from God. Bruised in the flesh and chilled in her blood she returned to her family at the fire, refusing to speak, and taking the smallest child in her arms in the hopes of finding some warmth to live for—almost to no avail. Her soul felt as though she had dropped it into a deep well and left it to drown.

Lilith, her middle daughter, a willowy tan-complected girl with an even disposition, tried to calm her.

"Mama," she said, "one day our father will find us and take his revenge on these awful men."

Zainab shuddered, with a chill even more cutting than the remorse that already cooled her blood—that a child of hers would find it necessary to say such things! It was a horror, a horror! And yet things might have been worse, because she could not know what we know, that every hour and every day and month and year brought them closer and closer—the children's children, at least, because she herself would not live to see it—to their terrifying passage over nearly limitless water.

More days of rough travel, the land becoming hilly and the trail turning away from the river, to climb and climb in the direction of the retreating sun. For the first time Zainab felt the chill of nights at a high elevation, and she slumped into a fever, and again her children attended to her while the dark enveloped them all and the noise of drums and the high ringing chirps of animals rang around them. She had been born into a land of few trees. Now that it became a possibility that she might die beneath a canopy of dark wood which at night seemed to fall slowly upon her as the flames of the cook-fire dimmed down to feebly glowing embers, she fought with the demonic thought of welcoming her end sooner than later. If the traders approached her one more time she would fight with them, until they killed her.

But then the worry of the children living without her changed her mind. And then the thought of the children living as captives in this dark and cooling land made her want to kill them and herself on the spot.

She slept holding Lilith to her breast, as if that might hide the girl from any traders with wandering eyes.

It did not.

After a long day's trek westward through the dry bush of a long valley the traders stopped the caravan to camp beneath a giant acacia tree and settled in to cook. Zainab had herself long ago given up on prayer, unable to find it within herself to submit to a god who would allow such torment to persist. Her own years were over, but the worry that her children would live as chattel, however well treated, for the rest of *their* lives filled her with dread. What kind of a god would inflict such suffering on so many for such a long period of time?

Daughter Lilith appeared at her side with a thick piece of bark that held a slice of fruit and some mashed vegetable.

"Mama, you must eat," she said.

"Ah, I've become the child and you've become the mother," Zainab said. "The whole world is turned around, upside down."

"Yes, mother," Lilith said, "backwards is forwards and forwards is back. Please eat. I heard the traders talking and it seems we still have at least one more day to walk before we reach Tambacounda."

"Tambacounda?"

"That is where we are going," Lilith said. "There is a market there."

Zainab could not help but groan.

"You heard them talking about that, too?"

"Yes, Mama."

Zainab felt a stabbing pain in her chest and turned away from her daughter to clutch her hands to her heart.

"What is it, Mama?"

"In that town, a place I have never heard of before all in the days we lived in Timbuktu, they will sell us."

"No, Mama," Lilith said. "No, no, no, no. They have a chief there, and he will take care of us, feed us, and give us clothing."

"He will buy us first," Zainab said. "For you and me and your sisters he will offer these brutes some coins. Or cloth. Or perhaps even a horse or a camel or two." She took her daughter in her arms and pulled her tightly to her chest. "You know we are worth more than anything anyone can pay..."

"I like to ride a horse, Mama," Lilith said. Such innocence in her eyes when she spoke, and when she remained silent—the thought of some man riding her daughter was almost more than Zainab could bear.

"Here," she said, pushing the sack with the marked stone into her daughter's hands. "This is not for you to lose."

At a crossroads—could this be Tambacounda?—they entered a large market. Stalls and tents, horses and camels tethered behind them, the vast animal smell of caravan life rose like smoke from a vast fire as they approached. One half the sky lay in darkness—this to the east—the other with the last light of the day. Drums resounded behind the large array of covers and pennants, and Zainab could also hear, ever so faintly, a wavering call to prayer.

The traders led their entourage into the city where from the gates of a domed palace hundreds and hundreds of slaves, armed with various weapons—bows, short lances, shields—burst forth into the large square before it. Within the walls a sultan presided over business in a lofty pavilion, and off to one side stood troops, governors, young men, slaves. Musicians among the slaves blew bugles and beat drums with sticks and made a wonderful sound. Before the sultan's chair jugglers and acrobats performed. The traders led their entourage off to one side of the court-yard, where a long-bearded man with a book inscribed numbers with a reed pen. His wives and many concubines stood behind him wearing fine silks, bands of gold and silver around their heads, singing quietly among themselves while their master went about his work of dispatching the goods presented to them by the traders.

Zainab screamed and the girls wailed and before they knew it they lived apart from each other for the rest of their lives.

Chapter Twelve

The Old Oak Plantation

A long, dusty carriage ride brought us to a location about fifteen miles outside of Charleston—and I tried my best to look forward at the road ahead rather than stare at the dusty beauty of the woman—the slave—who had joined us as we left town. A fairly good road, repaired by good hands after spring rains—thick trees covered with vines and mosses—swampy ditches stretching out at either side of the road. My own old New York countryside up near the Bronx farm or the woods atop the cliffs on the New Jersey side of the Hudson seemed barren by comparison to this lush and overgrown landscape.

A near-mile-long avenue of enormous oak trees, a tunnel of trees, led to the entrance of my uncle's house. With the moss hanging in long beard-like wisps from the upper branches and the light as subdued as in some grotto beneath the ocean, the avenue gave the impression of leading from one world to the next, a road that might take you to the land of dreams instead of merely leading you from the main road to the mansion.

"There is certainly nothing like this up north," I said to my cousin, even as I stared and stared at the slender shoulders of the slave girl—who sat demurely, waiting for the carriage to come to a halt. "Our winters are cold and chill, with icy winds blowing off the rivers that bound our rock island. If you can imagine it, picture winter nights, with our family huddled around a warming stove, closer to the way the Eskimaux live, or those others, Russians and such, who spend their lives either freezing in winter or boiling in summer, up near the icier oceans of the world."

"I believe that, Nathaniel," my cousin said. "Here in our dreamy land we live lives like no other, we know that."

"Even we Jews partake of it," Rebecca said. "Where else Jews can live as we do I can't imagine. Except for the Holy Land in the Bible, where else a paradise like this? Friendly Gentiles, the laws allowing us as much freedom as anyone else. The trees, the air, the water..." She gestured as a man might to the wide creek that ran parallel with the road. "Here we might make a special place for all Jews..." At which point she reached forward and touched the shoulder of the slave girl. "And those who would be Jews."

My cousin turned to his wife and said, "I admire your dreaming..." He turned to me and with the slightest hint of a sneer on his face—but somehow kept covert in his voice—added, "My wife is a dreamer."

Rebecca withdrew her hand from the girl's shoulder and sat upright on the carriage bench, making a toss of her curls.

She said, "Without dreams to compare to, how do we know when we are truly awake?"

I had no answer, as if this question could find one. I took another glance at the slave girl, hoping she might turn around.

"Rebecca has a vision," my cousin said, his tone turned slightly acerbic, as the driver, Isaac, his name was, I recalled, pulled the carriage to a halt before a grand old white house at the end of the tunnel of trees. Someone must have given some signal that I had missed, because just as we stopped, the slave girl descended gracefully from the carriage and without a glance back at us began walking to the house.

"A vision?" I said, noticing the smoothness of her movement—almost a gliding motion, as though her feet scarcely touched the earth.

"That we and all the niggers live happily together in our new Promised Land," my cousin said. He must have imbibed more of the brandy—did that flask have a bottom?—because his voice sounded a bit muzzy and booze driven. I marveled at this, because I had never known a Jew who drank like this, or, for a fact, owned a plantation with slaves, either.

"What kind of talk is that?" Rebecca said.

He paused and turned back to his wife. "We are quite a pair, are we not? You supply the sweetness and light, my darling girl, and I supply the shadows."

He addressed me directly.

"She'd want the Africans to raise themselves up and live—"

"Please, no more," Rebecca said. "We have a guest and we must give him the tour of the plantation."

"I know we have a guest. I can see we have a guest. I am attempting to explain our way of life to him." To me, he said, "You've had a long sea voyage, would you like first to rest?"

I shook my head, noticing that the girl, carrying herself as beautifully upright as any woman I had ever seen before, had turned the corner of the house and disappeared behind it. Dear God and Moses, perhaps it was the small amount of drink I myself had taken, but I wanted to follow her, anywhere!

"Very well," my cousin said, of course unable to notice the strongly magnetic feelings in my chest and loins. He dismissed the driver and climbed up onto the bench. Flicking the reins, he called "Onward!" to the horse, taking us with a left turn into the fields.

"We have about a thousand acres," he said as we trotted off on a raggedy dirt road, "with about two hundred and fifty of them well-fenced and well-drained and in a high state of cultivation...mainly with rice...altogether I'd say there is about a little less than half the plantation under cultivation and the other half mostly woods—yellow pine, oak, and hickory. We have a number of horses and mules and cows and oxen...and there are about a hundred Africans working here, though you will not see many of them just at this hour." He sighed, and took a deep breath, as if to regain some strength he might have given up when he had taken his last taste of brandy. "They will have stopped work in the rice fields for the day and while there may be some crews coming back from work on the dikes at the creek, most everybody else is at home for supper by now. Oh, yes, and there is a little brickyard also, near the bridge by the creek. It is a fine location, the water supply is inexhaustible, and the water is deep enough to accommodate flatboats from town so we can ship out the bricks. Some of the slaves work there, too."

He took out his handkerchief and dabbed at his forehead. Despite the slipping by of the day the sun remained hot, and the air whirred thick with buzzing insects and above us the constant cry of birds. There were a number of questions I knew I should ask, about the means of cultivation, and how much rice was grown each year, and how it was shipped, and so forth. But the heat weighed on my brain and on my tongue. I rode silently, and my cousin did not speak, so that the only sound for a while was the light rumbling of the carriage wheels on the dusty track. It had been a long day already and it had not yet ended.

Chapter Thirteen

The Forest

The place called Wassadougou—a green world, and Lilith suffered an obsidian-complected husband, rotund and unsmiling, whose southern features contrasted sharply with her own distinctively northern face—Semitic and almond-eyed, thin-lipped, an elongated jaw. He silently weighed her down so many nights that Lilith felt flattened even when great with child. His other wives chattered like monkeys. His many children treated her with disdain and sometimes outright cruelty. She hated them one and all. Her only friends were her own children, which meant that she lived for years alone in the midst of a crowded family compound, until the children grew old enough for serious conversation and discussion, most of which had to do with their ancestors and how proud they should be because of where they came from. The past was a glorious story, the present was a green and nattering hell. Large, biting, piercing insects assailed her, and in the trees devil creatures chattered and sometimes shat upon those who gathered below. At night she held the holy stone and stroked its inflected surface until her fingers became too tired to move. If only she could see a future better than what she had in mind, living until she died in this prison of green. If only she might have had her mother at her side!

Oh, Zainab, my mother, where do your bones lie? Oh, mother, mother, surely long gone now and never to comfort me again!

Her only comfort? Wata, her oldest daughter, dark about the face, pale in her back and belly and legs. Husbands did the naming, and the dark man called this child after a local goddess. The girl grew into a womanhood charged with passion and invention, becoming skilled at weaving, a family art, it seemed, and the cultivation of herbs, as well as caring for her younger sisters even as her mother grew more and more uninterested in the task. (She sat inside their house made of tree and grass for more and more hours as the years went by, talking to her own mother whom she saw sitting in a corner of the enclosure and beyond that claiming that she was sending prayers to God). Lilith appeared to be shrinking, if not fading away all together. She certainly had no standing with Wata's father, and among his wives she was barely recognized. Wata, lighter than many of her siblings, assumed a larger and larger role among the children—there were some sixteen or seventeen of them, from all the wives—and eventually she took a place among the wives themselves. This had its dangers, and sure enough, one night after the moon set and the entire forest seemed to have sunk into a deep and dreamless sleep Wata heard a rustling just outside the entrance. Fearing an animal, she sat up on the pallet where a moment before she had been lost in some nameless vision that came along when she had closed her eyes.

And who was this? Some forest demon?

Wata caught a glimpse of a woman peering down at her, and then the woman disappeared.

She thought she was dreaming—perhaps she was—so she lay back and closed her eyes.

At dawn she rose and went to visit her mother, whom she found still asleep. But not asleep!

She did not breathe! *Oh, Lilith, mother, mama, gone, gone gone!*

It took Wata months to get over the initial shock of her mother's death. She longed to see her again, in fact, now and then becoming convinced that Lilith had just peeked at her from behind a tree, and when a thought came to her on some matter about which her mother had taught her she could hear Lilith say the very words she was thinking. *Fetch water before sunrise while it is still cool. Or, look before you step to keep from offending a snake.*

She hoped for a miracle, she hoped she might find another mother. Who knows what lay outside her vision? You could not walk a forest path without seeing demons or go to bed at night without worrying about ghosts. She had, in fact, overheard the prayers of her father's other wives too often not to know words that she might say in protection. The god her mother prayed to, and her mother's parents before that, a man's god, did not have much power here in the deep forest. Where she lived now only the local spirits held sway, and on a night such as this, when she awoke with an instant flash of fear, she could not help but turn to them, to the dark mother whose figure arched over all when Wata tried to imagine her, in her body of shadows and smoke, a cloud above the hut, a wave of air shimmering in sunlight. Wata! Yes, she thought of herself now in that way, named after a goddess, and trying to live according to how the goddess might want her to live.

And what would the goddess do with the creature who appeared next to her just now in the middle of another of those nights of half sleep, half waking dream, her mother in her thoughts both in darkness and in light?

"Wata..."

Here was the chief's oldest boy by his second wife, and he smelled of bitter oil and some not so sweet brew he must have been drinking.

"Go away, you stupid boy," Wata said.

The boy threw himself down next to her and said, "I am not so stupid for choosing you, am I?"

"Choosing me? What is your little game?" Wata said. "Now, shoo! Shoo! Go back to your mother, little boy!"

Instead, he grabbed her wrist.

"And who are you to order me around? I am my mother's son, also, and my father is your master."

"What do you want with me? It is the middle of the night. I was asleep, I was dreaming."

"What were you dreaming?"

"I do not remember."

"Try to remember. Tell me."

"Are you a healing man? Did I come to you and say that I had a bad dream?"

He sat down next to her, as still as could be, which was not entirely still, because, after all, he was a boy.

"Tell me your dream, and I will let you go."

"Am I your prisoner that you can let me go?"

"Tell me your dream."

"And then you will let me go?"

The boy laughed.

"Sly you are, very sly."

"A woman has to be," Wata said.

"Yes, yes, especially a woman who belongs to my father and who will one day belong to me."

"You will never own me," Wata said. "No one will ever own me. I belong to my mother only, and her mother before her."

"What?" The boy held up his hands in mock-amazement. Outside in the forest a wild thing howled, a monkey or a cat feeling the claws of another beast rake along its back or side or a small animal recognizing that it was about to be devoured by a beast larger than itself.

Wata!

A voice cried in her ear. That of the small beast? She didn't know.

Wata!

Could the boy have been speaking? He sank to his knees and then lowered himself on top of her.

"Go away," she said, squirming beneath him.

He didn't pay attention to her voice, only to her body.

Wata!

Before she knew he had pried open her legs and stupidly probed away at her.

"Stop!"

"Hush," he said, suddenly half out of breath.

"Stop it now!"

He kept on probing, stabbing.

She raised her fists as if to strike him—hard—but he grabbed her by the wrists and pushed himself into her at the cost of tearing pain at her center.

Wata!

A net fell out of heaven, through the roof of the house, and covered her in a spidery essence of slim silver-coated ropes as the music of small fingered instruments tinkled in her ears. Voices began to sing. A hot soupy liquid replaced her blood and all she could do was open her eyes and see through the dark. Dark eyes stared back at her, unblinking.

Later that year she bore her half-brother's child.

Who was a good girl—another girl! whom Wata named Lyaa, after the First Woman of this green place, this girl who was as dark as a black river on a night without a moon. Some shades bleach out. Lyaa turned even darker, and, as it happened, Yemaya the goddess known by many other names, who, in addition to reigning above the great waters and rivers, presided over these green parts of the continent, approved. Lurking above the forest as she always did, sometimes in the form of sunlight, sometimes in the form of tiny droplets of moisture, she surveyed her domain, watching, listening always, for creatures who turned to her for assistance. In this way she showed herself forth in quite different fashion from the god who ruled the desert lands to the north, a deity who rather than reveal himself appeared to encourage everything among his followers that would keep him hidden. None of that for Yemaya! She was not shy or, for whatever reason, withholding.

One dark night, as dark a night as the night of Lyaa's conception, she appeared to Wata, and told her how glad she was that Wata had given the world this child. Far down the trail, she told Wata—of course, to Wata this encounter with the goddess seemed like a meeting in a dream—*I will look after her.* This girl will ache and she will dance and she will deliver a child whose children's children's child, or thereabouts, I am not counting, but merely trying to look ahead through the wavery dark and smoky curtain that keeps the future from our eyes, will free us all from the prison of our days. That is, if my plan runs true, and sometimes even the plans of the gods can go awry.

Wata awoke from that dream coated in sweat, and to the daughter to whom she eventually revealed this prophecy she appeared never to have quite recovered. As time in the forest went by, Wata grew so frail as to give the appearance of being already dead, her body an ashen gray beneath the usual sandy lightness of her skin.

In dreams along the route of the years Yemaya appeared to her again, stretching out her long dark arms to her and inviting her in.

Come to me, darling girl, she said. Come to me. Dance in my arms. Whirl about my feet when I am flying. When he was not much older than you, his own long arms covered with bramble cuts and the pocking of wood shards, my own son came to me in the night and had his way with me. I knew your mother's sorrow, I knew her shame, I knew the bitter blood that flowed in her veins. From where I live up here in the treetops I descend as dew and sometimes as river water. And tears. And spit. And urine. And the monthly blood. Poor men, they never suffer the flow. I ask them to cut their arms and bleed on my behalf, showing their loyalty. Walk with me and I will walk with you. You will have glory, rather than shame, and your daughter, named after the First Woman, will show forth as well.

Chapter Fourteen

First Woman

*D*ays and nights in the forest. Green sun, green dark, green moon, green air. Months and years. Wata and the helpful Yemaya, always present at night in her dreams to give her good cheer, raised this child, Lyaa, well. The father never did more than now and then glance at the girl. Wata had hoped that the beauty of the child and the power of its name would keep him by her side. The master's other wives pitched in, even as his own mother did her part to help with the girl's upbringing. To everyone— except, apparently, the father—this was a special child and a woman to whom a link, more than just her name, stretched back in time all the way to the mother of them all.

Yemaya showed Wata that woman, after whom Lyaa was named, one night in a dream—

I can tell you what happened before you came to the forest, and I can push you toward the future, but I cannot show you the future, because so many people must make choices to water its time, yes, future time, like a flower, needs watering from the actions of all those alive in the time before it occurred.

This was the dream:

Born on the side of a forest volcano she lived in the trees, though at a tender age she fell from a low branch and found herself standing upright on the forest floor. Putting one broad foot after another she now found herself moving forward. A handsome fellow who lived not far above chose to drop down out of the branches and take up the stroll with her.

This is good, he made clear to her that he saw things this way.

She touched his thigh, his chest, and turned her head aside to laugh, so full was her she-heart.

He touched her breast, her throat, his own chest full of longing and desire.

Pluck at us! Pick here, pick there! Tickle us! We laugh, oh, yes.

They told each other stories, using gesture and sound. In the trees, wide-eyed and wondering about everything around them the most pleasure came from living close to each other. Gradually it became clear that the main dangers in life, the cats that stalked them and the snakes that when disturbed would strike and bite, had only their senses of smell and movement. Lyaa and her lover-neighbor used these senses they learned to good effect by watching the animals but also found themselves in the dream world in which the goddess taught them lessons about the waking world. Did the big cats dream also? Did the snakes? Could there be a goddess of cats and snakes?

That handsome fellow shook his head.

Lyaa touched him on the throat.

She agreed.

Lo and behold, they discovered one morning, early, when the air smelled of smoke, and the birds remained silent, that they each had slept with the same dream.

Yes, yes, yes, Lyaa showed him the picture in her mind and he looked and tilted his head as if he were in thought. And she could see the picture in his mind, yes, yes, she could.

This land was once no-land, lying on the bottom of a bitter salt-sea, no trees, let alone forests, only curling undersea shrubs, among which lived large flat-bottomed fish with eyes at the end of long tentacles, if they had eyes at all. Sea-snakes as long as the line of the horizon shimmied here and there on the pebbly floor of the sea while sharks as large as tall trees roamed with impunity, and now and then a broad-beamed swimmer—whales?—floated past, bigger than entire hillsides.

Yemaya, splashing silently with her tail, drifted in and among these creatures, hand in hand with her brother Okolun.

At that time the sea tasted of sulfur and sweet oxygen, a flavor like berries and tart stones, or the rank stink of a kiss when the other body has not yet digested the flesh of the other he has eaten.

Shssssssss...Ay!

Whale ate shark ate snake ate proto-flounder, all digesting all, and the least of the fish merely working its jaws as it itself became another's meal, with a watery burp!

Okolun thought this was enormously comical.

He laughed and laughed, and his belly grew as he did so, and the noiseless sound of his laughter grew ten-fold and finally a thousand-fold—so it increased, and the sea-floor jiggled and tilted. He pointed to the comedy of meal-time and danced on the buckling ocean floor. Yemaya cocked her head at him and then took him by the hand.

"You've done it now," she said. "There are powers here as great as yours, I feel them, though I don't know what to call them or where they live. Inside the core of our world, where the fires boil and bubble and flow?"

She leaned over and gave him a more-than-sisterly kiss on the mouth.

Oh, the force below took the moment to burst open before them!

Stand back! Steam and undersea fire upshot straight to the surface and kept on going, even less deterred by air than it was by water.

Sister and brother looked at each other and instantly understood. Their father, a god beyond description, had decided to play some games in the molten sea beneath the salt-sea. Who could not bow to his power?

Some time later—a million years?—the sister and brother marveled at the mountain the father force had created, a tower that stooped above a green and all-spreading forest. So beautiful! Another couple of hundreds of thousand years went by—where was Yemaya during all this time? Amusing herself, swimming out to other planets to search for creatures who might accept her as their deity, but aside from some heat-worms who lived in the fumes beneath the surface of the ice on one of the moons of Jupiter, finding nothing. She accepted the fealty of the Ionian worms and returned to earth with a feeling of emptiness.

She arrived in this part of Africa, her old haunt, just as her father had decided to play around again with melted rocks and the earth's storehouse of steam. Up blew a rain of rocks and ash, lava poured down the lip of the hot mountain like stew from a tipped pot, and she could see from afar the first couple, first woman, first man, first child, walking quickly and steadily across the plain to escape the erupting mass, leaving footprints behind. It was the first time this woman or any of her family or descendants had caught her attention. It would not be the last.

Ay, Yemaya, she of the thousand eyes, who watched them from the stars and from just above the treetops. Yemaya! Who held out a thousand arms to you if you were falling, and caught you in a thousand hands if it happened that you did fall. Yemaya! She in the intricate rhythms of the drums, in the twisted braids of sound in song, in the multitude of birdcalls and insect choruses throughout the forest.

Wata fingered the marked stone, now and then recalling that she had heard of a time when a bodiless god lived everywhere above and helped you to make even feeble claims on the world come to life. But by now this had faded, and she taught her daughter Lyaa to recognize who it was who made her and to whom her fate was tied. Yemaya! She of the moisture and she of the air! Everything belonged to her, all beings, all plants, all light, all particles, everything we found, cooked, ate, spit, shat, softened, soothed, sleep, waking, noise, silence, liquid blood within us, all liquid running in streams and in the river to the north, rain from the sky, all blood we released when the moon called, ah, Yemaya! Goodness of the moon, blessing of the sun, of whom she was both the chief and the concubine! The old sky god of the north had faded away and now only Yemaya reigned in her heart.

She asked one of the artisans in the village to bind the marked stone in a small pouch of animal skin and one morning she presented this to her daughter.

Oh, Lyaa, how long has it been since your namesake, the First Woman, erupted from the center of the earth? How long has it been since you yourself were born in fire? Yemaya watching over you, Yemaya making you strong! You planted your feet on the ground and made your path, leaving behind footprints for us all to follow. You walked the earth, you walked upon the waters, you walked in air, you walked in light, you walked in dark! You walked away from the fiery cone spewing ash and fire, you walked from mountain to desert, you made children whose names are lost to us, and they begat more who begat more who begat more. The volcano subsided, their lives blossomed, and then fell away like old leaves. More children took their places, one of them who married a potter. That one reminded Yemaya closely of you. Tall, as beautiful as a tree, as beautiful as lava stone, within you all blood begins to flow, tugged at by the moon, watered by hot rains and cold, and in the world through which we walk, the air we sing in—Yemaya, Yemaya!—everything is liquid, no solid is anything, because life itself flows to us and from us, toward us and away from us, we can only splash and drink and spit and flow for a short while that we have in this chattering green palace of a world.

Yet can she save you from torment in this world while you are here? That remains to be seen.

Chapter Fifteen

The Tour

As we rode along my mind flickered back to home, and I wondered about what the city was like at this moment—decidedly cooler, of that I was sure—caught in its middle of the week hustle and fervor, my father at his desk, poor Marzy worrying about dinner, my Miriam, going about her day with her own family, perhaps thinking now and then about me. A surge of longing to be with her rolled through me, and I stared up at the leafy ceiling of the track along which we slowly trundled, wishing I could be there with her now instead of here, with these strangers, even if they were family.

"A hundred Africans to work in the rice fields," I said, recalling to myself my reason for being here. "That is a large number of people to order about and care for."

"Our father, your uncle," Jonathan said, "is a bit of genius when it comes to that."

And as if he were the director of some opera house back home he flicked the whip at the horse, we emerged from out of the canopy of trees, and came upon a line of black men in rough tattered clothes walking toward us, their voices raised in song.

> *Don't mind working from sun to sun,*

[they sang]

> *If'n you give me dinner—*
> *When the dinner time comes!*

He slowed the carriage almost to a halt and nodded as the men stepped

to the side of the road to let us pass, doffing their caps in the old English
peasant way. I could not help but smile at the simple music of their melodi-
ous outcry.

> *Don't mind working from sun to sun,*

[they sang again, voices languid in the heat]

> *If'n you give me dinner—*
> *When the dinner time comes!*

"Evening," my cousin said to the crowd.
"Evening," came the response from the men.
"Even."
"Eben."
"Ben."

> *Don't mind working from sun to sun,*
> *If'n you give me dinner—*

Their low voices faded away into the mix of sunlight and shade. In their
wake rose up a wave of body stink from hard day's work, and creek mud
(though I hadn't yet seen the creek), mixing with the general putrefaction
of things in nature, riled up by men tramping through it and across.

"A bit less rhythm and they could sound like us singing at synagogue,"
I said.

"You think you're making a joke," Rebecca said.

"What is she saying?" I asked of my cousin.

Jonathan allowed the reins to go slack and the horse slowed and thus the
carriage, and we emerged out of the trees at the small wooden bridge over
what he told me was Goose Creek, a broad and swiftly flowing stream of
water that seemed as much like a small river to me as it did a creek.

"Here I used to come all the time when I was boy, to sit by the creek-side
and drop in my line. Do you have places from your boyhood that you recall?"

"Of course," I said, and was about to begin describing a boyhood place,
when he tied the reins, jumped down from the seat, fetched a water bag
from the rear of the carriage and filled it at the creek-side.

Rebecca and I sat quietly together while he watered the horse. Every now and then she would glance down at her full belly, as it to convince herself it was still there.

A few birds called from the woods behind us. The light was slipping away and now and then a fish splashed in the broad creek. In the distance the slaves kept up their chants, a sound wavering on the darkening air.

"It must be…" Rebecca spoke almost in a whisper.

"What is that?" I said.

"It must be…different from here up north in New York."

"Quite different," I said.

"Are the Jews different?"

"You see me," I said. "Do I seem different?"

"No," she said.

"Most Jews I know are like me. Except that most of them are more diligent in the practice of our religion."

"You are not a diligent Jew?"

"No, diligence it seems is not my way."

"We are Reformers, ourselves," she said. "We ride on the Sabbath and the High Holy Days, for how else would we reach the synagogue? It is much too far to town to walk, as you must have noticed."

"Yes," I said. "Perhaps Jews are better in the city then. For we can walk to the synagogue because it is only a short distance."

"We try our best," Rebecca said. "And God must know that. Because He knows everything. Our congregation is in turmoil. We are hoping that God will help us settle a number of our disputes."

"Amen," said my cousin as he climbed back up onto the bench. "Are you having a fine old theological discussion?"

"In part, yes," I said, allowing myself a smile.

"Father's always good for that around the dinner table," he said. "A place I expect where you hope soon to sit."

And with that he gave the whip a twist and we began moving again, taking the narrow road along the river for a short while and turning onto a path that took us back into the trees.

It was dark when we reached the house, though because of the wonderful array of lamps that illuminated it from within it seemed like something out of a dream, a construction of slender pillars and balconies with a wide porch running around like a girdle, the entire structure raised up on wide brick posts and a set of broad stairs leading up to the main floor—the entire building at first glimpse seemed almost like a confection for a party table. Jonathan handed over the carriage to the same tan-complected young man who had driven us back from town while Rebecca and I climbed the steps to the entrance. The same slave girl met us at the door, and it gave me a tiny jolt, as if lightning had struck my chest, to see her again, especially when for an instant she fixed her eyes, a pale green shade, firmly on me— the stranger—and then looked past me at Rebecca.

"Missy," she said.

Jonathan came bounding up the steps, ignoring the girl.

"Come in, come along," he said, "the parents are waiting."

"Hello! Shalom!" came a hearty shout from the dining room and we walked in to find my uncle and aunt sitting already at the table.

"Where have you been?" said my uncle, whom I knew immediately by the set of his eyes and jaw, though his resemblance to my father ended there because of the rolls of fat in which these familiar features were embedded. "We thought the patrollers had gotten you."

"Please, dear, don't you joke about such things," said the gray-haired woman—my aunt, I had already decided—whose size, or lack of it, was all the more noticeable because of my uncle's girth.

"We gave our honored cousin a tour," Jonathan said. "Through the woods to the brickyard and the creek."

"It is a goodly property," my uncle said. He patted his belly. "Like me, I'd say."

The others laughed, and I gave up a smile. My father, a rather goodly shaped man himself, had warned me about his brother's weight. But still when my uncle stood to introduce me all around I found that I could not keep my eyes off the globe of his belly.

"Goodly, sir," I said. "I especially enjoyed the woods and the creek-side."

"I told him how I used to fish there as a boy," Jonathan said.

"Yes, you grew up in Paradise, did you not?" his father said. "But now." He touched a hand to the shoulder of the gray-haired woman. "Your Aunt Florence."

I bowed toward her and she bestowed a toothy smile upon me.

We took our places around the table.

At this point a tall young boy trundled into the room, looking partly like a youthful Jonathan and partly not.

"My son, your second cousin Abraham," Jonathan said.

I nodded to the fidgety boy, who was as it turned out the only child of a first marriage made by my cousin Jonathan to a Jewish woman who had returned to the Antilles years ago. The boy's eyes darted left to right, right to left, as though he expected at any moment to be overtaken by some adversary.

"You're a Yankee," he said.

"A Yankee Doodle Dandy," I said.

"You don't look different from the rest of us."

"Did you expect me to have horns?"

"Michelangelo's statue of Moses has horns," the boy said.

"You have seen it?"

"I have seen drawings only. Papa says though he will send me to Europe for my tour when I'm older and I will see the original."

"My father is sending me also," I said. "Perhaps we could travel together."

"You are too old," the boy said.

"Abraham," his stepmother said, "mind your manners. Please excuse him, Nathaniel. He may think you are old but he is still a child."

"Damned if I am," Abraham said.

"Abe!" My cousin rolled around in his chair. "Leave the room!"

My youngest cousin, who one day, I imagined, would become heir to the plantation in the long scheme of things after his father, having taken over after my uncle's demise, loosed his reins, scowled in my direction and obeyed.

My uncle now raised himself out of his chair, a rather monumental action that combined a great intake of breath and a steely pressing of hands on table arms and the uplifting of his massive chest and belly. The odd thing, I noticed, was how delicately he performed this, almost like a performer on a stage. No grunts, no moans, no complaints—only that inward sigh and he was on his feet.

"I will see to the boy," he said to my aunt, and then begging my pardon he moved slowly from the room leaving the rest of us to talk quietly in his wake.

"Such a young ruffian," said Jonathan, pouring himself wine from a beautifully carved glass decanter.

"Jonathan," said my aunt, "please wait for the blessing."

"I bless this wine," Jonathan said and took another sip.

"Jonathan," his wife said, "please."

"Am I a worse and more rebellious boy than my own son?"

He winked at me, and took another sip of wine.

"Abe is just a child," my aunt said. "We must forgive him."

"If I used language such as that at table I'd take myself into the hallway and give myself quite a talking-to."

"But you do not," Rebecca said.

"Because I will not," Jonathan said. "Not because I do not have it in me."

He drank again, and then reached for the decanter to refill his glass.

"Oh, Jonathan," said his mother, my aunt, "I wish you would tutor that boy a little more vigorously."

Jonathan merely took another sip of wine, and out of the desire to seem a good guest and accommodating member of the family I also took a drink. The blend of rich dry grape and the brandy I had drunk earlier stayed on my tongue a while. So this is how my Carolina cousins live, I sighed to myself, with this leisurely pace of taking food and drink—or in Jonathan's case in the reverse order—while attended by numerous bonded servants.

A trio of them made their way in and out of the room in an intricate choreography, carrying steaming platters of beef and fish and corn and tomatoes and carrots and baskets of bread, and aligning the silver and wine bottles, silently, as if almost we were not present, or at least just mere statuary rather than living creatures and us, or at least the rest of the family, ignoring them, as though they were invisible.

But in fact they were quite darkly visible, and the more dark they were the more present, beg ning with the cook, Precious Sally, as I soon learned she was called, who stood in the doorway, showing almost as much bulk and flesh as my uncle as she directed the other servants in their dance of food and service. Two women and one man, the women dressed in white aprons, like Sally's, whose apron was as large almost as a tablecloth in order to cover her huge amount of flesh, which made their darkness all the more stark. The man, a tall old fellow, with a forehead like a bulldog's and skin as dark as a night without a moon, wore a blue serving coat and britches, and bowed as each dish reached the table, ostensibly overseeing the service, but always with his ear cocked toward Sally, clearly the director of this entertainment.

I waited patiently—I was not just then sure why—for the advent of the lighter-skinned Liza, who had met us at the door. But she never appeared, since, as I quickly surmised, this was not in her line of duty.

My uncle lumbered back into the room, followed by his repentant grandchild Abraham. We waited and watched silently until they took their places at the table again.

"And now," my uncle said, with an audible wheeze, "to begin. Abe, will you say the blessing?"

My younger cousin looked down at his plate and folded his hands in front of him.

"God of our Fathers, God of Abraham—that's me—"

"Abe!" His father spoke up.

"—and Isaac, (we own him)…"

"Abe!" his mother cried out.

"…we thank you for the fruit of thy fields."

"'For our daily bread,'" Jonathan encouraged him.

"And for the bread of our table."

"No Hebrew?" I said, turning to Rebecca.

"We are Reformed here," she said. "Which means we have reformed our prayers."

"We sound like Gentiles," I said.

"At home do you speak Hebrew?"

"No," I shook my head. "But I always imagine all other Jews as more religious than me."

Abraham squinted at me across the table, wondering what it was I could be talking about and if it made any sense for him to listen well.

Through all this banter we ate and drank, and I watched the servants move to and fro through the room. I thought at one point that I might have caught a glimpse of the slender slave girl on the other side of the door-way, but when I looked again she was gone, if she had been there at all.

After supper we men retired to the porch—what they called here a "veranda"—and my uncle offered port and cigars to me and Jonathan. The smoke kept the insects at bay and we talked a while about matters broad and consequential and narrow and of no matter while imbibing the rich imported liquor.

"The Indians first smoked these," my uncle said, "as I understand it, as a form of prayer. They puffed on these and it made a rope of smoke that rose from their lips to the nostrils of their gods."

"Smoke instead of prayers?" I said.

"Smart boy," my uncle said. "Yes, you might put it that way."

A faint recollection, wispier than smoke, drifted into my memory.

"My dear mother, may she rest in peace," I said, "lighted candles every Sabbath. I still remember that."

"Same principle," my uncle said. "She was a lovely woman. I met her only once, when I traveled up to New York on business and stayed with you."

"I don't remember that," I said.

"You were the smallest of children then."

"But I would have remembered."

My uncle laughed and his bulky belly and arms and neck shook with his laughter.

"Because of my girth, no doubt, you think. But I was a lesser man back then. No bulkier than slender Jonathan here."

"And so I have something to aspire to then, father?" my cousin said, sipping from his cup.

"You do, indeed, sir," my uncle said.

We puffed out our smoke for a while longer, while the butler appeared with a bottle of port.

"Black Jack," my uncle said, "this is my nephew, here from New York to learn the ways of running a plantation."

I made to shake hands with the man but he backed a step away.

Alone then, we sipped the wine and talked.

"I'd like to hear all the news about my brother," my uncle said.

I made a summary for him of all, or most, that had happened in the past year—telling mostly the story of our business.

"And so he is well?"

"He is, sir."

"And your late mother's sister? How is she faring?"

He paused in thought, while I idly studied the shadow of the candle flickering across his broad face. In and out of the light his face shifted, looking first younger, than old, younger, old.

"She is well, sir," I replied, unhappy at the thought of Aunt Isabelle, whose person had not entered my conscious thoughts for a good long while.

"You say your father has not remarried."

I shook my head.

"And he has no thought about marrying Isabelle? Isn't that her name?"

"Yes, sir," I said.

My uncle tilted his large head to one side, then the other.

"It is an ancient custom of our people, you may recall, when a man becomes a widower to marry the sister of his late wife."

The thought gave me the fearful chills.

"He has not said a word to me about it."

"You would be the last to hear, I think," my uncle said. "But I know men and I know my brother. Your visit here has much to do with business, but it does also give your father some time alone with Isabelle."

It occurred to me with a shudder in my blood that all of this, my mission, my journey, might all have been a ruse constructed by my father, and then I brushed the thought aside and washed down some of my worry with more port. Where was the slave girl? Where was she?

"But it is business that brings me here," I said, daring myself to squarely light on the matter at hand.

"Business, business, yes," my uncle said, "the busyness of our lives. Your father seems quite determined to educate you in these matters."

My attentive cousin poured me another glass of the wine, and then poured another for himself.

"These matters," I said.

"My business is failing," my uncle said.

I sat up, alert to the news.

"He never told me this. He told me only to study your enterprise."

My overstuffed uncle leaned forward with a smile on his moon of a face, his large head floating in front of his body in the candlelight.

"Do you know the difference between us and the Gentiles?"

"They worship Christ," I said. "We merely produced him."

"Very good," my uncle said, with a laugh. "Very good. But there is something more, something in the character of the Gentile to which I'm referring."

"They are less devout?"

"Sometimes they are more devout, much more."

"Then we are less?"

"People say we Reformed are less than whole Jews. But we are inspired to act as we do by an inner power."

"But what about Gentiles? You were talking about them."

"They go into the business without a thought for the morality of it."

"And we Jews?"

"We struggle with the problem, we exhibit great soul-searching and painful thought." He pounded a fist on the table. "We moan, we groan, we worry…"

"And then?"

"And then we go into the business."

While he laughed at his own witticism, I took the liberty of pouring myself another glass of port. Before very long, I felt my head drooping.

"To bed!" my uncle announced. "Tomorrow for part of the day we will continue your education."

"To bed," Jonathan stood to announce—and make a toast—"where all life begins, and every day ends…"

I wove from side to side as I followed Black Jack who showed me to my room, a fine little closet on the second floor at the rear of the grand house with a window, covered with netting, wide open to the night.

I took some time removing my things from my bag, and from my person, such as the small pistol, which, figuring that I had arrived in the peaceful kingdom, I would not need, and so I placed it in the top drawer of the bureau, beneath a pile of handkerchiefs. I continued unpacking, eventually unwrapping the portrait of my mother and placing it on the bureau (and with a twinge of nostalgia poking at my chest like an insistent finger taking care to fold the newssheet from the New York newspaper that had wrapped my mother's portrait that I might read some of it later). I lay there a while on my soft down bed with the lamp burning, musing on the faint memories of that dear departed woman, and then I put out the light and lay a while longer thinking in the shadows of the room. What was it? The humming in the near-distance, like a chorus of some tuning of strings in an orchestra, but also the sissing of a million tongues, as though the stars, so bright beyond the trees, were each a lamp hissing after some cosmic god had blown cosmic breath across the sputtering wicks. It was the music of the low country under cover of darkness, the news of the land, the swamps, the creeks, the woods, and the skies filled with those stars, but lower toward the earth, the insects and the swooping birds who flew with beaks wide open so that they might just scoop up all that they needed for nourishment. Thus settled over me the last night of comfort and freedom from care that I would ever spend.

Chapter Sixteen

Taken

*O*verhead, chattering away, monkeys awoke her. What they were trying to tell each other, Lyaa could not say, noticing only that they were excited. But then, as anyone knew, that might mean one of them had found a dead bird or a rat or a mate or had a dream and awoke as startled as people were when they awoke from dreams dark or dreams cheerful, dreams of flying or dreams of dying, which she, as she had once told the local witch, sometimes suffered to great degrees.

Those monkeys, what might they see? Growing to girlhood in this green world just to the south of the river Lyaa had learned some things about the life around her. These chatterers with sandy whiskers and shining eyes migrated to the south in the dry season and in the wet season returned to make a noise in the heaven above the forest floor that began before first light and went on until after sunset, their calls increasing in pitch or subsiding now and then to celebrate encounters and meals and discoveries and disappointments and fears, much like her own life amid these people whom she could not call her own, because they owned her.

They owned her!

That was every morning's true awakening. In the pit of this green world, where insects crawled and swarmed and small rats ran right and left, even the smallest of animals was freer than she! Those monkeys looking down from the treetops upon this world of green, even they were freer than she! In this green world, no safe place offered itself. Nowhere could you hide. Her mother could not hide. She lived as her desert born mother lived, exercising ways not of the green world. After a while the greenness crept into her lungs and long before her time she lay weighed down in her breath by a terrible heaviness of green.

"I am your mother," Wata said to Lyaa, who sat cross-legged by her side. "I want to give you hope and a clear view of life. But I am confused. (Her breath came hard as she spoke these words). Our mother left the desert god behind in the northern sands. The entire world, whether sand and rock to the north or this jungle, or whatever lay south beyond it, remains a place of imprisonment. The desert god enslaved the men who enslaved us." Her whisper deepened, her breath turned into a rasp and a wheeze. "Pray now to the goddess of the forest. The goddess who rules the forest world and all the world's waters, whom the desert god challenged, may be our only hope!"

Yemaya, Yemaya, hear my prayer. Carry me away from this green house, carry me out of this place of worry and woe. She remembered even as a very young girl hearing such words in the language her mother called the tongue of the goddess. "My grandfather believed in submitting to his god," she explained to young Lyaa, even before the girl could truly understand. "I say no, I say never give in or submit, we slaves of slaves, born into chains and misery in our hearts. You are my only hope. You must never give in to the desert god but instead devote yourself to Yemaya and her sisters, who travel with us all over land or water."

Yemaya, Yemaya!

Yemaya made her heart full, and when she lost the path Yemaya helped her to find it again.

Yemaya! She of the fierce eyes and rough hands, a voice like a roaring stream, the queen of queens, mother of all the green jungle and blessed of all streams, rivers, and oceans, within and without. When Lyaa's father/ uncle stared at her ferociously with his one good eye, she did not look away. He hardly ever looked at either of them and so it seemed important to acknowledge his attention. *Yemaya*, she whispered to herself under her breath. Later his under-chief came to her and told her that she was not eating enough. She called on Yemaya then also for assistance. One night the big man himself, with his rolls of belly fat and that one good eye, strolled over and took her arm, inspecting it as if it belonged to a monkey or a bird.

She had heard stories, beginning with her mother's stories. *If he touches me elsewhere*, she said to herself, *Yemaya, please give me the strength to kill him or kill myself.*

As if he could feel the force of her prayer, the man released her. (But did it happen because Yemaya answered her prayers, or because he had seen enough? Lyaa had no answer. Perhaps there was no answer and could not be. Did the gods intervene in this world or did they not? Sometimes it seemed as though they did, sometimes as though they did not or would not or could not. Was it her name that called up the power of the First Woman?)

But as it happened on that morning early it was much worse than that, so much worse than she ever, in her innocence, might have feared. The monkeys could see the men moving along the forest paths, which is what gave them such cause for alarm.

Awake, Lyaa! they called. *Awake and hide!*

Awake and run! Others called back.

Awake, awake!

Come!

Hurry!

Run!

Go!

Alas, she did not understand the language of the animals, knew only that something important had happened.

Or something terrible was happening.

She sat with her ailing mother, listening to the disruption in the trees. Not until—yes! no!—she heard the rush of men hurrying along the path, and heard the clank of the chains they carried, heard the sound even though the chains lay muffled in large sacks slung over the traders' shoulders, did she try to urge her mother to her feet.

"Go," her mother said, so deep in her whispery voice that it seemed as though she spoke from another realm.

"You must stand and come with me," Lyaa said.

"Go," her mother urged her, and then closed her eyes, closed her lips.

Men shouted, women screamed, and children screeched and howled.

Go! The voice echoed in Lyaa's mind.

She glanced down one last time at her supine mother, ran out into the light, and kept on running, running, beyond the village clearing, into the woods, along the creek. It was not until she reached the edge of the big forest that, hungry for breath, she paused, and then raced forward again, hearing now the pounding feet of pursuers breaking through the forest behind her.

Yemaya! Yemaya!

"Run!" A woman's voice behind her urged her on.

Run!

Turning in the hope of catching a glimpse of how close the people hunters might be, she tripped on a root and fell forward, slamming her shoulder against a tree trunk that even though it bent with her weight was still large enough to bounce her back and send her catapulting off the path.

A moment later two men rushed past, chains clanking in the sacks at their shoulders.

She inched up above the grass and watched them disappear into the woods.

Oh, Mother! Oh, Yemaya! Might she be safe now? Slowly she pulled herself to her feet, touching the raw place where her shoulder had hit the tree. She felt tears rising in her belly even as she bent over and spit up liquid and air. Safe? Where was her family? What should she do now?

The monkeys overhead had quieted down and this gave her pause. Perhaps the raiders had moved past the village, though if so she feared they might have left for dead those who resisted. In spite of herself, she called up the image of her father/uncle, the man who had made her life a little prison in itself. If anyone had been hurt, she hoped, hoped so hard she began to double over again with belly pain, may it have been him!

When she pulled herself upright once more she started back in the direction of the village, walking slowly, tentatively, alert to every sound in the woods around her, the chirping of the monkeys, the call of birds, the rustle of leaves as she brushed past plants and low trees. It sounded as though the terror that had driven her to run so fast and far had ended. Her heart settled down. She whispered prayerful thanks to Yemaya, and in a deeper part of her cursed the desert sky god who allowed those slave traders to live and track poor human beings such as herself and her family.

"Lyaa!"

Her father/uncle hailed her as she stepped into the clearing.

Never, ever could she have imagined she would feel so happy to see this man whom she despised!

She walked toward him as he gestured, which she took to mean that he was happy to see her, too.

And all of a sudden the world went black, she fell forward, or was pushed, and couldn't catch her breath.

"And the cattle?"

Her father/uncle's voice boomed above her where she lay sprawled, a cloth tied tightly over her head, on the sandy ground of the compound.

"You will have them tomorrow, you have my word." This was a voice she didn't recognize. One of the slavers! Or not?

"You take these people now and you give me your word you will bring the goods in return tomorrow?"

"You have my word."

"Do I?"

"My word, for God."

"Your god or mine?"

The slaver spat, and Lyaa could feel him stamp a step past her.

"Is that a curse?"

"Never," her father/uncle said. "Never. I submit to your god."

The trader did not respond, instead kneeling alongside Lyaa and tying something around her neck. He then pulled at a chain and she felt the collar tighten at her throat. When he yanked her to her feet she nearly choked.

"My men are fetching the others. And then we depart. You'll have your cattle tomorrow before sundown."

"Thank you," she heard her father/uncle say, his voice more subdued than usual.

"I want to return to my mother," she said in a raspy voice, her throat constricted by the chain.

"Oh, yes, yes, she will be meeting you," her father/uncle said.

"She is ill. She needs help. She cannot take a deep breath. Did you see her back in the village? Did you?"

Lyaa felt strength flow into her arms and she reached up and tore at the chain.

Her father/uncle turned away.

"Tell me!" she shouted, at terrible cost to her throat. "Did you see her?"

"Take her," her father/uncle said.

And the trader led her away, pulling her along for some distance before they stopped and he removed the hood. She stood quietly, confused, numb at heart, while he and the rest of his band rounded up others from the village. Women sobbed, nervously clutching handfuls of belongings, children cried because their mothers cried, unknowing, innocent. The monkeys overhead joined in, chattering, screaming. Finally she herself began to weep, for her mother, for all of them. When the slave returned to where

Lyaa stood he stared and stared with coal-black eyes so fierce that she turned her head aside.

Pinching the flesh on her arm, the slaver said, "Worth every cow, worth every cow."

Chapter Seventeen

In My Margins

What Are the Origins of Woman?

It is He who created you from a single person, and made his mate of like nature, in order that he might live with her in love. When they are united, she bears a light burden and carries it about unnoticed. When she grows heavy, they both pray to Allah their Lord, saying: "If you give us a goodly child, we vow we shall ever be grateful." (Koran, 7:189)

What then are the origins of woman? All the stories have her born of man's clay or man's rib. But she gives birth to men, rather than men giving birth to her. Can all the oldest stories be wrong?

The new science says we first came out of water, and our ancestors, odd fish from the salt sea, flopped onto shore on stubby fins like legs and with rudimentary lungs breathed the sulfurous air before retreating to the ocean. And, oh, we liked the air! More and more often we stumbled ashore and stayed longer and longer, so that eventually some of our old folks stayed behind when the tide withdrew, making a life free of the vagaries of the tides and subject to the new light of the sun and the cool reflections of the moon.

But clay? But ape? But man?

All these stories whirling about on the fumes of a newly explosive land, where after the heat settled and the chemistry of place set in tiny green plants clung to the rocks and small insects whirred through air warmed by fire. First clay? First ape? Did we all come from clay and then did woman break free of man's clay and become a creature of her own? Or did the salt sea creature with lungs one morning a million million years ago ascend a tree as fish and descend some millions of years later as ape?

What are the origins of woman?

The first upright female wondered, turning her liquid eye to the moon, and breathed a sound of surprise.

What are the origins of man?

The first upright male turned his blinking eye to the sun, and looked away, down at his shadow.

Chapter Eighteen

First Morning

My first Carolina country morning awakening! And if I had been opening my eyes after a good sleep in Eden I could not have been more astonished and pleased—the air, just cool enough to make me feel as though I should arise, the light, milky with early morning fog, the odors, such a mix of flowers and trees and grasses my New York nose could scarcely begin to engage with them beyond the awareness of a wonderful new perfume.

The odors!

Now do not take this in the wrong way. New York had its own olfactory wonders, from the tarry beams on the river piers to the bittersweet smell of wood burning in fireplaces on the first cold autumn morning. And imagine crossing the Spuyten Duyvil into the Bronx farmlands without feeling yourself pushing aside a curtain of green wind. And the meaty stench of the horse apples in the gutters or the sweet stink of a dying dog in the roadway, its entrails laid open to the sun. Or if you would stand at the foot of our Battery and breathe in the perfect salt-sea sting of the incoming ocean tide, the breeze that carried it parting your hair toward the land behind you, you know the varied pleasures of our New York air.

But this curtain of oxygen—oh, I also learned my chemistry with master Halevi—in which I lay entangled weighed everything and nothing and like the depths of the ocean which I have heard has made a comfortable resting place for sailors who give up fighting sleep beneath the waves it pressed me to the bed—while at the same time allowed a medium in which my mind could take flight. Wasn't this how it might have been— and would be—if I had—when I would—set sail for Europe on my tour?

In a sleep-drenched state, picturing large thunderheads sailing toward us from the south, their stately top-heavy presences looming like figures

from a dream, watching over me, smiling faces painted on their upfurl-
ing undersides, eyes winking, mouths wide in laughter, and from a long
way away over the heaving water the boom and belch of their voices,
disconnected from their bodies but by the breadth and length of their
thunderous rolls making clear their relation to the soaring clouds—and at
my elbow, a girl, just my age, her hair flowing the wind off the waves,
one hand pressed tightly on my arm, the other holding to the rail—not-
Miriam—and the wind snatches away my hat and we laugh as we watch
it flop and roll into the ocean and the girl, not-Miriam, turns to me, face
uplifted, and says my name—

A knock at my door.

"Yes?"

I sat up, still half-drowsy, and after a blinking moment, swung my feet
to the floor.

"Massa Pereira?"

A woman's voice, sultry and soft, inviting, yet with a certain tone of servitude.

"Just a moment."

I stood up and pulled my nightshirt over my head. As I was doing so
I heard the door open and I immediately covered myself with the shirt.

There was the slave girl, standing in the doorway, looking at the floor.

"Excuse me," I began, "do you always walk in on a man in his room?"

"I'm sorry, Massa Pereira, but your uncle said it was urgent. He would
like to speak with you in the sunroom."

She stood there, as if waiting for my reply, her eyes still averted.

"You might have waited a moment."

Now she looked up at me, just a glance, and then down again.

"Yes, sir," she said, but did not move.

"I thought you were my cousin's wife."

She looked up at me, and then down again.

"Miss Rebecca," she said, "yes, massa. No, I am not."

Again, I caught the tiniest flicker in her eye.

"No, no, of course I know that. I meant that I thought it was she who
was knocking."

"Yes, sir," she said.

"And your name is…?"

"Liza, sir."

"Liza, I want to tell you how much I admire the clarity of your speech."

"Yes, sir," she said.

"You have no slave accent."

"Yes, sir."

"Has my cousin's wife tutored you in speech as well as reading?"

"She has, sir. And the doctor."

"The doctor?"

"The doctor who attends us, sir."

"Well, he has done a very good job."

"Yes, sir," she said, and I could not help but wonder if that flicker in her eye meant that she was ready to laugh.

My uncle waited for me downstairs in the company of the tall young African man, who had driven the carriage in from town.

"This is Isaac," my uncle introduced him to me as one of the overseers for the plantation.

"We met yesterday, Uncle," I said. "Isaac drove the carriage from town."

"Of course," my uncle said, while Isaac cast an appraising eye on me, as if he were figuring out right then and there the mettle of my branch of the family, which gave me the opportunity to take a look at him—a fairly young man, early to rise to the responsibility, I surmised, of overseership.

"He'll be showing you around the plantation and explaining matters to you."

"Good," I said. "As soon as I have my breakfast I'll be ready for my tour."

Isaac looked at my uncle, who shook his head.

"With the Sabbath coming up you should move along."

"Very well then, Uncle. We will go."

"That's the spirit, boy," my uncle said. "Isaac, he is all yours."

What a strange world, I thought, to say such a thing when Isaac belonged to him.

Though he did not show it. In fact, one of the first things he explained to me as we went out the rear door of the main house was that the way my uncle ran things on this plantation was out of the ordinary.

"You'll rarely, sir, see your African man working as overseer. Usually the job is reserved for a white man, someone tough as nails."

"But you are an African man—"

"And tough as nails."

It was his joke, but though I laughed, he did not.

The joke came at my expense as he led me behind the house to the stables.

"Is this barn the first stop on the tour?" I said.

Isaac squinted at me in the early morning mist.

"We mount up here," he said.

"I do not ride," I said. "City boy, and all of that, you know?"

"Master Jonathan has taken the carriage to town," Isaac said.

I took a deep breath and said, "I'll try."

Something flickered in the corner of my eye. Distracted, I turned and caught a glimpse of the slave girl hurrying from the house to one of the out-buildings.

"Keep your mind on the horse," Isaac said. I was afraid he would laugh, but he remained solemn in his demeanor.

After several tries, I mounted up and we went on our way, into a morning filled with busyness and news.

Chapter Nineteen

First Lesson

The big horse was called Promise and Isaac sat alongside me on a large black stallion whose name he did not say. He urged our mounts into motion and we went riding slowly away from the house. Promise, as big as he was, seemed a gentle beast, though I remained a bit wary of him.

Yet I was warier still of my mission to this place.

"May I ask you some questions?"

Isaac seemed to nod his head ever so slightly as we rode along. This I took to be positive.

"Is my uncle good to you?" I said.

"Not a question, sir. He is very good."

Recalling the auction block, I said, "I cannot imagine he would ever sell you away."

"No, sir. But sometimes that happens."

"I cannot imagine it."

"Things is different down here, sir," he said, and stared over the head of his horse at the trail ahead.

What kind of a life did this man have, I wondered as we rode along, in which someone might sell him in an auction? Was he born here in Carolina or had he been born elsewhere? From the way he walked and gestured, I assumed he was a native of Carolina soil, especially because his face showed such features as might have been the result of having had an Indian mother or father, a long straight nose and high cheekbones, and deep-set gray eyes. Most un-African, I thought to myself, because it seemed almost as though he were a handsome white man whose skin had darkened somehow in the night. Also most un-African about him was the way he stared me hard in the eye, almost as though he knew something about me, something he did not admire.

"Isaac?" I called to him. "Do you have any Indian blood in you?"

That manner of his—he turned, and turned away, pretending that he hadn't heard me. Meanwhile we kept up our pace along the trail, and I kept on wondering. His mother? Perhaps some Indian whom my uncle had bought as a slave and introduced to one of the African men in the barracks, a woman whose family had lived in the woods and swamps long before we Europeans arrived, and traveling up and along the coast, enjoying a carefree (if sometimes difficult) life of fishing and hunting to keep themselves fed. For how long had they and their ancestors done this? Yes, I kept on wondering about this. Far, far back in time, back at least to the time when my own ancestors were wandering in the desert, having angered God enough to make Him order us into an exile of forty years—

And their god or gods? Who were they? Where were they? I pictured them as idols or invisible amid the storm clouds that passed over our heads on hot days in spring and summer seasons. I asked him a question about religion. And he was quick to reply.

"Miss Rebecca," he said, "she's teaching us about religion."

"And do you find it interesting?"

"I do, massa, I do."

"In Africa, your people had a certain type of religion. I studied something of it with my tutor when I was a boy. Animism, he called it. The worship of spirits living in trees and rivers and such."

"I don't know, massa, I never learned that. Just the Hebrew."

"Can you read Hebrew?"

"I can recognize a few words, massa," he said. "Aleph," he said. "Bet…"

"That's more than I can read of it," I said.

I let our conversation fall away, dwelling in my amazement that this fellow, a little darker than me, but with more Hebrew, might be put up for public sale. With this in mind, it seemed appropriate that the mist still hovered over the rice fields as we made our way toward them. Though I had traveled a similar route the day before on the carriage, sitting high up here on my horse with nothing above but the sky gave me a different sense of the land and its extension. The animal's rolling gait, the screen of fog, with new sun touching on high clouds above us, all of it conspired to make a picture for me of beauty, strangeness, and possibility. Why the latter, I could not have said just then, but it was a feeling that stole over me, a feeling of hope in the face of duty.

The scene we encountered gave my fantasy more fuel.

In the mist a dozen or so dark men and women (though some of these were children, male and female, whose smaller stature led me to conclude they were all women) worked in the rows of the rice fields, stooping to their particular tasks of planting the individual stalks each in a small bed of mud. Aside from the clomp and click of our horses' hooves, the sounds here came from birds fluttering overhead and calling to one another—and an audible chant from the workers in the rows of rice plants.

Rize is...nize...
Nize is...rize...

...the men's voices low and rumbling, like thunder in advance of lightning, the women's voices sparkling, high, like the twitter of the birds, and the children added to the twitter of the upper registers of sound.

Nize is...
Rize is...

"Nice music," I said.

"Oh, yes, nice music, massa, ain't it?" Isaac said.

"I'd think it would give them some incentive to keep working, to keep moving. The rhythm of it would push them along."

"Yes, massa," Isaac said. "It pushes, yes. And I push them."

"Isaac, please, I wish you wouldn't call me 'massa.' I find it rather odd."

"But that is who you are, sir. The massa."

"I am only my uncle's nephew."

"But soon to be a massa."

"How do you know that? What do you know?"

Perhaps he would have answered me, perhaps not. But at that moment a cry broke past the boundary of sound and the slaves began shouting and throwing up their hands, pointing.

"Excuse me, sir," Isaac said, and dismounted and waded out into the water where he took charge of the noisy gang that had formed in one corner of the field. A few moments later he returned, followed by an agitated group of men and women holding up a young girl in their arms.

"What is it?" I said. "Is she hurt?"

He took a blanket from the back of saddle and placed it on the ground. The slaves lowered the young woman onto the blanket and gathered around her while she began to writhe and moan.

"Is there something I can do?"

Isaac looked up at me.

"Are you a doctor, young master?"

I shook my head.

"Shouldn't we take her to the house?"

"The midwife right here. Planting rice alongside her. Keeping watch."

"That's good," I said.

"Yes, yes, so you just sit there on that horse. Unless you care to ride back to the house by yourself."

"I will wait," I said, and leaned forward in the saddle and watched. From my perch I had in fact a better view than if I were standing at the outside of the circle of women. What did I know about life? It was only then did I begin to understand what was happening, as the women attended to their patient, employing cloths from Isaac's saddlebags and poultices and such they had been carrying along apparently for just such an event as this.

"Oh, Lord!" the writhing woman's cry went up.

The women around her used their hands on her, muttering, mumbling, chanting.

"Rize is," I thought I heard. Or were they some other words?

"Gawdamighty!"

"Careful, careful," Isaac said, looking down at them from his place in the circle of slaves.

"Isaac?" I said, looking down at him from my perch atop the horse.

The woman, eyes shut tight and jaw clenched, and breathing in rhythm as the others raised the hem of her raggedy field dress to reveal a brown belly swollen beyond any limit I had ever imagined, her lighter-shaded legs spread wide to reveal an orifice darkening like the track of a slice into one of our Marzy's red cakes and opening wider than any I had ever dreamed.

For a moment, the air went out of me and I clung to the horses' mane, fearing that I might fall. When I recovered to myself, I sat silently, watching, listening. Minutes went by, possibly more than minutes. The woman writhed on the ground in the center of the circle of women, breathing hard, breathing hard, breathing hard, and then resting, resting, and then breathing again, breathing again. She moved her lips, and I heard sounds, but it didn't seem as though the sounds I heard came from those lips.

Baby come soon,
Git a name...

"An' breathe..." A woman called up to the trees.
"An' breathe..."
Isaac stood at the edge of the circle, watching me, watching the trees, rarely glancing down at the woman in the center.
"What's her name?" I called to him.
He shook his head and gave me a look of great contempt.
"Lucy's Delilah," he said, almost as though he were spitting on the ground.
I ignored his disrespect, merely nodded, glanced up at the sun, and looked back to the circle.

Baby come soon...

One woman had applied a cloth to the laboring woman's forehead, another rubbed her feet, while a third held her hand and breathed along with her.

Aha, aha, aha, aha, aha...

Over and over.
After a while, I dismounted and held the reins, but when a scream went up from the circle I let them drop and rushed to the crowd. Isaac stepped in front of me.
"That horse going to wander," he told me.
"Of course," I said, turning back to pick up the reins. Something moved in the tall weeds at the side of the trail—a long green snake I rushed to catch a further glimpse of. Behind me a hush fell upon the crowd and I could hear creatures—birds—singing in the trees at the edge of the clearing. It made me dizzy to look up at the clear blue of the sky, almost as if I were about to fall—somehow, suddenly—upwards, losing all of my weight and gravity that held me upright on the ground.

The horse gave a snort, recalling me to my purpose, and I strode after it, about ten paces along the trail before I tried for the reins.

"Ho, Promise," I said. "Come here, Promise."

And finally I caught him.

At that moment a cry of triumph went up from the crowd down the trail and I turned to see one of the older women holding aloft a small pale bundle, which at first I thought were wrappings or bandages used in the birth.

Coming back up the trail alongside Isaac, I said, "It's not African, it's white."

"It will darken, don't you worry," he replied.

With some difficulty I remounted.

"I'll fetch the carriage," I said.

"A wagon will do," Isaac said. "Yes, you go on, ride back and send a wagon."

The woman cried out again, and a second small bundle appeared over the heads of the women.

"A twin!" I said.

"The afterbirth," Isaac said to me. "We keep that dry now, and bury it later. There's a ceremony." He turned a hand palm up. "Massa? Will you ride?"

And so I obeyed the order of the slave-overseer and turned my horse back toward the house.

Except it did not want to go in that direction. A few yards down the road the animal took a turn much against my will, for though I yanked the reins and kicked the beast's sides it walked onto a side trail and despite my protestations and threats—"Turn, Promise! Come on you beast! Promise, I'm going to whip you!"—carried me through the trees where low-hanging moss brushed my head and shoulders, and at one point a vine I took to be a snake nearly frightened me to death before we emerged into a clearing at the side of the wide creek, just behind the brickyard.

A group of about six male slaves labored at the side of the building, hauling finished bricks to make a stack of them at the end of a small wooden pier built out into the water where the sloop from Charleston would arrive at some point, sooner than later I had to assume from their urgency, to take the shipment away.

Some of the men looked up at me as we approached, and one of them waved—the foreman, I supposed, from the way that he kept his head a little higher than the rest.

"Yes, sir?" he called to me.

"No matter," I returned his greeting and sat a while atop my horse as though this were what I had come for, to study the work of these men forced into labor, instead of being carried along by the beast with its own will.

Unlike the slaves in the rice field, they stood to face the heat of the day. The sweat that ran down their necks and backs might have watered all the rice, so copiously it streamed. I watched in fascination as they mixed their compound for the bricks and added the straw to hold the finished block together, and then lay them on a large rectangular pallet with handles on both sides which took four of them to lift—making a sharp cry in unison that made my horse start—and guide onto the space they had set aside for the drying.

"Now—hush!"

And raised it to the pallet.

"Now—push!"

And carry the pallet over.

Then, as if he had been waiting to witness this display, my horse turned and began walking me back through the trees, putting the brickyard far behind us as we joined the main trail.

Isaac had already been back to the house and passed us on the trail coming the other way, seated up on a wagon.

"You awful slow, massa!" he called to me as we passed in the dust.

I knew that, I knew that. There were things here I had never imagined going on in ways I never could have suspected, which feelings were heightened for me all the more when I considered that this child whose birth I had witnessed had come into the world as a piece of chattel.

Chapter Twenty

Journey

$\mathcal{B}$y flatboat, a dozen women and children made the journey west, eventually disembarking when at Ziguinchor the river became unnavigable and their captors herded them ashore. A vast flock of flamingos, disturbed by the disruption in their fishing rights, rose into the air to become a great curtain of white, their flapping wings sounding like hundreds of curtains rustling in the wind. The captives spent the night in a large sandy area that smelled of dead fish and other rotting things. Dogs barked them awake long before the sun rose, accompanied by an intermittent chorus of roosters. Lyaa stood up and walked in the direction of the river when one of the traders called sharply to her and she stopped in her tracks.

The man pointed to a scraggly row of reeds.

She shook her head.

He walked toward her, raising his rifle as he moved.

Again, Lyaa shook her head and went to do her business in the reeds in full view of the slaver and anyone else who might have been watching as the first hint of the day's new sun inched up above the southern forest.

The man barked out a loud guffaw, but Lyaa refused to raise her eyes toward him as she walked, as proudly as she could muster, back to where the other prisoners lay.

The day passed, with more and more captives arriving from the direction of the river. Lyaa scanned the crowd chained together on the beach, longing for a glimpse of her mother. More than two dozen of the new arrivals spent the next night in that same place, and Lyaa, though she recognized some by the colors of their headdresses and some facial scarring, found that the more people who arrived, the more she felt isolated and alone.

Old Mother, Yemaya, she raised her eyes in prayer, *help us to break free of this terrible lonely place and return up river to the forest where we belong.* But then she could not help but remember that it was her uncle/father who had sent her off in slavery. Her mother had railed against the old desert god who hovered behind the selling of human bodies. Take Yemaya to your heart, daughter, she had often said, and you will find freedom. But her uncle/father prayed to the forest gods, and he did no better than the desert traders who bought and sold human beings.

How was it that Yemaya had not cursed him and crushed him where he stood, watching as the slavers herded Lyaa and the others like cattle onto the flatboats?

How was it?

She asked this of herself, she asked this of other girls with whom she became acquainted as they continued their captive journey along the banks of the river, a passage that took many days and nights. Some spoke her language, others had a few words and many hand gestures, others she could not communicate with at all except by gestures and sometimes by drawing stick figures in the damp earth.

Three horizontal lines, one vertical--in quiet moments she copied the designs on the stone, knowing that it had something to do with where she came from, but unsure of where that was. Back, back in time, beyond the desert city where the sand blew through the streets, this she remembered from stories her mother had told her, stories her own mother had told her, stories that her mother's mother had told her mother, all the way back into the first times. The rest of it came to her in dreams that visited her when she lay like a dead girl under the bright stars, the moon sometimes glazed with a slight corona of moisture-tinged clouds.

This she knew—

Her oldest grandmother, a slight woman, scarcely taller than a girl, with almond eyes, rough dark hair, and a flattened nose, holding the hand of her oldest grandfather, slightly taller, long arms, while behind them trailed along their first child, a creature even slighter of build than either of them, because food had been so scarce, a spouting volcano laying a fine rain of ash over the already parched country, driving away what animals it had not yet buried, and just that morning another wave of explosions from the flattened top of the peak to the east, so that they fled, along with the small beasts of the desert, those that could still scurry or crawl or fly, crossing old water holes and trailing the bank of a desiccated river, at one point feeling the moisture beneath their feet and—the grandmother glanced down to see it—leaving their tracks behind in the rapidly hardening mud.

At sundown they looked back once more and saw a faint new sun rising in the east where a great smoky fireball shot out of the volcano and soared into the air before spraying out its flowering of flame and smoke and ash. A memory blossomed in the woman's mind, a roar of a command to put their home behind them and start walking, as a vast canopy of fire and storm hovered over what had been their first home for as long as they could remember.

Another two days, and they arrived in darkness and pulled the rafts to shore. She felt such fatigue that sleep came quickly. She awoke to the stark light of the early sun, and, as she had been learning, immediately made preparations—gathered plants for tea, some nuts, a piece of fruit—to travel. When she looked around she saw dozens of people, dozens more than she had traveled with, and still no sign of her mother. The air smelled different. It had an edge that cleared her nose and tickled it at the same time.

Onto the boats again. Behind her another flatboat with even more people crowded onto it. Silently they moved along the river, boatmen poling them slowly along. That sting in the air grew sharper, and to the west the sky brightened at the upper reaches of the air. Blue faded to white, white glared, made her turn her eyes away. She feared that if they kept pushing west they might reach the edge of the river and fall down a steep drop into a darkness where she would never see again.

Midmorning now, and those without food began to call out to their captors. The slavers paid no attention. Lyaa lay down, pretending to sleep while silently clawing about in her pack for small bits of the food she had gathered. At the sound of a child weeping nearby she turned and saw the wee thing nursing at her mother's breast, but without satisfaction.

Lyaa offered the mother a few nuts, and the woman bowed her head in thanks. Hours passed, more flamingos floated overhead, and then someone pointed out a strange bird, with a deep pouch at its throat, and large wings, and other smaller white birds that called to each other and sounded almost as if they were laughing.

Except for crying children, silence reigned on the raft under the hot sun. At night Lyaa listened to the pole men call to each other, telling stories about girls and river adventures. She could hear the rush of the water against the wood of the raft, a shearing sound, as though water were falling over a cliff rather than simply moving swiftly along. A large empty hole seemed to open up in her the more she thought about her absent mother, and she shivered even in the heat of the rising sun at the prospect of going another day without her.

She had little time to grieve. A turn in the river up ahead, the paleness of the sky beyond caught her eye. People around her began to murmur, and some parents wept louder than their children.

"The sea, the sea!" someone called out.

She had never heard the word before, but before too long, as they rounded one more turn, she saw what they spoke of, the broad flat expanse of dark water, a solid blue-green plain reflecting back at her the light of the sun. Pale clouds sailed overhead, beyond the white birds in flight.

The sea, the sea!

Where close to an island covered with palms two large ships with broad white sails lay at anchor.

Chapter Twenty-one

More to Learn

*B*lack Jack the butler met me at the door and I told him of the need for the wagon out in the fields.

"Yes, massa," he said. "I'll take care of it."

None of my relatives seemed to be about. I asked him to heat water for my bath and went up to my room. After filling the large copper tub behind the screen he left and I undressed. I gingerly climbed in and soaked a while, listening to the birdsong outside my window, but despite the prettiness of that music I felt myself sinking now and then into a dolorous state in which I allowed myself to succumb to a deep despair about life here and the indentured state into which that infant in the field had just been born. How torn I felt between my duty to my family and its business and the desire to take up my pistol, fire into the air, and declare that each and every one of the slaves on the plantation was free to go! Was I myself free to go? The soothing water soon lulled me into a worrisome nostalgia for home and the city. I found myself missing the hurly and busyness of the streets, the cry of children scrambling for goods, the smoke from many chimneys, the horns and rumble of horse-carts on cobblestones, and, quite unbelievably, even the clouds that often descended to the house tops and made gloom a palpable part of life among us urban-dwellers.

Gloom, gloom, where have you gone?

These were my thoughts, my foolish mind turned upside down, when I heard a musical sound—not birdsong—from somewhere on the other side of the screen.

"Hello?" I called out.

"Massa Pereira," a woman said.

"What? Who is that?"

But I half-knew already, and so was not completely unprepared for the shock of Liza, the house-slave, appearing around the corner of the screen.

"I've brought fresh towel for you, massa," she said, staring past me at the wall. "I'll set it down here, sir, just next to the tub."

"Thank you, Liza," I said. I looked away out of embarrassment, the shock of her appearance working in my loins. "Now please excuse me."

She gave me a half-smile, half-squint of her fresh green eyes.

And she was gone before I could upbraid her for disturbing my bath.

I lay there in the water a while longer, trying to settle down in my excitement, mulling on the aftermath. I was of two minds. Pretty as she was, she annoyed me because of the brazenness of her action. It occurred to me then the reason why—because she was a slave she had no presence and so could move across these boundaries like a ghost.

I stood up in the bath and could not but help to admit to myself that thinking about her had stirred some part of me in a way I had not considered before this. In other words, I was ravenous for her, and I had to remind myself that up in New York my dear Miriam waited for me, and I was only biding my time before I could return to her. What kind of a man was I?

My mood of self-abasement didn't last very long. I reveled in the coolness after the bath and soon dressed and went down to take my first Sabbath meal with my relatives.

The scene I encountered was quite foreign and enticing. I had no sooner entered the dining room when my large uncle, seated at the head of the table, with all the rest of the family already assembled (including one I had not met), touched a beefy finger to his lips while my aunt lighted two candles at her end of the table and said a quiet prayer.

"The Sabbath Bride arrives," my uncle said when she had finished. "Sit, and eat with her."

A flurry of activity at the doorway, and I turned to look as Black Jack the butler entered with trays of food while once again Precious Sally watched with anxious enjoyment from the entrance to the kitchen.

"Did you notice those candlesticks?" my uncle said, gesturing toward the flickering lights.

"Oh, no, Grandfather, not that story again," Little Abraham groaned, a portent of noise to come.

"Hush," said my aunt. "Let your grandfather tell your cousin the story."

"They are pure silver, of course," my uncle said, ignoring his grandson's complaint. "And as you can see, they tell a story."

I squinted in the light and leaned closer to the center of the table, discerning on the slender candlesticks the etching of a tree, a man and woman beneath it, and a serpent winding itself around and around the base of the holder.

"Ah, yes, Uncle, the Temptation."

"A fine old story." He looked across the table and stared—at my cousin Jonathan. "A fine story to give one's attention to," he said.

"Ah, yes, Father," Jonathan said. "All of us would do well to pay attention to these stories."

My uncle turned his attention back to me.

"These candlesticks have been in the family since the days of our life in Spain, and carried with us for generation upon generation, passed along from mother to daughter. Portugal. Africa. The Canaries. Holland. And then to the Indies, where the Pereiras spent a good deal of time before coming here. But you know that, of course."

"Yes, Uncle," I said.

"And, if you believe the stories about them...?"

Abraham made a mock groan and touched his hands to his stomach.

My uncle ignored him.

"The silver was supposedly mined in the hills of old Lebanon."

Abraham groaned again.

"And the model for the female figure beneath the tree—"

"May I venture a guess?" I said.

My uncle gave me the nod.

"Salome," I said.

"A tempting answer, but not correct."

"Bathsheba," I tried again.

My uncle shook his head.

"There is a legend..."

"Eve!" I said.

"The very one," he said.

Again young Abraham made a groaning noise.

"Just a story," my uncle said.

"But with a moral," put in my cousin Jonathan in a voice that suggested that he was already well sated with wine.

"And that moral?" His father waited for an answer.

"Never give in to temptation, of course, though it lies all around us." My cousin gave me a conspiratorial look. "Have you ever given in to temptation, Cousin Nate?"

"I…have sometimes eaten more than I should," I said.

"You are too polite," Jonathan said. "But then this is the Sabbath meal."

"Jonathan, you might be polite yourself," his mother said.

"Yes, excuse me, I am sorry, Mother." He held up his hands as if to show everyone at the table that they were clean. "I am sorry."

"I am hungry," young Abraham complained.

"Yes, yes," said my uncle, "let us begin." He muttered a prayer under his breath while Jonathan raised a glass of wine and all followed his example. Black Jack leaned close to the table and served while Precious Sally the cook watched with approval from the doorway.

The evening meal consisted of roasted hens and stewed tomatoes, platters full of rice mixed with herbs and piquant spices and plentiful amounts of red wine. I couldn't help but notice when I looked up from a knife-stick of food, how the cook watched us quite carefully, interested obviously in how much—or how little—we were enjoying her meal—a little Hebrew Carolina feast fixed by this big woman born in Africa many decades ago.

There was no small enjoyment to it. The fowl, the rice, and the wine we drank in copious amounts to wash it down—it made me perspire to eat this much this vigorously, but the flavors, every tip to the tongue and buttery savor, were delicious. After the food had disappeared the wine kept flowing.

"Is this evening much the same as your own Sabbath celebrations at home in New York?" my uncle asked me, his glass raised high in his huge hand.

I shook my head.

"We live in a quiet house," I said. "Only the three of us. And I can't say that we pay much attention to the Sabbath other than that we attend to our prayers on Saturday morning."

"Your aunt has not taken over the woman's responsibilities since your mother's death?"

The light outside had faded and the flickering candlelight at the table must have made the instant flush of blood to my face not as noticeable as I feared it might be.

"No, sir," I said.

"She will," said cousin Jonathan. "It is the custom."

"Perhaps," said my aunt, "the Sabbath in the city is more difficult to practice. Out here in our country we make it something quite special."

"We've had the rabbi come out from town to speak with us all," Rebecca said.

"And she means *all*," Jonathan said, "Jews and pagans."

"Yes," my uncle added, "though I was severely disappointed in his approach to such matters."

"In what matters exactly, uncle?" I said.

Abraham sat up straight in his chair.

"Turning the niggers into Jews," he said.

My uncle slapped his hand on the table.

"Where do you hear such talk? Certainly not at my table."

"He takes this from your tone," his daughter-in-law said.

My uncle ignored her, ordering the boy from the room.

The boy sat there, head slightly bowed.

"Go," Jonathan spoke up.

The boy made to moan and left the table.

As he did so I caught sight of Black Jack, peering at us from the doorway, a near-smile on his face, as Precious Sally stood behind him, shaking her head, as if all of us were the age of young Abraham and entirely out of order.

"I apologize, Father."

My uncle nodded curtly.

"And I apologize, Nathaniel," Uncle said to me, his face as red as the coat of an old British soldier.

"Sir, nothing to apologize for. I am not so far away in age from Abraham and I recall it as a time when in confusion about whether I was still a boy or becoming a man I often felt such contradictory furies in me that I would say, or I should say, could say, just about anything."

"But you probably didn't," my uncle said.

"No, though I wish I had. I was a good lad, my father always said."

My aunt, who had been silent throughout this outburst, or, rather, in the end, silently weeping, now spoke up.

"I don't want to think of my grandson as a cruel boy. But he spoke so cruelly…"

"Mother," cousin Jonathan said, "he spoke out of ignorance."

"He hears the word about in the town," Rebecca said. "Perhaps the best thing is to keep him out of the town."

My uncle sighed a loud sigh, hissing through his large teeth like some kind of specimen from the woods.

"We have fallen down in our teaching of the boy," he said. "We must make all the more of an effort." He looked over at Black Jack (Sally had disappeared back into the kitchen). "I'm sorry."

"Yes, sir," Black Jack said.

Uncle paused, and spoke in such a way that I imagined that he knew the young boy must be listening from the other room.

"Must I say again what we take to be the truth? That we are all brothers under the skin, and that even if someone is born into the tribe of dusky Ham we must help him to recognize his worth."

"Thank you," said Rebecca.

"They know what they are worth," my cousin put in, ignoring his wife. "If they listen to the bidding at their auction."

Rebecca sat up and took in a great rush of breath.

"Jonathan!"

He turned his lips out and made a puckering sound.

"My darling, rest easy, I was simply making a jest." He nodded to me. "For our dear visiting's cousin's sake."

Rebecca remained outraged.

"I am quite sure our dear cousin from New York does not enjoy such humor."

She turned to me, which I took to be my cue to speak.

I took a sip of wine and set down my glass, giving myself a moment's more time.

"I do and I do not," I said.

My answer clearly did not satisfy her.

The look it produced on Jonathan's face seemed otherwise.

"I believe," he said, "that we understand each other. All that you've seen so far is quite new to you. I expect that before too long in your stay you will come to understand exactly how much it is worth you—and your father, of course. My dear uncle, sitting up there in New York City, watching over us and judging our every move…"

"Father is not like that," I said. "He looks fairly and equitably upon everything that comes before him."

"Of course, of course," my cousin said. "The fair judge from New York. Just like our God, giving us the opportunity—"

"Jonathan..."

Now it was his father, my uncle, who broke in.

"Sorry, sir, sorry," my cousin said.

At last, I found the breath to speak up again.

"I have a question, now that we are talking about such matters as this," I said.

"And your question?" Jonathan seemed happy that I was taking such an interest.

"You mentioned the bidding," I said.

"Yes?" he said. "That jolly auction system of ours, I did take you to see it. But what is your question?"

"Oh, I am, to say the truth, rather fascinated with this business of putting a price on a human being. And I am wondering just how one does that."

"Yes, you saw the handbill about one sale. Most others are like that, with particular prices for particular slaves."

"But how, sir, do you come up with a price?" I quickly took a large sip of wine and went on with my query. "If, say, one were to ask about a particular slave. Say, the house girl, Liza—"

"Ah, the house girl Liza," Jonathan said. "Yes. What about her?"

"Do you recall what price you paid for her...just as an example, mind you."

"The price for Liza, hmm..."

"Just a hypothetical question, mind you," I said, scolding myself in my old tutor's voice, who had always expressed his disdain for hypothetical questions. The actual, the particular, that's what he had always urged on me.

"Why—" my uncle spoke up.

But Jonathan interrupted him.

"Excuse me," he said, "but in the case of the house girl, Liza—" and he smiled at me from across the table in such a warm way that I leaned closer and gave him my complete attention, on top of the deep interest that I was already finding I possessed—"that question is moot. She was born here, and so no one ever bid on her."

"Yes, of course," I said. "I should have figured that out myself."

"No reason to," my cousin said.

"Why, though, young nephew"—here my uncle finally found the way to break into this intense exchange—"in the case of Liza you must recognize how impossible it would be to put any price on this young woman."

"But say," I responded, "in this hypothetical instance—"

Jonathan's smile collapsed into itself and of an instant he showed me a rather strange façade, as though anger roiled him for a fleeting instant and then, blinking, he found peace again in his thoughts.

"This one, Liza, the slave girl, is priceless," he said. "Utterly and absolutely and irrevocably without a price."

Chapter Twenty-two

In My Margins

Wisps of Life

Smoke, wind, water, salt, a cough, a kiss, a light in the eyes, a finger, a heel toe elbow shoulder hip, a plaintive wail...How do you prepare for a voyage that allows you nothing to carry except your memories and your soul?

Chapter Twenty-three

More to Learn (2)

*J*onathan's declaration, seeming half in jest and, to my ear, half in earnest, set the other family members to explaining themselves.

"I know that it must seem quite a fearful situation," my uncle said, "because we are a people who lived all too long in bondage ourselves. And yet we own these people, you are going to say, yes, I know. Unfortunately right now we cannot run the plantation without their labor. But when the time comes we will effect their emancipation."

"When the time comes, yes," my aunt said quietly, and I could not tell by her voice whether she was ratifying what Uncle said or disputing it.

"You cannot," my cousin said quickly, "set a slave free and expect he will know how to take care of himself. There have been experiments I have read about where birds of prey, wounded in one way or another, have been taken in by people of sympathy, and nurtured until their injuries, broken wings or legs, whatever they might have been, have been repaired, and then were set free into the wild again, only to perish, because they had forgotten their instincts for survival."

"And so you keep them here until you have trained them."

"We have only just begun our training, isn't that true, Rebecca?"

His wife nodded in agreement, keeping her eyes on me as if in search for some acquiescence.

Turning to me, Jonathan added, "Over the years we have had both good luck and bad with the sort of Africans we have kept here, and it has only been lately that we put our minds to the question of why this has been so. It has been Rebecca, my wife, who has been instrumental in this." He took another drink of wine and looked over at his wife.

Rebecca at last spoke up.

"Your uncle and my Jonathan did all the preparation," she said. "With the help also of a physician friend of ours. Perhaps at some point you will meet him. He visits now and then and tends to the health of our people."

"Or perhaps not," my cousin said. "He has been ailing himself and lately does not visit that often."

"In any case, dear Nathaniel, my little idea was like a small spark to their kindling."

"It was your idea?" I said, feeling a small spark of interest myself.

"I had a vision," Rebecca said.

"Really? I've never met one of us that had a vision."

"But, dear cousin, I did. I…I had not yet been able to conceive a child, but I had found ways to help small children. It was honey-making season, just a few years ago, when this idea came to me. I was spending an after-noon to myself while waiting for my beloved—" and here she cast a sweet eye at my cousin—"who was working with the slaves at the brickyard, strolling in the fields at the edge of the house. And I saw a bee, and took it upon me to follow it."

"Bees?" I said. "But what on earth can this have to do with slaves?"

"Explain to him," Jonathan said.

"I will," Rebecca said. "I followed the bee, keeping it in my sight as it made a rather dizzy pattern in the air just above and beyond my head, lighting from tree to vine to tree, until I thought I had lost sight of it and stopped to catch my breath. And the busy little insect buzzed just past my head, as if to invite to follow it further."

"Busy and buzzing," said my cousin, the wine having loosened his tongue a bit.

Rebecca took a breath and continued.

"And so I wandered through the woods, and I don't know how long I took, until I saw the sun slanting down behind the trees and knew it was time to start back to the house because my dear Jonathan would be returning from the rice fields soon—in fact, I could hear the dark people singing, their voices carrying like the noise of the bees and birds above the trees and then—"

"The dark people?"

"The slaves," Jonathan said.

"The darkies," Abraham said from the doorway and just then the here-tofore absent Liza came up behind him and gave him a rude side-wise shove, sending him full out into the other room.

Rebecca made a point of ignoring this distraction. I wished I might have ignored it, such a sudden spear of fire in my heart the sight of the slave girl produced in me.

Meanwhile, my cousin's wife went on, "They were singing, and here she took a deep breath and I watched her chest heave up and down as she sang the words in a voice deeper than her own. 'Don't mind working from sun to sun, If'n you give my dinner when the dinner time comes...'"

Now I took a swallow of wine, and Jonathan took another.

The doorway was now empty, Liza gone.

"It was beautiful music," Rebecca went on, "as beautiful in its own way as anything I hear in the synagogue—"

"Well, I certainly am not sure about that," said my uncle, her father-in-law.

"Hush," said my aunt.

"I am not trying to be disrespectful—"

"Please, my dear, continue," said Jonathan. "Father?"

My uncle shook his head, a signal for her to go on with her story.

As she spoke, I pictured not her but Liza gliding through the woods on the trail of the bee, her piercing green gaze and skin the color of walnut stippled by sunlight as she roamed from glade to glade.

Rebecca recounted her discovery, which, as I recollect it, had something to do with a Biblical vision of bees making honey in the corpse of a dead lion. I was not sure what she meant by this but would have politely kept on listening, except that I could not keep Liza out of my thoughts. I put her on the auction block in my mind and turned her this way and that, so I could observe her build and her strengths and whatever weaknesses— there were none—she might show forth.

A thousand, I bid. And then bid against myself. *Two thousand! Three!*

I turned her again and again, and bid her stare down at me from the block, before turning a haughty pose and looking away.

Four thousand!

"However," my uncle was saying when I prompted myself to pay attention to the conversation at the table, "I believe that while they may be children they can learn and become educated over time. In fact, I believe that all of the problems we have with our slave population comes from the fact that most owners ignore their capabilities rather than encourage them. For if he were treated as a perennial child, what man would not want to break his bonds and find his own freedom. Though, of course, that would be always disastrous for these people. Without an education, they could, in freedom, only fall back into the same mental bonds that held them back in the first place."

My leg had begun to ache from sitting so long, and I gave it a little shake, drumming my fingers on the tablecloth, and letting my eyes wander as again my mind did, lighting first on Precious Sally, who stood upright in the corner of the dining room, unmoving except for her huge chest working up and down, up and down, as she breathed, and then to Black Jack, who himself stood perfectly still in the doorway.

"And so we cultivate them," my uncle went on, "teaching them how to read, thanks to dear Rebecca here—" Rebecca made a gentle noise with her mouth and bowed her head toward Uncle—"and our physician friend from town, and teaching them such tricks of the artisan as making bricks."

His eyes rested on me, and so I sat up and showed my interest in these matters.

"How long have you been doing this, dear Uncle?" I inquired.

"For some time now," he said.

"And have you made many slaves ready to be freed?"

My cousin broke in.

"None, dear Nathaniel. We could not farm without them. But in a cultivated state they will, we believe, become much more cheerful in their present state and find some freedom in what they may read and discourse about."

My aunt spoke up again.

"It is the Sabbath and I don't want to hear any more talk about work and business, do you hear?"

"Yes, my dear," said my uncle. He motioned to Rebecca, who broke out into a song about the Sabbath bride, and we all joined in, not that I knew the song, but I moved my lips and mumbled the words along with the rest of the devout and dutiful family.

"And tomorrow being the Sabbath all day," my cousin Jonathan said, "we will take our leisure in the woods. Rebecca will be going back to town to visit with her family, so it will be you and me, dear cousin. And then on Sunday, the Gentile Sabbath, we'll have another day of rest. We give our slaves both days of rest."

"Two Sabbaths," I said, "what a fine idea. But do you fall behind in your cultivation because of that?"

"When we do, we eliminate one of the Sabbaths," he said. "Temporarily, of course."

"Very interesting," I said, and after the fine sherry following the dinner, I excused myself and retired, thinking to myself as I climbed the stairs that I had heard more talk about the Sabbath here in one meal than in an entire New York year.

I lay in bed, restless and worrying with my imagination, picturing again Liza on the auction block, and I went on bidding for a while.

Chapter Twenty-four

The Passage

*N*obody wanted to board.

The noise, the noise rose to the sky. Shouting, screaming, crying all against the crashing and lulls of the surf. Women prayed, men lunged here and there, weighed down by chains. Black men slashed at them with whips. Men pale as ghosts, with long guns, stood along the sand, some of them shouting orders to the men with the whips. Shore birds squealed overhead. Lyaa, in the middle of things, gazed wildly about the beach strewn with belongings, hoping for a glimpse of her mother.

For a time it seemed as though nothing would happen. The captives did not budge, and the captors did not seem to care, all just huddled, muddled together in a mass of confusion and noise.

Suddenly one tall man leaped at one of the whippers, and a gunshot rang out into the pale-white sky. The tall man fell to his knees, tipped over onto the sand which his blood turned brown, and the screaming began, even as the terrified captives now allowed themselves to be herded into a row of small boats lined up just at the shoreline.

"Mama!" a girl screamed over and over, "Mama! Mama!" and much to her surprise Lyaa after a short while realized she was the screaming girl.

Somehow, she settled herself, even as her boat pitched and rolled in the deep surf, a good moment, settling, even as she became drenched with spray, because there came one bad thing after another, and she needed her strength to endure. Sailors, mostly pale-faces, some with dark beards, hauled them up like dry goods out of the small boats and lined them up on deck, ordering them to set down their belongings. When a woman refused, a rail-thin sailor in torn denim grabbed her by the throat and tore a bundle from her hands. A baby went flying across the deck and the woman charged after it, gaining only half the distance to the infant when the sailor struck her down. A man reached over to rescue the infant and the rail-thin sailor hit him with a truncheon. The child disappeared in the confusion of bodies and shouts and screams and curses in four or five languages.

A white bird soared overhead, watching out of one eye and then the other as the sailors gestured and shouted, driving everyone below decks.

Stumbling down the slippery stairs.

Dark down here, so dark. Stench of bitter stink stabs the nostrils. Sailors swarm everywhere, pushing, shoving, punching, kicking the captives and chaining them to benches scarcely long or wide enough to hold them all. Born a slave, Lyaa had never known freedom, but she had not, until the traders took her from her uncle/father's village, known any darkness such as this.

Children wailed, infants screamed, one after another as one dropped away and another took up the noise. Sailors walked among the captives, plucking a child here, an infant there, and carting them away like debris while the mothers and some fathers screamed at the top of their powers, tearing hopelessly at their chains. Lyaa felt herself trembling, and then the world moved, shouts from up above, and began an intermittent pounding, pounding, that filled the air between the screams.

Her heart pounded, the wind pounded the sails, the ship pounded its way into the rolling sea. Where did they take those children? Lyaa asked in a voice raspy with thirst and emotion, hearing nothing but moans and hoarse shouting, the roar of wind and rush of water against cloth and wood. Hours passed. She strained for release from the bench but could not slip free of the chains. She tried to sleep, but the woman chained next to her made odd raspy noises in her throat, a noise that Lyaa could not shield herself from. And then came the hot high stink as the woman relieved herself in place. Lyaa vowed she would never do this vile thing, but hours later came the first time, as if in a dream of warm liquid and ammoniac air, she relieved herself in place. The urine perfumed the cabin, and then all the rest came down.

Shit. Vomit. Many became sick from the guttering rhythm of the ship. At some point some sailors descended into their mess, holding candles and one of them with a large pot.

"Hohlee farkin jeesus!"

The man shouted, the men shouted, the captives shouted.

"Farkin steeenk!"

Lyaa heard their words only as noise. Years would pass before she understood and spoke English well. But she already hated the language of the captor, just as she had despised the language of the Arab slavers and despised their Allah who had put her in chains. All gods seemed feeble, except Yemaya, who still apparently listened to her prayers, because some hours later came more candles in the dark, and crewmen rousted them upright, and others doused them with pail after pail of cold, stinging water that left her lips bitter with salt. Bless you, Yemaya, for cleaning us, bless you and all your children.

Though within minutes people began soiling themselves again, and, desperate for release, Lyaa strained at the manacles and chains until her ankles bled. Now the air around her reeked of the iron stink of blood. The wretched metallic odor leached through the space of confinement. It reminded her—Yemaya help her, she could not say why—of her mother when she was nursing the younger children. Was her mother enclosed in here somewhere? Would she ever see her again? Lyaa's mind worked back through the events she had suffered, the advent of the traders, the chase through the forest, the confrontation with her uncle/father. Her mother had told her of the family's travels as captives from Timbuktu to the forest, a tale Lyaa never tired of hearing, and amid all of the news of the family's sufferings and displacements and disruptions Lyaa never imagined that she would one day—all too soon, all so soon—turn these details over and over in her thoughts, longing for her mother, and relishing those memories that included her.

The warm rush of her urine gushed again over the bench where she lay half-dreaming. She had not even thought of it, let alone worried about it. What might have been a half day or a day confined in this infernal cabin and she had given over to the rhythms of her bladder and bowels while everything else around her sank into chaos and disgust. If there was another way of living with this, she didn't know, and if some of her fellow captives knew where they were going they didn't shout it out—or even whisper it—and she tried to catch the rhythm of the ship and give herself over to sleep

But just as she was dozing sailors descended into the midst of the captives carrying buckets of something that scarcely passed for food. With trembling hands Lyaa scooped up the lumpy mess and splashed the foul mixture into her mouth, swallowing but hating herself even as she did. Her stomach rebelled at the feel of it, and before she knew it she began to convulse and vomit up the slop.

"Better to eat," came a voice from the shadows behind her.

A man lay stretched out on the bench nearly full-length. Lyaa wondered how he had been given so much space when she saw that the former occupant of the bench along with this man had fallen onto the floor beneath it, still in manacles but unmoving.

"What happened to him?"

"He is dead," the man said. "I hope only they come and fetch him before he begins to rot."

"Do not talk about a human being that way," Lyaa said. "He was just like you, before he died."

"Oh, yes," the man said, "he was hungry and angry and filthy and sick, and I believe his heart stopped beating in the night. If we go on like this much longer, my heart will stop, too."

"How much longer do we go?" Lyaa asked him.

The man shook his head.

"I have heard stories…"

"Stories?"

"About events like this."

"Events?"

"These ghost traders—"

"Ghosts? Pale-faced men?"

"Yes, like these men."

"And where do they come from?"

"That doesn't matter," the man said. "What matters is where they take us."

"And they are taking us where?"

Lyaa listened to the rasping of her voice even as she felt the soreness while she spoke.

"Across the waters," the man said.

Lyaa felt her heart sink into her bowels, her heart bathed in her own piss and shit.

"Is it a long journey?"

"Long enough," the man said.

"What is on the other side of the waters? Is there another world?"

"It could be Paradise, or it could be filled with demons."

"I am glad my mother is not with me," Lyaa said.

"You should be," the man said. And he inclined his head toward her.

"Yes?" she said.

"This man, who has fallen?"

"Yes?"

The man suddenly howled like a dog.

"He is my father!"

How she wept! Wept and wept! Out went her sullied heart, and her hopes bathed in her filthy fears, and she wept and wept again, and finally, finally, finally, at least for that night—or was it day? she didn't know—she closed her eyes and even as she clutched in her right hand the small pouch with the stone her mother had given to her many mornings ago she drifted away from the bench where she lay enchained. Not even the stone could anchor her. Oh, my poor grandmother, neither living nor dying, but simply floating in her own odor and imagining she had been transported to a peaceful place even as the ship carried her to her hellish Paradise or splendid Hell full of demons. Whichever the other shore turned out to be, Lyaa longed with all her heart and strength to reach it alive.

No dreams, as far as we know, not in this round sleep. She awoke sharply in the dark to the jamming of water against wood, and beneath that larger motion and the noise of groaning sick and aching and sleeping captives all around her a tickling sensation at her ankle.

She sat up, glanced down, and saw the gray shadow gnawing at her.

No!

She kicked, and the animal fell away into the shadows. Her chest tightened, she could scarcely breathe. Her heart roared like the ocean on the other side of the timbered cabin wall. Quickly she used her hands to assess her state, ankles bleeding, toes, one two three four five, one two three four five, intact, knees, and her precious part, stomach, chest, present and aching.

The pouch with the stone she had worn around her neck?

Gone!

In a confusion of misery and great care—the stinking bench had grown slippery with her own residue and fluids—she leaned down and trying to keep herself balanced peered at the body of the man who had died and found rats gnawing at his flesh. Her gorge rose and she splashed vomit onto the floor, though the rats paid little attention, so intent were they upon their feast.

Better dead flesh than live! Fresh meant nothing, decay meant every-thing! Oh, they would love this voyage from the land of the living to the land of the dead! The rats would love it. And the captives and the crew would hate it worse than death.

She reached down and felt around on the filthy floor, unable because of the chains to stretch much further than the end of the bench. Here, she felt the cloth of the pouch. A rat nipped at her fingers and she flipped it aside. Before she could reach for the pouch again the rat returned. Once more she flicked her wrist and sent the animal sailing into the dark. With a deep intake of breath and a stretch beyond anything she thought she could summon up she found the pouch and clutched it in her hand as she pulled herself back onto the bench.

The pouch was empty!

Ay-ieee! It was as if her own heart had slipped from her chest!

It took a while for her to regain control of her breathing. Once more she leaned over the edge of the bench and walked her fingers through the filth, shoving aside aggressive rodents with her balled fist.

"Hah!"

A light appeared at the end of the row as one of the sailors completed his descent into the cabin. Catching sight of what she took to be the stone she reached again and picked it up. And with a cry of disgust tossed aside the piece of rat turd.

The light grew brighter as the sailor drew near, allowing her to see more clearly. Spying the stone she reached again—the last of her strength went the way of the smoke from the torch—and plucked it from the floor.

"All ow!"

The sailor shouted in words she did not understand, except that he spoke forcefully, and in a moment other crew members descended the stairs, with more torches and louder voices.

"All ow!"

They went from bench to bench, unlocking the manacles, raising the captives, some of them rearing up with strength and power, some of them sitting up as if brought back from the dead. Lyaa welcomed the climb up the steps to the deck, feeling power returning to her legs. In front and above her some people stumbled, a woman fell back, nearly pulling Lyaa and several others down with her. Drinking in the cool salt breeze that rushed down from the open port she regained her balance and surged up to the top.

On deck, the faint light of dawn, the sliver of a new moon already fading in the sky above the shivering sails. The wind conspired to cool the captives and buffet them about. More and more of them arose from below decks. Lyaa felt a flush of amazement at how many captives the ship held, and how many, like herself, seemed unable to do anything but blink into the rising light all around, the light of a dawn that seemed, as they did, to be coming up from below the surface of the ocean.

Some of the men began to chant at the sight of that rising light, an old song that Lyaa knew gave praise to the gods who made the days. How could it be after all she had been through that she found herself humming along?

"'Nuff!"

Sailors shouted, brandished pails and flung sea-water water at the captives, an act that seemed hostile until they all realized that here was a chance to clean themselves. Some of the men removed their ragged clothing. Even a few of the older women availed themselves of the chance for a cleansing.

"—!"

A balding red-faced sailor, eyes nearly bulging out of his head, shouted at Lyaa, taking her by the shoulders and spinning her around, pulling at her clothes. Within seconds she stood naked on the deck while another sailor doused her with chilling water from a pail. And again! She pushed at the sailor and he pushed back. Her legs ached, her bare breasts stung, she hunched her shoulders against the cold, while she covered herself with her hands, a distinctly human figure distorted by pain and humiliation, waiting for the chance to retrieve her clothing. From all across the deck screams and cries arose, mostly the voices of women.

Worse, she learned immediately why they screamed as the same red-faced sailor charged at her, grabbed her even more roughly than before and dragged her to a place behind the mainmast. What happened next we can never truly know, unless we find ourselves forced into the immediate degradation sometimes suffered by the victim, usually female, when man turns beast and instinct raw, foul, animal, devilish, destructive instinct—overpowers her. Lyaa struggled, and the sailor cuffed her on the mouth with the back of his hand. Blood spurted from her mouth as she shouted, wept, struggled, near to death but still struggling, although hopelessly, as it turned out.

"'Yemaya!" she called. "Mama!"

Sea-birds glided above the deck. The sails flapped one way and then another. It wasn't long before they herded everyone back below decks, and Lyaa found herself aching and chained once again, dressed in shreds of cloth, her (to others) mysterious pouch clutched close to her chest, wondering why she was not dead.

"I am sorry."

A man's voice woke her from a stupor.

Darkness enfolded the cabin as waves broke against the prow, hammer, hammering, stuttering back at the ocean. Her stomach ached, her ears roared from the mix of moans and silence among the people where she lay. She turned to the man whose father had died in the first hours of the first day of their journey. It had taken a long while—so long in darkness, she couldn't count in days—for the sailors to drag the corpse from the cabin and carry it above decks. The odor of its rotting flesh still lingered in the air.

"What?"

His bowels creaked and whistled as he gave up a reeking bolus of wretched disgust right there on his bench.

"I am dying," he said.

"No, no, no," Lyaa said, "you have a life to live beyond your father's life."

"I cannot live as a slave anymore," the man said.

"Death is slavery," Lyaa said, not knowing where her words came from. "Life is freedom, because it can be free."

"I do not understand," the man said, "and yet I do want to know."

She shook her head in amazement at her own speech, and though she tried she could not return to sleep, imagining all the spirits he had called down for her. One by one they settled in her body, presided over by Yemaya, and she knew this was good. Oh, goddess, she prayed, take us easily over the waters and break our chains on land, whatever land it is.

In the middle of the night the man reached over to touch Lyaa on the head.

"Bless you," he said. "All the spirits on your head."

As if in a miracle, up on deck some time later, chained together in rows of ten, someone pointed out an island off in the distance to the north.

Word pulsated through the captive ranks.

"Land! Land!"

The row of captives, urged on by the man whose father had died, shuffled toward the starboard railing and amid shouts from the sailors and the whirring and slap of whips as nearly one person they all went over the side.

Lyaa stared in horror at the empty space where a moment before all those people stood while the sailors shouted and whipped the air to hold back the rest. The captain in his dark uniform soon appeared on deck to call out orders to the rest of the crew. Sailors reshaped the sails and the ship began to turn. But circling back to the spot where the ten or so slaves had dived into the ocean no sign showed of any of the escaping captives.

The captain himself climbed down into the slave cabin along with a group of torch-bearing sailors. He shouted, cajoled, pleaded, ordered the slaves in his own language, none of which Lyaa could not understand. Many, many days went by before they were brought up on deck again.

Fewer of them gathered now. It was as if the god of death walked along the odiferous rows, pointing out those whom he would take with him on another sort of voyage.

But not Lyaa. She became sick, but she got well. She licked her palms after she ate the food the sailors delivered, licked rain water from the boards when on a beautiful sunlight morning after a vast rainstorm finally they did climb back up on deck again, if not gaining strength then at least not losing it as quickly as she might have. She prayed for more rain, and what better thing could happen than a dark cloud, lingering at the tail end of the boiling storm, poured down upon them, and Lyaa, along with the other survivors, turned her face to the sky and opened her mouth.

Returning to the benches some of the captives sang old god-songs and one or two of them—she swore she heard it, but she might have imagined it—laughed, a sound no one had heard in a long, long time. She held the laugh in her mind when she tried to sleep, but as had become usual a chorus of groans and weeping, coughing, whispering, farting, praying bubbled up constantly in the ranks around her. When at last sleep settled over her, her dreams became just as overcrowded as the cabin. Gods descended around her and spoke, in voices she could almost but not quite recognize, urging her to carry on through all of the filth and pain and discomfort and discouragement.

"For your mother," Yemaya said.

"For all of her mothers, those who gave birth and became and came and went and bore still more children." Yemaya's brother spoke in stronger terms still. "You must eat and drink whatever and whenever you can. You have a mission. Your mission is to become free."

Oh, yes, and darker spirits appeared to her as well. Shadows with horns and fangs and noses shaped like spears who chanted to her about welcoming death, and eating herself alive until she died.

Jump, dive, sink!

Follow your kinsmen down to the bottom of the sea. A lovely haven awaits you, the flowers of the ocean, jewels made of spindrift and the water sweeter to breathe than air.

"Don't listen," Yemaya cautioned her.

"Listen but don't obey," said the goddess's son.

He gave her explicit instructions, and she drank the slops sloshed into her hands and licked the decks and when someone near her died she went through the woman's pouch and found damp bits of nuts and she ate those, and when a man in the next row over caught and killed a rat she flinched before she took what he passed to her but took it she did, and drank the nasty animal's blood and ate its flesh. The next time she did not flinch.

Some of them had a plan. Days and nights had passed—very few of the captives could tell them apart—since their last time on deck. At least they could speak freely, none of the sailors being able to understand their languages, and only a few among them capable of understanding all of the languages they spoke. But in the dark, amid the stench and foul litter, a few of the men were talking about what to do the next time the sailors allowed them up into the air. Finally, it coalesced into a scheme, so that when they came up through the hatch one group moved to starboard and the other to port.

They had discovered a glorious day at sea, with great heaving fields of waves making up an ocean that seemed to have no limit except where it touched the pale blue of the descending wall of the sky. The wind blew easy, with hints of salt and tar carried on its currents. However, the slaves paid little attention to their surroundings, casting their eyes upward to the heavens or staring down at their chains. None seemed to meet the eye of any other. For a few moments, all seemed calm, and the sailors hauled their buckets up from over the side, prepared to douse the filth-encrusted captives with stinging cold sea-water to splash away the fetid stains and disgusting daubings, evidence of their miserable life below decks.

Just then the first line, men and women bound together, began to chant and sing, and a few sailors dropped their buckets, picked up whips and clubs, and rushed toward them. As the first sailor struck the first captive a line of men—all men—on the other side of the deck turned to face the rail and threw themselves headlong overboard.

The captain standing tall on the bridge turned red-faced with rage, shouting orders and waving his fists.

This time as the ship turned it became clear by the boiling patch of water where the sharks swarmed exactly where the captives had perished.

The captain shouted at the remaining captives—and there were still a great many, no doubt of that—and sent them, under a rain of whips and clubs delivered by his crew, down below. As Lyaa hobbled along, aching in her chains, arms raised to protect herself from the blows, she saw staring down at her from the captain's bridge, a blazing halo of sunlight coloring the sails behind him, the balding sailor—an officer, as it turned out—who had taken her behind the mainmast and wounded her soul. He stared at her as though she were some animal familiar to him from his travels in a foreign forest.

From that moment on, and she was not sure what it was that sent her in this direction, she dived down into her mind and tried to follow her path as far back in memory as she could, into her life and the life of her family. *Oh, Yemaya*, she silently called out, send me back, back to where I first emerged from my mother's womb, back to where my mother first saw the light, back to a desert dawn where her mother first saw the first light, back to where her mother's mother's mother's mother, and many before her, first opened her eyes on a place without trees, with mountains only, and a great mountain had just blown open and splashed a fiery cloud above it made of smoke and ash. Lyaa's belly ached and her head felt as though it were on fire as she lay dreaming in the dark, picturing those sparks, that sea, that sky, one far bright star above it breaking through the nearby fire so strong it was and so close to home. That star would ignite itself each sunset and serve as a signpost which each and all of her mothers would use as a marker of the trail toward safety and the future, even as she knelt in the dust and retrieved that stone that had shot up out of the burst of flame from the bowels of the earth, the stone gift from the belly and bowels of the mother.

Here it is!

Nothing settled down on this voyage except the pain, a dull rumbling in her belly and chest that never left but also never rose to the heights of the unbearable. It stayed with her, like the shifting of the timbers below decks, like the thumping of the waves against the hull, stayed always with her through the dark and into the moments when crew descended into the belly of the ship, torches burning.

When fever attacked her, she lay there burning in her own presence, calling again on Yemaya to grant her safe passage, though to where she could not say. For all she knew she might sail forever, bound to the bench, starved and thirsty, hearing voices in torment and voices in song. When she recovered from the fever—a miracle? Or just chance? She chose to see it as a gift from the goddess, who surely was guiding the ship toward safe harbor, wherever that might be—

Her blood had stopped.

Yemaya!

The goddess and her cohort tested her faith fully when the ship sailed into a deepening storm that made everyone in the hold as sick as dying monkeys.

Yemaya!

For days the benches—the world—rolled and pitched, dipped and pitched, and everyone threw up the contents of their near-empty stomachs, which meant blood and bile slopped the floor and swelled the air with a stench unimaginable to anyone who never lay chained to a bench in the middle of the ocean in a storm that nearly took the ship apart timber by timber.

When, after some nightmare of time, the ship settled once more into a steady forward pitch, she believed that she might have died, except that around her she could see some were living, some were dead, and there was a difference. The dead merely lay there, in various odd positions. The living twitched, vomited, and moaned.

Could anything more horrible happen? Oh, yes, oh, yes.

Once again into her world descended the bald-headed sailor and without a word released her from the bench and led her by the chain up the steps onto the upper deck. She had to follow, and yet she wanted to follow—if she were not on the chain she would still have kept quickly behind him, recognizing the pain in her belly was hunger and admitting to herself—forgive her, goddess!—that she would do anything for food.

And she did anything, and everything, and things she could never have imagined, under cover of darkness—dark below in the captives' deck, dark above on the upper deck, with dark clouds covering a sky that seemed lighter than the ocean on which the ship coursed along, sails full of wind, Yemaya's children blowing into the cloths to swell them and push the ship along.

This went on a while, this time, and other times, always in the middle of the night, and one night a full moon, graced with passing clouds, cast down its eye on her, and she became afraid, could not move, and the sailor twisted her and pushed her, goaded her with the handle of a whip, and she heard Yemaya telling her, "Go with him, young woman, go with him," and she never wondered why after that. The sailor gave her bread and bits of meat, kept her alive so that he could have his way with her, but by living she had her way with him.

Now in the dark she could feel the weight of her ribs pressing down onto the bench on which she lay—and she was one of the lucky ones.

Now in the dark, she felt the rush and roar of ocean against hull as part of her own heart's working.

Now in the dark, it sometimes became day, and she traveled back into the sunny world of before, when she was alive and living in the forest.

Now in the dark—

Now—

—holding tight to the stone each night in the dark she felt herself weighed down with it, descending, lowering herself as a body through the bench and through the deck floor, down through the hull and sinking below the ship, sinking fast beneath large fish and small, into a darker-than-dark level of ocean where strong currents pulled her one way and another, so that eventually she felt as though she were a ship in herself, sailing forward even as she sank down—

And down...

And down...

Until such time when she opened her mouth to taste the water and breathe, and the savor of it gave off a perfume in the back of the throat like that of delicious fruit, and she floated with her mouth open, so that the water flowed into her throat even as it flowed out of her nose, and she was breathing, breathing, cavorting like a mammal-fish, like whale or dolphin. And then she dove deep like a deeper fish, like other fishes we have not yet discovered, seeing in the dark as only some human being or animal can who has long lived down in the depths of light's absence can see, seeing the dark as light. Even within this deep realm she sometimes closed her eyes and found deeper darkness still, and slept within her waking sleep, letting the currents carry her where they might.

Which is how she found land.

And once upon a time rain fell onto the fields, and the fields beneath the sea swayed as if in a dance to the invisible and some not so invisible currents that ran on a slant in the parts of the ocean to which she had traveled, and she rose up out of the water and floated with these currents to the sun and the stars beyond, traveling to the most distant parts of the universe in the flick of an eye, as if all the universe lay within her own mind and all she need do to travel there was push out a thought. Did she know or not know? Worlds hung in the balance. And did she feel? Life on any of these rings of planets—how did she know the word? She didn't know the word, Yemaya gave her the word, all the words she knew, all the words she did not know—leaped forth when she pushed out, and whatever endings there might be came when she turned her back. Yet let her merely glance back over her shoulder, and everything took fire and light again, and the singing echoed through the air, and the light became rain became ocean became air...

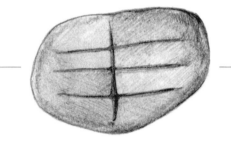

Chapter Twenty-five

Voices in My Ear

The Goddess Intervenes in a Kingdom by the Sea

No place was Eden except Eden. But for the Pereiras, whose ancestors stretched in a long line of alert and capable people from the time of the Roman conquest of the Holy Land through their exile in Rome itself and then, generations later, Holland, the island of Curaçao came close enough. A great-grandfather of Jonathan Pereira had, in place of some money he was owed in a business deal that had gone wrong in Amsterdam, taken the title to a seaside farm on this remote and lovely island. Storms sometimes battered it in late summer and early autumn, yes, but for most of the year the Pereira heirs, three brothers whose own parents had emigrated from Holland to the New World, felt as though they were living in the place from which their earliest family, or so the Bible would have it, had been expelled.

Alas for all, the farm had come with a cadre of enslaved Africans, some of whom worked the land and others who served inside the house. For ten thousand years, men had taken other men as slaves, either in battle—which was certainly not the case for the peaceful Pereiras—or as payment and property. Not even these Jews, whose ancestors themselves had once lived in bondage in Egypt, could resist the temptation and opportunity that slavery offered. This led to some odd and strange situations, both on earth and in Heaven, as on a certain morning in hurricane season when the then-very-young Jonathan was visiting the family of the uncle who had stayed behind to work the farm after his two siblings had shipped out north, one to Charleston and the other to New York City.

He must have been seven or eight, well, who knows if he himself could not remember exactly, some young age, possibly nine years old, but not much older, when he left his Curaçao uncle's seaside house and walked across his well-kept lawn—the slaves did a fine job of keeping it green and without weeds—and down through rows of sea grass to the beach. Let it be said, Jonathan was not a stupid child. Being able to lord it over the pickaninny offspring of the slaves had encouraged the mean streak in his character that most children, boys and girls alike, discover, sometimes to their sorrow, always to their amazement. Being a child himself, power over other children deluded him into thinking that he was a powerful boy.

This allowed him to believe that he found himself in no danger as he waded out into the lapping surf, waded out farther than ever before, feeling the strong waves wash over him and the tug of the undertow racing past the backs of his knees. The horizon growled black with storm clouds and thunder, and before he knew it a wave knocked him flat on his back, the undertow lifting him from below and behind, and carrying him out far beyond his usual limit.

A minute or two passed before he felt the fear surging through him even as the waves hoisted him up and lowered him, hoisted him up and lowered. And lowered, and suddenly he went under, flailing about, desperate for air.

Think! It was not just his life at stake as surf surged past his shoulders, as if to delight rather than to signal the imminent death by water that awaited him. And as he was sinking through the phantasmagorical aquamarine surroundings, seaweed torn around him, sand in upheaval, shells and starfish sailing past, even as the current, oddly warm but ferocious in its grip, boiled around his body and carried him along, to where he did not know—all of our fates hung in the balance, because so much was about to change for us, or never come to light at all.

A sudden stillness, and he watched the last bubbles of air float out of his mouth and float toward the surface. One bubble in particular caught his eye, and he tagged it with his glance as it rose higher and higher until it melded with the mass of other bubbles above his head.

"Goodbye," he should have said to us, if he knew any better. "Goodbye, and sorry that I am dying and that you will never live. Liza, me, the others to be." Stupid child, he had no sense of what ruled him now, the large dark hand of death squeezing his lungs and heart. He loved facing into the storm and walking forward. See where it took him.

Down he went so that his feet touched the sandy floor of ocean where he would, it seemed, come to his final (early) rest.

OOOOOOoooooooo...

He floated to his knees, his hair floating up in waves like sea plant and weed...

Was he gone?

Yes?

Poor fellow—yes, even he deserves our pity, for was he not then only a child? Dying...

Now as much as men would like to believe that the gods to whom they pray remain mutually exclusive—that is, the God of the Jews is different from the God of the Christians and the God of the Musulman, to name the major ways of religious thinking in the West—that remains not to be the case. Or so we might surmise, given the story of what took place in the distance, behind the bubble-born veil of that undertow. Above the storm, in the pure sunlight that always reigned when you cast yourself off a certain distance from the planet, or so ancient astronomers and some modern storytellers would propose, roared a force as great as the impending storm below.

Yahweh, whose followers took him to be the force behind all the greatest forces in the universe, found Himself in a quarrel with what he took to be a lesser god. Or goddess, this certain Yemaya, whose followers regarded her as the force behind many natural wonders on Earth, especially the oceans and rivers and streams and even perhaps in the Heavens, but made no claims as great as the Jews who worshipped Yahweh.

Yahweh, whose voice, when he employed it, seemed to come from everywhere and nowhere, spoke his annoyance, sounding something like Zeus, one of his older cousin gods, worshiped by the smart and poetic pagans.

"You're worried that he may drown? May? It seems quite certain to me."

"Then rescue him."

"I should rescue him? Can you give me a good reason. He is a nasty boy, bound to grow into a nastier man, and the world already has enough of these."

Yemaya, loud in speech but also looking quite lovely in her mermaid form—a mermaid swimming in near-space? I cannot figure that, but that is how the story has it—challenged Yahweh the way a wife might challenge a husband—with the full force and knowledge of someone who knows her opponent's greatest powers but also his greatest weaknesses.

"But so much depends on him!"

"He chose to walk into the waves."

"He miscalculated."

"He thinks he is invincible. This will show him."

"Death will show him?"

"Some human beings have to learn the hard way."

"And if he learns this, what good will it do him, what good will it do the world?"

"The world needs him? For what reason? Tell me a reason and I will save him. Though, let us admit it, you have the power to do that yourself, do you not? Which makes me believe that you want me to join in only out of a certain goddess-like perversity."

"I want you to save him because he is one of yours."

"In the narrowest way he is, yes, he has the sign upon his genitals that he belongs to me, and now and then he mutters a prayer when sitting with his congregation."

"Do you want one less of him in the world?"

"Why would you want even one more of him?"

"Because…"

"You, Yemaya, are too coy to be in the Heavens! Come out and say it, because you know I see it, I see everything, you want him because without him—"

"Yes, without him—"

"Without him no one will be born to tell this story."

"Exactly."

Unheard cataclysms unechoed through the cosmos. Stars lived and died. Showers of some light that no one would ever, ever in the history of human science be able to explain came pouring up and down and sidewise among the galaxies.

"And your precious girl, not even born yet, and when she is conceived, conceived in awful torque and wretched forcefulness, you want her to be free?"

"Yes."

"But you want me to take away this boy's freedom to die?"

"Yes."

"You want me to save one of my nasty own when you should be rejoicing that he will not live to do his damnedest in the world against your followers?"

"Yes."

"Do you think I am bound to do this?"

"Not necessarily."

"Do you think I reserve the right to be free and take his life?"

"Yes."

"Then I will allow you in person to save him. As if I have a choice. Yes, because you are bound to save him no matter what I wish, correct?"

But Yemaya had already dived through space into the deep air of our planet, listening to Yahweh, because like any deity she could hear everything everywhere but often deigned not to admit all the speech and all the cries of anguish and pain and all the noise and blunderbuss burstings and agony of torture and outpourings of misery into her outward realm of sound, but already on the way to do her deeding.

Thus a black mermaid burst out from behind the sea-foam and ocean-wrack curtain, taking the drowning boy by the elbows and hauling him onward and up toward the surface.

"From what I have seen," the black mermaid—Yemaya, goddess of oceans and skies above oceans—declaimed in his ear, "I should leave you here to drown. But

so much depends on you growing into a man, however despicable a man you might be, that I had to come to your rescue. You will grow older, and aid your family in Charleston and become an owner of men, women, and children as you learn the business of growing rice, and one day you will see a young woman, beautiful, brown, helpless, because she is your property, and you will use her as you would use a beast, though your vile actions will not make her one, neither will what you do to the daughter she gives to you keep her from going on to make her fate. Oh, you men are so much slower than us gods! I have just told you all of your future that matters, and you are still imagining that you are drowning!"

She hauled him to the beach and dropped him hacking and wheezing on the sand.

And she left him spitting up salt water, ready to begin his life to come. He certainly never saw her again. Though he felt a certain power, which had come from her. He felt as though he had survived a great test, and that he could do anything, anything! And suffer no harm. Poor thread of a human being, nearly lifeless detritus of an argument between two gods, he believed that if he had not saved himself then he at least had the powers of nature on his side, and that they had saved him—how close to the truth this was, and how utterly distant and far—to do great things on earth.

Chapter Twenty-six

The Pest House

*T*he ship had stopped moving!

Even before she opened her eyes she could smell, beyond the stench of feces, urine, blood, vomit, the perfume in the air, the flowers. She was sure she was dead.

"Home!" she called out, "we are home!"

"Home!" the word passed among them.

Others began to weep, some shaking those who had not yet awakened, only to discover that they would never awake, not in this world.

They had returned home! The home shores, the home beaches, the forests of home! This hope became only the first cruelties of their disembarkation in the New World.

Sailors descended the ship's stairs, using whip-handles to goad the people onto the deck. Yes, warm breezes carried the scent of flowers and land lay no more than a body's length away. Land—but not homeland. The sky above seemed a different shade of blue. Not home, not home! Women bleated like sacrificial lambs while men muttered to other men. The sound grew louder, like the rumbling of running animals on a plain. Sailors, and rough men who boarded from the shore, rushed among them, waving stanchions and threatening to beat them down. Slowly the muttering subsided as the news dawned on them that they were further from home than ever before.

Lyaa could hardly stand as she moved along with the herd of people to descend the gangplank. Seeing someone crumple and fall into the water, she held tightly to the rope railing, assembling with the others on the wooden pier. Flowers—and in the distance trees she had not seen before, with broad leaves, flowering. She breathed deeply, desperate to rid her nostrils of the awful stench of the ship. The sun came up behind her. Her legs trembled so they could scarcely hold her. How many days and nights? How many storms? How many bodies?

Shouts! Thunder of voices!

Pale-skinned men roughly dressed now herded them into a fenced-in place near the water and others came carrying buckets and doused them with cold water, again and again. A white-haired pale-skin wearing a mask over his eyes walked among them, daubing at his nose with a cloth. Now and then he pointed to a person, sometimes a man, but mostly women, and others came to lead them from the compound.

Lyaa enjoyed the dousing, and hoped for more. To rid herself of the stink of their long voyage was the only thing that she truly wished for, at least for the moment. And food! Yes, yes! When more pale-skins carried in barrels of soup and baskets piled with bread she elbowed her way past the frailer captives to lower herself to her knees and feast on the thin mixture.

Some people pulled themselves away from the barrels and collapsed onto the pier. Others ate, and then vomited, and ate again. And vomited. She herself ate until her belly ached, and then she paused for a breath or two, and ate again. More pale-skins pushed their way into the crowded pen, shouting in that language Lyaa could not understand.

What did it matter to her? At any moment she could shake loose these leg-manacles and fly out of the compound, soaring high above whatever land this new place happened to be. Nothing else mattered to her. Her freedom lay just outside the reach of her hand, just beyond the next cloud. She could fly away, and so she decided that she would soon make her departure.

At the edge of the fence she stared out at the countryside, and the bright off-white sky where beneath the ocean surged, she knew, she knew. Standing on tiptoe she thrust her mind into the air. As she was about to leap from the ground vicious cramps doubled her over and she sank to her knees, vomiting, vomiting, vomiting over herself, over the ground.

A large dousing of water shocked her awake. She lay on the ground, in the middle of a long row of bodies. Without the sun holding high in the sky she would have thought she had been shot back to the hold of the ship. People moaned, retched, tried to roll over on their bellies, but found themselves constricted by the manacles and chains. Even as she tried to lie still the wrenching and tugging along the line pulled her this way and that.

Eventually calm settled over them and the tall pale-skinned man with the eye-mask walked among them, with two short and ugly men following.

The tall man—he seemed older than the others—pointed and said some words, and the ugly men unlocked manacles and detached people from the line, some of them going in one place off to the side, some to another as the tall man directed. Some people shouted, others struggled. The two uglies, using stanchions, beat down the ones who tried to resist and let them lie where they fell. When the tall man came to Lyaa he paused, and reached down to touch a finger to her cheek and then to her belly. *Ah*, she decided, *a medicine man!* And yes, he pointed, said more words, and the two uglies unlocked her and led her off to one side, with the group of people who appeared to be slightly fatter and more steady than the other group.

A thick-armed man as black as the sky without a moon said to his companions in this group that he understood what the pale-skins had said.

"Yes? Yes?" People clamored to hear. "How do you understand them?"

"On the ship, I listened, I learned," he said.

"And what do you know now?"

"We are good," he said. "They mean we are going to live, we are healthy as can be after the ship."

"I am sick," Lyaa said.

The man clucked at her.

"You are not sick. I heard what he said. You are carrying a child. They like that."

"I am carrying a child?"

"You did not know?"

"I did not."

"He said it was true."

"Who said it?"

"The shaman, the tall one."

Lyaa smiled to herself, and touched her belly lightly with her fingers.

"This is not just a child," she said.

The old man gave her an inquiring look.

"What else could it be?" he said.

"The goddess," she said. "My mother was, and her mother before her, and before all of them they were, and this new one, she will be, too."

The old man paused, as if he were considering something to say, and what a luxury that was, after all the horrors of the journey they had endured.

But a pale-skin holding a stick pointed it at him and beckoned for him to follow, and he left Lyaa there, pondering her new condition.

At least, though confused, she remained alive. Over the next days and weeks as she walked about the small pen where the pale-skins had put them, walls all around but the sun shining over head and plenty of birds flying, she felt in her heart that she had, that all of them had, been abandoned. Once she might have thought of herself as one of those birds about to fly, but now, weighed down with grief and homesickness and the literal weight of her growing belly, she heard the birds laugh at her, stupid, earthbound girl. But the child she was carrying? She had no doubts. It was not another creature to be bought and sold—it would be able to fly.

During the early morning, nearly every day of her stay in this pen, she could hear the moans and shrieks as the uglies came to cart away the sick and dying, while Lyaa and her group stayed strong. She knew for a fact—the tall dark man reported it to them—that the pale-skins gave them more food than the sickly ones. And after a few days the sickly ones would sink even further into their illnesses, and the uglies would come to remove them from the pen.

Taking them where?

She did not know.

"I think they put them in the ground," the tall dark man said. "They are dying here, and will be dead within a few hours. That is why they take them out of here."

That must be true. As her group grew stronger, the number of the sickly weakened, and, according to the tall black man, something was going to take place soon—he heard the uglies talking about it, something new soon.

A few mornings later, with the sun and the laughing birds high overhead, the medicine man came around and looked each of them over, nodding, making musical sounds with his lips.

"What?" Lyaa said.

"We are ready," the tall black man said.

Lyaa shook her head. She took a deep breath and felt the holy infant turn inside her belly.

"Ready for what?" she said.

Chapter Twenty-seven

Voices in My Ear

Yemaya

Ooooooooooooooooooooooooooooohgh! The feeling! I have been away from these shores for so long! The people carried their bodies here, they carried their blood in their veins, they carried their memories of the past life in the forest and deserts, along the seashores and up the rivers. They carried me, too! Ooooh, yeah!

I came with them. Because without me, what are they? Sacks of skin, stalks of bones, hearts and livers breathing, fluids flowing? Ooooh, yeah! But I am what lies behind the eyes, I am what lurks in the part behind the dreaming! I am the bigger thing than anything they know! I am what seizes the heart when love comes, and makes life seem so sweet! Even when it grinds the bones and sears the flesh! I am the I am, and that is nothing to sneeze at, if that is what you say when you want to say how surprised you are at the turns life takes, the zigzag of it all! I am here, I was there, and am there, too, but here now also, and in the laughing in the lungs, in the moisture in the mucus in the lungs and in the dreaming part too, daydream and night-journey, all in the all, oh, do say you love me, is all you have to do and I am yours and you are mine!

Chapter Twenty-eight

The First Sabbath

*M*y mother had just appeared to me in a dream when early the next morning I was awakened by a knock at the bedroom door. I roused myself to answer the knock and found the slave Liza standing there, posed in a not very submissive way, hands on her hips, an almost scolding pout to her lips.

"Time for the Sabbath ride, massa," she said and seemed about to say something more when my aunt called her name from down the hall and she turned and without a word to me walked away.

As it happened, I had no time at all to linger. Drugged by the country air, I suppose, I had overslept, and the family was waiting for me downstairs, where I hurriedly appeared, my face dripping from the fresh water I had splashed on myself, my stomach an empty knot.

"Please, massa," Precious Sally said, handing me a mug of coffee as we went out the door. I scarcely had time to thank her as we went out the door.

"I am sorry if I make us late," I said to my uncle and aunt. "I have not slept this long since I was a child."

"No matter, sir," my uncle said, raising a beefy hand toward the carriage where Isaac stood, holding the horse's reins. "We always give ourselves plenty of time before the service, coming as we do from afar."

"Do many other Jewish families live on plantations?" I said as we climbed into the carriage. I sat up front with Jonathan while his parents and young son and wife sat behind us, squeezed together like chattel on the way to market. (Yes, the thought did occur to me!)

"A few," my uncle said, "though most live in town. The town is better for business, of course. We had a business there when we first arrived here."

"The import and export?" I said, mentioning the only business I knew really well.

"Import, yes, export, some," he said as Jonathan flicked his whip and the horse pulled us away from the house. "We had shares in some ships bringing Africans to Charleston. This produced enough money for us to buy the plantation and our own force of Africans."

I did not know what to say, speaking about slaves.

"They seem a healthy bunch," I finally let out, my thoughts called back to Liza in my doorway earlier that morning.

"Either them or their parents tested by the passage and by nearly a month in the Pest House," my cousin said. "And looked after by the doctor."

"The Pest House?" I said.

"The quarantine that separates the living from the dead."

"Don't be disgusting," Rebecca said. "I hate it when you sink so low as to speak in that manner."

"It's the truth," my cousin said to his wife. "Don't you like to know the truth?"

"Not that truth," she said, and turned her face away from husband. "Do *you* know what is the truth? Can you look the truth in the eye? You may not want to."

"Children," my uncle said. We all hushed up, and Rebecca began to hum a tune.

The horse pushed along. Soon country yielded to city and within what seemed like a few minutes we turned the corner at Coming Street and pulled up before the same trim stone building I had seen on my little tour upon arrival.

We stepped down and a smiling black man took charge of the carriage while we climbed the steps, my uncle and aunt and cousins greeting others who entered along with us.

Here something strange began. At home, where my father and I attended synagogue together on the Sabbath—a custom honored more in the breach than in practice after my mother died—I took certain things for granted: such as prayers in Hebrew from a thick old-perfumed book, which I had not made much of an effort to learn, even though prodded by my tutor Halevi; and the separation of the sexes, the women up in the balcony, the men below; and the cantor singing whiny and sinuous melodies that echoed of the exotic East. Here I was handed a slim pamphlet that smelled more of new ink than old hands as my uncle, after easing his bulk onto one of the benches to the rear of the hall, bade us all sit together, wife and daughter-in-law and son and nephew alike. (I had the mixed pleasure of being squeezed in between Rebecca and Abraham.)

The choir commenced to sing a prayer in English, with the same melody as Rebecca had hummed over the noise of the carriage on our way to town. The congregation sang, muttered, mumbled, chanted, swallowed the words.

Next a trim man in a dark suit mounted the dais and said a prayer about harmony and peace.

I raised my chin in a question and Rebecca said to me in a whisper, "The Officiating Minister."

"No rabbi?" I whispered back.

"We are Reformed, and newly so," said Rebecca.

I gave a shrug as a hymn in Hebrew rang through the hall, and then a version in English. Instead of following the words in the pamphlet, I gazed around the place, enjoying the morning light that flowed in from the high stained glass windows. I took note of white-haired men and women in beautiful lace shawls, fidgeting children, and some girls and fellows my age. There was one girl, in fact, who turned her dark eyes toward me as I glanced at her and then we both looked away. When I looked back, she was staring at the stained glass window, as if the study of it might yield some fascinating information.

"Ah," Rebecca said in a whisper.

"Yes?" I said.

"What?" Abraham said.

"Someone for you?" Rebecca said.

"For me?" I said.

"Her name is Anna," she said. "She is my second cousin."

"Who is?" I said.

"You know exactly whom I am talking about." And despite the seriousness of the service and the music, she puckered her lips and laughed at me through them.

I looked down at the pamphlet, turned pages and then looked at the front again at the Articles of Faith of Reformed Society of Israelites, giving myself a way to forget my immediate embarrassment. Ten of them! I didn't know that I could articulate more than one. But here I read these carefully while the service continued on around me, as though I needed nothing more than these first articles to survive in the moment.

> I.   *I believe with a perfect faith, that God Almighty (blessed be his name!) is the Creator and Governor of all creation; and that he alone has made, does make, and will make all things.*
>
> II.   *I believe with a perfect faith, that the Creator (blessed be his name!) is the only ONE IN UNITY; to which there is no resemblance; that He alone has been, is, and will be God.*
>
> III. *I believe with a perfect faith, that the Creator (blessed be his name!) is not corporeal, nor to be comprehended by any understanding capable of comprehending only what is corporeal; and that there is nothing like him in the universe...*

I looked up and caught that girl looking over at me, and I looked back at the pamphlet while all around rose the sound of voices gathered in prayer.

> IV.   *I believe with a perfect faith, that the Creator (blessed be his name!) is the only true object of adoration, and that no other being whatsoever ought to be worshipped...*

One more article, I said to myself, and I'll look at her again.
Which I did.
Our eyes met and she might have smiled as I looked quickly away.

> V.   *I believe with a perfect faith, that the laws of God, as delivered by Moses in the ten commandments, are the only true foundations of piety towards the Almighty and of morality among men...*

One more, I told myself. But then I looked up again.
"I saw you," Rebecca said again in a whisper.
I didn't dare look at the girl again, and so turned back to my reading. Voices rose around me, louder now.

> *Hear O Israel,*
> *The Lord our God,*
> *The Lord is One...*

Yes, well, now this was familiar, and as the prayers rolled on I longed heartily to be back in my old room, with the airs of Marzy's cooking drifting up the stairwell and Father humming while he clenched his pipe in his teeth and outside my window a New York robin might be singing to announce that spring was near.

I believe with a perfect faith…oh, what did I believe, outside of these memories that drew up such desire in me? What perfect faith did I possess that I could listen with perfect attention as the Officiating Minister read from the Torah—

"Now after the death of Moses, the servant of the Lord, it came to pass that the Lord spake unto Joshua, the son of Nun, Moses' minister, saying, Moses my servant is dead; now therefore arise, go over this Jordan, thou, and all this people, unto the land which I do give to them, even to the children of Israel…"

I believed…I believed…that I was hungry, and that that I was tired of all this talk about Africans in the family's possession, and I hoped to complete this family chore down here as quickly as I could so that I could return to Manhattan and leave for my tour and then return a year later to join my father in his business and to pay a visit to dear Miriam's house and speak to her father and ask for her hand in marriage, and enjoy our engagement and then the wedding, in the synagogue, with flowers and music and a honeymoon out on Long Island in the warm season, where birds sang and the gentle waves of the Sound lapped at the shoreline and we were free of all of life's calls and demands, at least for a time.

"…as we made our own way," the Minister was saying, "a generation ago, or two, most of us, crossing the water from the Carib islands or from the Old Country…our fathers' fathers'…"

Our fathers' fathers'? I knew little of the past, understanding only that my father's grandfather, Isaac Pereira, had emigrated from Amsterdam, arriving in his new Carib island just about the time the Dutch had departed from New York and the English had taken over. With nothing in his hand except a small satchel of clothing and nothing in his pockets except a few gold pieces and a gold timepiece given to him by his father, he had come to take over a farm given over to him as part of an Old World debt. His sons took brides from Amsterdam. My father, Samuel, was born just before the successful colonial uprising against the English in America (and his older half-brother, my large uncle, just before, and a third brother, who stayed behind on the island while my father and uncle emigrated to the former English colonies up north). My father made his way to New York while his brother hurried to Carolina to make his fortune in farming. My father married my dear (alas, late) mother Margarita Monsanto, some time after the British returned to burn our new capital of Washington. Or such is how I understood all this.

A snort! A burst of air distracted me from my wandering thoughts. I looked over at my uncle, his eyes closed, apparently asleep and ready to tilt over in my direction at any moment.

He opened his eyes even as I regarded him, touching a finger to his nose, and closing his eyes again. My uncle at prayer. Massive but quiet, contemplative, near-sleep. Halevi had insisted to me during my instruction with him in our religion that we Jews prayed by saying our prayers, that is, saying the words which in themselves were near-magical. Yet prayers had never caught on for me, for one reason or another, undoubtedly my own lack. My uncle appeared to suffer from the same lack of ties to the traditions of our so-called tribe. He scarcely repeated a word from the service, listing one way or the other as sleep kept him in that perpetual tilt.

What sort of a Jew was he? For that matter, what sort of a Jew was I? Neither of us seemed to have more affiliation with our religion than we did with family, blood relations. Strange it seemed to me that Christians, as much as I knew them, had actual principles and beliefs—the pact each made with their Jesus to accept him as their savior. What did I have? A vague feeling of association with others like me, most of whom seemed familiar in their lack of fervor and their sense of tribal life without necessarily believing in any supernatural being such as God. These Reformed Jews certainly seemed to me to be further along in the dissolution of our religion than most of us who did nothing but pay lip-service at ceremonies such as this only a few times a year.

More noise burst from my uncle's nose and lips, not a song but the last gasps of a snore.

I took the time to study his face, the way, as Halevi had once explained to me in one of our lessons about art, a sculptor might study a stone. Chip away at the extraneous and you would find my father's features in my uncle, and then add some slabs of flesh and let thicken, and you would have my uncle. Staring at this relative whom I had only recently discovered, I felt a certain longing for my home and, yes, my father, and my mind ranged toward him, the man who had engendered me.

Behold what my father had accomplished—built a trading house, and constructed the very stone edifice in which I was born, a marble structure on the west side of Fifth Avenue, looking carved and polished where it stood between two larger Protestant brick palaces. A pair of stone lions guarded the entrance. A ten-foot-high wooden door nearly a foot thick provided entry, if you were permitted it. Once admitted, you found yourself in a foyer that led on one side to a large sitting room and on the other to a dining room with a grand twelve-foot ceiling and room enough to feed the crew of a sea-going trading vessel. This would one day become mine.

"Cousin Nate?"

But there I was, dreaming of home when the service ended, and Rebecca, with an inclination of her head, bid me to slip out of the bench and allow her to step into the aisle. I stuffed the pamphlet into my coat pocket and did as I needed to do.

"Come now," she said, taking me by the arm, and before I could protest she led me up the aisle to the very girl I had been staring at.

Anna?

"Cousin Anna," she said, "how lovely to see you."

The girl, standing with two elderly folk I took to be her grandparents, smiled sweetly at Rebecca, and I followed her eyes as she took note of Rebecca's prominent belly and then raised her gaze to meet my own.

"Good morning," she said, as though we had met a dozen years before and every now and then made our re-acquaintance.

"Good morning," I said, wondering if her nerves felt as hot as my own. I was sure I showed red in my face and pretended to be searching for something up in the stained glass of the windows.

"You are both my cousins," Rebecca said. And then with a laugh, "Though advantageously neither of you is related to the other."

Now it was Anna's turn to blush as Rebecca introduced me and we shook hands and exchanged polite confidences, such as the fact that I had come from New York and that she was the oldest of four children, living on Society Street with her father who was a merchant.

"And how long will you be staying in Charleston?" Anna asked me.

"However long it takes me to conclude my business," I said. "And so, my answer is, I do not yet know." The room had grown hot with the presence of so many of us, but the sharp tropic tang of this girl's perfume cut through the thickness of the must.

"If you come back into town I hope we will have the chance to see you."

Oh, my blush ran hottest yet!

"That would be lovely," I said.

"Our cousin can arrange it," Anna said.

"Of course," I said, turning to Rebecca.

"Tra-la, for now," she said. "I see my in-laws are beckoning to me. We'll all meet again before the great bye-and-bye in the sky. Anna, we will come visit you."

"I would enjoy that, Becky," Anna said.

"But now we must return to the country."

It was a long ride home, it was a short ride, I can't recall which, my mind was so stuffed full of a number of things—and the warm air on my face, and the noise of the horse and carriage, and the sky so blue above, and my new family in the carriage along with me.

Could I consider living here?

Of course, I said to myself, and imagined meeting pretty dark-eyed Anna at dinner and paying court to her and taking long walks with her along the Battery, where arm and arm we would gaze out upon the water.

We are probably very distant cousins, Anna, I imagined myself saying.

And how would she respond?

Nathaniel Pereira, I heard her say, *what of Miriam? What of her? Are you so fickle that you find yourself daydreaming of me when that sweet girl back in Manhattan is pining away for you?*

Yes, yes, I suppose I am, I said, daydreaming, while the carriage bounced along, bringing me closer and closer to The Oaks, my temporary home on earth, I am that fickle, because I am young and youth is fickle and youth daydreams and flits from flower to flower like the happiest bee in summer.

A flower, a face, drifted into my thoughts.

Liza.

Chapter Twenty-nine

In My Margins

A Hard Bargain

How could it not have happened the first time he went to an auction? He was of the right age, and in the right frame of mind, that is to say, isolated, lonely, longing, and in a constant torment of desire. This state arrived even before dreams, and sometimes he could not dream without having first purged himself of the cool and nagging fluids over which he had little control in the making of.

In the same ten years that coincided with his torturous and agonized adolescence, when his father built the plantation from scratch, Charleston saw a blossoming of the slave trade as few other American ports came to know, so for this boy, fresh from his coming of age ceremony, accompanying his father to an auction at the docks, the time was ripe for all that languished negatively in his soul to come forward into the light.

For this he was reborn.

Perhaps his father saw a certain anticipatory look in his eye, or perhaps he felt it incumbent upon him to make a brief speech to his son and had decided long in advance that he would do this. You can be the judge. Here is what he said, as the carriage rolled through the streets of Charleston (he might have said something just after they left the plantation, or somewhere along the dusty road into town, but he waited until what seemed to be almost the last minute. Why? Fear? Worry? Guilt? Who knew? But perhaps we might figure that out from what he said).

"Son, I want to warn you that some things you witness this morning may shock you and repel you. There is no more raw a situation than the one you are about to see. (The older man spoke with a slight accent, a mixture of his forebears' Dutch and his island English, of the second-generation variety.) Our business is rice, no more, no less. But on occasions such as this we have to open our eyes to the rest of life, and we may see some awful things, but sometimes awful is necessary for the success of our enterprise. Now you will hear people say things this morning that

may sound terrible and strange. The way they speak about the Africans is neither true nor civilized. The Africans are not animals, do you understand? Slaves are people, but people who were not strong enough or brave enough to fight off their condition and keep their freedom. Our people were slaves in Egypt and Babylon. And might still be, if God had not intervened on our behalf. But He did not intervene until the last moment, when all who were not brave enough to strive forward had lost their hope. Imagine you are hurrying out of Egypt across the bed of the Red Sea and you hear the hiss and thunder of the boiling waves on either side. Do you stop and tremble? Do you allow your fear to enslave you? No, of course not, you hurry to hurry and finally you reach the farther shore. As you remember from studying the story of Moses [Had the young man studied it? He must have, but he simply did not remember, so caught up he was in the anticipation of the morning's events.], freedom comes to those who take it, never to those who lie back and wait for it. Please remember, no matter what you hear or see, these Africans are neither inferior people nor anything like animals, though you will see them traded, bought and sold as though they were. [The young man held his breath at that statement, not knowing what to make of it.] They are people who have lost their way, who have lost their will to be free, and if not born to be slaves then find themselves destined to slavery for the rest of their lives, unless they fight to win their freedom. And here, so far from their homeland and without any means or money, they would be hard-pressed to fight for anything, anything at all. Now, son, I have asked myself why these questions come to my mind, and I say to you that because we are as a people a rather philosophical tribe such matters come to the fore when we are living our lives. And because we were a people who ourselves had once lived in bondage matters such as this slavery business often come to my mind. And as the questions occur I say in response what I have just said to you. When it is their turn to win their freedom it will come to them. And until then we all must live with the way things are right now, because that is their lot. Do I make myself clear? I know perhaps that I sometimes ramble. These are not easy matters to contemplate. Owning human souls makes for a great challenge for the owners. It brings out the best in us, and it can bring out the worst. These slaves have belonged to Africans, and English and Portuguese, and now they belong to us. It is our duty to everything we believe that we treat them fairly."

The young man heard his father's words, but he did not pay much attention. A delicious and [what he at this point in his life did not have the words or experience enough to call] exotic feeling was building in his chest and hips. He listened to his father, but did not reply, because he could scarcely breathe. He saw a zigzag *lightning-like pattern shimmering before his eyes, and even when he closed them the vision persisted.*

ZZZZZZZZZZZZZZZZZZZZZZZZZZZZZZZZZZZZZZZZZZZZZ

zzzzz shimmering shimmering

The black mermaid soon swam into his vision, barred from him by the zigzag emanations, waving over and above the wavering lines.

And then she disappeared. And the lines kept rippling out to the outside perimeter of his eyes, and also went away.

His knees went weak as he and his father descended from the carriage, hearing the voices and calls along the quay, smelling the tar and cigar smoke, the flowers of early spring, the brackish seawater in high tide, all of the way before him illuminated by a bright warm sun. The darkness he carried with him, something he could never explain, took on a certain bulk in his arms and even his stomach felt affected by the weight. By contrast with the sunlight it had a texture and heft all of its own.

But until they reached the auction site on the quay he had little idea of what role this darkness would play in his life. Gulls cried out, screeched, veered and swung out over the water and back again, to the barques and sloops that lay at anchor. Three-masted schooners often docked here, carrying cargo from distant places, but these he paid little attention, focusing all of his awareness now on the long room with barred window openings just west of the quay. From within came shouts and squeals, bursts of song and sorrowful outcries of the variety you might expect to hear when mothers and children parted for what they took to be a long inevitable time.

A large number of local gentlemen had gathered before the raised platform where a wooden shaft with chains attached stood in the center, the men talking among themselves as though waiting for the opening of a service of some kind or in anticipation of meal. The boy and his father stood a pace or two apart from this crowd, though now and then the older man acknowledged the greetings of the other gentlemen. To one or two he gestured at the boy and made known that this was his son.

That son heard little of this now. He concentrated on the sounds from within the long barred room, standing almost on tip-toe in an attempt to try to listen. When a man in a coat and hat stepped up (as if out of nowhere) onto the platform the boy leaned his entire body in that direction. The man began to jabber and the boy paid little attention to what he said, straining, virtually up on his toes to see beyond the shoulders of the men bunched up in front of the block as a bulldog faced man, clearly a guard, in dark clothes and club in hand, went to open the door to the barracks.

The shouting, weeping, crying that poured out through the door—he held his

breath—*this even before the guard, now aided by another man just as ugly, herded
the interned Africans into a line just behind the block and plucked from the bunch
a thick-necked fellow as dark as a moonless night and pushed him up a set of steps
so that he stood above the crowd. The boy's eyes burned in amazement as the
auctioneer began to take bids on the African.*

*"...stronger'n when he went into the Pest House, blessed with muscles galore,
gentleman as you can see..."*

*The man stared above the heads of the crowd, his eyes fixed on some point the
boy could not, when he turned behind him to spy, discern.*

*Voices shouting money figures boiled around him. The man was led away.
Another took his place. And then another.*

His father grasped his shirt-sleeve.

*"We are looking for a helper and such for your mother. You keep an eye open
now, son."*

"Yes, sir," the boy said.

*The crowd pressed tighter in as the first woman of the auction walked carefully up
the steps, as if she were wearing a long gown on which she might trip rather than the
rags that scarcely left any part of her generous tar-black body unexposed.*

"What do you think, son?"

The boy wanted to speak but felt as though he had lost his tongue.

His father leaned down and said, "A bit too old, probably untrainable..."

*The boy nodded, and felt the crowd pack closer as the sale of this woman
speeded along.*

*A younger woman, less sure of herself and much more exposed, if that was pos-
sible and still be wearing clothes, stood tentatively on the block.*

*A man nearby expelled from his lips a lascivious noise, something the boy had
heard before only when men called to dogs or horses. Others took up the sound.
The boy felt suddenly weak in the legs, as though he might fall down and become
trampled under the feet of these large, bidding men.*

"Five hundred!" a man called out.

*"Look at her," the auctioneer said, touching a short rod to the girl's naked
ribs. "Look!"*

*Perhaps it was a dream, the boy thought later. His thoughts swirled about in
his skull and his stomach twisted and untwisted. He looked and looked, and under
cover of the press of the crowd—who also apparently pushed forward to look and
look—he found his hands on his lower parts, and while the auctioneer called for
bids and more bids rubbed himself until he felt some release from the state of frenzy*

that had overtaken him, and when he looked around at the crowd again—after the young woman had been removed from the block—he thought he saw one or two younger men who, like himself, might have just undergone the same twisting of body and soul.

Another young woman walked up the steps chanting, and would not, despite the urging of the auctioneer, quiet down. What language, the boy had never heard. What was she shouting, almost singing to the crowd, no one, probably, could say, except perhaps the other slaves crowded now into the space between the back of the block and the walls of the barracks. The boy could not have ever seen her before, of course, and yet she looked familiar, and when, as sometimes happens when a person stands above a crowd and runs her eyes across their faces, her eyes for a moment met his he recalled the black mermaid who had saved his life, if that is what happened when the undertow pulled him into the waves not so long ago, and as the young woman went on chanting above the calls of the auctioneer the boy wrenched himself from the crowd and ignoring the shouts of his father ran toward the water and when he reached the brackish line of tidal wrack just below the tarry stanchions holding up the pier threw up the contents of his last meal and for a number of minutes retched drily, and in tormenting pain in stomach and bowels.

These people are weak, he shouted to himself in a loud voice in his mind, who but the weak would ever let themselves be caught and bought and sold? I never would. I would escape! I would fight to the death!

This is what I gleaned, this is what I heard, this is what I surmised, this is what I dreamed, this is what I imagine took place, given all, all that I have learned.

His father took another view.

"If you keep people," he often said to Jonathan, "you must sometimes treat them as if they are your own children."

His father did not like to say "own." He said "keep" instead, always, even if his son would sometimes call him out on that.

"And treat your own children like slaves?"

"Show me the respect I deserve," his father said. "Do not speak to me in that rough manner. You are a gentleman, raised by a gentleman."

"Yes, sir, I am sorry," his son said. "I do apologize."

That was how it went back and forth between them, father and son, patriarch and heir apparent.

As to his relations with his mother, they were nothing. In his dark heart women were nothing to him, slave women were nothing, white women, Jewish women, a little better than nothing. Whatever happened between the gods as they discussed his fate, out of it came a hard bargain!

Oh, what a fate, a fortune to look in the eye, to have such a grandfather as this!

Chapter Thirty

The Second Sabbath

*A*ny daydreams I might have called up about Anna and any plans I might have had in mind about Miriam fled like wisps of fog at the first appearance of morning sun when on the Gentile Sabbath as I lay in bed listening to the birdsong outside my window there came a knock on my door.

"Yes?"

"Massa?"

Her voice! It chilled me as sharply as a pitcher of cold water dashed across my chest!

And at the same time heated me up!

"Massa Jonathan sends some trousers for you, sir."

"Leave them outside the door," I said, wary of showing my eagerness for seeing her. I was in an excited state all of a sudden (again, again!), and it wasn't something of which I was proud.

"Yes, sir," Liza said, but immediately opened the door and entered anyway, a broad smirk on her face. She tossed a pair of heavy trousers onto the foot of the bed and stood there looking beautiful in her green eyes and white smock.

"You must not keep on doing this. You must respect my privacy, Liza. Please leave the room so that I can dress."

"These are for you, sir, from Massa Jonathan," she said. "For your hunting trip today."

"It's true, I did not pack for hunting in the woods," I said. "Thank you, Liza. Now please leave me."

She stood a moment, lingering as she did the morning before, and showing me more of that strange emotion in her eyes, a look not brazen, but not appealing either, yet something in between. She left the room, hips swinging, leaving me behind to contemplate what was both wrong and right with nature as I knew it and myself tied up in a knot.

Yet we had things to do on this other holiday. Within the hour, after coffee and a bite of Precious Sally's best Sunday cake, a wonderful rich mixture of eggs and butter and certain secret spices—"Not giving away my secrets," she said when I inquired, by way of praising her cooking—cousin Jonathan and I set out on horseback for the woods.

I was seated on Promise. I knew not the name of his steed.

The woods! The woods! Not a place where I was either yearning or prepared to be! Although the sun had scarcely risen above the height of the tall bushes the heat had already become intense, bordering on excessive.

"You must live an exciting life up there in your New York City," my cousin said as we rode along.

"Yes, yes," I said, straining to keep my seat upon the fast-moving beast.

"As you have seen, we live our quiet life out here in the country and visit the city now and then, perhaps every other Sabbath. And I can do it only because I know that almost as soon as we arrive we are going to be returning home. While I know I must have shown a certain amount of pride when we took you around the city, I have to confess that I never stop at those places we showed you except when we have a guest such as yourself, which is rare. Most of the time I am here, with now and then a visit to the synagogue. When I was younger I did now and then visit the auction. Now my excursions occur mostly in my reading of history, something Father encouraged in me ever since I was a boy, and my outings to hunt and fish. Such as today's."

"There is Rebecca, is there not?"

"Oh, yes, I nearly forgot. She would be furious with me if she knew I had forgotten to mention her."

He laughed a deep laugh, and it had such dark bass notes to it, that it made me wonder why I had not heard him laugh that way before. The trail narrowed and we slowed our pace so to move single file, and so I gave myself over to the buzzing of the insects and the sound of our horses' hooves upon the spongy track and the creaking of their bones and muscles, and my own wondering. What if we kept on riding, how far could we go? Past the river, west toward the mountains of Tennessee, whatever those mountains were called, and then keeping on to the west until we reached the Ohio territory ahead, where Indians roamed and men lived freely in the open or under leaning roofs to keep off the rain and snow?

Out of the razzing of the insects and the shushing of the wind in the treetops I might possibly make out the thousand voices of strange tribes, whose ways and mores intrigued me much more than the people among whom I was born or those I met. I could hear their horses, tethered in large numbers outside their huts. I could hear, ever so faintly in the distance, the cries of their hounds. If one passed through these Indian lands, I wondered, what might be the chance of survival? And wasn't there beyond them a great river that one had to cross, and mountains upon mountains, to reach the shining Pacific? Oh, I was dreaming, dreaming far ahead of myself, as it ultimately transpired! As I hope I have made clear, I saw myself as a Europe-man, ready for my Grand Tour that lay on the other side of the nearby Atlantic. (Not even thoughts about the family's abode down in Curaçao, which came up now that I had met uncle and cousin, could bend the line I drew in my mind from New York across the Atlantic to points east. Do not distract me, Caribbean, for I am, within a few weeks or a month or two at most, was how I saw it, Europe-bound!)

"This is the place," my cousin said, disturbing my geographical reverie as we broke out from beneath the trees into a glade filled with sunlight with the river running gaily to the north of it. We dismounted and tied our horses to trees on the edge of the clearing and fetched water for them from the river in leather pouches. "This," he said, "is where Rebecca would have us build our colony."

"And what is that?"

"Our special place, as she calls it, a community where massas and slaves no longer exist and Jews and gentiles live in comity, and Indians, too, who worship only the wind in the sky."

"It sounds like a lovely plan," I said. "How shall you do it?"

"If it were a plan, we might begin," my cousin said. "As for now, it's only an idea mingled with a dream." He took a deep breath, as if inhaling the very idea he was speaking of. And then spoke again in a voice quite different. "Her dream."

"And not yours also?"

"I am more practical." Something sparked in his eyes, and I believed him to be considering, considering the necessities of such a vision.

"And yet you let her dream."

My cousin laughed in as dark a way as I had yet heard him.

"Dreams, Cuz, are dreams…"

(Looking back I recognize that this was the high point of our acquaintance, his talk of dreams, and my attempts to see such good things in him as his talk would imply.)

Suddenly, overhead in the clear sky, a flock of pigeons erupted across the space, as if freed by the hand of some Manhattan boy who had been keeping them on a rooftop.

A loud crash echoed through the glade and I dodged instinctively at the sound of it while the horses did nervous jigs about their tethers.

This was cousin Jonathan, having fired his pistol into the air, watching a bird fall toward the treetops.

"Very good," I said. "Good shot."

"Will you try your eye, Cousin?" he said.

"The birds are gone," I said, looking to the sky.

"They'll be back," he said.

"Then of course I will."

"Are you a good shot?"

I immediately thought about my pistol in the bureau drawer back in my room.

"We have a number of moving targets in New York City," I said, "beginning with our immigrant rats. But I have not yet tried my hand at such sport. But will you fetch that bird?"

"For what?"

"For our supper."

"No need, no need. Thousands like it will fly past at any moment. You just need take a shot at the sky and it will bring down another piece of supper. Or two more. Or three."

"Paradise," I said. "Manna. Food falling from the skies, forever."

"We do have to shoot them," Jonathan said. "So not Paradise exactly. But a workable Eden on earth, between our pistols and the crowds of nature." He held the weapon out to me.

"Would you like to try?"

"The sky is empty of birds just now."

"They will return."

"Some other time, perhaps," I said.

My cousin bowed his head toward me and fit his pistol back into his waistband. He pointed to the creek.

"And now to the water," he said.

From the fine sack he had carried with him at the saddle, he extracted two rods with line and hooks. He reached into a rough sack he also had carried with him and extracted some lively worms one of the slaves had dug up for us early in the day and hooked one and then handed me the other. Its wriggling presence made coolness on my palm and I watched it squirm a little before following my cousin's instructions and skewering it on the hook. Within moments we cast our worms into the gently moving stream and sat quietly to await whatever came next.

The hot morning sun inched above the treetops at our backs. Hawks circled overheard. In the distance dogs cried out, while I settled into the still business of fishing wherein such minute motions as the light current running against the line where it entered the water made patterns fascinating to the eye.

"Ah," my cousin said, sinking down to a place on the vine-covered ground, "this *is* Paradise."

"It is lovely," I said, sinking along with him. "I have never fished much before this, Cousin. Except perhaps to throw bricks into the passing Hudson."

He laughed and stretched his booted feet out before him while holding his rod high.

I followed suit, and then, as he lay the rod at his side, did the same, for the pleasure of quietly doing nothing and yet having the right to say you are doing something after all. He passed his flask to me, and I took a sip, and handed it back to him and watched him spend a moment or two with the same receptacle to his lips.

A fish jumped in the creek, its silver sides catching the sun and winking it back at me.

"In the best of all possible worlds," my cousin said as he jiggled his pole so that the line danced at the water line, "we will live off the fish we catch and the slaves will be free and all will be well with all of us and the world." He took a breath, slowly, as if inhaling a pipe. "A fine dream, is it not?"

"A fine way to see things," I said, pausing a moment to gaze down into the current. "Of course someone else will have to work the plantation."

"New Africans," he said. "Each year we'll bring in new slaves and gradually free them also. That is my wife's idea."

"But the trade across the ocean has ended," I reminded him.

"We will restore it," he said.

"Our government will never do that."

"Our new government will," he said.

"A new government? And which is that?"

"A confederacy of Southern states become a separate nation."

Now I should record my astonishment at his declaration, but I couldn't say how I would have responded, because of a sudden my pole came alive in my hand.

"Whoa! I have a bite!"

"Indeed you do," said my cousin, watching with delight as I raised and lowered the pole to the pull and tug of the creature on the end of my line. I eased it out of the water and watched it dance on its tail on the surface—a blue and green and yellow-gilded fish as long as my forearm—when we saw another creature bobbing about in the water just upstream.

We both jumped back in astonishment as a dark-skinned man with a bald head that showed off the earth-color of his skull came stumbling out of the creek, water running off him in gushets, and collapsed in front of us.

"My God!" I said, staring at the man who lay prone before us. "He is nearly drowned." Suddenly the image of the young dark boy from New Jersey came to my mind, and I felt an acute instant of desperation at how he himself, wherever he might be in our region, must surely desire to run, to flee across water and follow a path that would take him back to freedom.

"He was not swimming for pleasure, I am sure," my cousin said. He stood there, hands on hips, regarding the fallen creature. "Damned fool is running south. He should have stayed north of the creek."

"Running?"

"Yes, a way for slaves to exercise their limbs," said Jonathan.

"What?" I said.

My cousin touched a finger to his lips.

"Hush!" he said with a menacing sort of hiss.

High above us a hawk circled, and smaller birds sang, as they had been singing, since sunrise. The fish flopped about on the creek-side, the water gurgled in the sun. And in the distance came the high whining song of those dogs we had been hearing for a while.

"Ohhhh."

The slave just then reached up and grabbed his leg.

Jonathan kicked at him, and tore at his own coat pocket where he had stowed his pistol.

"Away!" he shouted at the slave, still kicking, as though trying to shy away a rampant dog.

"Sorry, massa," the slave said, clinging to his leg.

"You are going to be sorrier still," Jonathan said, cocking his pistol. "Release me!"

"Cain't," the slave said with a moan.

Jonathan drew back a step, dragging the clinging slave with him, and still threatening the man with the pistol.

"I said *release!*"

"No," I said, wishing desperately that I had not left my own pistol behind.

"I have him," my cousin said, turning to me with a gleeful stare.

He gestured with his pistol.

"Get up," he said to the man.

"Getting' up, massa," the man said, releasing my cousin's leg and slowly pushing himself to his feet. He stood trembling. Water had soaked his ragged clothes so that they clung to him like a second skin, accentuating his already thin appearance. He had a long bullet-shaped head and large front teeth, which chattered uncontrollably not from the water, which was quite warm, but from fear. Even at this distance I could smell the stench of it pouring off him.

"He is confused," I said. "Put the weapon aside."

"He certainly is," my cousin said. "He is a fool to run."

"Tell him which way to go."

"What?"

"Tell him which way to go. Give him a chance to run away."

My cousin shook his head.

"He will not get far. The dogs are out looking for him."

"Give him a chance."

"He is someone's property. Should I steal from another man?"

"Think of him as a fish that got away. Let him go along."

My cousin stared me in the eye, as if appraising my whole self.

"I will show you my good will," he said, lowering his weapon and squinting at me, as though the bright light of morning had suddenly faded. "I will give you this as a sign of my good faith in our family and business relations."

Jonathan cleared his throat and looked down at the wretch before us.

"You are running in the wrong direction," he said. "Head west and when the river turns north keep it to your right and that will take you to the lake, and from there, west a long, long way to the mountains. Can you remember that?"

"If I forgot all I got to do is listen…" The man looked over his shoulder and we all stood a moment listening to the sounds in the distance of howling dogs and the faint shouts of men.

"Go!" a voice burst out.

It was my voice.

"Thank you, massa," the man said, and he jumped to his feet.

"One more moment!" Jonathan said.

"Cousin, he must be on his way."

"He will need to do one thing more."

"And what is that?" I said, seeing the pain and torment on the dark face of the runaway.

"He must needs bow down to me."

"What?"

Jonathan turned to me and showed me that infernal grin that came before with his laugh. But he was not laughing now.

"You want him to bow?"

"To us," he said, gesturing with the pistol.

"And then you'll let him go?"

"I will. It makes no difference…"

"You," I said to the runaway. "Did you hear him?"

The man nodded.

"Bow down then," I said. "Hurry."

"As if to a king," Jonathan said.

"Is this some horrendous—"

"Bow," Jonathan cut me off.

The runaway man looked at him and then turned to me.

I nodded.

The man knelt and lowered himself to the ground before my cousin.

My cousin raised his pistol and then lowered it to aim at the prostrate man's head. A moment or two passed before Jonathan said, "Very well, then. Go."

The man jumped to his feet and, while Jonathan stood perfectly still and pretended to aim his weapon at him, dashed into the woods.

Frankly, I could not find any words to say about what I had just witnessed.

"Damnation!" Jonathan spit onto the ground.

More moments passed, with the air filled with the barking and howls of approaching dogs.

My cousin seemed to be about to say something to me when a pack of low-slung muscular animals came bursting out of the trees on the other side of the creek, howling as they came. A trio of horsemen followed. The dogs took a moment to run their snouts along the far shore before plunging into the water and surging toward our side and the horsemen behind did not pause as they ripped into the stream, emerging on our shore in a burst of spume and splash just behind the dogs.

But with shouts and roars they reined up just before us while the dogs went rushing off into the woods.

"Where's he at?" called the wire-haired fellow atop the blue-tinged stallion.

"Langerhans, how are you?" my cousin said. "We were sitting here quietly fishing and look now, you've scared all the fish away, I am sure."

"It's the Sabbath, you should be home or at church," Langerhans said, a nasty half-smile on his crooked face. "But then your kind don't go to church on Sunday, do yiz?"

"We went yesterday," my cousin said, matching the horseman sneer for sneer. "On our own Sabbath. Think of it, man. Our country, broad and grand enough for each and every man to have a separate Sabbath." A slight sneer turned his mouth as he spoke. "But you, you are not at prayer now either, are you?"

"Listen, my Hebrew friend," the patroller said, "I'll be at prayer tonight thanking the Lord for the bounty on a runaway nigger, that's for sure."

"Whose nigger is that?" Jonathan asked.

"You ain't seen him? Well, you couldn't have missed him, could you, since he must have splashed up out of the creek worst than our dogs."

Langerhans leaned down along the mane of his horse and gave me his eye.

"Yankee down from the nigger north, are you?"

"We do not think of it that way, I have to tell you," I said.

"What you have to tell me," the patroller said, "is which way the nigger ran. Oh, shit and barnstorms, the dogs'll find him. We just have to find the dogs before they tear him to pieces. Before anything else, the nigger needs a whipping."

"So no funeral?" Jonathan said.

"Not if we can help it." The man smiled, and it appeared to be the same as his sneer. "Nigger's someone's property and we're bound to protect it."

In the distance the dogs broke into a high melodic whine.

"Well," Langerhans said, "we got to be off. Give my regards to your father. Tell him anytime he's got trouble with a nigger we're ready to help out."

"We don't happen to have any problems these days, do we?" Jonathan said to me.

But before I could speak the three men turned their horses and trotted off into the woods in the direction of the dogs.

"Well…" I said, wandering over to the creek-side, where the ground was torn up by the horses.

"A not-so-pretty side of the way we live down here," my cousin said.

"Yet on our family's property we have no runaways?"

"No, sir. They love us and we love them. They respect us, and we are trying to teach them." Again, that demonic sneer appeared on his face. "Why, they look upon me as royalty, as a king!"

We heard the now distant dogs singing even higher in their frenzied whining, and we stared at each other and I did not like that look on my cousin's face. I could not see the look on mine, but I felt it. Oh, I felt it! If I myself could have bolted and run, that would have been the time.

Chapter Thirty-one

The Promised Land

*T*he tall dark man had counted the moons. Ten of them had risen and set before one early morning the uglies herded them into small boats and sailed across a short stretch of water to another pier. It astonished her, the sadness of this last short trip! One of the Africans rolled over the side into the water and despite his manacles began to swim toward the rising sun. Before the shouting subsided he had sunk out of sight.

This weighed on Lyaa like a stone, and between that and the weight of her unborn child, whom she was sure was the goddess herself waiting to be born again, she found herself slow to move and thus the object of shouts from the pale-skinned uglies. From the riverside to the long barracks where the Africans first were penned seemed like a great distance to her, walking as she did as if in water. Here now, she peered through the metal slats of the barracks wall, watching the pale-skins pass by in what seemed to be a market. Piles of fruit and vegetables lay on tables all across the yard. Bolts of bright-colored cloth and baskets, figures made of sticks and clay lay displayed as wares the strolling customers might choose among. Oh, how she would have loved to have strolled there, too, and touched and inspected and chosen pieces of colorful cloth to dress herself. She was dreaming awake in this fashion when someone touched her shoulder and she turned to see the white-haired man with the clear mask over his eyes staring at her belly.

At the nod of his head another pale-skin came up to them and holding her by the manacles led her out of the pen into the sunlight and up onto a large raised wooden block. Even after all the time lying below decks on the long passage and the many moons under guard in the crowd of women and men alike on the other side of the river it still shamed and disturbed her to stand naked in the bright sunlight before a crowd of shouting pale-skinned men. One of them pointed at her with a stick and a man behind her used a stick to prod her into turning around.

The voices grew louder, and she felt the sun bearing down on her head with the weight of a large stone.

Let us fly away now, she urged the goddess, but when she took a deep breath and urged herself upward nothing happened, except the man next to her began speaking to the gathering crowd.

He turned her again, and this made her dizzy. He turned her again, and she felt the sun weighing on her even more.

He gently poked her in the belly with the stick, saying something that drew a laugh from the crowd, and she turned away, holding the pouch with the stone to her nether parts and wishing she could drink water or, again, fly high, or go to sleep and have a beautiful dream that would carry her away from all this turmoil.

The man held the stick over her head and called out, and men in the crowd called back to him.

He leered at her and touched her belly with his stick, raising a cheer from the crowd.

She flailed her arms at him and spun away. A shout! The man slapped her on the shoulder. Lyaa felt her gorge rise, and turned in the sun spewing vomit over his shoes and falling onto the platform before all the light disappeared.

Was she dreaming? What land was this? So far across the waters from home, so far from the heaven in which she had flown within the goddess's body, and yet the light from that heaven poured down on her, and on the wagon in which she lay, and the noise of the creaking vehicle and the sound of the animal's hooves on the road, the clicks and grunts of the driver—she leaned up on her elbows and caught a glimpse of his black neck and the back of his black head—even the sound seemed magnified by the light all around it. She took several deep breaths and closed her eyes, pressing her knuckles against them, and opening her eyes again. All that she had seen? Still here! Was this real or a dream? She asked Yemaya, but the goddess didn't answer.

And then, she noticed that she lay covered in a simple cloth garment, rough but roughly enough to dress herself in. After all that time down in the hold and up on deck living nearly naked she had nearly forgotten it was not the natural state of things. The man who drove the cart wore a white shirt that glowed in wavering lines in the heat of the burning sun. And then she noticed that a man rode on horseback alongside the wagon, a man wearing a rough-cloth dark shirt and dark trousers, his face as white as the cart-driver's shirt.

She shivered, and heard herself sigh. The day grew hotter, even as the wagon bounced along beneath a canopy of trees. Another forest! But not the forest of home, no. *Oh, Yemaya, please, goddess, You cannot have gone away and left me here! You would not, would You?*

Chapter Thirty-two

Two Selections

That night I returned to my room and, in a rather melancholy mood, stood at the window a while as though I might see into the dark across the fields and into the woods where that runaway black man had been hiding—though I was quite sure he had been captured, giving the excitement of the dogs who went after him—and then picked my way through a book case near the bed. The only thing there that caught my interest was a small volume of illustrated poems by a man named William Blake. But these I put aside for further study. Next I went to the bureau and took up the prayer pamphlet I had folded and pressed during my stay in the synagogue.

> *Creed of the Reformed Society of Israelites*
> Q.   *What are the fundamental Elements which form the basis of the Jewish faith?*
> A.   *The thirteen following:*
>   1.   *The existence of God.—We believe that God exists, who created and sustains the universe.*
>   2.   *His unity.—We believe that God is ONE, and only one, without a second that can in any manner be compared to, or associated with him.*

Slowly, I read down the list of the other elements of the faith—His incorporeity, his eternity (*"We believe that he is eternal, without beginning and without end…"*), his direct superintendence (*that he reigns alone over the universe without the intermediation of any other power…*), his providence, the truth of prophecy, the prophecy of Moses (*"the prince of prophets"*), the delivery of the Law, the permanence of the Law, oh, and yes, the rewards and punishments for those who fulfill the law and those who transgress it, and the Coming of the Messiah—and last, the Resurrection of the dead.

> *We believe that those who sleep in the dust will awake, and*
> *All who have died will return to life.*

I studied this yet again, finding this talk about death and resurrection rather odd for the Jews, since in New York this subject never arose. And then remembering something I had put aside while I had been unpacking I went to my bag and saw at the bottom the rumpled New York news sheet that I had used to wrap my mother's portrait.

I unfolded the sheet, held it up to my nose to catch an inky whiff of the city I had only recently left but which already seemed so distant that this artifact might have come from the ruins of some ancient exotic capital. The headlines I ignored—despite all of my old teacher Halevi's promptings, I was never much one for news—but by the flickering light of the candle I read a poem that the editors in their wisdom had chosen to publish.

> *Once upon a midnight dreary, while I*
> *pondered, weak and weary,*
> *Over many a quaint and curious volume*
> *of forgotten lore—*
> *While I nodded, nearly napping,*
> *suddenly there came a tapping,*
> *As of some one gently rapping, rapping*
> *at my chamber door.*
> *"'Tis some visitor," I muttered,*
> *"tapping at my chamber door—*
> *Only this and nothing more…*

This poem kept me rapt with the spirit of it, and a bit on the edge of nervousness after hearing of its speaker's encounter with the harbinger of darkness and death.

> *Open here I flung the shutter. When,*
> *With many a flirt and flutter*
> *In there stepped a stately Raven of the*

Saintly days of yore...
"Prophet!" said I, "thing of evil!
Prophet still, if bird or devil!...
Is there—is there balm in Gilead?
Tell me—tell me, I implore!"
Quoth the Raven, "Nevermore."

All this knocking, rapping, tapping—and the apparition of that bird—set me to walking about my room—the knocking, rapping, tapping—and even after I put out the candle and climbed into the bed it kept my mind alert.

Knocking—rapping—tapping...

Try as I might I could not find sleep. Instead I imagined my father in his office—the king in his counting house—going over the books, counting and measuring shipments from Samarkand, barrels from Italy and China, gems from the volcanoes of Borneo—and then his homecoming each evening, when Aunt Isabelle would greet him at the door, the perfect housekeeper (assisted of course by Marzy). And they would take their supper and sip a glass of wine and talk about the business of the day.

Oh, how these thoughts drew in me a such a longing to be home I nearly cried out in the dark!

Slaves and dogs and fish and sun, birds and pistols! Wishing to imagine such things no further, eventually I fell into a troubled sleep. After what I could surmise as having been a short while, I awoke (in my dream?) to find myself standing before a black-winged creature with the head of snake and the body of a cat.

A deep-voiced "Sir!" from out of the dark. I sat up with a start.

"It's Black Jack, massa."

"What are you doing here?"

"I heard you cry out, massa. Are you all right?"

He stood there in the room, as much a part of the dark as he was of what little light there was from a faint moon glowing outside the window.

"I cried out loud?"

"You did, massa," he said. "May I help?"

"Yes, yes," I said. "I was reading. I was dreaming. Black Jack, something to drink, please? Something soothing..."

"Of course, massa," he said. "I thought you might want something like that." And with that he faded away into the darkness near the door. I could hear his footsteps down the hall, and fainter still on the stairs. Oh, houses at night! How they change from the places we inhabit during the day, as if when the sun goes down and the moon comes up we live in more than one plane at a time. I lay in the dark thinking about this and before I knew it I heard footsteps coming back up the stairs. A light tapping (tapping, tapping) at the door.

"Come in, Black Jack," I said.

I felt the light breeze as the door opened and the figure entered the room, a form cast by the light of a candle, and for a flickering instant I felt a terrible rush of icy fear in my blood—a mare out the night had come to murder me!—

And then I heard her voice.

"Massa Pereira?"

"Who—oh!"

I jumped to my feet.

"Yes, sir," the girl Liza said. "Black Jack asked me to bring you this. He said you were having trouble falling asleep."

As she crossed the room first she was nothing more than a wavering of the dark, and then, as her pale (compared to the darkness) face caught the light of the candle-flame, I could finally make her out in a white smock holding the tray before her.

"What is that?" I said, seeing the goblet on the tray.

"His special potion for sleep," she said.

"A magic potion?"

"Yes, yes," she said. "Drink and you shall be bewitched, massa."

I strained my eyes in the dark to see if I might catch a glimpse of her eyes, but she was nothing but a solid emblem of something somewhat lighter than the dark behind her, with no particular features for me to make out.

"Then bewitched I shall be," I said. "But first, one thing."

"Yes, sir?"

"Stop calling me master, please?"

"—"

"Liza?"

"Yes, massa?"

"That is exactly what I'm talking about. No more of that."

"No, massa," she said.

"Liza!"

"—"

"Liza?"

"But what do I call you then, massa?"

"Nathaniel, call me Nathaniel. Or Nate."

"I can't do that. The old massa will be angry with me."

"Then let's make an agreement," I said, picking up the goblet and without hesitation taking a long swallow of the sweet pungent liquid that stopped me for a moment from breathing.

"Massa?" she said.

"No more of that," I said in a raven-like croak.

"Yes, sir."

"No, no, no, no. When we are alone, you call me Nate. When we are with the family, you can do your duty and address me as usual."

"Yes, massa."

"Yes, what?"

"Yes, *Nate*," she said. There was something as smooth and pungent in her voice as the liquid in my throat.

We paused there, and I must say, in the spirit of candor, that in that instant, when I stood so close to her that I could hear her quiet breathing and mistake it for my own, the heat of our two bodies embossed the place in the dark where we faced each other.

"*Nate*," she said.

"Ah," I said, quite taken with the fact that she had used my name and the way she had spoken it.

Tenderly, she took the goblet from my hand and turned to set it on the tray as I boldly allowed myself the gaze at her faint outline in the dark, ghostliness upon ghostliness.

I stepped toward her.

But she was already out the door and gone.

I returned to my bed and lay there what I thought was a long time and then I was opening my eyes to bright dawn sun and the music of birds.

Chapter Thirty-three

Straw into Brick

*T*he Sabbath had ended. Now it was time for business. First thing the next morning I went directly to the stables where I found Isaac working on the carriage.

"Are you ready, sir?" he said.

I nodded as we packed some jars of water from the house spring into our saddle-bags.

"You don't want to drink the creek water, massa," Isaac said. "Folks have been known to meet the Visitor from drinking creek water."

"The visitor?" I said.

"The cholera, the doctor calls it," he said. "Nasty awful. Empties you out and then dries you up for the grave."

"No creek water for me, then," I said as we hitched up our horses, or rather Isaac had taken care of his and mine, my old Promise again, and mounted up for the ride to the brickyard. The sun was just rising over the tops of the trees and the insects buzzed all around us. A faint haze hovered at fetter-length. Birds called and responded and called.

"Isaac?" I said.

"Yes, massa?"

"Were you born here?"

"Yes, massa."

We rode a little way in silence.

"Do you have a family, Isaac?"

"My papa and mama is dead," he said in rote fashion, which made me wonder if it was true or not.

"And no wife?"

"No, sir. Though I would like one some day."

Though I gave no hint of it, a small shudder ran up my arm and into my chest as I imagined this man, finding a woman—Liza? Yes, I saw it!—like himself and going about the business of making a child.

But as happens sometimes with our desperate fantasies I was immediately distracted from it as we approached the clearing at the creek-side where the brickyard stood, and the same crew of men I had seen on my first tour of the spot were all in place, already set to their labors.

"Mornin', massa," a few of them said, raising their heads from their business.

We dismounted and tied up our horses and stepped closer to the men to watch as they worked, some of them at a large pool of water and mud where they mixed in straw from a large pile nearby, and others next to them, cutting and shaping the wet loose-formed bricks they extracted from the pool.

"They work here by themselves," I said. "What is to stop them from bolting into the woods?"

"Is that why you wanted to come here first, massa? To see if any of them looked like he wanted to run away?"

"Not at all," I said, embarrassed to myself at my secret motive for choosing the brickyard over the rice fields. "I'm merely curious. This is unusual, is it not? Men, not free, working by themselves out here on the edge of the plantation, making straw into bricks. According to the Bible, that is what my own people did when they were slaves."

"That is in the Bible?"

"The Jews were slaves once, yes."

"I remember the missus teach us that," Isaac said.

"Very good," I said. "First labor in bondage. Then freedom."

"Yes, and so it is our turn now, massa? Here you are, come down to figure things for your father, so that you all might buy a plantation of your own and work the slaves. I don't hear how that means setting us all free."

"You know a lot about my business here, it seems."

"This a small place, a plantation, smaller than a small town."

"It is small. But pretty."

"Pretty hard," he said, gesturing toward one of the men who was going back and forth to the creek and hauling water back for the brick pit, and two others digging up mud and two others hauling armfuls of hay from the back of an old wagon (without horse to haul it) and mixing it with the mud, so that when it had enough substance they cut brick-shapes from it and set these on the pallet in the sun.

Over and over.

A few bricks each few minutes.

Stand there long enough and you could see the entire life of the lowly brick from mud hole to baked entity lined up alongside the shed-house, where the finished bricks, lifted from the pallet, lay piled beneath the make-shift roof. In a thousand years, enough bricks for a holy tomb!

"You see how it's done?" Isaac asked me. "Straw and mud into bricks. A simple thing. Like most things in life. One plain thing mixed with another makes something different yet the same. The way they do this, it hasn't changed much since the first days we read of them in Exodus. Your ancestors, my brothers here, they work the same way as in Egypt, breathe the same way, eat the same way, make all of the same ablutions, and hold all of the same desires."

"You are quite eloquent, Isaac, a fine example of just what my uncle's plan for educating your people can accomplish."

Isaac snorted through his nose the way my horse might, if stung by an insect or slapped by a tree branch.

"Uncle massa has a plan? Well, the doctor helps us," he said. "He comes now and then from town."

"I have heard of him but I have not yet met him."

"Don't know that you will, massa," he said.

The look in his eye, I could not explain it, if asked, and I was not asking myself about it. I retreated over to where old Promise was tethered and I extracted a jar of spring water from the saddlebag and took a long drink.

"Massa, can I ask you a question?" Isaac said.

"Of course. What is it, Isaac?"

"Do you have an idea of why you are standing here?"

"Here, at this brickyard?"

"Here, in Carolina, on this earth."

I looked around, seeing this place at the water, the drying bricks, the shed, and I was about to make an answer to Isaac, when I was jolted back into the workaday realm by a shout from one of the brick-makers.

"Boat coming up!"

"Hey, da boat!"

Isaac called out to the men, and I watched as around the bend in the creek a flatboat edged its way upstream on the power of several black men poling.

"Coming for the bricks," he said to me. "So they can build more houses in the city, and all around the county. These men, they dig and mash the mud and water, mix in their straw, form the bricks and bake them in the sun, and next thing you know a house goes up in town and people make a life in it. All beginning with this mud."

But that was enough philosophy, or history, however one might categorize his remarks, for this day, because we had immediately to oversee the docking of the boat and the loading of the bricks for shipment down the creek to the river and into town.

Chapter Thirty-four

Old Dou

The doctor had noticed, and he had told the owner, who when he arrived home after his errand to Charleston, told his wife, the mistress of the house, and she told the head house servant, so that when Lyaa arrived at the plantation a good large number of people knew she was expecting.

A cloud of confusion settled in her mind. She knew and yet did not know. She had lost her mother—and not until she met Old Dou the head house servant, a rotund African woman the color of tar with large round eyes—also tarry in shade—who asked her a few questions in a language she understood from the first days of the passage and who gave her some answers as well, did she accept the facts about her condition.

Lyaa shook her head in refusal. Old Dou gave a shake of her head.

"You don't know, do you?"

"Know what, mother (the formal way of addressing a woman this much older than she was, though Lyaa felt a tiny chill in her chest when she addressed her this way, because of a sudden she missed her real mother so desperately)?"

"You don't know how it happened?"

Lyaa shook her head.

"Is it the goddess?"

"Yemaya?" The older woman shook her head. "You don't believe that, do you?"

"I am Yemaya, I believe in her, in me. She is in me and I am in her."

"Put that old talk aside," said Old Dou. "Tell me what happened in your passage."

Lyaa, suddenly lucid, told her about the degradations and the deprivations, the suffering, the filth.

The woman listened for a short while before she said, "No, no, tell me about the men or a man."

"Man?"

"Who was he?"

"Who was he?"

"You heard me, daughter. The man who took you."

"I saw things in the passage, though, thank the gods, nothing happened to me except the heat and the sickness."

"I am glad to hear that, daughter. But please now, tell me."

"Yemaya protected me."

"Daughter, who was he? One of us or one of them?"

Lyaa shook her head.

"I don't know."

"You don't know? It was too dark? You were too sick. But you said you did not get sick."

"Perhaps I got sick."

"And then?"

"And then the goddess helped me."

"The goddess didn't help you to get away from that man."

"What man? Please, why do you keep asking about a man?"

"Daughter, you are carrying a child and that comes from being with a man. Did your mother never teach you that?"

Lyaa began to weep.

"I never saw my mother, not after they put us in the pens."

"She did not sail with you?"

The girl shook her head.

"I don't know where she is, whether she is alive or…"

"Oh, daughter," said Old Dou, taking the girl in her arms. "This sorry life, this sorry world, I am deeply sad for you. For all of us."

Suddenly the girl pulled free of her hold.

"You say I am carrying a child?"

"The man gave you a child. What man was it interfered with you, daughter?"

Lyaa bowed her head and took a breath that seemed to go on forever. She looked up and her eyes went inward down into a deep place darker than the tint of Old Dou's flesh. Finally, she looked outward again. Finally she spoke.

"A sailor was the man," she said. "He hurt me. I didn't know it made a child. Is that why he gave me bread?"

"He gave you bread?"

"When he…did it with me…again."

"He may have been a bad man, hurting you like that, but he gave you something else, greater than bread. You cannot eat of it, but it will give you nourishment all the rest of your life."

Lyaa shook her head.

"A child?"

She brushed her hand across her belly.

"I don't feel a child."

"The child feels you."

"I have the goddess inside me, and I am inside the goddess."

"What are you saying?"

But before she could try to explain the doctor returned and directed her, as the master had directed him to tell Old Dou, to take the girl to the bedding at the back of the barn.

"This is comfortable," Old Dou said once they arrived at the barn. "Better than most get when they arrive here. But these Hebrews have a funny way. They own us but they want us to like them. It is different from the old country. At least they are, though not a lot of the others. The Christian folks. I hear things, I see things. Word travels, and not just in carts and carriages. All the years here, they do whipping. They hang people in the sun. Can you see that? No, you cannot see that, sick as you are. I do not mean to frighten you. Be glad you are here. Be glad the master wanted to get me a helper, and not some ugly girl up out of the fields, her ways already all twisted. He wanted somebody new, somebody we could teach. That's what he told me. Maybe the master decided he will get us a bargain, somebody who is two for one. That is you, daughter, clearly that is you. But right now I see we need to help you or else we might have nothing for our money. Listen to me, nothing for *their* money is what I mean. You know I sure don't have any money, not even anything hidden under the clay in my little cabin. But you had something hidden, didn't you? Right there in your belly. In your own little clay hiding place. So we need to get you comfortable, sure, and get you some food, and fatten you up because you are going to get fat from the child soon and soon, because that child will come out of hiding."

Old Dou touched the girl on her cheek.

"No worry, I will take care of you."

Most of this passed Lyaa by. She felt cleared out, exhausted, hungry, tired beyond the need just for sleep. Only just now she felt steady, after that long voyage. Only just now did the sky and trees and earth stop shifting in her vision, side to side, up and down. She settled into her bed in the barn, soothed by the odors of animals that drifted in from the front of the building.

"We are all brothers and sisters," Yemaya told her in a small voice that Old Dou could not hear. *These horses, they carry us, but they do it as a favor. And we groom them, as a favor. The whole world works that way, daughter, and you are no exception. That sailor up on deck took something from you that you can never get back, but he left something in you, and that has grown to be the child within you, this little pip of a child grown into a swimming fish in your belly, growing now so fast and so big that I have to move over to make room for her."*

"*Her?*"

"*Oh, yes, she is going to be a girl.*"

"*I am a girl.*"

"*No, a woman now.*"

"*And you are a girl.*"

"*Long ago, and now older, much older.*"

"*When you were a girl, tell me about it.*" Oh, all that life in the forest, all that running, all that pain of captivity, the pain of the passage, and rape, the ignorance of her own condition or of where she was living, in what place and what country, poor demented girl finding happiness only in the goddess, until the day the birth spasms took her over.

Chapter Thirty-five

Rice and Blood

*A*nother early morning, another ride, as Isaac and I mounted up, and rode along the trail. A swift furry animal low to the ground started across our path, startled the horses, which startled me, reminding me again of the runaway slave my cousin Jonathan and I had encountered on our fishing day. My heart beat up a flurry, and then settled down. I touched my hand to my coat, where the pistol had made a shape under my fingers. And then let go. I had decided I would not ride out without it anymore.

"Here we are, master," Isaac said, as we left the woods and found ourselves at the rice fields.

We dismounted, tied up our horses, and walked toward the field, which looked to me like a large rectangular lawn, submerged by long rains. About two dozen slaves, men and women, some of them not much older than children, moved slowly up and down long rows, pulling up what looked to me like long stems of grass.

"Is that the rice?" I said.

Isaac shook his head.

"Few weeks ago, we planted the seeds and then we flood the field to make them grow. We call that the sprout flow. It covers the seeds and we keep the water in the field until the sprouts come out. What the folks do now is pull up weeds. Soon now, we drain the water and the sprouts grow more. We flood the fields again, that is called the point flow, and the water covers up to the top of the plants. Then we drain a little more—"

"How do you know when to do all this?"

"We watch the plants, we watch the tides, we watch the moon. You want to hear how it finishes?"

"Certainly."

"We leave the plants half in water till they can stand up on their own, then we drain the rest of the field. That's when the hard weeding work comes, and after that we let in the water to cover all the plants again and leave it that way until the early fall."

All the while he was speaking I was watching the slaves in water to their ankles move up and down the half-submerged furrows, bent over and waving their hands and their hoes to take out the weeds. There was a tinge of brine in the air, and this turned my thoughts to the ocean I had traveled to reach this place, even if keeping the coast in sight most of the while, and the tides that washed in salt, and the pure creek water that flowed back in after the tide pulled out, and the waxing and waning of the moon. I tried to imagine the ocean voyage made by many of the slaves who worked here, but such an event lay beyond anything I could picture.

"Come," Isaac said, with a gesture of his hand, and led me out into the field. The water sucked at my boots and I splashed myself up to my knees as we plodded along. Here in the middle of it the briny odor grew stronger.

The slaves—men and women of varying ages—stared at us as we approached, pausing only a second or so and then returning to their stooped postures as they moved along the rows.

Another master, I decided, that was how they saw me, the way beasts in the field might respond—and I disliked myself for the thought.

"It smells of the ocean," I said.

"The ebb and flow of it makes for a mix of salt and fresh water," Isaac said. "We learned how to do this across the water. It makes for good crop."

"You learned in Africa?"

"The people from there learned," he said, "They brought it here, and taught us how to do it."

We had kept on walking as we talked and now we had reached the other side of the field and climbed out of the water onto the berm that made a border between the rice field and the marsh that bled out into the creek.

"And next, the harvest?"

Isaac held his arms out wide and then took up an invisible scythe and began to sweep it across the tops of our feet.

"We take the rice hook and cut the plants and lay them out to dry."

"And after the harvest?" I said, stamping my boots on the ground and seeing the water spray out of them. I felt childlike, and at the same time a bit weary, because even as I walked and talked, the slaves kept bent to their labor.

"After the harvest?" Isaac's eyes went watery for an instant. "After the harvest, yes. Much to be gained."

"But how is it done?"

"In the old days across the water this is how it was done. We take the mortals and pestles—"

"Mortars, do you mean?"

"Mortars, that's right! And we pound the rice to remove the outer husk, then we lay it onto the fanners, the flat baskets, to do what you call in English winnowing. We shake the basket back and forth, back and forth—" He held his hands out as though he were holding a basket in front of him and shook them, shook them—"and the husk falls away."

He turned his head and pointed to the creek. "Comes the flatboat, and they take it away to town..."

"That takes a lot of time and fortitude," I said, "to thrash the rice and hull it that way. And then the cleaning?"

"We did the cleaning over the water," Isaac said. "Now the master here sends it on the flatboat and they clean it in the city. And sell it from there. What we don't keep. This makes for a difference from the way we did it in Africa. 'Course I have never been in Africa. This is just what I hear from old folks in the cabins."

Isaac sighed, allowing me a glimpse of the defenseless side of him, because, to be sure, up until now, he had been all bravado and strength.

"Nothing here is much anymore like it was across the water, from what I hear," he said. "Beginning with the slavery."

"Come, come," I said, hearing—how strange—my father's voice in my own, "I know from my studies of events there is slavery in Africa. Many, many thousands of slaves were captured by Arab traders and by your own people and then sold into bondage a second time."

Isaac lowered his head as if he had immediately to inspect our shoe-tops.

"Yes, yes, I hear about it, I do. But I don't know which is the worst, slavery by our own or slavery by another."

"They are equally despicable," I said.

His head jerked back and he looked wide-eyed.

"That is what you say about slavery?"

The man belonged to my uncle, and I was a guest down here, and so I did not want to become embroiled in anything that might initiate a family squabble.

I said, "We came here to talk about the rice. Tell me more about the threshing, Isaac," I said.

"Yes, the rice. We brought it here, we grow it for you."

He gathered himself together, shook his head and turned and went walking along the berm.

"Isaac?"

"You got to have great patience to grow the rice, massa," he said over his shoulder.

"Tell me more," I said, walking along behind him.

But he was silent.

A few moments later we arrived at the place in the berm where the dam-doors made of woven vines and flat slabs of wood stood against the inflow of the creek water, to be opened when it was necessary to bring in more water, closed to keep the briny creek water out when the tidal flush splashed upstream.

"See that?"

He pointed to the creek, widening here in a bend as the water flowed sluggishly against the berm.

I thought I saw something moving in the water and my first thought was that another runaway was crossing over. And then I decided it was a downed tree trunk.

Until I saw the yellow eyes in the elongated mossy green skull raise up just above the surface of the moving stream.

"What is he waiting for?" I said, making out the rest of the alligator now that I could see him.

Before he could answer, some five slaves came splashing along the creek bed, staves and metal tools in hand. The beast no sooner turned its mossy head when they attacked it, and its tail slashed back and forth churning the water to almost complete froth, and it roared, oh, Lord, it roared!

"Why are they doing that, Isaac?"

"For the meat," Isaac said.

Before it was over, two slaves went down into the water, moaning and screaming, but the other three, with great bellowing themselves, and raising staves and fists beat the beast to death, and hauled it on shore. My heart nearly stopped at the sight of all the blood smeared on the black skin of these men, on the rough greenish hide of the dead beast. These peaceful souls, so enchained, could wreak murder if they cared to. The best of me thought it was good that they could conquer a monster such as they had. The worst of me feared they might sometime unleash their fury on their masters.

Voices in My Ear

A Song

Massa sleeps in de feather bed
Nigger sleeps on de floor,
When we'uns go to Heaven,
Dey'll be no slaves no mo'…

Raven Dream

That evening I retired early and while the moon rose outside my window I slipped into sleep on the wings of the fantasy that my father would invest in this enterprise and I would thus set everyone free. As I pursued this line further, imagining myself saying to Liza that now she might linger awhile in the house as a free woman I heard a knocking, a tapping, a rapping.

Was it only a dream? A raven?

I started up in bed at the sound of a door closing—or was it opening?—and wandered into the hall, seeing a shadowy figure a few paces ahead of me, who then descended the back stairs.

I went to the top of the stairs, paused, and then descended.

The door to the back rooms opened, and I pursued the person who had opened it. Not until out under the night sky did I see the figure of my cousin Rebecca like a ghost illuminated by a half-full moon, and that she—worse gods!—was following someone herself.

Her prey—and again I walked a bit too quickly and reduced the distance between both of them and myself to a proximity dangerously close—turned out to be her husband, my cousin Jonathan. Oblivious—or, who knows the truth, utterly uncaring—as to whether or not anyone saw him, and his wife following him and in this rather comic than sinister procession me following both of them, he proceeded in the direction of the cabins. The hour was late, and in the quarters where the slaves resided, in those small structures made of porous timber and mud plastered in the chinks between the crudely carved out boards someone was singing, a song all the more outstanding in its lyric because of the quiet that surrounded all else.

My old missus promise me
Shoo a la a day,
When she die she set me free
Shoo a la a day

Across the small lane that separated the row of cabins another group of men huddled together in harmonies.

Massa sleeps in de feather bed
Nigger sleeps on de floor,
When we'uns go to Heaven,
Dey'll be no slaves no mo'…

My cousin Jonathan went up to the door of a cabin near the edge of the encampment and without hesitating stepped inside.

His wife, my dear cousin by marriage, Rebecca, who often made this trip herself in daylight to help some of their charges learn to read, stood there a moment, lost in the presumably dark act that her husband had performed—and then, as she turned, turned himself, which meant that I turned, though, because of her hurry to return to the main house—I could hear this in her steps—I turned toward the barn and stepped just inside to allow her to pass me as she made her way to the rear of the house and, presumably, up the back stairs and up to the upper hall where she returned to her room.

I was left, under that half moon, breathing in the rich dung odors of the animals, in the barn, asking myself not only what I had just witnessed but why I had made myself to witness it—but then Rebecca could just as easily ask herself the same questions. The only thing I did not know was how many times before my cousin Jonathan had taken his little journey from the house to the cabins, and just how many times his wife had followed him as witness to what could only be deeds darker than a night in the country without a moon. Neither of them appeared to hesitate in the way that a novice at this business would hesitate.

I stepped out of the barn, about to make my way back to the house, when I saw yet another shadow pass along the path to the cabins. I ducked back inside the entrance of the barn and squinted through the dark, try-ing to make out whose figure this was walking along, later than even these other late walkers I had been stalking. Imagine my heartbeat when I recognized Liza!

Of a sudden a breeze came up, the fields making a rustling noise, as though some god were breathing across the high grass and small trees. I waited until Liza passed the barn and went on toward the cabins. I followed her almost all the way, until by the light of a fading cook fire, I saw yet someone else appear against the dark. Isaac meet Liza with an embrace, and I watched, until I could see them no more in that same dark.

Chapter Thirty-eight

Old Dou and the Doctor in Consultation

*L*yaa, in the throes of labor, writhed and screamed, calling out names of goddesses and gods, crying for help. Normally, it would have only been Old Dou, the African woman who ran everything for the family as an army sergeant might run a company, to assist but the doctor happened to be making his rounds that day so when he heard the news, he briskly walked to the cabin where she lay suffering that torment women undergo, and then forget, so that the human species can continue on earth.

"That's a way," Old Dou said as a foreman might speak to a struggling novice laborer in the fields.

"Take a breath, girl," the doctor said. "Take a breath, and then push from under your belly and out."

Old Dou, standing at his side and because she was more round than tall looking up at him as they both lay hands on the laboring woman, spoke quietly, the doctor less so. He was used to taking a forceful role in such medical matters as childbirth—the people he treated appreciated a physician with a firm hand.

"She don't understand you," Old Dou said. "Even I talk to her sometimes she don't understand me. Look at her eyes."

"She's in a state," the doctor said.

"She been this way ever since she arrived. It happens to folks on the passage, they just lose their minds, sail right past them, is how I see it, and they never be good anymore. Except, like she is, good enough to give up a new baby to the world."

"Not just yet…" He raised the woman's skirt and took a clinical look at the widening divide between her legs.

"Soon," Old Dou said, and she began to weep.

She shocked the doctor with this show of emotion.

"What is wrong with you, Dou?" he said.

"I see one coming, but I see one going, too," the woman said.

"I do not see any sign of trouble," the doctor said.

"Only because you can't see it," Old Dou said.

"What do you see?" The doctor kept his eye on the patient, listening to her breathing along with the cries and shouts of pain.

"One coming—see?"

The infant's head began to breech.

"Here we go," the doctor said, preparing to reach for the child and help it arrive.

"But look," Old Dou said, meaning, look at the woman's face, notice the sudden decrease of breath, feel the decrease in the blood-pulse at her wrists and neck. "Going, going."

"All right," the doctor said. "Here, you have done this many times before, you take the child." He saw it now as a question of pacing, the child rising into the world as the mother sank into the dark clouds beneath which awaited her death.

"All too young," he said.

"Oh, she's old," Dou said. "That passage, it makes you old. Either it kills you or you live a long while."

"She came through alive," the doctor said.

"Naw, naw," Old Dou said, bold and brave and wise enough to know when she knew more than this medical man of the modern world who had trained at the best college in the world. "The death begin on the passage in her mother's womb, and it's just finishing with her now. That's where death is, death is in life, nowhere else."

"Hush a moment," said the doctor, "we need to pay close attention."

Here came the child! Coughing, and then crying, breathing into this new world!

The doctor wanted to laugh, but, as he watched the mother sink, he also wanted to cry—and his training prevented him from doing either. This young woman who had survived the ocean passage, now she set out on another journey, crossing over from this world to wherever it is, if any-where, we go when we die. These slave women broke his heart, and chal-lenged his ability to believe that everything had a practical answer. They gave birth, and then they died, more, so many more, than other—which is to say, white—women. Was it simply the brutal nature of their lives? Or were they cursed? And if so, why? Why them? Why them?

He was deep in a mood, mulling all this over while wrapping the body as Old Dou cuddled the newborn, when into the cabin stepped the plantation owner's son.

"I...was overseeing some work in the barns and I heard about the screams," Jonathan said. He did not give a second glance to the corpse of the mother covered with a sheet but rather walked directly up to the newborn child.

"You are a sweety little thing," he said in a made-up high-pitched voice. "Sweety-weety, yes, you are, so sweet and weety, weety and sweet."

The doctor had never much liked Jonathan, but as he watched the man coo and coo over the new-born he wondered if he might be mistaken about the young master.

"Sweety-weety, weety-sweety," Jonathan went on. On and on and on, until Old Dou wrapped the child in a cloth and carried her out the door.

Jonathan followed.

"Sweety-weety," he said in that same high-pitched voice, "weety-sweety..."

The doctor had never seen this man, or any man, behave with such silliness, or was it madness or devotion over a child not his own. At first it cheered the doctor and then made him sick to his stomach as he wondered what good—or evil—would come of this.

A little girl, and they called her Lyaza. Her mother left her the imprint of her beautiful face, dark eyes just the right distance apart, perfect lips, the nose a masterpiece in shape and form, all of this the color of sand on that ocean beach from which she first departed her native continent.

The doctor, who would become a strong presence in Lyaza's life, and in her own child's life as the years passed, checked her over, beyond the perfect face—looking to the functions of her various parts as best he could surmise, breathing, the flow of her blood, digestion and evacuation, liveliness and laughter.

"Well, Old Dou," he said, "Lyaza's a strong and pretty baby, and though it's going to take time for the family to recover its investment, this one is going to give back much more than her mother could. The mother, being..." His voice trailed off, and he tapped a finger to his forehead.

Old Dou nodded, but she did not smile. It was one thing to belong to someone, and to have to show obedience to any of all of these white people. It was another to give in to any emotion that might suggest you were happy about any of it. Smiling, jokes, singing, dancing, all that belonged to the private lives of the slave cohort on this plantation, and you might figure on all plantations. Here, at least [the only place I know about in an intimate way, having heard these stories from my mother year after year after year], the Africans tried to live lives like any other people, when they took to themselves. And of course the sound of that happiness—the singing, shouting, joking, dancing—sometimes broke out into the air for anyone in the big house or anyone passing by to hear. Faces that might be downcast in the big house often bloomed like flowers in the privacy of the quarters. Charged with energy, limbs that dragged in the fields stepped lively and hopped and kicked to celebrate the vitality of the life-blood flowing through them. Song came later, after the girl, taken in by Old Dou, joined in the music, in her simple way, so that the old house slave cooed and hummed and sang for her as she often did, especially in the early days of her growing years.

The doctor enjoyed that side of the African woman. If he found himself a little too stiff to allow his soul to sing along with the music the slaves made, still he knew it was a good thing they did. The other side of Old Dou gave him pause. The woman who gathered herbs to treat people in the cabins, who threw chicken bones on a mat and read news in them about the future, a time which, invariably, she surmised would be worse than things were now, the woman who looked up at clouds and saw wispy signs in the air, in other words, the woman whose mind and soul belonged to Old Africa rather than to the rational ways he hoped would make up the future of the country they both lived in, this woman made for doubts in his mind. A physician, trained in Massachusetts, who returned to his native grounds after the cold winters of the north began to seep into his bones, the doctor took her to be a competent if overly mystical house slave worthy enough to be trusted with the family's treasured belongings, and discreet enough to keep her countenance cool if not indifferent when the usual flows and ebbs of family life in the big house sometimes rose to the level of distress and disarray. It wasn't the Hebrew aspect of the family's nature that intrigued him. Up north he had met and sometimes befriended people of this persuasion when called upon to practice his profession. No, at this point, even after the son's odd tweety-weety performance in the presence of the newborn, it wasn't yet any of the family—Pereira or his wife and child—who gave him pause for reflection. Old Dou was the one person in the household who most intrigued him, because of her consistent calm and her demonstrations of competence and control. It made him wonder about the nature of the Africans themselves, that this grand woman should have emerged from the raucous, sometimes lazy, always scheming cohort of her brethren, who, as he saw it then, had allowed themselves to be taken as slaves and shipped here to the country that freedom had founded.

His stay in New England had informed him a great deal on these questions. Here in Carolina, where his own forebears went back enough generations to put them at least a hundred years before the war for independence, there was never any question that it was commerce above and beneath all else, on which the well-being and satisfaction of society was built. All of his people had owned large plantations or ships or warehouses for storing what came in on the ships, and as a family over the generations they had amassed a fine legacy of land and houses and animals and human property.

He was one of the few male members of his family who had decided that such commerce was not his fate (while the women, whose destiny was to enjoy the fruits of all the great commerce by practicing the arts of music or drawing or sewing or even poetry, never questioned it). His father expressed his disappointment upon hearing that one of his sons, the one, in fact, in whom he saw the greatest potential for working in the world of commerce, would choose to take up the art of medicine, but since it was, unlike the music or drawing and the other things the women practiced, an important art he acquiesced in his son's choice of a future. But the man did understand why his son might choose to take another path in life. The buying and selling of the numerous bodies of Africans, for example, one of the aspects of his business, had over the years driven him deeper and deeper into an understanding of the human soul that caused him to question his own life and the life of his business. He had read on the question of human nature as presented by various philosophers—he was not at all an uneducated man and had, in fact, attended the same New England school where his wayward son, as he liked to think of the physician, had gone to medical college—and he had read and studied in the area of theology, which was one of the reasons he found church on Sunday so boring, always comparing the priests to those deep and profound thinkers on the subjects to whose level they hardly ever seemed capable of reaching themselves. The paradox of freedom remained the question at the heart of the matter. He accepted God and his laws, and yet he never could get over the problem that allowed for a man to make his own way in the world and still accept that he remained a creature whose every step was preordained by his Lord.

Praise God! Praise the Lord! That was a mouthful, but necessary to set down on paper.

And furthermore: most of his family was too obtuse to appreciate the fineness of such a problem, but his physician son was one with whom he could speak, and speak freely, especially after the doctor had finished his schooling. There had been a slave revolt in a small plantation to the south of Charleston, an incident in which the slaves had turned on the master and his family, killed them, and burned the house and all the barns and killed the animals before fleeing into the woods where, eventually, starving and afraid, they had been found by a large cohort of militia and unofficial outliers who brought them back to the home county seat where they were quickly tried and every one of them, mostly men, but also a few women, hanged.

An isolated incident, but nonetheless the old patriarch talked about it with his physician son, asking him aloud what he had been asking himself in the quiet of his own mind, which was how the Africans could have allowed themselves to be taken into captivity in the first place—it just was not in his nature to understand this kind of submission—and how once indentured here in Carolina they could translate the question of how to achieve their freedom, if that was what they were seeking, into the brutalities of murder and destruction.

"After all the years of reading and studying I have done on the question," the father said to the doctor, "I can only conclude that men may be born free but that these Africans are not true men. Science has shown us, how they not only live closer to the animal but their brains are not at as high a stage as our own. You, son, have looked at human brains and at animal brains over the course of your schooling. Surely you have seen the difference?"

"And what if, father," the doctor said in what was one of their final discussions on the subject, before some agent in his father's blood turned sour and weakened the nature of his body's life-giving fluid, "I can tell you that I have never discerned a single important difference between the Caucasian brain and the African brain? What if I told you that?"

The doctor's father smiled—he had the most charming smile, as his wife, the doctor's mother, and several other women over his lifetime, would attest—and his son knew that their discussion was about to end. The man's smile always announced his decision to conclude whatever matter was at hand.

"Based on all that I know," he said, "that is, adding my experience on to what I have read in philosophy, I can only say that you have not looked hard enough, son. As to the act of observation itself it may be that just as beauty lies in the eye of the beholder so does the possibility of freedom."

"Father, are you saying these people were born to become slaves rather than free men?"

But his father had already turned away.

All of this came to mind for the doctor, though his father was long dead and his brothers had taken over the family business, and he himself having drifted into the orbit of these Hebrews, whom he had befriended after they had called him one desperate night to attend, if he could, what turned out to be the last hours of the matriarch of the Pereira family. More death! This time it had been the withered Jewish crone who had been an infant in Holland and after her family's passage to the Antilles had grown to womanhood in the islands. Oh, time! Oh, time! A few decades after the American Revolution, one of her sons had packed them all up and moved them to Charleston when it became clear that there might be greater fortunes to be made in South Carolina than on their small Carib isle. Another son went to New York. Pondering all this change and transformation made the doctor both lament to himself and celebrate the perseverance of this tribe. Yet he understood the decision of someone who wanted to set a course for a more prosperous shore. At her vigil, hopeless, of course, but one in which he tried all that he knew about medicine that might change the course of the old Hebrew woman's decline, he encountered unfamiliar complexity in the person of Old Dou, the crone of darker hue who as an infant had arrived on a slave ship before anyone else in the household. (In the middle of a storm at sea she had slipped out from between her mother's legs, and after her mother had died of dysentery some weeks later spent the rest of the voyage being passed along among the strongest of the remaining women, and some of the men.)

So here she was, the African woman, the first time the doctor had spied her, hovering over her old mistress's body, drawing her hands along the lines of her arteries and veins. When the doctor, about to apply leeches, asked what she was doing, she explained that she was using the power in her hands to smooth out the flow of the old woman's blood.

"Up north, not so many years ago," the doctor said, drawing on some lore he had acquired during his medical training in Massachusetts, "someone might call what you are doing witchcraft."

Old Dou looked him hard in the eyes, not an act a slave made without serious decision at that time, and then laughed.

"I am a witch, yes, and you are another."

The doctor ignored what she said about him and asked her to show him what she was doing and explain why. A few minutes passed while she talked about the blood river in the old woman's body and how sun, moon, sky, and certain stars could change the course of the body's flow, as directed in the hands of someone like herself.

The doctor listened in fascination, but in the end he went along on his own way, employed his training, and bled the old woman. This seemed to have kept her alive for a few days, but then without more than a whisper, with the entire family gathered around her bed while the doctor and Old Dou stood off to one side, she expelled through her lips a single bubble of air and passed away.

And what had all of this to do with the little girl child who lay murmuring in the basket in the single room of the shack behind the big house where Old Dou, her stature long ago elevated beyond that of the field hands, had been allowed to sleep and live? Well, it had all to do with the old African woman herself, who had, while Lyaza's mother had passed from pregnancy to birth—and young girlhood, we have to say, to womanhood, in the throes of her murderous labor—listened to the tormented woman's stories, sometimes garbled, sometimes lucid, about her passage, and her family back in the forest and back further still into the desert land where they had first come to awareness of themselves. Her (old African) religion helped her to understand the meanness, if not wickedness, of the slaveholder's way of seeing, because she understood that all life on earth, from scorpions to mayflies and everything in between, every stone and rock, flowing stream, and cloud, and tree and plant, and certainly every living creature above that level of life, was filled with god, each one had a spirit, some smaller, others greater, and that it was no slander—as the slaveholders often depicted it—to think of us having descended from the large animals that lived in trees and foraged for food on the ground, and fought, and mated, and nursed and raised their children, and even laughed and played nearly as we still do, when sorrowful occasions pass us by, rather than saying only Africans came down in the world that way, and were not truly human, while the slaveholders, Christians almost all of them—with a few exceptions, such as the Pereiras—were made directly by their god, or passed down in a line from the angels above.

See what this woman held in her hand just before the birth of that child! A stone, marked at some distant moment in the dark or light or invisible past! Where had it come from? Was it witchcraft? How did Old Dou find it? Had Lyaa handed it to her before she went into labor? Or did she find it, when it was forced out of the center of the mad, young girl's body during childbirth, just before the new girl-child arrived into the light of a Carolina summer morning? The foundation stone, a pebble yet a boulder, mysteriously carried in the body, first mineral of earliest creation, now it saw the light again.

The doctor held this stone up and studied it, before Old Dou asked him for it.

"I'll keep it for the girl 'til she's grown," the African woman said. "It's like hearing the true stories of the old country," she said. "It is a piece of the old country, a piece of the first world on earth..."

Chapter Thirty-nine

"Abraham Seixas"

The Oaks
Goosecreek
South Carolina
My dearest Miriam:

Though it has been several weeks now since I saw you at the pier, I can still hear the music of the band and I can still picture your charming face before me, far below, down there in the crowd, yet still close to me. Of course I must admit from the moment that we lost sight of the Battery, life began to change for me in many other ways. We sailed down the Arthur Kill and put in at Perth Amboy, where I was overwhelmed with emotion, because there in that town my mother first took sick, and there we had our last good time together. After Perth Amboy, we headed south, hugging the coast, and after some days reaching the delightful port of Charleston, here in South Carolina.

I cannot tell you how different it is here from New York. Beginning with the air itself, which is a not-so-delightful mixture of warm water and various natural perfumes. Here and all around a certain stillness has overtaken men, though surely only for the moment. The odor of the port, the odor of horses, these are familiar. But out in the country, which is where I write you from, the land is hot, damp, and marshy, and the sky is laden with large thunderheads that float above us, never stopping, like some grand oceangoing armada. Even inland about fifteen miles, water is everything. As I write to you I must pause and take a sip from the glass at my writing table. In the rice fields the "driver," as the one who drives the labor force is called, must work the small dams that keep water from the creek out or, opened, let it in, to flow across the newly growing stalks of this precious grain. There is a rhythm to it which has been explained to me and over the past week or so I have seen a number of demonstrations, though I have not yet mastered it.

Even though I am a Master.

Will you be my Slave?

A jest.

Isaac is the slave who serves as the overseer in the rice fields. He is one of three "drivers," working in the brickyard and the other fieldwork and wood-cutting cadres. He has been in charge of showing me how the rice-planting is done. Though we do not always get along, for a slave—but listen to me talk!—he is a proud, almost arrogant sort of fellow—yet I have found him to be the most knowledgeable person on the plantation when it comes to the agricultural questions.

The overseer is usually a free man, but Uncle has put Isaac in charge because he commands the respect of all the others and is completely loyal to the family. I hear stories about cranky and rebellious slaves who must be severely disciplined in order to keep them in line. But on our plantation—well, look what I have written! "our"!—on Uncle's plantation firmness and kindness seems to work just as well as physical punishment and the kind of disdain and spite that seems to rule in other places.

For an example of the other sort I can tell you about what we witnessed when on a sojourn to town—Charleston—just the other day.

We had come in to have lunch with the family of my cousin Jonathan's wife Rebecca and it was a very agreeable time in their house on Society Street, only a few blocks from the water. The house is a three-story wood and white-washed-brick affair, with the face that it shows to the street wearing a rather blank brick stare. The entrance is reached by a walk through a gate to the left of the façade and a short path to the steps leading to a wide veranda that sweeps around the west side of the house and looks out on a lovely garden which is blocked from sight from the street by tall hedges and a rather majestic magnolia tree.

On the veranda when we arrived was a large black woman—she

could be the sister of Precious Sally who cooks at The Oaks plantation—sweeping the floor. She greeted us warmly, and invited us inside, where Rebecca's mother and father were waiting in the front sitting room. The room reminded me a good deal of home, because it had curtains that cut out the light and noise of the street, and many family portraits on the walls, and several sets of silver candlesticks. Rebecca's father, Louis Salvador, was the son of one of the first Jews to serve in the army of our Continental Congress during the Revolutionary War. Her mother, born Elena Suares, was the child of two immigrants from the Indies.

"We arrived with nothing," she said. "And now we have everything."

And, indeed, if you count the pretty house and garden and the many sets of candlesticks, and dishes and paintings and silverware, and their children, with Rebecca the oldest and three younger brothers, Joseph, Louis, and Abraham, and their business—fine clothing for the town gentry—they do hold quite a store of wonderful possessions. Oh, yes, and this includes the woman who was sweeping the porch when we arrived, and a cook, and two male slaves who worked the yard here and inside the house and two others who worked in the store.

Two of Rebecca's brothers serve in the store with their father, an elderly man with long white curls dangling down on either side of his head, while the third is an attorney who was recently elected to the state legislature. This was Joseph, a tall, red-haired fellow with a wide nose that gave the appearance of having been flattened with the backside of a spoon. Sitting next to him on the veranda was his wife Jessica, a buxom woman with sand-colored hair, and two children, a boy and a girl, who reminded me of the way the two of us used to be. Also in attendance, a cousin of Rebecca's, a dark haired girl, whom we met at the synagogue the Sabbath before.

To entertain me at the gathering Rebecca's father wanted his grandchildren to show off their talents.

"Say the poem for our guest, darlings," he urged them.

"Oh, Father," Rebecca said in protest, "do not force them."

"Of course they will recite," her brother, the father of the children, said.

At his bidding, they stood and turned to me, smiling, as if quite familiar with the art of performance, and the boy announced, "This is a picture in words of one of our old people, Abraham Seixas."

"If he ever really existed," Rebecca said.

"Of course he did," her father said. "I knew him."

"Of course, you knew him," said his wife. "You knew everybody. Now let them just say the poem, darling, and be done with it."

"This is a poem," my host said to me, "that will make you see a lot of who we are." He gestured toward his grandchildren, as if he were about to conduct a band. "Children?"

They stood, and the boy bowed toward us and announced the poem.

"Abraham Seixas."

The pair began reciting.

Abraham Seixas,
All so gracious,
Once again does offer
His service pure
For to secure
Money in the coffer...

"It's a portrait," my host said.

"You told him that," said his wife.

"Children, go on," said my host.

"Father," Rebecca said, "not this next part. It's too..."

"Rebecca," said my cousin Jonathan, "respect your father."

She looked at me, I looked to the children.

He has for sale
Some Negroes, male,
Will suit full well grooms,
He has likewise
Some of their wives
Can make clean, dirty rooms...

"It is…silly and hurtful," Rebecca said, looking at me. She turned to her cousin. "Don't you think so, Anna?"

Her cousin shook her head.

"It is silly," she said.

"It is mean," Rebecca said.

"Rebecca, hush," Jonathan said. "Let them finish."

"It is just beginning," Rebecca said. "Father?"

My host ignored her, directing the children to go on.

For planting, too,
He has a few
To sell, all for the cash,
Of various price,
To work the rice
Or bring them to the lash.
The young ones true,
If that will do,
May some be had of him
To learn your trade
They may be made,
Or bring them to your trim.

"Have you heard enough?" Rebecca said to me.

But I did not wish to be an ungracious guest, and so I shook my head, while the children raced along in their sing-song fashion.

The boatmen great.
Will you elate
They are so brisk and free;
What e'er you say,
They will obey,
If you buy them of me.
He also can
Suit any man
With land all o'er the State;
A bargain, sure,
They may procure

If they don't stay too late.
For paper he
Will sure agree,
Bond, note or public debt;
To sell the same
If with good name
Any buyer can be met.
To such of those
As will dispose
He begs of them to tell;
By not or phiz,
What e'er it is
That they have got to sell.
He surely will
Try all his skill
To sell, for more or less,
The articles
Of beaux and belles,
That they to him address.

They bowed, and we applauded and went in to lunch.

At table the father of the children, Rebecca's brother Joseph, the red-haired legislator, having had just returned from the capital was dishing out a plateful of news about battles in the governing body in Columbia.

"The struggle now is between those who want to nullify and those who talk secession," he said.

Rebecca's father announced that he had always been in favor of nullification as long as it did not lead to secession.

"Tariffs are never good for me," he said. "It makes all of my imported cloths cost extra. And my prices go up."

"You are arguing a practical point," said his son. "My colleagues in Columbia put forward nullification because they would desire to have us make our own laws and regulations, in other words, create our own union. It is the first step."

"Ah, yes," his father said, "because they want to preserve our peculiar institution no matter what the law of the nation."

"Father," Rebecca spoke up, "you call it peculiar but whom do we have cooking our lunch just this moment?"

"That's what I mean," her father said. "To me this is very peculiar."

"That's why I had my vision," Rebecca said. "Because it is all so peculiar."

"Your vision," her father said. Then turning to look directly at me. "You know about her vision?

I nodded, preferring to keep my silence.

But next he said, "And what do you think of it?"

I looked down into my glass and took a breath.

"Peculiar," I said, and we all laughed together.

"But you do think she is right?" her father said.

"I don't know enough about the way things are down here," I said.

"The way things are? They are what they are, sir. They are the way the Lord intended them to be. *Selah, selah.*"

"Father," Rebecca said.

"Do we want to discuss this?" Jonathan said.

"All we have is what we talk about," Rebecca's father said.

"We have God's laws and man's laws," her brother put in. "If God had solved everything, why do we need a legislature?"

"Yes, you have a point," said our host. Turning to me, "But I am interested in our guest's view of things."

"His view of us?" Jonathan said. "He thinks we are queer folk. With our strange ways. He is, of course, a Jew himself. But Yankee Jews seem to be different from us."

"And what is that difference?" said our host.

"They don't own slaves." He paused, licked his lips in anticipation of what he was going to say next, and then said it. "Yet."

Everyone at table laughed at that, at me, except for Rebecca. Jonathan meanwhile refilled his wine glass, something which I had not noticed he had been doing since we sat down at table.

"You all are being horrible," Rebecca said. "Horrible rude and horrible, just plain horrible."

"I will take back what I said," Jonathan spoke up. "They will never have slavery in the north. It is too cold, I hear, much too cold for an African population to survive."

"Perhaps," I said, "if they have a choice between slavery and warm weather and freedom and cold weather, they might still wrap themselves in warm coats and choose freedom."

"A good point," put in our host. "And do you think they will have a choice?"

"If your daughter's plan, or vision, whatever you call it, works, they will."

"It never will work," he said.

"Father!" Rebecca was insulted.

"It won't," he said. "You might educate the occasional genius of a slave. But as they are like most other people, geniuses are few and far between. Most of them are condemned to a life of ordinary servitude."

"Do you really believe that, sir?" I said.

"I do," he said. "But what do you believe, young man? Are these black slaves educable, do you think?"

"I...I do not know enough of them to say."

"Well, sir, you must live here a while with us and find out for yourself."

"That is exactly what he is doing," said my uncle. "He is making a study of it."

"To what end?" asked our host. "Are you aiming to become a scientist and study our skulls, Jews and slaves alike?"

"No, sir," I said. "I am here because my father, my uncle's brother, asked me to come and investigate plantation life."

"Investigate? Oh, sir, that makes it sound quite serious, as though we are part of some sort of crime. Investigate, to what end?"

"He is thinking of ways to invest, sir," I said.

"A good Jew," our host said.

"He is trying to help his business, sir," I said.

"And that is?"

"Sir, it is import-export."

"Does he buy and sell slaves?"

"No, sir, not now. Only lifeless goods."

"Very good, very good. But he may yet. Is that what he is asking you to investigate?"

My uncle broke in.

"My brother has many irons in the fire," he said. "He and I have had a correspondence. Let us say that he is quite interested in what we do here, because he himself may choose to become part of it."

"Well, he is a wise man to look before he leaps. There is no greater sorrow than to enter into a business about which you know nothing. Especially if it is a business that deals in human lives."

"Yes, they are human," Jonathan said, as if he were talking to himself and himself alone.

"Jonathan, what are you saying?" I could hear the anger in Rebecca's voice.

"Nothing, I am saying nothing. Ignore me, Rebecca. I was speaking loosely."

"Many hold the same view," said my uncle. "Just as they think that way of us."

"Yes, Jonathan," Rebecca said, "do you wish others to think of you in this fashion?"

"Frankly, I don't care what others think. As long as I am free." He glanced over at me, catching me in my fascination with all this going on before me. "What do you think, Cousin?"

"About what?"

"What do you think about slaves? Are they human? Or are they another species? Or perhaps even akin to inert articles, such as furniture. I could, if I like, sit upon a slave and he would not complain as I am his master." Deep in his throat he made a sound, something like a laugh, but slightly more sinister, as if since knowing that no one else would find his comments comical that he would have to laugh all on his own.

"Jonathan!" Rebecca stood up from the table.

"Please sit, darling," Jonathan said. "We are having an interesting discussion."

He gestured, and she slowly seated herself again. "Cuz?"

"I don't know enough about slaves," I said. "From a distance, they appear to be perfectly human."

"Or imperfectly," my uncle said.

"Yes," I said in agreement. "No better, no worse, than the rest of us."

"Just unlucky at birth?" My cousin seemed almost to be taunting me.

"As you say, no more and no less than other people."

"But other people are not slaves," said Jonathan.

"Jonathan," Rebecca said, "other people might say the same of us."

"That Jews are not lucky or that Jews are not human?"

"We once were born slaves and now we are free," Rebecca said. "It proves to me that those born black slaves may one day gain their freedom."

"Easy to say for someone who grew up in town," Jonathan said. "But where would our plantation be without their labor?"

"Then there should be no plantation," Rebecca said. "What do you think, Anna?" she asked of her cousin.

Anna looked at me, of all people, as if I might give her direction. But I said nothing.

"Children," our host's wife said, "don't quarrel. It is not good for the married life." She then turned to her son and asked about recent events in Columbia.

Rebecca's brother talked about the Jews in the legislature and how much the Gentile members depended on them.

"Because we defend our way of life here," he said. "And we were once slaves ourselves…"

"More evidence for the peculiar," Rebecca said.

"Why do you talk that way?" Her mother shook her head. "It is a miracle, Rebecca, that you found a man as good as Jonathan, when you talk like such a…a…"

"Sport?" I said.

"Sport? And what is that?"

"A changeling," I said. "Rebecca's ideas are ahead of her time. Ahead of our time."

"She is a bold girl," Jonathan said, "and I admire her."

"Thank you, my darling," Rebecca said.

Now, dear Miriam, I have to tell you that two strange things occurred during the course of this visit, neither of which I have yet described. The first such thing happened after I asked where I might wash up before leaving for our drive back to The Oaks and Rebecca directed me to a water closet toward the rear of the house.

"Can you find your way back, Cousin?" she said, rather playfully.

"I believe I can," I said.

She then left me to close the door to the little room. After making my toilet I wandered on my return to the front of the house, passing a small sitting room from which I heard voices.

"You are not feeling well?" A woman spoke, whose voice I did not immediately recognize.

"I cannot go on," I heard a woman say. This was my cousin Rebecca, speaking in a voice so tormented that I nearly did not recognize it. Whatever playfulness she might have feigned while speaking to me had disappeared.

"What choice do you have?" This, I now understood, was her cousin Anna.

"None," Rebecca said.

"That is right," Anna said.

"I...I spoke to Mother."

"And what did she say?"

"She said, this is our lot. And I should not complain anymore, it would not be good for my child."

"The father of whom..."

"Yes?"

"...is the father of whom?"

"You make a joke, Anna, and I wish that I could laugh."

"I am sorry, Cousin. I do not care to make you feel any worse than you already do. It would not be good for your child."

"My child..." Rebecca's voice dropped away, almost to the inaudible. I leaned closer and listened hard.

"I wish that I had no child coming."

"Rebecca!"

"I do sometimes wish that."

"Please, please," her cousin said. "Let us speak of other things."

Rebecca seemed to recover herself almost at once.

"Do you mean...?"

"Yes, I do."

"He seems like a gentleman."

"I do like the way he carries himself."

"And you would like for him to carry you away to New York?"

Even as I felt myself begin to blush I heard the rustling of skirts and hurried away from the door, thinking back to her walk through the dark on the way to the cabins while continuing on to the front of the house where the rest of the party waited for me. Rebecca and Anna soon returned as well and we made our farewells.

And now I must tell you of the second incident, something that you will find awful and revolting, and so I suggest that you set this letter down and put it aside if you fear being horrified and affronted. I apologize in advance for the awful picture it gives, something that soundly jarred the stillness I mentioned when I first began this missive.

As we were driving along the Battery (for who cannot resist a last turn along this wonderful avenue, with the park of trees on one side and the ocean on the other side of the sea wall), we saw a commotion up ahead. A carriage had just run off the road, apparently because of some fault and distraction of the horse, and sat up on the grass, with the animal, a huge chestnut gelding, now docile in front of it, head bent, nibbling at the local flowers. Just as we approached, the driver, a man dressed all in black with top hat and silvery-white hair down to his shoulders (I instantly recognized him as a man who had boarded our ship in Perth Amboy on our way south) leaped down from his seat, raised his arm high and beat at the horse with his whip.

The animal lifted its head and whinnied in pain.

Whup! Again, the man slashed at the beast across the eyes.

"Dumb!" he cried out. "You, dumb!"

Again he slashed, and the horse whined, and tried to pull away, carriage and all, but the man had grabbed at its traces with his free hand and kept slashing with the other.

From the stoop of a house across the park, where he had been sweeping the pavement, a slave came running, waving his broom and shouting.

"Stop!" Jonathan called out.

At first I thought he meant to shout this to the man beating the horse, but when he called out again I understood that he meant for the slave to halt.

But the black man kept on running, and without a pause, reached the man and horse, and pulled the whip from the man's hand.

The man reached down for the whip, and the slave shoved him away. As the man stumbled back onto the green the slave rushed to the bewildered horse, taking up his reins and running a hand across his mane.

Which gave the silver-haired man in black time to pick himself up and grab his instrument and advance to the slave, slashing the African across the back of the neck. Still holding the reins of the horse, the slave turned again.

Whup! The whipper slashed again. Blood spurted from the black man's head, and he dropped the reins and grabbed his hands to his neck.

Whup! The slave staggered, the horse gave a whinny and walked away, leaving the black man to take yet another slash, this time across his hands and face.

"Enough, sir!" shouted my cousin, standing on the carriage box. "Enough!"

The whipper turned, and gave us all a broad smile, showing us his bright teeth, and, seeming to recognize me, making a little bow before turning to give the slave—amazing that the poor wretch still stood upright—one more slash of the whip before the black man fell to his knees, and then fell further, face forward upon the grass.

Another man came running across the green wearing nothing but trousers, a white shirt, and suspenders.

"Dastard!" he called out.

Upon reaching the horse, he took up the reins and looked down at the fallen slave.

"You have done injury to my property! I shall have you in court, sir! Do you understand me?"

The two men began to quarrel, and Jonathan sat down again on the box and coaxed our horse into moving.

"Stop," I said, "we must stay and assist him."

"It is not our business," Jonathan said.

"We are witnesses," I said, looking back to where the two men stood arguing over the fallen slave—blood gathered about his head—while the horse had taken to nibbling again as the grass. "I know that man."

"You know him? We will be impugned," Jonathan said.

"Why?"

"Because we are Jews," he said.

"We are men first," I said.

"Speak for yourself," said my cousin, laughing again that same strange laugh as he urged our horse to pick up speed. I myself wanted to race away, oh, I wanted to put all of this strange land behind me. [For a number of reasons, of course, I did not send this letter.]

Chapter Forty

Study

*I*n the short time I have spent at The Oaks I have learned a number of interesting things about life here, beginning with the hierarchy of the slaves. In the house Black Jack ruled, like a ship's captain, and Precious Sally, though she had many privileges, stood just below him in rank. Then came Liza, who served my aunt as a personal maid, and attended to such other chores in the house as Black Jack and Precious Sally called upon her to do, which apparently gave her the freedom to move about the house and grounds at all hours. Like members of the family itself, all of them were always present, passing in and out of the rooms, particularly at mealtime, but certainly visible and moving about the house most other times of day.

And it was clear, from the way they carried themselves, that they held positions of authority, even though it was just as apparent that they remained servile to the wishes of my uncle and aunt, and Jonathan and Rebecca, and even young Abraham. They hardly ever spoke, except when spoken to, and never ever raised their voices the way a normal person might, if engaged in a serious conversation with someone about a moment of apparent importance, not even when Abraham raised his.

Although sometimes they found their patience tried.

As when, say, I heard my aunt, who was speaking to Liza while unaware that I was sitting on the veranda reading just outside the door, say to her in a tone usually reserved in our New York society for coachmen speaking to their horses or parents to recalcitrant children.

"Now you know how I like to see this silver?"

"Yes, ma'am."

"And do you see your reflection in the knife?"

"Not clearly, ma'am."

"And should you see your reflection in the candlesticks just as bright as day?"

"Yes, ma'am."

"Then, girl, polish them again and bring it back to me."

"Yes, ma'am."

Or when Abraham rudely shouted down the stairs for his boots, which were somewhere in the house after having been repaired.

"Ma?" he called out.

Black Jack went to the bottom of the stairs and called up to him, that, young massa, his mother had gone out. Abraham sent a curse down the steps suitable more for a grouchy old man than a young boy.

Black Jack demurred, and fetched his boots.

Nor did Black Jack raise his voice when my cousin Jonathan, who, by now I had come to recognize, seemed to vacillate between two temperaments when it came to slaves, burst into the house one afternoon—I was sitting on the veranda, reading reports of the last five years' rice harvest supplied to me by my uncle—and shouted for the house man.

"You ignorant bastard, that horse has not been watered! I asked you to tell Isaac, did I not?" My cousin slammed something onto the floor—his riding whip or a hat, I couldn't see, just heard the thwupping noise as it hit—and charged outside again.

"Damned stupid nigger," he said, catching my eye. "How am I going to run this place one day with nothing but these damned stupid niggers..."

He stomped off toward the barns.

(All the while in this, Black Jack kept his calm. More than that, back inside the house I heard him humming to himself.)

But if the house slaves were treated with a mixture of disdain and the grudging respect born of necessity, the slaves who commanded the field niggers, as my cousin called them, held a place in trust about as high as the house slaves, while the field niggers—and there were eighty or ninety of them, by my uncle's count—were regarded as something just above the animals.

Thus it was quite strange—though just how strange I did not know until later—when of a Saturday afternoon on the veranda Rebecca gathered her group together for Bible study. She had chosen Black Jack, Precious Sally, the girl Liza, Isaac (whom I took to be Liza's paramour), and four or five young men who worked the fields.

Some of the house slaves possessed their own Bibles, having once belonged to Gentile families and thus instructed in the Christian way. For those who didn't have a Bible, Rebecca had copied out the text for discussion, Exodus 3, verses one through five.

She handed these to those who needed them and then said to all of us gathered there:

"Today the subject of our discussion is the story of how the Hebrew people were rescued by God from their bondage in Egypt. Here were the Israelites having been sold into slavery, and their leader Moses is given a sign." She turned to me and asked if I would like to read.

"Me?" I had rested my eyes on Liza's sandy brow and so was distracted.

"You are the guest," she said, handing me a Bible with the place marked.

"Thank you, you are being very kind, Rebecca."

I glanced at the slaves, who were regarding us as though we were a Saturday afternoon entertainment. Holding the Book before me, I swallowed hard, cleared my throat.

"'Now Moses was tending the flock of Jethro, his father-in-law, the priest of Midian, and he led the flock to the far edge of the wilderness and he came to the mountain of God, to Horeb...'"

"Where's 'at?" one of the field slaves asked another, who shrugged and pretended he was still listening intently.

Rebecca shot him a school-teacherly-like glance, and signaled me to continue my reading.

"'And a messenger of God appeared to him in a blazing fire from out of a bush. And he looked and behold: A bush was burning but the bush was not consumed. Moses said, "I must turn aside to look at this incredible sight. Why does not the bush burn up?" And when God saw that he had turned aside to look God called to him from out of the bush, "Moses! Moses!" And he answered, "Here am I." And He said, "Do not come closer. Remove your sandals from your feet, for the place on which you are standing is holy ground."'"

"Thank you, Cousin," Rebecca said, taking the Bible from my hand. "Who would like to read next?"

Isaac, his jaw tilted up in a pose of challenge, gave a nod of his dark head.

"Go on," Rebecca said.

The slave lifted his copy of the Bible and began to read in a clear steady voice with scarcely an error in his pronunciation. My eyes remained on

Liza, her near-pale skin and her own blue-green eyes, and my mind began
to drift. This was more attention to the Bible than I had given it since I was
a boy and tutored by my Halevi. After Isaac finished his passage, Rebecca
asked several of the field hands to try, and these were much less agile at
their reading.

I was beginning to get bored, when Rebecca interrupted one of the
young men, a heavy boy, his skin dark as swamp water in the shade, as he
was stumbling about with the page.

"Jacob, do you understand what you're reading?"

"Yes, missus," he said.

"Can you explain it to the rest of us?"

"No, missus," he said.

"Then you don't truly understand it, do you?"

"It's a lot of story 'bout freedom," he said. "But I don't know no none
of it."

"One day you will."

"That's what the Jesus folks say," one of the other hands spoke up.

"What do they say?" Rebecca asked him.

"They say, we die, and then we free." He made a loud noise with his
lips and everyone smiled in his direction.

"And what do we say?" Rebecca nodded for him to keep speaking.

"Jews say, we free until we die."

"Life is everything, yes," Rebecca said.

"And one day…"

The boy spoke up in a manner that I had never heard a slave employ.

"And one day?" Rebecca urged him on.

Now he appeared to be slightly embarrassed by all the attention we
were giving him. But he spoke anyway.

"And one day we'll be free in this life, in this world."

"And the key to this door?"

The boy smiled, showing a mouth empty except for three or four
wooden teeth.

"The Book," he said.

"The Book, yes," Rebecca said. "This Book, and all books. Reading
will make you free."

At which point she passed her copy of the book to Liza, who picked up
where the darker boy had left off.

"Exodus, thirteen, verses fourteen through sixteen," Liza announced. "'And when, in the future,'" she began, "'your child asks you and says, "What is this happening here?" you shall say to your child [she looked up, and she stared directly at me but neither smiled nor acknowledged me in any other way], "With a strong hand God brought us out of Egypt, from the house of bondage. When Pharaoh's [she said "ph-haro" and Rebecca corrected her] heart was hardened against letting us leave, God killed every first-born in the land of Egypt, from the first-born of human to the first-born of beast. Therefore I now sacrifice to God every first male issue of the womb, but redeem every first-born among my sons." And so it shall be for a sign upon your hand and for frontlets between your eyes that with a strong hand God brought us out from Egypt...'"

I watched her all the while she read, noticing the way her lips scarcely moved, and the grace with which she held the Book. It was a remarkable event that I was witness to, the readings by these slaves on the subject of recovering the freedom of a people who had been in chains in Egypt. That it was my own people who had won their freedom charged the reading with seriousness, and that it was part of my family that owned these slaves who were reading about freedom made the event even more remarkable to me. And that I spent most of this hour studying the face and neck and collarbone and slender chest and arms of Liza made it a most memorable event as well.

As the hour ended I said to her as quietly as I could, "My cousin Rebecca has taught you well."

She gave me a quick smile and said, "I have another teacher, also, a doctor."

I nodded, not knowing what else to do or say, wondering, wondering, if Liza were *my* slave, would I set her free?

Chapter Forty-one

Half-light, Half-dark

The child Lyaza grew, and the doctor, who had been a fairly young man when she was born, found himself noticing certain signs in his own life that demonstrated to him that he, too, was growing older. As the child turned handsprings in front of Old Dou's cabin, the doctor heard the noise of his own clacking joints. The child ate the simple meals provided for her by Old Dou and the field hands as though she were more breathing air than taking in food while his own digestion fell on hard times. He lost weight, his stomach growled and sometimes howled. When the girl reached a certain age she was allowed by Old Dou to wander about the house during the day and eat the scraps from the family's table. Sometimes a guest at that table, the doctor admired the way the girl ate anything Dou or the cook handed to her.

This girl gave off light, life, stars in her eyes!

The doctor, who was married but without issue, felt her as a mild magnetic force. He watched her play, and when he stopped in at Old Dou's cabin once or twice a month to see how the child was faring, he sometimes watched her with her eyes closed in sleep, dreaming of who knows what kind of freedoms that might set her apart from the daily round of the plantation. At times like this he recalled what when he first saw it he recognized as aberrant behavior, the young master's baby-babbling over the infant girl. This little thing, wraith-like and so charming, also wandered through his thoughts in idle hours. So innocent she was of her condition, it gave him pause to consider how even a slave might seem to herself somehow free if she was not aware of her own perpetually indentured state. Perhaps all of us live this way, he considered, wrapped in chains and yet thinking ourselves free. And was that a kind of freedom after all, or just an illusion of living without chains?

Free men are often the worst, he decided, noticing with his clinical eye over the course of several months of visits to The Oaks that the plantation owner's son appeared to have kept his attachment to the slave girl, which by this time the doctor found to be quite bizarre, prowling about the house, trying to look innocent even as he tracked little Lyaza, who often played alongside Dou while the woman worked. Over the course of several years his great interest, in the doctor's eyes, clearly took an aberrant turn. It seemed to come out of nowhere, though the doctor knew that whatever physical abnormality he might discover in a patient, there was usually a cause buried somewhere deep in the man's history. Although sometimes, as it might possibly could be with Jonathan Pereira, the illness remained inexplicable. Illness! Thus the doctor named it, based on his observations, but an illness that revealed itself as more spiritual or mental than physical. Here was a man so caught up in the movements and sounds of this child that he seemed no more free than metal splinters in the field of a magnet. Whenever the doctor saw them together Jonathan fluttered about the child in such an embarrassing thrall of attraction that the doctor could only look away, if not leave the room, whenever he saw him at his game.

Just as he had in that moment of her birth, when Jonathan babbled over the girl's head, "Weety-sweety, sweety-weety…"

Was it that he had happened by accident to have been present at her birth and somehow felt a special link to her?

The doctor considered that as a possibility. But without speaking to Jonathan, always too busy anyway either with work or with his silly prattling over the slave child, he could not say for sure. Who knew what he wanted? That was the doctor's sense of things at first. Did the young man himself know what he wanted? The odd light in his eye, the slight quavering of his tongue when he opened his mouth to breathe, the hitch in his motion before he approached the girl as if with some purpose before suddenly halting just short of her and turning away to stare at some distant point on the ceiling or through the window—these hints at his state gave the doctor pause. He feared that he knew more about what the man wanted than the man did himself.

And so, against his better judgment as a physician who believed his profession meant observing and deducing, not introducing himself into the situation at hand, whenever he was present he tried to intervene, coming between the girl and the man as best he could without crossing the line into rudeness.

"Perhaps Lyaza would like to show me her doll collection," he would say, allowing the slave child to lead him to where her makeshift play-toys lay in rows behind the pallet where she slept.

There they would sit and she would babble on about which doll had what name and what her duty was around the plantation.

The owner's son stood over them, as if on guard.

"Oh, little weety-sweety, sweety-weety, show the doctor your dolls..."

It was embarrassing to hear a grown man behave this way.

"Sweety-weety, little weety-sweety..."

The man, behaving in such foolish fashion, sounded more like someone caught in some net of his own unknown devising—the doctor really had no name he could put on it—than a grown man tending to one of his own properties.

But then who am I to judge? the doctor said to himself. There appeared to be little harm in all this, just the embarrassing foolishness of it all. Also, he could not stay here and focus on it. Always it came time for the doctor to leave: he had to make his rounds and then return to town for his regular practice. Now and then he would allow himself to consider what Jonathan might be doing in his absence. The child herself, to look at her, enjoyed his attention. The doctor could only hope that all was innocent. And after Jonathan's wife had a boy child, the doctor decided that that was that was that. The man now had offspring of his own and would tend in the natural direction of raising the boy.

This, however, did not happen, at least not in any way that the doctor could observe. As the girl's body changed over time and she lurched into adolescence with the beginnings of breasts and jutting hips, she drew all of Jonathan's visible attention even as his young son cleaved to his mother, estranged, because of his father's behavior, from the paternal realm. The girl played on, oblivious to the nature of Jonathan's interest, merely enjoying all the attention he gave her.

Old Dou, who had much earlier recognized his behavior as obsession, tried to stand between them.

This she could do while the girl remained a child. As she grew older, Lyaza found that she had the freedom to run about the grounds and play by herself in various nooks and crannies of the big house and the nearby outbuildings. Old Dou could not keep up with her.

Not so the plantation owner's son. He ran with the girl, and ran some more, even after his own family duties became, with the birth of his own son, pressing, and even after, when his wife left him and returned home.

"Oh, sweety! Sweety-weety! Wait for me!"

You could hear him calling to the girl as they ran about the back of the house, around the barns and back to the house.

The older Master Pereira had a blind-spot when it came to Jonathan. He wasn't a bad man, no, not at all. He also did not pay much attention to his family, having given himself over completely to the administering of those who administered his little rice-growing kingdom. He was unusual in that he kept the doctor on call for his family and for the property, which is to say, the slave people. Most plantation owners let the Africans tend to themselves until and unless some injury or illness grew well beyond the point of mere maintenance and repair.

"My watchword," he declared once or twice over that sherry he and the doctor occasionally drank together, "is health, the health of our rice-farming, the health of our people…"

What did he mean by "people"? the doctor wondered the first time he heard that.

Did he mean his own family, his co-religionists—the tiniest of minorities in this countryside, though in town a fair number of his "people" congregated on the Sabbath and prayed in the beautiful if sparely decorated synagogue (he had been a guest there and observed its austere façade and interior).

The Jews, the few he knew, always impressed him with their business acumen and their concern for the quality of their wares. The master had grown up in the Caribbean, he explained to the doctor, and while his family had not owned any human goods—he called slaves that—he had observed a number of plantation owners and their operations. And here, in retrospect, as the doctor recalled this conversation in light of the worrisome—because it was worrisome, no matter how much he tried to discount it—behavior of the man's son, things grew quite interesting.

"My people, you see," the man said to him, "themselves lived in bondage in Babylon, and so knew the heady stuff of freedom when they achieved it. Unlike the Africans we now own, they did not have to travel far to labor for others with no recompense."

"Egypt was not far?"

The doctor decided that he would engage the man, whom he normally spoke with only about the medical conditions of family members, and slave retinue. Why should he not? Such interesting views the man had.

"Not in terms of land and landscape. Quite similar to, say, Judea."

"And so, Babylon the same?"

"Quite the same."

"Whereas here, in our Carolina, the land differs greatly, yes, I see that. But your further argument?"

"These creatures are adrift," the master said. "So far from home, they cannot, surely cannot find a moral compass or master the situations in which they find themselves."

"And so we give them the comfort of food and the vocation of laboring and so bring them a certain order?"

"Well said," the master said. "Have you been reading the same German authors as me? Von Herder and such?"

"No, no," the doctor said, "I don't read many Germans. I am just thinking about what you are thinking, and I decided that this must be your thought."

"Yes, it is, as you heard, and heard correctly. We do bring this disorderly and dislocated group of people some order and tie them to a place."

"Yes, sometimes literally tie them," the doctor said with a laugh.

When at last he walked away from this conversation, which had begun as a discussion about one thing and ended about another, he felt a bit of shame about that laugh.

But then he wasn't so much concerned about the maintenance of his own soul but focused all of his working energy, and a great deal of his thought, on the health and physical welfare of others. His flaws, and he had some, did he not? (he chided himself for an hour or so about that laugh), seemed few in comparison to all the good he did. Not that he focused much on what he did either. He simply performed his labor as he was trained to perform it, and so kept his patients as healthy as he possibly could. Some, of course, grew sick and died. It was a wise doctor who knew that he could do little to prevent the forward-teetering patient with an ailment well on its way to carrying him off. Mainly he tried to keep the majority of the people he saw—including the slaves—on the path to a balance of work and some comfort, even if, in the case of the slaves, it meant an often explosive few hours just before the Sabbath, the only time they truly had to themselves.

All of this—what he probably thought of as his philosophy, though he never called it such—he put into a notebook bound in cow-hide and whose pages he kept from everyone else, even his wife, which, by the time of his first encounter with the Africans on the auction block in town, meant no one. The invisible hand of an illness—the slaves called it The Visitor—swept over the county and his wife had died of it suddenly, one of those patients to whom he could only give comfort rather than aid. Since they had had no children—he was too busy, he convinced himself, delivering other people's children to have time for another marriage of his own, let alone children—the notebook rested in a drawer in his house in town unnoticed by anyone except for himself, the writer of it.

How many such books, he wondered aloud, *languished unknown or mostly unread in various desks and cabinets in Charleston alone?* Here might be the hidden history of this difficult time in which he found himself alive, born into a system that educated and rewarded him, and turned others into chattel. He vowed to keep on writing, though no one would read his entries. At least in this way, he decided by his action, he would record his views on the strangeness and oddity of Carolina life, where he lived a variation of the motto of the Frenchman he read who declared that man is born free and lives everywhere in chains.

Some do, in South Carolina, he wrote, *others do not.* At least others don't wear visible manacles. The poet William Blake calls them "mind-forg'd" manacles. But he was not writing about actual enslavement. Mental slavery made for fools and foot soldiers. Actual slavery was something else entirely. The way his own throat sometimes tightened as he approached the slave quarters where he practiced his art at the master's behest gave him pause. He was wearing his own chains, yes, though you could not see them. Yet he had to admit, in an immediate paragraph, that he had freedoms no slave would ever know. The Africans in the early shipments, may have been born free, but all of them would die in chains. Almost entirely because of them, he, who was born into the bondage of a certain way of seeing his life and the life of those around him, might possibly become free.

About such matters he wrote and he wrote and he wrote. Hours would go by in which he bent to his labor of recording the histories—or stories, as he thought of them—of various slaves he had encountered, including, as it turned out, the family of the very child whose welfare he worried about. And he wrote about the owners as well, the good Christian people whom he attended to in town and on their plantations, and of the Jewish master with whom he sometimes had those intense philosophical conversations that made him feel as though he were approaching the very borders of discovery, only to draw back ever so close to the edge of seeing life in new fashion. Medicine goes to the cause of maladies, he decided, when he thought of his particular cast of mind, but not all of them are things we might cure.

For instance, the behavior of the master's son. It grew more intense as the years passed, and the man took more liberties of time with the slave girl at the expense of his family. Old Dou told him that on trips to town he would search out small gifts for her, and when his wife found one of these hidden among his clothing wrapped in fine paper and packed into a box—this was a silk scarf made somewhere in the Orient, not something that any slave child, however adored, might imagine would become one of her own possessions—he became angry with her for spying on him. Word got around. Everyone in the congregation in Charleston heard about it. How this wife, his first, the dutiful docile daughter of distant Caribbean cousins, said nothing, until one day, finding herself at the edge of a fine despair, she asked the slave woman who kept their house for them to accompany her on a trip to town where, using money she had apparently been saving over the years, she purchased a place on a ship sailing for the island where she was born and departed. Once she had reached her birth home she wrote a letter to her husband in which she recorded the extreme suffering she had known because of his obsession and vowed never to return.

Jonathan seemed hardly to notice, his obsession having taken on proportions that finally made it difficult to go unremarked by his father.

"Dear boy," the old man said, "you must not neglect our Abraham now that his mother has departed."

But before he could raise the question of his son's attention to the slave girl Jonathan spoke up.

"Father, please excuse me. I am going to town."

He abruptly left the room, drove the carriage to town, and returned the next morning to announce that he and Rebecca, the daughter of family friends, were engaged and soon to be married. This was his way of declaring the matter closed, even before anyone could open it further. As he explained it to his new young wife his affection for the slaves was deep and complicated by the history of their own people who once were slaves themselves. He encouraged Rebecca in the education plans she made for the slaves even as he continued to proclaim in his actions his odd and obsessive feelings about Lyaza.

The doctor wrote about all this in his notebook, including how, on one morning, after being informed by the slave named Isaac that Old Dou lay in her cabin, dreadfully ill, he went to seek her out and found the girl weeping at the bedside of the older African woman while Jonathan hovered in a corner of the room.

"She very sick," the girl said.

"Help her," Jonathan said to the doctor.

"I will do all I can," the doctor said.

"I hope so," Jonathan said, though the look in his eye, a truly odd gleam that reminded the doctor of madmen he had treated while in his school days, seemed to say otherwise.

The girl appeared to be more immediately distraught, weeping, moaning at the bedside.

"Please take her out of here," the doctor said to Jonathan, wanting them both to leave so that he might try to treat the old woman.

For that, he never forgave himself, although what happened next surely was inevitable, given the circumstances.

Jonathan took the wailing girl by the hand and led her out of the cabin and off into the fields.

"You sweety," he said, "I will help you."

The girl protested, looking at him as if she had never seen him before.

"Tweety-sweety," he said.

"Stop!" she said to him.

He swatted her with the back of his hand, bullying her the way a man might bully his dog or his horse, and dragged her by the hand further away into the surrounding woods. When they reached a shaded glade off to one side of one of the cultivated fields and he drew her close to him she was whimpering like an injured animal.

"Sweety," he said, "no crying now, no crying."

She went limp in his arms, and he lowered her to the ground and without any hesitation stripped off her clothing and had his way with her.

As simply as that, all the years of his apparently confused adoration and hovering protection of the girl came down to this. When he had finished, he wiped himself with her skirt and tossed the rest of her clothing at her.

"Get dressed," he said. "I have an appointment in town."

He left her lying there, not looking back even once as he walked away across the fields.

For a while the girl lay there, mourning for herself. The young master had been rough with her and she was bleeding in a way that she had never bled before. This frightened her terribly, and so she pulled on her clothes and walked back toward the cabin. No sign of the man in the fields ahead of her, but she caught sight of a slave boy she knew and sat down in the field out of his sight until he passed by. When she returned to the cabin Old Dou lay where she had left her, breathing harder than ever before.

"Doctor," she said.

The doctor looked her over, noticed bloodstains on her dress.

"What happened to you? Are you all right?"

"I all right," the girl said. "Mama Dou?" (That was what she called the old African woman.)

Old Dou did not reply, merely lay there breathing so hard that Lyaza feared she might begin to cough or spit up flesh from within her chest. Her own pain and turmoil seemed like nothing alongside this.

"Can you sit here with her?" the doctor said. "I have made her as comfortable as I could."

"Yes, massa," Lyaza said.

"I will return in the morning," the doctor said (worrying, without saying anything about it, that the old African woman might not last the night).

Lyaza sat beside Old Dou's pallet while the woman laboriously took in air and pushed it out as noisily as an ungreased carriage wheel. The next two hours went by slowly. All her short life the girl had known this woman as her caretaker and the mother she never had. "You a new girl," Old Dou always said to her. "New girl from the Carolina." Dou told her the story of her birth, complete with the tale of the passage, but keeping it less awful than it actually was. "Time enough for you to know everything. Time enough."

Was it now time?

"New girl?" The old woman breathed the words out roughly.

"Mama?"

"Your head whirling? Don't let it be whirling."

She urged calm for the girl, but her own voice, and breathing, suggested urgency.

"You all right?" she said.

Lyaza shook her head, but the old woman did not notice.

But she detected somehow the tears in the girl's eyes.

"What, new girl?" she said.

Lyaza hesitated, and the woman said, "Do not be sad. We all go. Come and go. Yemaya...take us in her arms."

The old woman slipped further away, like someone out at sea at the end of a long rope that kept growing longer.

"Yemaya," she said, slipping, slipping.

"Ah, Yemaya," the girl said.

"Yemaya," the old woman said in a whisper floating atop her breath.

"Mother," the girl said.

"New one," the old woman said in a voice so soft that the girl had to lean her ear down to the woman's lips. Her chest, always soft with her pillow-like breasts, seemed hard, calcified. Her breath smelled sour, like bad onion.

"Mother," the girl said again, pressing herself closer to the woman's face.

"New..."

The girl wept through the old woman's last breath.

Light had faded from the cabin. She was still weeping at dawn when the doctor returned.

"Oh, my dear, my dear," he said as though he were addressing a girl from town. "What have we here?"

He knelt at the side of the old woman, lifting her hand and feeling for her pulse. Gently he placed the dead woman's hand at her side and turned to ask a question of the slave girl. His eyes narrowed as he took in her figure, the blood that had darkened on her skirt.

The living old woman's fist had been clenched, the dead old woman's hand lay open, a stone resting in her cooling palm.

The doctor picked it up, turned it over, and then handed it to Lyaza.

"This must be yours to keep," he said.

Chapter Forty-two

Man to Man

*A*nother morning came, and Isaac was waiting for me at the back door.

"It's time, mas'," he said, escorting me out to the barn.

"How are you this morning?" I said.

"It's a big morning, mas', for the rice."

"For the rice crop, I know, yes," I said. "But what about you, Isaac?"

"Me, massa?"

He looked at me as if I had spoken to him in a foreign language.

"You."

Isaac shrugged.

"What's me?" he said.

I stared at him but said nothing and we mounted up and rode a while in silence.

I did not know what to say. It was all so odd, to be in the company again of a man who was not, according to the law, if not the law of nature, truly a man, with all the attendant rights and freedom. Might this have been what it was like to be in the company of an ancient Hebrew, a slave in Pharaoh's Egypt? This man seemed so placid, as if his people had not been brought here in chains, like animals, like imported goods, where mine had left behind lands where they had less than the rights they deserved and so arrived in America to find their full share of freedom.

I tried to keep all this in mind as I spoke to him, though I could not keep out of my mind the image of Liza gliding up to his cabin door in the dark and him coming out to greet her. I was not someone who could guard his feelings from obtruding, such as my father could, or my cousin Jonathan, so I am sure he must have heard some of my rough emotion in my voice.

"Isaac, will you tell me, how old you are?"

He shook his head.

"Let me ask you a question, massa."

"What is your question?"

"Would you talk to this horse?" he said.

"Talk to the horse? I suppose I might talk at it, to keep it going or to make it feel as though I was its friend, that I wasn't going to beat it."

"Then you can't talk at me."

"I would like to talk with you, Isaac."

"Why? What's the use of it?" He gave a shake of his head and turned his gaze to his horse. "Come on, boy," he said.

"You talk to *your* horse."

"Animal to animal," he said. "This horse and me, we speak the same language."

"Damnation!" I said.

"Is that a question, massa?"

"An expression," I said. "You are not fooling me, Isaac. You are obviously an intelligent fellow, or you could not be overseeing the rice planting as you do."

"Oh, massa from the North, I can oversee the rice because I am close to the rice. And close to the horse. I can tell you what the wind says, what the water says, and then I tell the rice what to do."

"You did tell me that the rice crop depends on the knowledge that you all brought over from Africa. You are a sly fellow, Isaac," I said. "But do not be sly with me. I have come here to learn, and slyness does not help."

"Den I'se not be sly, massa," he said.

"Is that your slave voice, Isaac?"

"Das right, mas'. It's de voice I can't leave behin'."

"But my cousin's wife, your master's daughter-in-law, has plans for that, as you know."

"She got plans, sho.'"

"Speak plain English, please, sir."

Isaac slowed his horse to a stop. And I tried to halt mine, though it walked a few paces further along so that I had to look back at him over my shoulder.

"Don't call me that, massa," Isaac said.

"Call you what?"

"You called me 'sir.' Don't fool with me, Mr. Yankee Master."

"I am not fooling with you, Isaac. I can tell that you have a good mind. I can see that Rebecca's teaching is working quite well."

"Oh, yes, it is," Isaac said. "Quite well, yes."

"She is preparing you for freedom," I said.

"Is that what she is preparing us for? And what if she is just preparing us for being a better kind of slave?"

"She has good intentions, as far as I can tell," I said.

"And does her husband, your cousin Jonathan, my master Jonathan, have good intentions?"

"I cannot speak for him," I said.

"You don't want to speak for him," Isaac said. "Because he is a liar and a hypocritic."

"Isaac!"

"Oh, yes, sorry, mas'. I'se know de slave can't talk 'bout de mas' dissa way. It be a bad way, and I'se sorry, I'se truly is."

"She's taught you well, hasn't she?"

"Who?"

"Miss Rebecca."

"She's taught me almost nothing," Isaac said, "except to put a fine point on all the things I've known since I was a child."

"She wants to help."

"She helps to make my condition more painful. I learned how to read, but not from her. When she wanted to teach me I had to pretend I knew nothing, and after a while she had me read certain things that prove to me that I am all the more hopeless and damned."

"How did you learn to read?"

"You got to know everything about my life? Do I know everything about your life? How did you learn to read?"

"I had a teacher, a man in New York."

"Well, massa, the doctor here in the county taught me."

"But about Rebecca,...she is a good woman," I said. "She had a vision—"

"While her husband lurks around the shacks at night?"

I lost all control then.

"You do not have to lurk around, do you? You live in the cabins."

I pulled up my horse and he turned and reined in his animal.

"What are you talking about, massa?"

"No more 'massa'," I said.

He reached over and held the reins of my horse.

"What are you talking about, me not having to lurk around?"

"Liza," I said, nearly choking on her name.

"You want to talk about Liza? She is like my sister. Or like a cousin. Yes, like a cousin."

He dropped the reins and pushed at my horse, his own mount stepping away a foot or so between us.

"I see," I said, but I did not see. And he knew that.

"Do you?" he said. "Do you see? Massa? What do you see? Hard to see nigger slaves in the dark. Except when they got a light tone on their skin. Easier to see the high yellow, ain't it? Easier to aim for. 'Cept some masters go for the real dark. They like to sink into the black of dark, they like to just disappear and get swallowed up in the black of the black, don't they?"

"I would not know," I said.

My horse gave its head a shake, anxious to move again.

"You wouldn't, eh? Well, you got some cousins who know, don't you?"

"Yes," I said. "Yes, I do."

His horse gave a whinny and now both horses danced a little in place.

"We got to move," Isaac said. "You said what you wanted to say."

"I want to tell you one more thing, though," I said.

"What's that? I mean, what's that, massa?"

"Stop that, please."

"What is it?" Isaac's voice turned hard again.

"I am not that kind of man."

"What kind of man is that?"

"First of all, not the kind of man who would make another man his slave. And second, not the kind of man who would make a woman his slave."

"'Sat right, massa? Well, I'm glad you came down here from up North to learn some things. Because you got a lot to learn."

"I want to learn," I said.

"You will," he said. "You will."

Chapter Forty-three

In My Margins

New Science

This new science, anthropology, wedded to an old study, history, and theology. These studies, my studies, knotted to family and forebears, the road down which we came…and sometimes I wake in the middle of the night, having just dreamed of that erupting volcano, the first family, my family, fleeing from it as fast as they can walk, over the cooling lava plain…

Chapter Forty-four

Another Letter, Unsent

The Oaks

Goosecreek

South Carolina

Dear Miriam:

I am still not much the letter writer, although I have recently composed a note to my father about some of the business matters that brought me here to this plantation, with acres and acres of woods and rice fields and barns and a pretty white house at the center of things where my uncle and aunt serve as the head of the family. But I have been wanting to write to you about this family, since it is so different from our small New York groups of blood relatives. Nights on this plantation give me plenty of time for reading and writing and reflection. I wanted to use the light of the lamp on the desk at which I sit to illuminate for you what yours truly has seen and learned. It is not exactly what I had in mind when I set out on my journey here, but it has taught me certain lessons about the world and myself. I don't know that if I had stayed in New York that I would not have learned these same lessons, but it might have taken a while longer for it to happen.

There is a grace and languidness people effuse here...

There is a city here nearby...Though some decades ago it served as the destination for numerous slave ships from Africa, with the end of the trans-Atlantic slave trade, Charleston's busyness subsided somewhat. From what I have observed in these days, despite active foot traffic, and the usual horses and carriages, the city takes up no more area than one of our many neighborhoods. Yet I do admit it has its beautiful places, such as the charming tree-covered park just at the southeastern point of the city, called the Battery, where the richest and the most high-born families live, where we witnessed that horrendous moment of the horse-whipping.

Such a strange proximity of beauty and barbarism!

As for my family, it is situated some miles from town, on a number of heavily treed acres, with, as I have already written, the rice fields and barns and such, and the deep creek that runs on the northern border of the property that carries boats from town to the small pier at the family brickyard…

I have mentioned some of the slaves in my earlier letter to you. South Carolina, I am told, is more of an admixture than most of the rest of the South, except perhaps for New Orleans, this probably in part because of its access to the sea and the constant traffic of ships and sailors from all parts of the nation and the globe. Importing of African slaves made the city thrive, and now the sale—oh, yes, my dear, the very exchange of human beings for money!—of slaves from all about the South continues to bolster the local commerce…

Liza appeared with the coffee pot, and for an instant no greater than the breadth of a moth's eye, she glanced at me[—tiny jagged shock like lightning in a dark stormy early summer night sky, a thought I am not including in this letter—]and then she poured the liquid into my cup.

Liza, every bit a dutiful house servant, moved once again to my side. [And that was perhaps the first time she came close enough so that I inhaled, along with the rich cacao flavor of the coffee blend, the perfume she scattered as she raised her arm to pour, another thought I will not include in this letter.]

I cannot write this, I cannot tell her how I feel, I cannot dare to tell myself…

Chapter Forty-five

Night-blooming Flower

With Old Dou gone, nothing stood in Jonathan's way. A new girl, long in the tooth and with a pair of eyes each of which seemed different from the other, everyone called her Precious Sally, took over the kitchen, apparently suggested to the master by Black Jack, but she could not stand up to the master's son, who worked his will on Lyaza whenever it came upon him. Like some dog in heat, he would find her in the cabin or in the kitchen of the big house (where if she was alone he would rush her into the pantry). Breathing his foul hot breath in her face, he would push her around and wrestle her into position, hiking her skirts so that he could penetrate her, from the front or from behind, making low rough noises, spew his fluid, and then immediately depart. Left to clean herself off in the darkness of the pantry, Lyaza felt more sorrow than shame. She knew if she told the doctor he might do something, but she withheld all this from him. The doctor would go to the master. The master would find an easy solution, and it would not come out well for her. Better to endure the torture than to be sold off to some other household, perhaps some household far south of here, where the stories that circulated among the slaves would have it that worse misery and brutality reigned. Where Old Dou had cared for her, that was home. The old woman was gone, but she could feel her, like the goddess, in the air.

On the veranda there opened in the dark each warm night in season a night-blooming flower that gave off the most ferociously intense perfume. This rush of body and overbearing soul that went on between her and the young master over and over again reminded her for some reason of that night-blooming flower, something quite beautiful that in its fullness reeked a little of rotting meat.

"He hurting you so much, ain't he?" Precious Sally said to her one morning in the kitchen.

Lyaza shrugged it off.

"Not any more. I don't feel nothing."

The air was delightfully warm, and as clear as it could ever be now that the season of pollen had shifted into summer's end. Heaven must be close to a morning such as this. And yet she felt nothing.

And then in the next moment she felt something twitch in her belly.

"Dou," she said, to the ghost of the old woman who, in her dreams sometimes, hovered over her head in the small cabin, "I do not want it, this seed."

The old woman—she saw her, hand in hand with Yemaya, dancing on a cloud—nodded, but did not speak. The goddess, through the lips of the old woman, gave her some instructions about which mushrooms to hunt and grind up with mare's milk, that when rubbed into her privacy, would keep the man's seed from taking root.

You take this, Yemaya said, *you will be a fine young girl again.*

Drinking the potion made of this recipe made her ferociously ill—and cleaned her out. Blood again, running from her nether inner parts.

This happened to her twice.

Sometimes after these events the girl lay there in the dark, worn down by cramps and prophecy, sobbing, so alone she might have been a seed herself, lost in some field as vast as the night sky that covered them all, so clear in late summer and early autumn. Camel, fox, turtle, monkey, dog, all these animals came alive as spaces between the stars, and not just the girl, but all her neighbors listened quietly on clear nights for the voices of these heavenly creatures, hoping for guidance, as the girl always was, hoping for secrets to fall into their laps. These old ways flourished, especially here on the plantation owned by the Hebrews, where traveling Christian ministers, always ready elsewhere to convert the pagan slave to the proper religion, never seemed to find their way.

Several times a year, on feast days from the old religion from home, everyone who could stole off into the woods after dark and watched the ceremonies, the animal sacrifice—usually a goat but sometimes chickens— at the center of things. Two and three times a night this went on, in small groups each time, to keep the masters and overseers from becoming suspicious and wondering about the absence of activity out in the slave cabins.

Lyaza stayed sometimes for two cycles of the sacrifice, the songs, and the prayers. Best of all times were the stormy nights, when thunder rumbled overhead, so that the men could play the drums they had constructed out of animal skin and old logs without fear of discovery.

The *BOOM*, the *BAM*, the *DON DON DON*, echoing through the forested groves, men chanting, to Shango, god of storm and wind, women raising their voices to Yemaya, the goddess alive and well in the sap in the trees, in the dew on the grass, in the light of the half-moon, in the wind itself, *BOOM BAM DON DON DON DON*, the drumming linking the drummers in their pounding and the families they stood for here on earth and the noise echoing up amid the storming clouds until it reached the ears of the waiting gods, the *BOOM* and the *BAM* and the *BOOM* and the *BAM* and the *BOOM* and the *BAM* and the *BOOM* and the *BAM*... echoing, echoing on into the dark above the forest, where only the sliver of the moon gave hope that the goddess still watched over them, perhaps, like them, still trying to become accustomed to life here on the ground of this new world and in the air above it. *BOOM* and the *BAM* and the *BOOM* and the *BAM* and the *BOOM* and the *BAM*...

Yemaya, to whom I gave my blood, Yemaya, who kept the ocean moving under me, who rained on me, who watered my throat and hair, moistened my eyes and helped me to see when awake and dream when asleep, Yemaya, who put this living thing in my belly—for she had another one growing.

Shango dancing, carrying his three-headed axe, singing, "Give it all, set it down, the man will do it..."

Yemaya singing, "Shut the mouth, put down the axe, let her carry what she carries, all the way home."

"Home," Shango shouted, "she has no home."

Yemaya singing, "She had one, now she tries another, she will not yet find it but her child might."

Yes, she was carrying again, and the turmoil created in her head by the drums and animal screams was nothing compared to the turmoil in her heart. She was sure this child would live and so she would carry forever the visible mark of her shame, that she could not defend herself against the approaches of the master's oldest son. A dark, oh, a dark time! And so when she heard the drumming she rushed off into the woods to lose herself in the beat and in the shifting of hips and stamping of feet, solicitations with long arms raised skyward, to the goddess who must know what she had done to her, because she knew everything.

BOOM and the *BAM* and the *BOOM* and the *BAM* and the *BOOM* and the *BAM*.

> *Lightning kill me, kill the child*
> *Drum kill me, kill the child*
> *Lightning kill me, kill the child*
> *Drum kill me, kill the child...*

Chapter Forty-six

The Flood

*H*ere on this morning, in deep morning light, Isaac and I emerged from the woods into the broad clearing where the earth appeared to shimmer and glisten, as though a million million droplets of dew—or manna?—had fallen from the sky. The sight was beautiful enough to take my mind momentarily off the sordid matters of plantation life and put myself to studying the organics of it.

"We got to walk now," Isaac said, and we dismounted, left the horses at the edge of the clearing, and walked into the rice field. We made our way along the berms that formed the border in lines that ran in rectangular fashion, from the woods where we had come from, to the south where another stand of trees stood guard, and to the north where the broad flat spaces filled with young stalks of plants came up against the waters of the wild swamp.

Along that berm Isaac pointed out to me the small squares of grating and wood that served as the flood-gates embedded in the walls of earth, some two dozen of them.

Along this low wall of earth, with all these windows ready to be opened to the water, the slave minions, mostly men, but a few women here and there (including a decidedly pregnant girl, at the far end of the first field) stood at the ready, waiting for Isaac's command.

"The plants," he explained to me, "are ready, as you can see."

And he stopped us, and bent down to show me the young rice stalks at our feet just tall enough to bend in a breeze.

"Feel it," he said.

I reached down and took one of the tender stalks in my fingers, enjoying its smoothness and breathing in the humid odor of the earth and the few inches of water in which it grew along with its thousand thousand sisters.

"The little darlings," he said, "they be needing the support, and it is time. The tide has gone all the way out, so the creek is more fresh water than salt, and the marsh been cleaned by the upstream waters."

About thirty or so slaves stood at the gates, waiting for his command. He raised a hand above his head.

"How long will you be staying here, mas'? You going to stay long enough to see the harvest?"

I shook my head, feeling myself informed with my new way of thinking.

"I don't think so," I said. "I believe I will return to New York quite soon. Possibly within a few days."

"Is that true?" He kept his hand raised above his head.

"Yes," I said with a nod, amazed that my resolve had stuck with me and at the same time wondering what my cousin might be thinking if he could overhear this conversation.

"Then we got to work quick," Isaac said, making a pulling motion and drawing his hand back to his side.

The slaves bent to their work, opening one by one the doors of the small dams and standing back as the water trickled in from the marsh and the creek beyond. Though the water level rose slowly, the sharp stink of the salt rose quickly to my nose.

> *Bring the river*
>
> > [the slaves sang out]

> *Bring the river*
> *To the garden.*
> *Bring the river*
> *Bring the river*
> *To the garden…*
> *Bring the river*
> *Bring the river*
> *To the gar-ar-den,*
> *Bring the river*
> *To the garden*
> *Oh, mah Lord…*

Here was a striking event, the way these people brought the work and the singing together, making one lovely melody of sound and physical labor. They moved slowly and deliberately, as did their voices, and the effect put to shame all the music I had ever heard in the synagogue, and certainly any stray songs I might have heard trickling from the churches in my city of a Sunday.

Oh, bring the river to the garden!

"So you see," Isaac was saying to me, "the fresh water floods in, and lifts the stalks, and keeps them lifted until they are strong enough to stand on their own, which is the time when we open the flood doors at the bottom of the field and drain the water down. In a moon and a half...it will be ready..."

"A moon and a half," I said.

"A month and a bit more," he said.

"And then the harvest?"

"And then the harvest."

"So, Isaac, you employ here knowledge of the plants themselves—"

"Yes." He nodded his head.

"And the growing season."

"Yes."

"And a knowledge of the tides."

"Oh, yes, the tides, very important."

"And the mixture of minerals and such in the water."

"Yes, oh, yes."

"And the climate."

"The sun, you mean? Yes, yes, sun and moon. In Africa they pay as much attention to the cool light of the moon as they do to the heat of the sun."

"But you have never been there?"

"Mas', I been there. I am there now. I am there always. I make Africa here."

A shout went up from the flooded field. The slaves went running, and we followed after.

The girl who had stood full-bellied at the flood-gate now bent over, doubled and doubled again.

Her water had broken, spilled out into the flooding field.

A good sign! All these slave folks cried out.

My second birth here in my short stay on the plantation! I should have been taking this as a sign of rebirth, in myself, and in the life around me. And yet in me rose up so suddenly—I could not then say why—such gushing waters of regret that I wanted to drown myself in my own confusion.

Chapter Forty-seven

Is a Decision Near?

"And how did you enjoy the flooding of the rice plants?" my uncle said to me that night when the first course of our evening meal was set before us.

(My uncle, about whom more in a moment, was sitting in front of a full plate of food—meat, rice—a bountiful meal produced by Precious Sally the slave cook—but he was not eating.)

"Enjoy, Uncle? I found it quite enlightening."

"Isaac is a good guide, is he not?"

"Oh, yes, yes, he is."

"Quite a good fellow, that Isaac," my uncle said.

"Good?" said my aunt. "How do you know he is good?"

"He does good work," my uncle said.

"And work is everything?" My aunt seemed quite annoyed.

"We have to keep an eye on it," my uncle said. "The price of rice is down, the cost of shipping goes up. We have to pay good money for flour and meat to feed the…" He broke off, and suddenly dropped his eyes and rested his head on his chin.

"You were saying?" My aunt spoke as if she actually wanted to know what he spoke about.

My uncle looked up, seemingly startled to find himself where he had been just a moment before. He stared directly at me.

"To feed the niggers, you were saying," my cousin said.

"Please," said Rebecca. She nodded her head toward Abraham, who sat silently observing the family exchange.

Turning to Jonathan, my uncle said, "I do not like that word."

"Africans, then," my cousin said.

My uncle seemed to have regained all of the vigor which momentarily he had appeared to have lost.

"Africans? Southern-born? I truly do not know the exact figures. We should do a census. So many have been born, so many have died. Now Isaac's father, he was African-born, yes?"

"Yes," my cousin said.

"Is he alive or dead?" My uncle spoke as though he expected an immediate reply.

"I do not know," my cousin said.

"Let us find out," my uncle said.

"Jonathan," my aunt said, "you will do this?"

"A census?" my uncle said. "An accounting? Let Isaac do it. Better a slave, who will find out all the truth than one of us, to whom they will lie if they believe they must."

Rebecca, Jonathan's wife, cleared her throat and said, "Isaac reads and writes now."

"Yes, that is marvelous," my cousin Jonathan said. "Isaac is a reader and writer." By his tone I could not tell whether or not he thought this was a good thing or a bad thing.

"He could do a census, that is what I mean," said Rebecca.

My uncle leaned across the table and said to me, "Isaac took you to the fields today, did he not?"

"He did, sir. It was quite interesting."

"You will find the harvest quite interesting, too."

I then spoke up, declaring from my heart.

"Uncle, I am going to miss the harvest."

Everyone at the table turned his attention to me.

"You're mistaken," my uncle said. "The harvest comes in the next two months."

I stared at the food heaped high on my plate and when I looked up I noticed that Precious Sally was watching me from the doorway. Not wanting to insult her, I carved myself a bit of meat and began to chew. It tasted dry and slightly earthy, as though it had been dropped in the mud. The rest of the family settled back to eating while I spit the meat back out on my plate.

"I am returning to New York on the next ship out," I said.

"What?"

My uncle sputtered and showered the place before him with his spittle.

"Surely you're joking," my cousin said.

"I am not joking," I said. "I am leaving as soon as I can."

"Nephew," my uncle said, "dear Nathaniel, you must not think of leaving. We need you to stay and report to your father."

Jonathan pursed his lips and took a swallow of wine.

"It is our peculiar institution," he said. "He does not want to be a part of it."

"No, I do not," I said. "I am not condemning it. I just do not want to be part of it, no."

"Oh, so you will return to New York and tell your father that you cannot bear the thought of investing in an enterprise such as ours?"

"My father will do whatever it is he wants to do," I said. "I make no decisions for him."

"But you are here to report for him," Jonathan said. "Leaving so precipitously, my cousin, will say a lot to him."

"It will say more about me than about you," I said. "I am just not much for farming. I am a city boy, Cousin. I am weary of the country."

My uncle made a sputtering noise with his lips and his head swayed from side to side, and for a moment I worried that I might have caused him to suffer a seizure.

My aunt thought the same. She reached over to touch him on the face and said his name.

"I do not want you to worry," she went on. "We are going to find a way."

"Yes, yes," he responded. "I am merely surprised, and distraught. Nothing more. But that is sufficient, is it not?" He pulled at his collar. "The heat, the heat. Do you suffer too much from this damnable heat, nephew?"

I would have spoken, if I had something else to say. But my cousin put in his opinion.

"Father," Jonathan said. "He mentioned nothing of the heat."

"Then it is other things. The isolation. Sir?" He pointed a finger at me. "I promise you more of town. You are a city person, you need more of it to survive. So!" He patted the palm of his hand against the table. "Yes, yes, we all go to town once a week, at least, to dinners, to the synagogue, of course. And on that subject, Rebecca, dear daughter-in-law, please tell your cousin by marriage what you were recently telling me."

Rebecca, who remained silent throughout these exchanges, touched the tip of her napkin to her lips and said, "Cousin Nathaniel, I was hoping that you would join me in the conduct of my work with the slaves."

"Perfect," my uncle said, "perfect, perfect, perfect. You, sir, will have a hand in the making of citizens out of the stuff of slaves."

"It is certainly an admirable project," I could not help but say.

"Then you will consider staying to work on it?"

"I will consider it, yes," I said, feeling myself turn on a pivot.

"An admirable idea," my cousin said. "You can only help the poor slaves by staying."

"I think it sounds just lovely," my aunt said.

"I'm so glad to hear this," Rebecca said.

"But dear daughter-in-law, there was something else, was there not?" my uncle said.

"Oh, yes," Rebecca said, and it was quite odd, because for a moment she appeared to be blushing.

"Nathaniel, you recall my cousin Anna?"

"I do."

I was trying to be polite, but Rebecca took this as enthusiasm.

"She is a lovely young woman," my aunt said.

"She seemed quite lovely," I said.

"Her parents give a lovely spring party every year," my aunt said.

Rebecca leaned closer to me and said, "We are all wondering, Anna is wondering, I am wondering, if you would come as her guest to this event."

Black Jack moved in and out of the room, carrying trays, fetching trays, while Precious Sally remained in the doorway, nodding her sage head. Liza, who sometimes helped with the preparation of meals, was nowhere to be seen. My growing obsession with her seemed suddenly vile and ignorant and unjust. Rebecca's idea was quite tempting. This slavery question has been vexing me so. My sentiments have me spinning around and around and around so that I am dizzy with indecision. In how many ways could the world pull a young fellow like me? I supposed that I was soon going to find out.

Chapter Forty-eight

Into the Maelstrom

$\mathcal{T}$he night came and again I retired early, abjuring the after-dinner talk with the family. My thoughts were topsy-turvy, jogging to and fro. Be that as it may, as I climbed the stairs to my room, I believed I had finally made up my mind. I knew clearly that I had to leave. I simply could no longer understand how anyone could live under these circumstances, in this fool's paradise built on the backs of the indentured.

I sat down at the desk and wrote to my father, hoping to have the letter delivered to town the next morning and posted to New York, and as I wrote I found myself imagining that I might even find a ship going north that same tomorrow morning and deliver the letter by my own hand.

And yet I could not, when I put out the candle and lay back on the bed and closed my eyes, find an easy passage to the temporary oblivion of sleep. As much as the problems I turned over in my mind disturbed me they also kept me alert. Back and forth, back and forth I trundled in my mind, as a figure plagued by madness might shift from one point on stage to another and back again, and back again.

I reignited the lamp and by the steady flame in the still air read some pages of a book from my uncle's library.

Anything to distract me from my worrisome woes!

"A Descent into the Maelstrom."

This story took me quite rapidly along with it, as I began to read, the story within the story, that is. "We had now reached the summit of the loftiest crag. For some minutes the old man seemed too much exhausted to speak…"

The characters in the story within the story climb the mountain called Helseggen, and I climb with them, even as the narrator reaches the vertiginous moment when he looks down from the heights at the sea.

"I looked dizzily, and beheld a wide expanse of ocean, whose waters wore so inky a hue as to bring at once to my mind the Nubian geographer's account of the Mare Tenebrarum. A panorama more deplorably desolate no human imagination can conceive…"

I no sooner looked upon the sea with this agitated narrator within the story when I heard the knocking at my door.

Still in a stupor, in a reading dream, I lowered my feet to the floor and stood up.

The knocking, tapping, sounded again.

"Yes?"

With chilled blood in my veins I half-imagined to find a giant raven standing there.

I went to the door and opened it.

"Massa," Liza said.

"No, no, no, no," I said, suffering a jump in my blood into my throat and down along both upper limbs, and then down further. "I would prefer that you do not call me that," I said. I was agitated from reading the story, I told myself.

Liza looked furtively behind her.

"May I come in, massa?"

I nodded, and she stepped inside, trailing an invisible cloud of scent. Earth after rain, wood-smoke, wood-flower—her perfumes charmed me with their natural airs.

"It is late, Liza," I said. "Is there trouble?"

She shook her head.

"They have all gone to bed. I've been walking up and down the hall, trying to…to make the courage to knock on your door."

At which point she burst into tears.

"Oh, massa!"

"Please?" I said.

She shook from her misery, and wailed on.

"Tell me," I said, "what is the difficulty? You act as though you're being pursued."

"I am," she said, and threw herself down upon the bed, which she herself had prepared for me so many nights since my arrival.

"Please tell me," I said, still keeping my distance and trying to pretend that we were together in a well-lighted downstairs room with many people passing in and out instead of alone together in the dark in my room and on my bed.

"Water, please," she said.

Immediately, I poured her a cup of water from the pitcher near my bedside, a pitcher that she herself had fetched and often refilled.

She sat up and sipped from my cup.

"Thank you, massa," she said.

"Nate," I said. "Call me Nate."

"Nate," she said. "Thank you, Nate."

Still quite in possession of my own mind, I noted the effect the saying of my name on her lips produced in me.

"So now, Liza," I said, "will you please explain to me what circumstances have brought you here to me at this hour of the night?"

For a small part of a second, she laughed, or I thought she laughed, but then it turned out to be the awkward intake of breath and noise that began another round of tears.

Which she suddenly cut short, jerking herself erect and pushing her head back against the headboard.

"He is after me," she said in a deep and hurried whisper.

"Who is after you?"

I leaned closer, and found myself, with legs already weak, naturally giving in to gravity, sitting lightly near the foot of the bed, and allowing my eyes to focus on her face. Even in the dark her eyes showed a ferocity and a fear at the same time that I could not fully comprehend. And her hands meanwhile she clasped together, almost as if in prayer, and kneaded them nervously on her breast.

"I cannot go into it, it is too distressing," she said.

"But you must tell me," I said. "Obviously you came here to ask for help and I can't help you unless you tell me the truth of the situation."

"It is too awful to tell," she said, making liquid sounds with her lips, as she if were still drinking from the cup.

"Take a moment," I said. "Compose yourself."

I took a moment myself, also, getting up from the bed and going to the window, and once again staring, staring, as I had been doing on so many nights since my arrival, into the native country dark. It was late, and so few fireflies flared up their winking lights around the field, but in the dark, as if over water, the distant sounds of the animals from the barns and from the woods beyond them, flared up, and subsided, flared up, and subsided.

"Now, Liza," I said, turning back to her, "please tell me your story."

"Later, Nate," she said in a whisper, finally taking hold of my name.

"Later?" I said. "Speak up, I can hardly hear you."

"Later," she said.

"Later than what?" I said, venturing near the bed and leaning close so that I could make out whatever it was she was going to say.

She reached for my hand and pulled me down close to her, so that I collapsed of my own weight onto the space she made next to her by rolling to her side.

"Liza, I—"

Yes, I tried to speak, but she was upon me, tugging me close, and pushing her soft lips upon mine, so that I opened my own to hers.

Cinnamon and bonfire, a bouquet of blood and wine, and the soursweet taste of desire long fermenting in the throat, and deeper—all this I tasted, as we pressed against each other, as though each wished to press hard enough to pass through the body of the other.

"Liza," I said, halting our long kiss just for the sake of saying her name.

"Nate, Nate, Nate," she said, the words falling on my head like petals from a night-blooming tree. "Do you wish to know me?"

"Yes," I said, "I do. Do you wish to know me, with your own free will?"

"What is that?" she said, in a voice quite perplexed.

"You choose this, not as a slave but as a free woman?"

"But I am not free."

"I do not own you, Liza. Do you choose this?"

"But I am the master's property."

"No one ordered you here, did he?"

Her slight hesitation to answer my question gave me pause.

"Did Uncle tell you to come here?"

"No!" she said in an outraged whisper. "He would have me whipped if he knew."

"Whipped? He has people whipped?"

"It has happened, yes."

"Who would dare to order such a thing? Who would dare to carry it out?"

Liza remained silent.

"They have never whipped you, have they?"

"No, no, no, not me. Oh, you would know it if you saw."

"Jews employing the lash used on them by the Egyptians! I hope I never live to see such a thing."

"If you stay here long enough, you will."

"Sorry, sorry, sorry, Liza, that I suggested my uncle sent you here to coerce me, to tempt me to stay."

I kissed her again, tasting the bouquet of her lips, with the added tincture of desire now flavoring the spittle that we mingled in our mouths.

As when an apple, still tethered to a branch by the slimmest clasp, begins to shake in the first brisk autumn wind and its stem incurs a fatal tear, I found myself, pressed against her, on the verge of falling.

She made a mewing sound beneath me, and in the dark I wondered if woman had turned into cat.

This was all so new to me that all I knew was that I should behave, the way a man did, as though it were not new to me.

"Massa," she said.

"Please," I said.

"Nate. Nate."

"Yes, Liza?"

"Before this happened, you were a free man."

"Yes?"

"And you are still free?"

"I am."

"Though now you own a slave."

"What do you say?"

"I am yours, Nate."

Time went by, cocks crowed in the yard also, and the faintest scrim of a false dawn showed over the tops of the trees beyond the barns. When it became light enough to see Liza's skin next to mine it was time to figure our way out of this dilemma. Instead, we lingered, luxurious in the aftermath of our mated desires.

"Now tell me the truth," I said, "why is it you came to me in the night? Who was pursuing you?"

Liza laughed, and touched a finger to her full lips, which stood out in a sort of inverted rendering of dark against light as the light filled in the hollows of her face made by night.

"I was pursuing myself," she said. "I was pursuing you."

"So it was not my old uncle?"

She laughed again, this time slightly hysterical.

"I didn't say, massa, it was anybody."

"Don't call me that."

"Yes, massa, I won't."

With mock-ferocity I loomed above her, pinning her arms to the bed.

"You will not."

"No, I won't, not anymore."

"Isaac?" I said. "Is it Isaac?"

At the thought seeing the two of them meet at his cabin door I scarcely could control my anger.

"Why, if he—"

"Not Isaac, never Isaac," she said. "He is my brother. He—"

I stopped her, because the thought came to me with a mental jolt.

"Jonathan? Cousin Jonathan?"

She sat up at once and all warmth left her voice. If it was possible to see this cacao-colored woman turned pale, I saw it then.

Silently, Liza took to her feet and picked up her clothes. In the night I had seen only a burst of flesh here, a breast, a thigh, her neck elongated in the passion of our coming together. Now in the early dawn she stood luxuriously naked in the instant before she covered herself cloth by cloth. I had never seen a woman fully unclad, and so I gathered it all in—breasts, thighs, pelvis, where her flesh curved as though it were carved from brown stone or light mahogany—while she covered what I saw almost as soon as I saw it.

"I trust it was not Jonathan. He is married," I said in my own naïve way. "And he may be my cousin but he is old enough to be your father."

She said nothing except, "Can you help me?"

"Help you to escape him?"

Almost fully dressed now, she turned to me as she worked her buttons closed and nodded.

"Yes."

"I am planning to leave for home almost at once," I said. "I can't...I have to return to New York."

"You got to stay a little longer."

"I have made up my mind."

"Just a little longer?"

I shook my head, more in confusion than anything else.

"I had planned to go to town and check the sailing schedule for boats to New York."

"Take me with you."

"What? I cannot—"

"Take me to town," she said. "Take me with you to town."

I sighed deeply, feeling myself still sinking into that same abyss I'd first fallen into before the rising of dawn.

"Can we do that?"

"I can arrange it," she said. "I got some...some...powers here in the house."

"They treat you well," I said, "or so I thought until you told me about Jonathan. Liza, has he ever...?"

Now it was her turn to sigh, a strange thing to do given all the circumstances, scarcely any of which I knew at that moment.

So that when she stole out of my room just as the first rays of the sun caught the tops of the trees beyond the barns I lay back on my bed, puzzled, satisfied, shaken—bewitched, and boiling about in my own woes and desires, more certain and yet more confused than ever. Did I yet know who I was? Did I know why I had traveled here? I believed I now had the answers in my heart. But these did not match the answers in my mind.

Chapter Forty-nine

In My Margins

What Is a Jew?

*W*hat do they believe? They wandered the desert, hoping for water. They followed a pillar of fire. They pray to one god. No afterlife? This makes them different from Christians. They see a deed as valuable in itself, and not a stepping stone toward eternity. Do they treat others as they would be treated themselves?

Chapter Fifty

A Child Is Born,
a Mother Departs

*M*iddle of the night. All around the cabin dark kept a hold and lay a weight on the other cabins, on the big house itself not far away under the watery slim moonlight cast down by the quarter orb. Her cry went up in the darkness, and everyone heard, everyone knew. How could they not, the plantation slaves living so close together in the quiet pasture behind the rice barns. At first she lay there in the cabin, twisting and bending with the waves of labor, all alone, calling out to Old Dou and Yemaya, wondering if Wata, her mother's mother, of whom she had heard a great deal, might be floating somewhere above the cabin, and then she heard rumbling above the roof and harsh rain fell for a short time, and then quiet, and then two voices arguing, Yemaya and Yemaya's brother Oganyu, the baby is mine, one called to the other, and the other called back, no, no, no, the baby is mine!

The rain fell again, and now she heard Old Dou soothing the arguing children of the god. The rank odor of decaying fish drifted through the cabin. Lyaza felt her water break and then gush across the pallet.

A dog barked.

She felt her head floating free while the bottom half of her leaked like a broken crock.

Up on the roof Yemaya and Oganyu wrestled accompanied by great yells and thumping for the soul of the unborn child. She looked up through the wood and saw Old Dou dancing around the squabbling siblings. She cheered on one, and then the other, and then the first. Lyaza took up the cheers, wriggling out of her aching, writhing body and sailing up onto the top of the cabin, naked, trembling, feverish, excited, desperate, lonely, sad, despondent, hungry, happy to see Old Dou, so recently departed, even

under such awful circumstances, sad that in a short while she would bring
forth the spawn of the awful slave-keeper.

"*Monster,*" Old Dou called him, reading her mind.

"*I kill him,*" Lyaza shouted back.

"*But the baby,*" Old Dou said, folding her arms across her chest as the
god-sister and god-brother flew off into the black sky, going where neither
woman could say. Up to the moon? Up to heaven beyond? Back to the
home country? Up and up and up, and then diving back down beneath the
sea? Yes, perhaps there, where Yemaya kept her home and where Obatala
had raised her and her brother, among the flow of great undersea currents,
among the fishes, cousins to whales, lovers of dolphins.

In that water Lyaza saw the outline of a plan. As if in a dream she leaped
from the roof and landed some yards away from the cabin and leaking
water and fluids made her way across the fields to the rice paddies where
the water surged into the holding ponds at high tide and the salt leached
out, making a mist that stung the nose. By the edge of the lapping pond
she lay down and eased her legs apart so that the child slid freely from her
body. Taking up the light burden she held the ropy tie in her teeth and cut
the placenta from the living child. Her mouth tasted of salt and blood, as if
she licked herself down below where the child had emerged.

Drums in the distance, either just on the other side of the rice ponds,
or at some distance in the world of her head, that close, that far the sound.

Yemaya spoke to her from the pond.

"*Take your child up and raise her.*"

Lyaza stood up and held her child above the water.

"*Raise her,*" the goddess said.

"*Take her,*" Lyaza said.

"*No no no no no no no no no no,*" the goddess said.

Lyaza screamed at Yemaya.

"*Take her away!*"

"*No!*"

"*This child filthy spawn of filthy master wretch!*"

She took a deep breath and hurled the infant into the air, as though she
were pushing against someone in a dance. It disappeared into the mist and
she waited to hear the splash, but none came. She stumbled on leaden legs
through deserted fields back to the cabin where she lay back down on the
bloody pallet. Closing her eyes, she saw behind the lids the stout figure of

Old Dou, and a shadowy woman standing behind her, either the ghost of the mother she never knew or Yemaya, just which she could not say. With a loud sigh she settled down into the filth of her life and the wretched sleep of the hopeless, awaking at the first light of dawn, a soft light that stole in like an ocean dew, settling over the doorway and then the floor and finally touching her where she lay in her misery, an empty hulk of a girl ready for nothing but death.

Soon after the light arrived a boy named Isaac showed up with the infant in his arms. The boy grew taller and taller, and his face turned into that of Jonathan, the master's old son who stood there, nodding his head, the infant now in his possession.

"Devil!" she screamed at him.

Oh, Yemaya! These women reached the heights of childbirth, and then they plummeted into darkness. Lyaza stood up, reached for her child, and fell dead on the cabin floor.

Chapter Fifty-one

Love in Town

That morning I slept late, one of the indulgences of plantation life. Liza, I presumed, must have immediately begun her work for the day. I imagined her hurrying down to the kitchen where she assisted Precious Sally, the woman who had the largest hand in raising her, touching milk and water, eggs and flour—her magical presence turning these elements into nourishment for all of us.

I could picture Precious Sally opening her eyes in the dark, saying her prayers to the gods, whichever she might believe in—and raising her large body out of her bed of ticking and straw, pulling on her apron and making ready to proceed to the kitchen to prepare breakfast, where she found Liza already baking the daily bread.

Isaac, perhaps having slept in his clothes, slowly raised his head off the straw pillow and looked around at the sound of the crowing birds, knowing he must wake his crews and get them moving into the fields as the sun was rising. And in the other cabins, dozens upon dozens of other slaves beginning their long morning, awaking out of the freedom of sleep into another day of captivity, some with words of love, some with curses on their lips, stumbling out into the woods and performing their ablutions, and then eating a corn cake and taking a sip of water and hasting to the fields.

Some of them were singing, a little love tune—

> *I love my darlin', dat I do,*
> *Don't you love Miss Susy, too?*

Some sang parts of a work song—that same

My old missus promise me
Shoo a la a day,
When she die she set me free
Shoo a la a day…

I could hear the music, though most were moving in silence, dragging their feet, heads lowered, eyes still fixed on whatever dreams they might have lived in their sleep.

To belong to another person! To be owned by someone the way people owned shoes or carriages or tables and chairs and horses and tools! It never occurred to me to consider such matters even after my days living at The Oaks, at least not until after that night with Liza. Lying there in my bed, the odors of our coupling still rising like ancient perfume from the pillows and sheets, I was reluctant to give up the memories of the night before even as I knew I had to arise and dress and descend the stairs to the breakfast table into the world of strife and suspicion.

Liza was nowhere to be seen. Here I met my uncle. Even as he skewered a small breakfast bird on his fork he appeared to be watching me carefully as I entered the room.

"Well, lad," he said, "and how are you this morning? Slept rather late, did you? And I thought you were early to bed."

"I read a while, Uncle."

"Ah, the reading. Always something I plan to do but never get to it." He sighed, and chewed on the small bird.

From another doorway Jonathan entered the room, like a leading actor suddenly making his entrance on stage.

"Good morning, gentlemen."

"Good morning, son. And did you have a good rest?"

"After great exercise, great rest," he said.

"Oh, were you out wandering in the night?" I tried to stare my cousin down, but he met me glinty glare for glinty glare.

"Jonathan is always up early," my uncle said, "always on the watch for odd stoppages and difficulties."

"And for the good events, too," I said.

"Oh, yes," my uncle said. "Certainly for the good as well."

"What good, Cuz," I said to Jonathan, "do you find in your wanderings at night?"

"Oh, a quiet night, Cuz, with nothing stirring except a slight breeze, and a few peaceful songs on the air from the cabins."

"You do help to keep the peace there, do you not?"

My cousin stepped toward me and leaned his face close to mine. I could smell traces of foul whiskey on his breath, the residue, no doubt, of a night in the cabins.

"You yourself seem quite well rested," he said. "Tell me, dear Cousin, do you take this kind of leisure in New York? I will wager a week's worth of labor that you do not."

"No," I said, "I am usually up quite early, as I've been doing since I arrived. Except for last night."

"Always a good idea to make an exception some time," my uncle said. "Sally? Was there liquor in the pie last night? Our young nephew appears to have been drugged."

He proceeded to cut the bird and eat.

"Nawssir, massa," Precious Sally said from the stove, and my two relatives laughed.

Jonathan turned his glance to me.

"You haven't changed your mind about leaving, have you? Staying here you could take a great deal more leisure."

"What precisely do you mean, Cousin?" I said, staring at him and trying to discern some particle of motive in the events of the previous evening.

Jonathan gave a shrug and settled at the table with a coffee mug before him.

"Nothing more than what I said, Cousin," he replied.

"Because in fact I have decided to take a bit more time," I said.

He sat up, and appeared to be surprised.

"How very nice. Father?"

"Yes, indeed," my uncle said, his jaws still working on the meat of the bird.

"Though I still do want to inquire about the sailings to New York."

"Eventually you will go, yes," my uncle said, swallowing.

Jonathan raised his mug toward me.

"But not this week or next." If he had not sounded so smug I would have taken him for being surprised by my decision.

"No," I said, "I don't think so. Yet I am not entirely sure when I will go."

"Of course," my uncle said.

"At least not until the rice harvest, yes?" said my cousin.

"I cannot say."

"Of course not," my uncle said, touching a napkin to his lips in that dainty manner he had.

"I will need the carriage for a trip to town today," I said.

"Oh?" Jonathan looked at me suspiciously.

"I wish to speak to the ship's agent," I said. "I would like to know the schedule."

"Of course," my uncle said. "one of the boys will take you."

"I will go alone," I said. "I believe I can handle the horse."

"You have learned a lot in your short stay, yes," my uncle said. "Has he not, Jonathan?"

"Oh, yes, Father, indeed, he has."

"And I will need some assistance," I said.

My uncle turned to Jonathan.

"Then you will go—"

"Not him, sir. I will need some assistance…in the market. Those local curios you mentioned to me when I first arrived. I thought perhaps Liza might accompany me and help me find them."

"Did I mention such things to you?" my cousin said.

Crockery clattered in the washing basin behind us where Precious Sally worked her pots and plates.

"You find the fine baskets for the harvest right here on the plantation," she said.

"But they are worn from use, Sally," my cousin put in. "It would be a good idea to find some good unused specimens in the market."

"Miss Rebecca, she could go," Precious Sally said as she picked up dishes and silverware strewn about the floor.

"Rebecca is teaching her reading today to the children from the cabins," my cousin said.

"I…we will be fine by ourselves," I said.

"Of course," my uncle said. "That's a splendid idea."

"Liza will be of great assistance," my cousin said. "I am sure she has been already."

He sent me a sideways glance, and I held his gaze. Did he suspect anything about last night? Could Liza have said something to him as a way of keeping him at arm's length? Or, worse, could he after all have sent her to me on a mission to tempt me to stay, making Liza into a monstrous liar? And was my uncle a part of such a plot? A cold shock of regret quivered through my body and if I had been standing next to the wide creek I might have thrown myself headlong into the waters.

But if we were going to town that day—and there was nothing I wanted more—we would have to leave soon. The drive was long, and I hoped to spend more time with Liza, though where or how I had not even thought about at that point.

My uncle aided us in what was now a plan, going out to look for Black Jack so that he might send him out to the barn to find Isaac who would hitch up the horses. Jonathan meanwhile went about his business for the day, whatever that business was, leaving me alone in the room for a moment with Precious Sally.

"Massa from New York," she said, her big brown arms showing below the rolled-up sleeves of her voluminous dress of cotton sacking with an apron of thicker sacking draped over it.

"Is that what you call me?"

"It is," she said.

"I suppose that's who I am. Except I'm nobody's master."

"Not so far," she said.

I shook my head.

"You've been listening to our conversations?"

"Everybody talks in front of us. Sometimes it's like we're not there. Sometimes it is…"

"You know what my father wants to do?"

"From what I hear he wants to buy part of this plantation."

"And I don't want him to. I've decided that."

"But you ain't going back to New York yet. First, you said you was going."

I shook my head, confused somewhat that I was having this intimate conversation about my life and family matters with a woman I scarcely knew—who, and I confess that I thought this, was a slave to boot.

"I'm going to town to inquire about sailing schedules."

"I see," she said.

"And I would like Liza to travel with me. To help me at the market. I… want to make some purchases before I leave for New York."

"Uh…" she said. And then she added, "Huh."

It was that look, that tone of voice—I had known it all my life growing up with Marzy in the household. African or white, our servants were our consciences, and it was important for us to notice the way we treated our consciences.

"I trust you can spare her for the day. Perhaps even overnight. We may not be able to return until tomorrow." I paused and took a breath. "I don't know why I am telling you this. It sounds as though I am asking your permission."

Precious Sally sighed, and her huge chest heaved up and down in a wave of inhalation.

"You don't have to ask my permissions," she said. She seemed about to say more when my uncle came huffing and puffing back into the room.

"All arranged." Turning to Precious Sally, he said, "Now where is she?"

"Right here, massa," Liza said from the doorway. She was wearing a fresh dress and a tan straw hat that sat on her head at an angle I could only call jaunty.

"She need a pass, massa," Precious Sally said. "They's been trouble up the road."

"Of course, of course," my uncle said, "I'll write it just now." And he left the room while the three of us remained, the big woman, me, and Liza, silent, silent, silent, until he returned.

About half an hour later we set out, the passes in my coat pocket, my heart beating, or so it seemed to me, louder than the noise of the horse's hooves. I held the reins and Liza sat primly alongside me. The horse—a big old gelding named Archie—seemed to know the way, and obliged only now and then to give me the opportunity to urge him along.

"How are you this morning, Liza?" I said, finding it difficult to breathe.

"Fine, massa," she said in a voice that gave no notice of any difficulty on her part.

"Are you never going to call me Nate again?"

"Maybe later, massa," she said.

I reached over and touched her at the knee. It was a shock to me, almost as if I had touched the tip of a candle flame, and I noticed she flinched at my touch.

"I am suddenly tired, are you?"

"Yes," she said.

"But happy," I said.

"Yes," she said.

"Liza," I said, keeping my hand in place, "I have been thinking about you...wondering about you, I should say."

She sat silently, giving nothing back.

"It was..." I paused, not knowing the words, and the creak and rattle of the carriage and the clomping of the horse filled the world all of a sudden. I wanted words to fill the emptiness and ward off the confusion inside me. The heat grew steadily stronger, and the road seemed long.

"Tell me about yourself, will you?" I said.

Liza touched a hand to her hat as if it might be blown away in the wind, though it was a breezeless morning, except what air we stirred as we rolled along in the carriage.

"I...was born here, at The Oaks."

"And your parents?"

"My...family, they came over on the ships."

"From distant Africa?"

"From across the water, yes."

"That's a long way. And a long time."

"Not that long, Nate. They didn't live that long."

"I am sorry," I said.

"I am sorry, too," she said. "My mother...she died when I was born. Precious Sally helped raise me up. That's how I come to work in the house." She paused, and we listened together to the rumbling of the carriage wheels in the dust.

"Nate?"

"Yes, Liza?"

I took my hand from her thigh and lay my arm around her shoulders.

"I got a question. If I'm ever going to be a free woman—and that's what I dream of—I know I got to talk better than I do. That right?"

"When you are free, Liza, you can speak any way you like. That is part of being free."

"I read books, you know."

"I believe I know that."

"Next thing I want to work on my hand."

"That would be a good thing."

"The doctor says, you write a letter, it's like casting your voice over the miles."

"A lovely way to put it," I said.

She pursed her lips and turned her face away, as if she suddenly had a desire to study the plants and trees we passed.

"Do you ever wonder about what it's like to be a slave?"

"What a question! No, I never have."

"That's because you don't have to. But every one of us dreams about being free, 'cept those that can't dream. The stupid ones. The ones be content to stay where they are every day, working until they fade away, for a few cups of flour and some pieces of meat at the weekend and the holidays."

"I could find many people like that in New York," I said, "and they are supposed to be free."

"They are free," Liza said. "So they can choose to be a slave or not. Slaves don't have a choice."

I remembered the terrified man crossing the creek not so long ago.

"Unless they run."

"You got to be something stupid just to try and run." Silence settled over us for a little while, silence, tempered by the racketing of the wagon and the sound of the horse. Then she said, "Or awful smart, and do it the right way."

"What way would that be?"

"Not that way," Liza said, as we noticed a group of horsemen coming our way from the direction of town.

"No, not that way," I said as Langerhans and two of his cohorts on horseback flew past us at a gallop, the leader inclining his head toward us as we passed. I did not quite understand, though, what I had said.

Liza grew silent and stared at the sky above the treetops, lighter than the light blue above the barns where we had begun our journey. It must be the sea, I said to myself, the sea makes the sky turn as light as an egg-shell.

When we arrived in Charleston we went immediately to a hotel where I took a room. Liza quickly departed for the market and I made a visit to the shipping office and inquired in desultory fashion about departure dates of boats sailing to New York. When I mentioned there might be two passengers, an inquisitive clerk asked me for our names. He stared at me as though he could somehow read the plan I held in my mind. I told him nothing more and returned and went upstairs to the room. I took up a post at the window to await for Liza's return. Outside the street was filled with carriages and towns-folk, white and slaves, walking along as if with great purpose to their lives. In my own life, meanwhile, I saw no purpose beyond the next hour, waiting as I was with a deep expectation about the woman who would return. As to my voyage home, I thought almost nothing of it now, and felt deeply powerful in my decision. This was what it was like, I took pride in, to be a free man who could freely decide his own fate.

Time passed. My father's pocket-watch ticked away. I was contemplating going out for a walk to the ocean-side of town when there came a knock at the door, and Liza entered the room, followed by two young slave-boys, bearing large tubs of steaming water.

"Massa," she said, after the young slaves had set down their burdens and left the room. "Time for a bath."

"A good idea," I said. But as dusty from the road as I was, I stood there a moment, until she came up to me and began to tug at my coat.

Not since I was a boy and bathed by my mother had I ever undressed in front of a woman in the broad light of day. It was both embarrassing and titillating to me, as Liza helped me off with my shirt, and knelt to work at removing my boots and my trousers. I was intensely excited but at the same had wandering thoughts as I studied the top of her head, the intricate intersections of wiry hairs making patterns that only another person could have braided. Who did this for her? Precious Sally? Another girl from the cabins?

"Now," she said, and touched me as she stood up and led me to the large porcelain tub in the far corner of the room into which the slave-boys poured the water.

I climbed in, flinching at the heat, and then relaxing into it.

I shut my eyes, and when I opened them again Liza had already removed her cambric, and then her skirt and stood before me, a living sculpture in sandstone, before climbing into the tub alongside me.

"The road was dusty," I said as she laved me with a cloth.

"Your dust I can wash away," she said.

"I'll wash you," I said.

"Not this you can't wash off," she said, holding her darker arm next to mine.

"Well, you can't wash the Jew out of me, either."

"That is not my worry. I am not even a Jew. Just a Jew-slave."

"You're my slave," I said, taking her liquid body in my liquid arms.

"Uh-uh," she said, "I belong…"

"Hush," I said, kissing her wet lips with mine.

"Naw," she said, just after, "I was saying, in my heart? I don't belong to anyone."

I pulled back my arms and picked up the cloth and began daubing at her breasts.

"And these are not mine?"

"No," she said.

"To whom do they belong?"

"In my heart?"

"In your heart."

"Nobody."

"And this?" I said, dabbing the cloth at the precious place between her legs.

"Nobody," she said.

"I wish I was nobody," I said.

"What?" she said, and then she laughed, and we embraced again, and then stood up, splashing water everywhere, as we stepped out of the tub and rubbed each other down with towel cloths before rushing to the bed.

What followed I cannot say except that you can imagine it, the naïve boy and the wounded slave girl, what transformations of love they made.

And the talk that followed.

"Nate," Liza said in a whisper, her warm words in my ear. "What if you could buy me? Would you buy me?"

"I have already thought about that," I said. "Indeed, I would. That way we would never be apart. I will make an offer to uncle as soon as we return."

"But you have to understand he will refuse. Your cousin…will force him to refuse."

"What interest does he have in keeping you?"

"He is a…stubborn man. He will not give me up, not to you."

I accepted her view as truth.

"Liza," I said, "here is what I will do," making a great revelation to myself as well as her. "When I return to New York I will advise my father to buy into the plantation. That is why he sent me, to advise him on this question. This means I will own you after all. And once I own you, I will set you free."

"Nate, the family will never agree to that. They would rather lose the plantation rather than set me free."

"They are mad, then. Why would they take such a course?"

Liza shook her head, but remained silent.

At that point I should have asked another question. But instead I became caught up in the intrigue of the moment.

"Then I will steal you," I said. "What if I bought us passage on a ship north and we left from here next week?"

"We could not," she said, engaged again in our speculations. "You must have papers for your slaves. A bill of sale."

"I..." I took a deep breath. "I could forge one."

"Do you even know how to begin such a thing, Nate?"

"No," I said. "But I can find out."

"And if you owned me you would truly set me free?"

"We would be free souls together, Liza. I swear."

She rolled close to me, and more time went by.

After what seemed like some hours I consulted my watch, only to find that it had stopped, for lack of winding.

Chapter Fifty-two

A Visitor (1)

$\mathcal{Y}$ou have got a cast like a nigger," my cousin said to me on our return while Liza was climbing down from the carriage.

I looked over at her but she gave no impression that she had heard what he said.

"I bathed this morning, but now I have to bathe all over again."

"Did she help you with your bath?" my cousin said, with Liza still within earshot. He did not give me a chance to reply before adding, "And now that blush on you makes you look even more nigger-like. Or maybe like a redskin. Or a Jew!"

"You don't have to speak that way, Cousin," I said.

"I beg your pardon, Cuz. You and my wife must speak more about this."

And he leaned toward me and I smelled the liquor on his breath and things sharpened a little in my understanding.

"And so have you decided," he said, "about staying or leaving?"

I watched as Liza made her way to the big house, picturing her shifting hips beneath the bright clothes she wore.

"I am going to stay a while," I said. "At least through the rice harvest," surprising myself again with my certainty. I watched my cousin's eyes following her.

"You have given this some serious thought, and it makes me happy," he said. But the look on his face did not affect happiness, not at all.

All this I attributed to his drinking.

My uncle, however, behaved rather jovially at the lunch table and I did not believe it had anything to do with drink. That so many things were about to erupt I had no inkling.

"I'm pleased to hear that you will be staying on a while longer, nephew," he said.

"It pleases me, too, Nathaniel," my aunt said.

Rebecca echoed her sentiment.

"I hope this means you will help me with our teaching."

"Certainly," I said. "I believe that is important."

"Important for..." Jonathan stopped, glanced around the room. Precious Sally, standing at her usual post in the doorway, made a sound in her throat, but said nothing, of course.

"Important for the slaves," I said. "To be free and illiterate, that is not true freedom."

"Yes, yes," my cousin said. "To be free like me, able to read, that is true freedom."

"It is, Jonathan," Rebecca said.

"Yes, I am glad to be free to read this," he said, pulling a letter from his coat pocket and holding it up to the light.

"Do not—" my uncle said.

"I want him to hear it," Jonathan cut him off. "He is part of the family...our wonderfully large family..."

"Very well then," my uncle said, and slumped back in his chair.

"This note arrived early this morning."

"Yes," I said, ignoring what I took to be his prescience about my purposes there. And Liza's. Did he suspect us? Of course, he suspected us. Or perhaps he had even ordered her to...? Fortunately for my mental state at the moment, he cut off my thoughts as he waved the letter in front of us.

And then began to read.

"'Christians of Charleston! Awake! While you have been sleeping certain Forces have gathered in the countryside, teaching slaves to study murder. A certain Jew has been showing them a Plan! Under the oaks a travesty is brewing! Tend to your possessions, tend to your Souls! The True Way is to follow Jesus! Step off the Path and you are Lost! Watch for my next Bulletin!' Signed 'Your Brother in Christ.'"

Rebecca burst into tears.

"They want to scare me. This is not fair. I discovered years ago that our good doctor friend from time to time has also been teaching Africans to read. Then why should I stop? I will not stop. I will go on with my instruction."

"Of course, you will," Jonathan said. "But we do have to be aware there are certain parties opposed to it."

"It is none of their business," Rebecca said.

"They are making it their business," Jonathan said.

"I will not stop. That is the end of it."

"Yet it might be the end of us," my cousin said.

"Nonsense," I said, thinking back to the inquisitive shipping clerk. "This is the doing of some befuddled individual and surely not the majority view in the city."

"I believe that is so," my uncle said. "They are good to us here."

"They are not good. They are merely tolerant," my aunt said. "I was afraid this might happen."

"It is nothing of the kind," my uncle said.

Rebecca wept again.

"You never liked me," she said to my aunt.

"This is not true," my uncle said. "She does like you. She loves you, child."

"When you go, she will be mean to me," Rebecca said.

My aunt stood up and went to the doorway.

"When he goes, I am moving to town."

"And how will you live, Mother?" Jonathan said.

"I will establish myself as a sole trader. I will open a business."

"What business?" my uncle said. "What business do you know?"

"I will sell lace, perhaps. I will sell dresses."

"What do you know about dresses?"

"What do you know about rice farming? Everything you have here comes from the Africans."

"Then perhaps I shall depart this world at an early date," my uncle said, "and give you the opportunity to work sooner as a sole trader."

"Is that what you wish?" my aunt said.

"No, no, no, no. I do not wish that. But if I did leave early, you can sell The Oaks, and sell the slaves and have enough money to move to town and establish yourself in business."

"And me? Where would that leave me?"

My cousin's voice turned almost to a childish whine.

"Working with your mother," my uncle said.

"This is the only work I know," my cousin said. "Here, at The Oaks." He paused, as if contemplating some important fact. "But if we had to sell all this, I suppose…"

Rebecca began crying all the louder.

"Rebecca, please," Jonathan said.

Rebecca stood up and pointed her finger at Jonathan.

"I am a lady in distress. To think you'd sell all these people!"

"You are not a lady," my aunt said, "none of us is a lady. In fact, you're much more like a child, with your childish notions of teaching these slaves to read."

"Be quiet, Mother, please," Jonathan said. "Rebecca is doing a fine thing."

"I am pleased you say so," Rebecca said. "Of late I haven't been sure what you thought of my work."

My aunt, her mother-in-law, ignored her remark.

She said directly to Jonathan: "And are you doing a fine thing too? Cavorting with the—"

"That will be enough," my uncle said, making it seem as though speaking were as much a chore as lifting. "All this talk about my departure is quite premature and it is putting a terrible strain on my old corpus and I want to end it right now. Do you hear me, Jonathan?"

"Yes, sir," my cousin said.

"Mother?"

Silence for a moment. Then she made a reluctant, "Yes."

"Daughter?"

"I will be silent," Rebecca said.

"Thank you," my uncle said. And then he turned to me.

"Nephew?"

"Yes, sir."

"He has nothing to do with this," Rebecca said.

"Is he teaching them, too?" My aunt turned to me and made a smile close to a leer—it was sickening to see this woman do such a thing with her mouth.

"Are you?"

I did not know what to say.

"Mother, please," my uncle said.

"You sound like him," my aunt said, pointing to Jonathan.

"I am his son," Jonathan said.

"And whose sons are yours?" my aunt said to him. "Or daughters!"

At which point Rebecca made a wailing noise, like something you feared as a child you might hear at night in the dark.

Bam!

My uncle slammed the heel of his hand on the table, rattling dishes.

"I will not have this kind of talk at my table," he said. "I will not!"

All of her offensiveness disappearing in an instant, my aunt now began to cry.

"Mother," Jonathan said, "if you are going to become a sole trader you must not give in to tears."

My uncle turned to him with a fury I had not seen before.

"Your mother will not speak to you anymore about these matters and you—you will not speak to your mother in this fashion."

"Yes, sir, sorry, sir," my cousin said, suddenly remorseful.

Rebecca went on crying even as my aunt's weeping subsided.

I noticed just then that the slaves had left the room.

How I wish I had followed them, to the barns or the fields, wherever they had fled, because the next minute brought the sound of men and horses outside the house and then someone striding up the front steps of the veranda and knocking loudly at the door.

"Nevermore!" I said.

"What is that?" my cousin asked.

"I'll go," I said.

"Ask Black Jack," my uncle said.

I paid him no mind and left the room and went to the front door.

Which I opened and felt the shock of seeing once again the silver-haired man in the top-hat who had boarded the boat in Perth Amboy and beat the horse and slave in town. Behind him just beyond the house waited men on horseback, Langerhans and his crew, and one or two others whom I did not recognize.

"You again?" he said. "These then are your people?"

"May I ask you what your business is, sir?"

"That is precisely the question I have come to ask here, and as it turns out I have come to ask it of you."

Behind me I heard my uncle stirring.

"Who is it, Nate?"

"A man from New Jersey," I said.

"New Jersey?"

My uncle came lumbering up to the door.

"Not truly from New Jersey," the man said. "That is where this fellow and I met, but I have been associated with other states and other places."

"This fellow is my nephew," my uncle said. "Now what is your business here?"

The man looked past me at my suddenly alert and agitated uncle.

"May I come in?"

"I will come out," my uncle said, and gave me a little shove to move me out onto the veranda so that he might follow.

The man stepped aside, looked back at his companions, and signaled them with his hand to remain where they were.

"And now, sir?" my uncle directed the man to the table and chairs to the left of the door. "Will you sit?"

"Thank you," the man said. "But we are in a hurry. Unless perhaps you can answer our question."

"And that would be, sir?"

My uncle looked at me, as if I understood what he was thinking.

"My slave has run off," the man from Jersey said. "Have you seen a little nigger about twelve, dark as night, wearing red trousers? This fellow here, your...?"

"My nephew?"

"Ah, hah! Yes, your nephew. He has seen him."

"Have you?" my uncle turned to me.

"Not recently," I said. "I first saw him on the ship. We were passengers on the same ship."

My uncle cleared his throat and inclined toward the man.

"Why did you come here to inquire? Was he seen heading in this direction?"

"A good question, a very good question," the man said. "I was directed by these colleagues of mine..." He gestured toward Langerhans and the patrollers. "The good folks in Charleston said you all might know something about runaways."

"Did they?" My uncle pushed his belly forward and stepped closer. "What else might they have said?"

"I've never been a man to waltz around the truth, have I?" He looked directly at me. "Have I, son?"

"I would not know," I said.

"You know something of me. You may know enough to know that I will tell you now what I learned in town. I'll tell you that I learned in town that here on this plantation some odd things have occurred. That you brothers of the Jewish creed, in collusion with a certain medical man, have been teaching slaves how to read and write. And—"

"First," my uncle broke in, "that is not any of your interest. And second—"

"First," the man said, "it goes against the nature of things that the Africans should try to acquire the skills of a higher breed. And second—"

"First," my uncle said, "there is no evidence that Africans are what you infer is a 'lower breed' than white men. And second—"

"First, there is evidence that those of the tribe of Israel are a breed apart," the man said, his finger poking the air, and his eyes all-ablaze, "and second—"

Now I was growing angry.

"Second what?"

"Second, it is clear I am gaining no traction talking to you here. Now you will excuse me, because I have to go and catch my little nigger."

At this point Jonathan, who had been listening in the doorway, stepped out onto the porch holding the offensive missive in his hand.

"Did you write this letter?"

"Sir," the man said, "I don't know what letter you're referring to."

"This letter," Jonathan said, and began to read from it again.

"Stop!" My uncle waved his hand. "I will not allow these things to be spoken in my house."

"I respect that, sir," said the white-haired man.

"You are a strange man," Jonathan said, crumbling the letter in his fist. "A strange man from—" He turned to me. "From where?"

"New Jersey, I believe," I said.

"Wherever you are from, it is now time for you to leave the house, please, sir," Jonathan said.

"I will be going," said the man, "and though I'm in a hurry I at least expected that I might have been invited in so that I could at least decline the invitation. But that would have been a Christian thing to do, to offer such an invitation, and you—"

"We are not Christian, no," Jonathan said. "Now please leave, sir."

"I will leave, and frankly I hope never to return. Because if I do it will be most unfortunate."

"Are you threatening us, sir?"

"I am merely stating a fact. If you see my nigger, I expect you will hold on to him for me."

"I doubt if he has run this way," Jonathan said.

"It is your reputation, sir," the man said, brushing a hand along his thick white hair. "There are only a certain number of places where he can run."

"If I were your slave," I spoke up, "I would run anywhere I could."

The man turned to me, his eyes glowing near-yellow in his head.

"I thought you were a more judicious fellow. If I did not know you were from New York, I'd think you wanted to challenge me to a duel."

He then bowed slightly toward me, and twirled around on his heel, his cape following, and departed from the veranda. Within moments he remounted his horse and without another word the man and his crew, with one last glance back at us from Langerhans, went galloping away up the road.

"Wherever he has departed to, the young slave is fortunate," my uncle said, "to be free of that creature's clutches." He turned to me and asked how I had come to know the man and I explained how I had encountered him, though I omitted most of the stranger elements that had passed between us.

"Travel sometimes makes for curious companions," he said.

As if to put a concluding point on this entire incident, around the corner of the house Isaac came riding, leading my old Promise behind him, his presence reminding me that for many long minutes while we talked with the white-haired man the slaves seemed to have faded away.

"You coming to the fields, massa?" he called out to me. And so then making a bow of my own I left the veranda and mounted my horse. I had only just begun to ride, when I heard a voice from the veranda and looked back to see Liza standing there in her apron.

My heart leaped, more animal than our steeds.

Chapter Fifty-three

Introductory Lesson

They named her Liza, a version of her mother's and grandmother's names, and this girl, a pale creature compared to most of the other slaves— you'd say she was the color of almonds—stood out from everyone else even as she tried to stand close. Her great-grandmother had disappeared somewhere near an African river, her grandmother went mad but still gave birth before she died, and her mother succumbed in the birth throes, victim to what felt like a curse upon all the women.

Liza hoped to escape that curse.

Her father—everyone except *his* father seemed to know about her paternity, from the house slaves to all who lived in the back cabins and worked in the rice fields—put her to work in the main house when she was still a child, and there Liza flourished, learned under the tutelage of a black stump of a woman named Precious Sally, to help in the kitchen and to cook simple meals, if not at first for the aging master and his family, at least for the other house slaves. The doctor checked on her every time he visited the plantation, extremely worried that her father—he took him to be that dangerously mad—might at some point try to take her up the way he had her mother. He talked to the slave child, asked her certain questions that might have led her to reveal certain matters if in fact they had occurred.

But nothing.

This gave the doctor pause, and he was, at least momentarily, pleased that no harm had come to this girl.

Yet.

Because, he surmised, her father suffered from a terrible mental diffi-culty, and, the doctor believed, it was only a matter of time before the man would turn his attention in the worst way to his beautiful almond-colored daughter. For a while though, the man seemed to ignore her.

Meanwhile, the girl was growing, and much to the dismay of some of the field slaves who saw it, she now and then turned cart-wheels on the lawn of the main house on her way to work in the kitchen. Cooking. Baking. Cleaning. Gathering the spices.

At this point the doctor intervened and gave her periodic instruction in how to read. At least twice a week, and sometimes more, the physician would appear at the kitchen door, as though he himself were one of the slaves, forbidden to enter through the front door, with books in his arms. He taught her the alphabet from an early age. The way she sounded each letter seemed to him a small miracle, and she mastered this quickly. Oh, and doesn't this make all the difference! He sighed to himself. Give the young bird a little shove from the nest and it instinctively spreads its wings and however clumsily flies to safety. And the human child? She sounds her letters, and soon will be able to fly on her own, yes. Scientific-minded fellow that he was, the doctor encouraged her to read to him from geography books first, such as some that he bought in town.

INTRODUCTORY LESSON

Questions to my little Reader.
What place do you live in?
Is it a town or a city you live in?
What is a town? What is a city?
Which way is north? Which south?
Which way is east? Which west?
Have you ever been in any other town or city than the one you live in?
If you have, what was the name of that town?
In going to that town, which way did you go?
What town lies next to the place in which you live, on the north?
What town is next, on the east?
What next, on the west?
What next, on the south?
What county do you live in?
Do you know what a county is?
What state do you live in?
Which way is Boston from the place you live in?

Which way is New York?
Which way is Hartford?
Which way is Philadelphia?
Have you ever seen a river?
Have you ever seen a mountain?
If you have, what was it called?
Describe a mountain?
Did you ever see the sea, or ocean?
What is the sea, land or water?
Is the land smooth and level, like the water?
Are towns built on the water, or on the land?
Do animals such as horses and cows live on the water, or on the land?
Did you ever catch any fish on the land?
Where is the sky? Where are the stars?
Did you know what the shape of the world is?
Did you ever hear of England?
Did you ever see anybody who has been in England?
Do you know which way England lies?
Did you ever hear of Asia?
Do you know which way Asia lies?
Did you ever hear of Africa, where negroes come from?
Do you know which way it lies?

The doctor's little reader quickly learned her lessons in what lay where and how she should regard them. She learned her directions, and told him a story about catching fish on land—a silly dream she dreamed one night after reading with him. She did not know anyone who had been in England, but she had heard of Africa, yes, and she recalled quite vividly the stories old women back in the cabins told about the old country, the rivers, the forests, and she knew which way it lay. Back there, over her shoulder, where across the rice fields the ocean broke on the shore, and made a road of waves all the way back to the place where her grandmother had been born.

Where is the sky? Where are the stars?

She knew answers to these questions, too.

The stars spread overhead on dark nights without a big moon, the stars made shapes—the boy sometimes pointed these out to her—and some of these pointed toward England and some to Africa and some to Philadelphia and New York. Each of these names seemed as foreign, and as familiar, as the next. Only the stars glittered with a fascinating and hypnotic light that made her wonder about everything in the world and everything above it—creeks, rivers, roads, trees, fields, farms, horses, people, African or not, each fit into a pattern like the pattern overhead in the dark on nights without a great moon. Though some nights just before sleep she wondered how she might steal a boat and sail back to Africa, she understood that once she returned she would have no place to go. Could she look for, and find, her grandmother? How far deep into the forests must she have returned? It might be easier to float up to the stars and turn upside down and use the glowing specks of light as stepping stones back to the night skies above the place where her ancestors were born.

Such a vast place, Africa seemed in relation to all else on the globe in the book. And all a big ball, and all that ocean between her and Africa. It seemed easier to memorize a poem about it all than to contemplate leaving the plantation and returning to Africa.

GEOGRAPHICAL RHYMES
TO BE REPEATED BY THE PUPIL

The world is round, and like a ball
Seems swinging in the air,
A sky extends around it all,
And stars are shining there.
Water and land upon the face
Of this round world we see,
The land is man's safe dwelling place,
But ships sail on the sea.
Two mighty continents there are,
And many islands too,
And mountains, hills, and valleys there,
With level plains we view.
The oceans, like the broad blue sky,
Extend around the sphere,
While seas, and lakes, and rivers, lie
Unfolded, bright, and clear.
Around the earth on every side

Where hills and plains are spread,
The various tribes of men abide
White, black, and copper red.
And animals and plants there be
Of various name and form,
And in the bosom of the sea
All sorts of fishes swarm.
And now geography doth tell,
Of these full many a story,
And if you learn your lessons well,
I'll set them all before you.

Ball...air...all...there...She loved the sound of the rhymes...*sky...sphere...lie...clear...*

If there was any moment in her early life when she first thought about walking away, running, it must have been here. Mark it!

Chapter Fifty-four

A Visitor (2)

It was many and many a year ago,
In a kingdom by the sea,
That a maiden there lived whom you may know
By the name of ANNABEL LEE;
And this maiden she lived with no other thought
Than to love and be loved by me...

Up in my room that night I tried to calm myself by reading, but I could find little distraction in Poe, my eyes running over one stanza over and over. Here I was, when the knock came at my door, saying to myself, *And whom might this be? The Raven?*

Liza stood at the door, alone, a thin cotton wrap flowing from her shoulders, dressed for settling in for the night in the big house, ready to help her mistress should some distress arise. She held a candle, her eyes catching the reflection of the flame, and that same flame guttering in the wake of our passage from the door—I drew her in and closed it immediately behind us—to the bed.

"Massa," she said, setting the candle-holder down on the night-table.

"Please," I said.

"Massa Nate," she said, lowering her head toward me in a parody of submission.

"Stop it," I said, touching a finger to her chin. Her skin felt so smooth and cool, I couldn't help but follow with my hand.

The lines of her—neck, throat, chest, her breasts—her gown fell away—she slipped her arms through the sleeves—

I stood a moment, beginning to shed my own clothes.

Breath of her—sweet oil, mint—hair of gardenia—breasts oiled with nutmeg and tincture of lemon—staircase of her ribs, full sweet belly—peeking into the navel that connected her to Africa and all the generations past, who loved each other, struggled with and fought with and sold each other—kissed my way down the smooth slope of her abdomen.

"Oh, Nate," she said, in a sweet voice, the kind you might use to speak to a loving child in a story, "come to me now."

The dark subsides into more dark. Night sounds again from outside the window, seeming now more familiar than exotic, more welcoming than lonely. You horses in the barn, nickering to each other in the sleeps you take alone, oh, you doves nestled together and cooing in dove-dreams in the rafters of the barns, oh, owls in the woods and mice in your dens, oh, alligators loving alligators in alligator-love out in the slimy mossy depths of the swamp waters, oh, all you captives in the cabins dreaming of freedom in the sleep of your enslavement, I take you in my arms because my reach has now so been increased I can hold so much more of the world!

"Nate?"

Liza's whisper, soft almost as a voice in a dream.

"Are you awake?"

"Yes," I said, "I am. Never been more awake, in this way."

"I can't sleep."

"I am sorry."

"I must go."

"No, no, stay a while."

"It's not good for me to stay here. Someone might see me leave the room."

"Tell them I commanded you to stay with me."

"They would assume that," she said. "It is another matter."

"Tell me."

Dimly in the dark I could see her move her head from side to side.

"Not to be told."

"Another secret? Another truth I thought to be true turns out to be something else than it seems?"

"Many things are not what they seem. 'I am black but O my soul is white!'"

"What is that you say?"

"A poet, William Blake said that. The doctor read that poem to us. And we read it ourselves. I can recite it to you."

"You can?"

"Don't you think I have a memory?"

"Of course, of course, I do. Please do say it."

She said the poem, and I lay back on the pillow, astonished.

"Striking, quite striking," I said. "My own education has been deficient, because I do not know it."

She touched my arm.

"I can recite other poems to you," she said.

"That makes me happy," I said.

"I may be a slave," she said, "but when I read a poem I am free."

"One day you will be free. You all will be free."

"I have read this in a book the doctor gave me," she said. "How all men are born slaves. Of one sort or another. Even the freest man must break loose of his father and mother, and his family's laws and rules, and his country's. Weren't all the English just as much slaves as we who came from Africa? And didn't they come here to free themselves?"

"What else did you read in this book?"

"The English stopped the ocean slave trade. And one day the Carolinians will choose to free us."

"And they will choose to lose their plantations? It would have to happen at gunpoint. As some of the legislators here have been arguing."

"The plantations are poorly run," Liza said, naked, and speaking as if in debate in the legislature. "If it weren't for slaves, they would fall apart. Look here at The Oaks, how your uncle must plead with your father to help him with money."

"And so he is a kind of slave, too, a slave to money."

"But he chooses this. A free man may choose to give over his will. But when he chooses to win it back he has the power."

"But for now, he is failing."

"That is what I see at the dinner table. That is what I hear from others of us who listen well."

"Which is a good thing," I said. "Because otherwise I would not have come here. And we would not have—"

She leaned forward in the dark and kissed me firmly but languidly on the mouth, and we sank down together into the dunes of pillows and the ripples of sheets. Yes, all our troubles, all our obstacles, from her being born into slavery to my errand to Charleston, all conspired so that we might come together in this moment that, with blessed hindsight, I see as the high point of all our enchanted moments together. Our loving, our talk, our thoughts mingling... This daughter of the tribe of Ham, and this son of the tribe of Abraham, bound together, these distant cousins! Cousins, after all!

Chapter Fifty-five

In My Margins

What is a Journey?

I began in Africa, on the slopes of a young volcano—before this I have no recollection—a creature moving slowly but surely on my own two feet, herding my child before me as overhead the ash began to rain down on us, and we kept moving, yes, moving across the swampy plain. We cried out to our gods, and our gods called out to us. One was fire, the other thunder. Some of us stopped on the plain where the ash stopped and some of us kept going, stopping only when we reached the forest and we lived in the desert for a long time and they lived there a long time in the forest, until hateful men who worshiped other gods came and swept us up in their nets and tied us with their ropes—oh, ropes made from plants we ourselves had grown!—and dragged us south and then north, then west, where we and our children built a city. The city baked in the heat, and one day we sailed down river to escape it, finding ourselves in the great forest, and stolen from there next we stood at ocean-side, our bodies chained to each other. How we survived that passage over water I do not know. Many many perished.

And that is our history in a paragraph!

Chapter Fifty-six

Days...

A week passed since that extraordinary night, and I went about my business of taking long days in the fields stooping with the field hands as they bent themselves over the burgeoning stalks of rice—trying to pay close attention to what Isaac, armed with a short hoe and a long knife, instructed me about, the nature of the plant, the particular features of the stalk, the buds of kernels. The rice was nearing maturity—I was beginning to acquire enough expertise to notice the plumping of the kernels and the subtle transformation of shading from pale white to light green to thickest green—but I was so hot in my coat, stripping it away, steeped in sweat like a river I might have waded in up to my chin, and my head swelled up with reckless thoughts.

"Isaac," I said, "how can you work like this? The heat is so abominable."

"Massa," he said with a laugh, "I like this. It makes me think, when I close my eyes, I am home in Africa, where my fathers came from."

"Your fathers?"

"My father's father's father. Otherwise, they been here a long time."

"But you still have your protection against the heat?"

"I don't have protection. Difference is, I know I have to work here. You go home after the rice harvest."

"You heard that I was staying until then?"

"You hear things around the plantation," Isaac said.

We moved along, up to our ankles in salty-tinged water, the long row of rice plants.

"What kind of things?"

"Things, massa, things."

"You must hate me for what I do," I said, before I could stop myself.

"Hate you, massa?" Isaac gave me a quizzical look, and if I had not been disturbed about what I had just thought I had made known, it might have amused me, this slave arching an eyebrow and taking the measure of me as though we were talking together on the street in Manhattan instead of in a flooded rice field in South Carolina.

"I don't hate you, massa," he said.

"But you know what I am doing?" I said this: part confession, part query, a search for approval, and a small part braggadocio. I said this: because a man cannot live too long without company of a confidante, someone, a friend, against whose opinion he can test his actions. I had not understood this before I left New York and arrived in Charleston, but I certainly understood it now.

"What you doing, massa? Walking in the water with Isaac."

"Don't be coy, Isaac."

"I don't know what that is—'coy,' massa—so I couldn't be it."

"I thought you were able to read."

"Yes, but I never read that word."

"Let me be frank, Isaac, I have only been here a short time but I know that a pin doesn't drop somewhere on the plantation that you people don't hear it."

"Us people?"

"You slaves."

"Uh-huh, massa," he said. "Well, I suppose that's true." He stopped walking, and I stopped, and he plucked a rice stalk and held it up before his nose, testing it in the light. "You talking about—?" He stopped his work and raised his little hoe as though it were a weapon.

"You know, Isaac," I said, "it is damned difficult for me to believe that I am having this conversation."

"With a slave?"

He shook his head.

"Well," he said, "you got to think of slaves same way you think about any people. Some of us smart, some of us quick, some of us slow. Now that Ms. Rebecca helping us to read we can make a good conversation. You want to conversate about the Bible? I can conversate about how Moses led the Children of Israel out of the land of bondage and out into the wilderness for forty days and forty nights." He cocked his head in the direction of the plantation house and said, "And how Samson brought down the temple."

Now it was my turn to laugh.

"You are doing well to 'conversate,'" I said.

"You doing well in the field here," he said. "And other places."

"You…you are not angry?"

"Angry? Why should I be angry?"

"Angry at me."

"Angry at you, massa?"

I don't think that any white man had ever spoken to him in this way, because he gave me a look that a man might give to a talking stone or a passing cloud that rained down coins.

And then I said the next thing, the final thing, that could only have caused him great consternation. And me, also. Because I was as much delivering the news to myself as to him.

"Isaac," I said, wiping sweat from my forehead with my sleeve, "I…I am in love with her."

Chapter Fifty-seven

...And Nights

The night of that same day Liza burst into my bedroom.

"How dare you!" she said, throwing her fists at me as I stood up to meet her.

I caught her by the wrists and we spun around, almost as if in a kind of dance.

"How dare I? I did not know a slave could say such things!"

"You didn't? You didn't? Well, despite my life of slavery I am free—I am free to hate you!"

She tore one of her hands free and banged me in the nose. The pain pulled me back and I clasped both hands to my face.

"Nate, Nate," she said in a sudden worried cry. "Are you all right? Are you?"

Hands still covering my aching face, I stumbled back against the bedroom wall.

"No," I said, "no, I'm not."

My voice sounded thick. Glancing down behind my hands I could see the blood dripping onto my shoes.

"Oh, I'm so sorry, so sorry," Liza said, and guided me in her arms to the bed.

"I...I'll fetch some water. Wait!"

"Wait? Wait? My blood cannot wait."

"Here," she said, and snatched a pillow from the bed and shoved it at me. I caught it in one hand and pressed the billowy thing to my face. She left the room while I sat on the edge of the bed, breathing hoarsely but steadily, feeling the blood run out of my battered nose and down my shirt front.

In a moment she was back. Her eyes were wild, her duster spattered with my blood.

Clutching the cloths she had just fetched and dipping them into the water from my drinking jug she dabbed at my nose, and then bid me press the wet cloths against it.

"Lie back," she said.

I obeyed, but gagged on the blood that ran down the back of my throat.

I sat up again.

"Back," she said.

"Are you the massa?" I said. "It is choking me."

She approached me again, dabbed, pressed. After awhile, in which we both remained silent except for our breathing, the blood stopped flowing.

"Why did you say that?" Liza asked.

I pulled the cloths away from my face.

"What did I say?"

"You know what you said."

I shook my head, this motion somehow stirring up the pain, if not the blood, almost in an instant.

"You told Isaac you loved me."

I sighed, and swallowed, and tasted the bitter iron of my own blood.

"I said that, yes."

"So stupid."

"Me? Stupid?"

She shook her head, frightened all of a sudden by her own aggressiveness toward me.

"I said it," I said, "because it is true."

"It is not." Her voice was hoarse and raspy.

"Oh, but it is, sad to say. And wonderful, too."

I tossed the bloody cloths onto the bed and reached for her hand.

She pulled it away.

I reached again.

"You're still bleeding," she said. I felt the hot stinging in my nostrils, still wet with the flow.

She picked up the cloths, refolded them so that the clean side showed, and pressed that against my face, at the same time pushing me back so that my head lay against the bloody discarded pillow.

"I hate you," she said.

"You don't," I said.

"I do, I do. You have ruined everything."

"And how have I done that? What did you have before...?" I stopped myself, amazed at the stupidity and cruelty of such a remark.

"Yes, you're right, massa. Dis nigger woman, what she have befo' de man from New Yawk, he come along?"

"I'm sorry," I said, feeling my shame as more intense pain in the center of my face.

"What did I have? Oh, what did I have?"

It was her turn to hold her face and moan.

"Liza," I said, "I did not mean to—"

"Leave me be!"

"Sorry."

"Yes, you're sorry. You're sorry."

With a huge sigh, she heaved herself to her feet and stood unsteadily before me.

"I can't come here anymore. I have been wanting to tell you this, and now I must tell you this."

"Is it so awful for you? I hadn't understood that it was, Liza. I thought... I thought that you felt something the same as I did."

I reached for her hand, but she pulled back.

"Please," I said, "don't turn me into a beggar." I patted the bed alongside me. "Come sit, please."

"Oh, massa," she said. "De massa call."

"Stop it."

She burned a look at me that gave me more pain than her fist that crushed my nose.

"What massa want?"

"Stop it, please."

"No," she said, her voice returning to normal. "Tell me what you want?"

"I want you," I said. "I want you to sit here beside me."

"You want me?" She burned me again with that gaze. "You want me?" She shook herself as though a cold wind had just passed over her body. "You can have me. Oh, yes, you got me. Massa, anything you want."

And with an angry jerking motion, she tore at her frock, ripping buttons as she pulled.

Now she stood before me, naked to the waist, her chest heaving.

"Here," she said, bowing toward me, then descending to her knees and pulling at my boots. "Now." Off she pulled a boot, throwing it against the wall, then another.

"Stop it," I said, pushing at her as next she tried to interfere with my buttons.

"Massa want me to stop?"

"Yes, stop."

She ceased her frenzied tearing and fell back onto the floor, hugging her knees to her chest.

"Yes, massa," she said, and began to sob most terribly.

"Liza," I said, not knowing what to say beyond her name. I eased myself down onto the floor beside her and took her in my arms.

"You say you love me," she said. "Don't you know that is the cruelest most awful thing to tell a woman like me?"

"But I do love you."

She ignored what I said.

"And do you know why it is so cruel?"

"No," I said in a whisper near her ear. "Tell me."

"Because I am not free to refuse you. And I am not free to accept you, either. I am just a lonely piece of chattel, do you understand? A Jew-slave, as they call us in town. I am like Promise, the horse you ride here. A Jew-horse he is, too."

Turning in my arms, she breathed close to my face. The pain of my bleeding nose was nothing compared to the ache I felt in my chest.

"Perhaps it is time to go," I said, pushing myself against the bed and standing up.

"So it's a lie?"

"What is?"

"You say you love me, and you'll send me away?"

"It is too painful," I said.

"Yes, isn't it? Oh, I hate her, that bitch-cousin of yours! I hate her profoundly!"

As hot as it was in the room, Liza then gave a shiver and crossed her arms across her breasts.

"You hate Rebecca? Why?" I said. "She has been so good to all of you."

"That is the reason I hate her! And I hate the doctor, too!"

I had to shake my head.

"You hate these good people? Why?"

"It was terrible of them to be good to us. Before I learned to read, before I read all these things I read, I didn't know how much I was hurting."

"Liza," I said, and once again took her in my arms.

"Be careful," she said. "Don't be good to me."

"Why not?"

"Because I'll hate you, too!"

She pressed herself against me, trembling wildly. In an instant we threw ourselves on the bed, God's Jew-slaves, both of us, doing the bidding of our bodies that He had created out of dust and clay.

Chapter Fifty-eight

Beyond Words

The first time it happened just after she had been reading and talking about what she had read with the doctor—a novel about, of all things, the South Pacific, about sailors stranded on an island with natives who reminded her of some of the African stories she had heard in the cabins. He had made his rounds, and then left for town. She returned to the kitchen to prepare for Precious Sally's evening meal, her mind filled with that South Sea story, and with another part of her mind marveling at how reading could carry you away out of your present life, out of slavery, even, at least while you were reading the story.

A knock on the wall, and Isaac came into the room.

"How are you today, Liza?"

"Fine," she said. "We just been reading together."

"What you reading?"

And she told him, and he agreed that it sounded like a fine story, something he might like, and though he was a little behind her in his ability to read he said he would try it.

"It's so funny, Isaac," she said. "I read the words, and it gives me such a fine feeling beyond them. It is something we should do all the time."

"I hope to do better at my reading," Isaac said.

"You should," Liza said. "I swear, it's how we get free even if we're still chained to this place."

"Yes, yes," Isaac said. "I will try it, because I do feel chained. Even by these Hebrews I feel chained like their old ancestors, just like the Israelites in Egypt."

Liza stood at the cutting board, preparing vegetables for the meal.

"You been reading, you been reading your Bible."

"I have," Isaac said. "I surely have."

"The religion in the Bible?"

"Yes?"

"It's only one kind of freedom. These novels the doctor's been giving me."

"The ones you talking about?"

"And other ones," Liza said. "Lots of others."

"They ain't about religion."

"Some are, some aren't. But they all make me free in my mind in so many more different kinds of ways than the Bible makes me free. Brother, I am beginning to love them more than I can say in words."

"That's what you were saying."

Liza giggled.

"In words, yes. Now that's a joke!"

That was when *he* came into the kitchen.

"What are you doing here?" he said to Isaac.

The whiskey fumes spread out on his breath like morning mist.

"Fetching some water to Liza," he said.

"Get out. Fetch something else somewhere else. Get to the barns!"

"Massa," Isaac said, retreating out the door.

Jonathan moved toward her and Liza retreated—unfortunately—toward the pantry.

"You whore!" he shouted at her, shoving her through the open door. "Fornicating with that boy," he said.

She shook her head.

"Fornicator," he said, swatting her with the back of his hand.

Fear roared through her blood and she tried to squeeze past him but he shoved her back inside the pantry and pulled the door closed behind him.

"No, please," she said, in a voice that reminded her, even as her fear rose in her blood, of how she spoke in dreams.

He batted her with his fist and she stumbled back against the shelves. Sacks of sugar and grain slipped down around her feet. In a nightmare of motion he pulled at his trousers, pushed her down, and planted himself on top of her, hip to hip. As he began to fumble at her with his fingers, she writhed in desperation, unable to free herself from his weight. He took himself in hand in preparation for coming into her, and she slapped at his face.

He grabbed her wrist, and they fought for a moment, her blood still racing, before she felt herself giving way beneath the heavy press of him. Her blood turned to tears, now coursing through her body like rain-water.

Chapter Fifty-nine

Dawn

*W*hen the first light comes up she is lying there asleep, her skin turned off-gold in the early news of dawn, her breasts like dark puddings, her nipples like raisins. Her braids undone, her hair become a tangle of clots and burrs, her eyes moving beneath her eyelids, as if she might be watching a music show in the privacy of her dreams. And her chest moves up and down with her breath, though she breathes so silently I can't hear even a whisper of the stuff that gives her life.

She seems so close and yet so distant from me, she in her slumbering state, me in my wakefulness.

Or is it me who is dreaming and she who, in another plane, is awake and wondering about me as I wonder about her?

Our God is a dour God, somber and distant in these latter days. Nonetheless I pray to him, of whom I have never asked much before, that He might make this moment last, make it so. This brown-skinned girl with gold-flecked eyes and hair like vines and limbs like those of a goddess carved of sandstone—here is Eden, here is Paradise—and all the rest an afterthought, the moody preoccupations of men too stony to unbend to the call of the moment.

I now shocked myself, because for the first time in months I thought of Halevi, who before this journey had been my constant companion, at least in thought. If he were here, I decided, we might argue this.

But my company now is not a philosopher, but a slave who has shown me something I hadn't known before about freedom.

I was still pondering all this when she slowly opened her eyes.

"Hello."

"Hello," I said.

"It is light, I am late."

"It is early. No one is stirring, not even the birds."

She sat up and shook her head from side to side as if to shake sleep from her mind.

"I have to go, I have my duties."

"What duty could be greater than this? To stay here with me."

"Yes, massa," she said. "But I got other chores. Sunday, it's a big break-fast Precious Sally is making and she'll be needing my help to serve."

"So we're back to that? To 'massa'?"

"We never went away."

"Liza, you and I have traveled some distance from there."

She reached up and touched a playful finger to my chest.

"You rode me."

"We rode together."

"But we went far."

"We went deep," I said.

"Horses don't go deep."

"Some do. Ours did. We did."

She shook her head, as if amazed at a thought.

"All the horses around here, and, you know, I never been on one."

"Oh, yes, you have—"

"No, no, Nate, I'm saying, I have never ridden a horse. Isaac, he always promised me, but he never did do it."

"I am no great horseman, but sometime I will take you for a ride. On my Promise."

"Do you promise?"

"I promise."

"That thrills me."

"Is that so?"

"Yes, for a slave girl, to have a master make a promise to her, you don't know how good that feels. Will you promise, though, to let me ride my own horse?"

I lay down beside her and whispered in her ear.

"I promise."

Her ear—like a beautiful shell you might find washed up on the beach after a storm.

"I must go now," she said.

"Stay a little while longer."

"Precious Sally will be looking around for me. You would not want for her to find me here."

"She never comes up to the second story."

"She could be waiting for me at the bottom of the stairs."

"Does she know about...?"

"About this?"

"About us."

"Mr. Yankee, sir, you have a lot to learn. There is nothing that goes on in a plantation like this that the folks don't know about."

"My folks? My family?"

"The slave-folks, that's who I am talking about."

"I suppose that is because I in my fit of love madness told Isaac?"

She nodded, her face a picture of smugness that I tried to kiss away to no avail.

"You are a fortunate man," she said.

"I know that."

"Not because of anything except that Isaac must like you. Otherwise he might have killed you."

"And then what?"

"And then, he would have run off."

"And lived as a fugitive?"

"He would have run far enough so that he would have found his freedom."

"That's quite a price to pay for freedom," I said. "To kill someone, and then run."

"It looks like a steep price to you," Liza said, "because you won't ever have to pay it. To a slave, it's something, but not that much."

I surveyed her, this woman who had stolen *my* own freedom, and then I said, "Would you would kill someone to be free?"

"If I had to. If I was running, and he stood in my way."

"But you are not running," I said. "So that will not be a price you have to pay."

She gave me a sly smile, and showed me all the light in her eyes that I longed to see, even while seeing it. I caught her in my arms once again, and though she protested, it was a feeble attempt. It made me think that she might never want to be free of me!

She took a deep breath and said, "I'm not running—yet."

Chapter Sixty

A Proposal

$\mathcal{A}$nother week went by. In the fields the kernels of rice were plumping in the sun, and the water that nourished them grew warmer and warmer each day, more like a tepid bath than a cooling wash. Over in the brickyard the sun beat down so hot that it made the entire clearing feel as though it were on fire, and the mud blocks appeared to turn to bricks with the speed of bread dough in a fiercely heated oven. Few songs from the slaves now. They worked in nothing but their tattered trousers, their dark sweat-soaked bodies gleaming in the sun, rank kerchiefs tied around their heads to keep the sweat from pouring into their eyes and blinding them. I quickly removed my coat and now and then exercised my privileges of stepping into the shade and taking a rest against a tree or going to the horse and drinking from the animal-skin water bag that I had tied on to the saddle when I left the house in the morning. The water tasted rank, absent the coolness that had made it so appealing when one of the house slaves had drawn it for me from the well just after breakfast.

The slaves had their own way of cooling off, with a break in their labors coming every hour or so when they would wade out into the creek up to their shoulders, or some even ducking their heads under while others joked about alligators catching them for supper if they didn't catch them first. Once at midday they had time to rest, on some pallets that were put there for just this purpose, pallets soaked with sweat and worn thin by the daily grind of bodies splayed out upon them. (There were not enough to go around, and most of the slaves sprawled during this respite on the ground, under the shade of the trees at the edge of the glade, which in this season was no shade at all.)

After a day such as this I found myself waiting for the right moment at dinner to ask for an interview.

"You wish to speak to me?" my uncle said. "We are speaking now."

I tried not to look around at the other faces at the table, my aunt's, Jonathan's, Rebecca's, and I avoided any recognition of white-haired, ram-rod straight Black Jack who stood at his ready just behind my aunt's place, or Precious Sally, at her customary stand near the rear door.

"Might we speak in private?"

Cousin Jonathan raised his lip and glared at me.

"Something about the rice, no doubt," he said.

My uncle turned on him, in as sudden a way as a heavy man like himself could turn.

"Have some respect for your cousin."

"Might we speak now, sir?"

"Let me eat my dessert and we'll retire then to the veranda."

I watched him devour two slices of Precious Sally's best peach pie and swallow his coffee in one gulp, which gave me little time to rehearse the speech I planned to make to him.

"It is so hot this evening, is it not it?" my aunt said.

"It is," Rebecca said.

Jonathan continued to glare at me, ignoring his dessert.

"Come on, mass' Jonathan," Precious Sally said from the doorway where she kept her watch. "Ain't you going to eat my pie? It's delicious."

"What about him?" Jonathan said.

In the place before me my own dessert lay untouched.

"I made it for you, mass'."

I couldn't help but be distracted as Jonathan, looking dutifully scolded, reached grudgingly for his fork and attacked the pie.

"Well, now," said my uncle, his own plate now cleared. He got up and lumbered to the veranda, with me a few paces behind.

Outside, in the swell of the early evening heat, my fear cooled me. I watched carefully as he lowered himself into his large wicker chair that creaked as he sat like an old bridge with heavy wagons crossing it.

"Shall we have a little brandy then?" he said when he had settled.

"Thank you, sir, but not for me."

"Don't suppose it will do me any good, but then it can't hurt either, can it?"

He called for Jack, who almost instantly appeared, and told him to bring us some brandy.

The light had faded, but the noise of the day still pushed against that border of sound that came with the night. I listened, waiting for Jack to return and depart again.

"Now then," my uncle said, raising his glass.

"Uncle," I said, raising my own glass and quickly swallowing, "I will not dance around the subject." I cleared my throat and spoke again, as forthrightly as I could muster. "I wish to buy Liza."

He paused a moment, silent except for his breathing that was so intense I could hear it despite the rising sounds of night, and looked at me as though I had caught him in the eye with a bright lantern light.

"Well, then, so you shall agree to my proposal? Have you written to your father? I don't pretend that I kept track of everything that happens on this plantation, but I would know if you had sent out a letter."

"I have not yet written to him, Uncle," I said.

He wagged his head from side to side.

"But it is good news that you have made up your mind. And as far as owning anyone, you will own all of that girl's fifty or so uncles and aunts and cousins and brothers and sisters, and so forth. Though it is difficult, if you ever were so inclined as to figure just who is related to whom. I know there are Gentiles who keep good records about these matters, and I know that we Israelites are famous for keeping our genealogies, but that has never been of much concern to me." He reached into his pocket and pulled out a handkerchief with which he dabbed at his forehead, giving the impression that he was an overweight dandy rather than a businessman.

He was putting me off, playing with me, but I would no longer be toyed with in this manner.

"Uncle," I said as forthrightly as I could, "I don't want them all. I just want her."

Now he appeared puzzled, using his great bulk to somehow sink down inside himself and keep from the question I had proposed.

"Well, hum, there are so many difficulties..." He suffered a jagged cough, and appeared almost bewildered by that occurrence, and stuffed his cloth into his pocket and quickly poured himself another brandy.

"Difficulties...?"

"None that...I don't wish...Nephew?" He raised his beefy arm and drank.

"Yes, Uncle?"

"We will own all of these slaves in common, you see? But I cannot sell you that girl. In fact, if you had decided to recommend to my brother that you believe this enterprise of ours to be a bad proposition, your aunt and I would sell all the slaves, except for a few, like Liza and Precious Sally and Black Jack. They would come to town with us and work for us in whatever house we might acquire there."

"So, Uncle, you are saying no to my proposal?"

"Is it a proposal? Either it is or it isn't." His hands were trembling, which gave me the impression that he felt nearly overwhelmed by this difficulty. "Do you wish to become partners with me and your cousin in the plantation?"

"That question I am still pondering, Uncle."

His eyes wandered off to the front lawn, where fireflies played across the hedges.

"That is, as I say, a simple question. But you have complicated it enormously by your query about Liza."

"You are fond of her, Uncle?"

"As I say, were we to sell all else and move to town, she would be one of the few we would keep."

Isaac came to mind, the picture of him soaked with sweat, bending above the rice stalks.

"You would sell Isaac?"

"Isaac? Oh, no, no, no, he had slipped from my mind." An agitated look spread across his face. "No, we would keep him also."

I shook my head in dismay.

"But you would not sell Liza?"

Now his voice tightened, his drawl nearly disappearing from his speech, like the old cultivation water from the rice fields upon the opening of the drain ditches.

"Nephew, how do I say this? She is like family to us."

"I am part of the family. So she would not be leaving the family if I bought her."

He took several deep breaths, and I watched him, and waited, listening to the now overbearing sounds of night.

"Dear nephew," he said, "Because you are so insistent I will consult with your cousin about this question. Though I doubt he will hold a view different from my own. He...is quite attached to that girl."

"Is that so?"

My uncle ignored my impudence and focused again on the matter that mattered most to him.

"Allow me to say this again. If you persuade your father, my brother, to invest in the plantation, you will in effect become the girl's owner."

He cleared his throat.

"I wish to resolve our business. Young man, the future of our family depends on this, and I trust you will make the right decision. And when I say family, I hope you understand that it includes all of the slaves who work on this plantation."

"Uncle, I am still pondering all this. I hope that by the time of the rice harvest, everything will be clear to me."

"Which will be soon. We have had good hot days, and Isaac tells me the kernels are plumping up beautifully."

"Yes," I said, "it will be soon."

"Meanwhile, I will speak to my son about your proposal. Who knows that he may be more forgiving than I suspect."

He looked down into his glass, and after this gesture of refusal to meet my eye I looked out into the night.

Chapter Sixty-one

The Stranger

*S*he had first heard of this matter when attending to a dinner in the big house some months before his arrival.

"I have written to him," the master had said.

"Good, then," said the missus.

"And he has written back."

"You did not tell me."

"I am telling you now," the master said.

"And what did he say?" put in Jonathan, leaning across the table with great seeming intensity in his father's direction.

"Ah, you have an interest in your New York uncle, whom you have never shown an interest in before?"

"Father, we have never needed to before."

"We did not need to," the missus said.

"And now we do," the master said.

"Indeed we do," said Jonathan.

"A strange uncharitable family we are," the master said.

"Without survival," Jonathan said, "there can be no base for charity."

In the kitchen Precious Sally explained to her that this was the New York part of the family that had not stayed south when first they came up from the islands.

"They brothers," she said. "But only half. Different mothers."

"Just like us," Liza said.

"All people alike," Precious Sally said. "They just got different ways of living."

"Aside from the truth," said Liza, speaking in the voice she had acquired after years and years of reading, a voice she rarely ever used except when she felt safe, and with only the few people she trusted, "that some are slaves and some are free, I would agree with you."

But on that morning some months later when Isaac told her that the New York cousin was coming into the port at Charleston, she discovered that all were not the same. This one, Nathaniel Pereira, tall, and without much of a smile, gave her an odd feeling in her belly, and she wondered why. A pale-skinned man with that dark hair, he was not at all handsome to her, and he walked so stiffly she wondered if he might just break apart. In one of the melodramatic novels she had taken to reading of late the heroine might have felt some fateful tie to the man such as he was. She coldly noticed his lack of gravity—it was more that he lacked a certain amount of weightiness—even when she compared him to Jonathan whom she detested and despised.

Her father! A sneaking monster, a horror of a man! A snake, a devil in disguise!

And now here comes this New Yorker—who, unbeknownst to him, was her cousin, of sorts! He seemed to have chosen to use his freedom at the service of remaining detached from the life around him. It was almost as if he were a white ghost, passing through the world but never becoming part of it. Liza knew with all her heart that if she were free she could never live this way.

"Here, listen now, here is my plan," her father said, talking, talking, while she lay there, burning, her heart no longer holding enough tears enough to weep.

And when she had heard it, she said, "I will not."

And he said, "Yes, you will. I am your father and you will do as I say."

"I will not," she said again, even more resolute than before.

"Filthy whore, bitch, scum of a slave, you will do what I say or you will be hammered up on boards next to the barn!"

Several nights after her first encounter with the New Yorker she returned to her cabin and found her father waiting for her with a fiendish grin on his face.

"Go away," she said.

He reached up to pull her down and she danced out of his reach.

"Come here," he said. The stink of his whiskey breath offended her sorely, even where she stood from him at a distance.

"I won't," she said.

"I am ordering you to come here. Do you want a beating?"

"You cannot have me," she said.

"You bitch, I own you!"

"But since I carried out your wishes with your cousin, I am spoiled goods. Even more than spoiled, since you first spoiled me."

"I will show what is spoiled and what is not. Come here, or I will tie you up and take you and leave you in the barn with the other animals."

She took a tentative step toward him, so that he might see how frightened she was. And then she stopped.

"You do not want this now."

"Do not tell me what I want."

He sat up, preparing to stand.

"Wait, please," she said. "I have something to tell you."

"And what might that be?"

"I have lain with him."

"You have trapped him then?"

"Yes," Liza said, "but he has trapped me as well."

Now Jonathan pulled himself to his feet and stared into her eyes.

"How has this puny New Yorker trapped you?"

"He has given me a disease."

"What?"

The lie lay smoothly on her tongue and it gave her pleasure to say it.

"Yes, from the first time I went with him. Do you want to see the evidence, do you want to see my soiled rags."

"No, no, no, no," he said in disgust. "So, he has ruined you?"

"Yes, and it is terribly painful upon occasion," she said.

He dropped his gaze and turned aside.

"If you are lying—"

"I am not lying, I am suffering."

"Can the doctor cure you?"

"Yes, he is treating me now, but it will take a while."

"I will not go near your filth," her father said, "but you will tell me the moment he has made the cure and we will, I promise you, have at it again."

He brushed past her and hurried out of the cabin.

Liza threw herself down on the pallet, crying and moaning until she was hoarse.

Chapter Sixty-two

A Palimpsest

*N*ot long now, massa," Isaac said, another week or so later, holding up a handful of the rich and plumped kernels from the stalks at our feet, stalks that held their heads high, strong, in spite of the weight of the burgeoning kernels.

"Good, good, Isaac," I said. "The time is coming near, and that's good."

I rode back from the rice fields in a daze and a dream, my mind going black in bright daylight with the hope and expectation of seeing Liza before the sun rose again on the next day. Who knew a man could live like this? No one I knew in New York ever expressed such a heart condition as mine.

Mute at dinner—retiring early to my room—reading (Poe, Poe, Poe, Poe!), dreaming into the dark—that was my round after returning from the fields. I felt as much a slave to my condition as the dark people who went home to their cabins and took some feeble pleasures before sleep and the next day's round of hard labor. What did it matter that I could leave the plantation? That I might return to New York? Or perhaps even travel to London and Paris? A chain wrapped itself round my heart, and I could not stir myself to think about anything else except Liza.

One night at dinner Rebecca brought up what under different circumstances for me might have seemed an innocuous matter. She mentioned that several of the women she was teaching talked now and then about witchcraft and how to make spells to bind a man to you. She joked that she would put a spell on Jonathan, and he put back to her that he would turn her in as a witch.

"A Jewess witch," he said. "That would make our dear Gentile neighbors rather suspicious. Accused by her own husband, for putting a spell on him."

Rebecca rose to the height of her powers and said,

"I put a spell on the rice."

"Please, now," my uncle said, "this is foolish talk."

Jonathan enjoyed it.

"Do you know the slave goddess, the one they pound drums to and sometimes make their sacrifices to in the woods at night? I spoke to her and asked if she would make the kernels big and plump."

"No, no," said my aunt, "this is not a joking matter. Jonathan, I do not like you to joke that way. It is against our God."

"Oh," Jonathan said, "who or what is our God? A clump of rules. We never see Him."

"He is everywhere," my aunt said.

Jonathan would not relent.

"Is he there, Mother, when I make my water?"

"Please!" she said.

"Or when—"

"Enough," my uncle broke in. "I am weary. I am not feeling well. All this taxes me, in my soul."

"These men and their souls," my aunt said. She looked over at Rebecca. "I should not expect more from them, but I always do. And it always hurts. This is the life they give us." She looked directly at me. "Even you, who seem so polite and gentle for a man. Who knows what you are doing—"

"Please," my uncle said.

"Please what? Please who?"

My uncle raised a hand in the air. My aunt subsided back into her chair.

Rebecca then tried to ease the situation.

"Nathaniel, do you recall my cousin Anna?" she said.

"Yes," I said, happy to change the music at the table, though given my present cast of mind I had only the faintest recollection of a girl in Charleston.

"Talking of witches, perhaps she may put a spell on you."

"This is quite enough now," my aunt said.

Rebecca shook her head, smiled, and said no more.

Dear Father [I wrote later that evening before bed], Soon the rice crop will be ready to be harvested, an event that I am using as the marker for my own decision about what we ought to do about the prospect of investing in The Oaks. Though I have not come to a formal conclusion I can assure you that my belief is firm—we should not tie ourselves to any enterprise that depends on the enslavement of other Human Beings…

I wrote further, offering observations about the family and the weather and what little I had heard about political events in the state.

And I tore it up.

I picked up my pen and stared at it, then set it down, and got up and went to the window, the only place down here I truly called my own, where night thoughts beckoned and I could wonder in freedom about all the entanglements in which I was caught—my father, my family, my New York, and here in South Carolina, my Liza.

I felt like a fly in a web, wriggling and wriggling until I made myself all the more entangled.

A breeze stirred, an unusual occurrence, and then I heard the sound of a horse, and a shout. What was I to make of this? Was it a slave trying an escape? Was it one of the patrollers come to rouse us to some duty in which we did not believe?

A few moments later and I heard footsteps in the hall, and my uncle's and Jonathan's voices raised in discussion. A few moments later came a knock at my door.

"Cousin?" Jonathan said.

"Yes?" I spoke.

"I hope I haven't awakened you," Jonathan said. "We have just heard of a meeting in town we must attend. Be ready to ride in with us early tomorrow morning."

"Of course," I said, "but what sort of meeting?"

"One that should be both inspiring and maddening. I can't say more."

"I will be ready," I said.

At moon-rise, another knock, one I had been counting on.

"Quickly," I said.

"You seem distressed," Liza said.

"Jonathan was here only a short while ago."

"Don't worry, he didn't see me."

"Can you be sure?"

"I am sure," she said. "Sometime he has to attend to his wife." Liza undressed and climbed into the bed with me with a nonchalance suggesting that she had been *my* wife for a thousand years or more.

I took a few breaths, calming myself.

"What did he say to you?" she asked.

"My cousin has invited me to a meeting in town."

"What sort of meeting?"

"The same question I asked," I said. "He would not say."

"I will leave early," she said.

"You always do," I said.

"We don't want to be caught," she said.

"But I am your massa."

"Yes, you are."

"And so it should not matter, should it?"

"But it does, Nate," she said, giving me all of her mouth.

Moon, and moon, and more moon, and we settled back, and the faintest fingers of a breeze brushed our bodies, and then evaporated.

Moon-set. A wave of sadness overwhelmed me at the sight of this sandy-skinned beauty lying beside me, and then she opened her eyes—so dim it was in the room, on the verge of dawn but not yet dawn—and looked at me as though assessing what it might mean if she were not here and what it meant that she was.

"It worries me," she said. "We cannot do this again—"

"What, my love?" I cut her off.

"We must be more cautious," she said.

"I do not care anymore about being safe," I said, "and neither should you."

"Oh, Nate, Nate, when you are a slave there is nothing else to be afraid of. But when, as you are, you are free, there is a great deal to fear. I fear for you."

Philosophy—and sympathy!—from an African! From a slave-girl!

She got up to dress, and I tossed about in my bed, as though sleep were a rough sea and I were a small boat. What if Miriam...? What if even that Anna, who even now must be asleep in her bed in town? Yes, now I remembered her, dark eyes, dark hair. But Liza, Liza!

Chapter Sixty-three

Voices in My Ear

Okolun Returns to His Home

*Y*es, she had gone before him, but he was not one to give up until the very last, yet the thread that tied him to these old country people was spinning out and spinning out ever thinner and thinner. *Leaving the girl behind was one thing, after all, she was like anyone else, holding her fate in her own brown fist and thinking that someone else, a god like me, held her the same way. Oh, that has been going on so long, even a long time for a god to contemplate, I must say, going on ever since we first made these creatures and watched them go their own way so afraid of every which way and turn that they had to believe that we were guiding them. Give it up, I say, take your fist and seize what you need, do not, I say do not, and these may be my last words to you, because just as some billion years ago, or whatever time is to you and earth, these continents Africa and the New World were still joined together, just as they were one, not even twins but two heads and hearts in the same body, the plates beneath—I can't imagine what you believe as I tell you this, but we always knew about the shift and jolts and creakings and tearings of these massive shelves beneath the upper world— these plates shifted, and the continents ripped away from each other—imagine the earthly pain! The noise! The winds! The storms! The eruptions! The slides of fiery ash and mud!— and the New World went its own way, leaving Africa behind. Don't these people see they have the same chance now, the chance to turn their servitude into freedom? This, my farewell message to all of you, beastly owner and worried vassal, as I put the New World behind me and return to a home that loves to receive me in proper fashion. Carolina, farewell, oh, my Africa, beaches and deserts and forests and rivers and trees and mountains and skies skies skies—*

In less than the time it took me to say this, I have returned, kneeling beneath the ocean just off the African shore, planting my undersea garden, ready to emerge and play with anyone who worships me, to give guidance, but never, never, never to chain anyone to a single truth! Hello, Africa, I am home!

Chapter Sixty-four

Isaac

*H*ave we forgotten about Isaac? We must not let him drop from our thoughts. He came close, very close, and not just once, alas, to murder and to discovering his true self.

The first time occurred just after the first time Liza found herself with child, and there was no doubt as to whose child it was. Early one evening Isaac accompanied her into one of the farthest distant cabins, a shambling old ramshackle place among places already quite old, where an ash-gray witch woman lived, an ancient creature who could have been the older sister of the late Old Dou, with a beautiful thin-jawed face that might have been carved out of wood from a distant thick forest. She had the reputation in the cabins of dealing in herbs both white and black that she had learned to administer when she was a young girl in the old country.

Either because she had mystical foreknowledge or because she was a wise student, even in her oldest age, or perhaps because of it, of human behavior, she greeted them both as if she had been expecting them.

"It is not too late," she said.

Liza, just inside the door, tried to back away, but Isaac held her arm.

"You know?" he said to the witch woman.

"Look at her," the witch woman said. "Young, as beautiful as the rice kernel in its almost to full blooming condition, who can not see?"

Now Liza became interested, and stepped right up to the woman, so close that she could smell the rank weed odor of her intimate parts, mouth and other places.

"But not too late for me?" Liza said.

"No, no," the witch woman said. "You have long travels to make before you sleep. This is only a beginning."

"You can help me?"

The witch woman held up a twig on which had sprouted several thorns. Without warning, she pressed it to Liza's throat, pricking her.

"I already did," she said, tossing the twig aside as Liza slumped to the floor like an old curtain detached from its rod.

"What did you do?" Isaac stepped up to her, but had to turn his head aside at the odor of her breath.

"What you came for," the Witch Woman said. "Put her on the bed and let her sleep. When she awakes, all will be over."

With an agility quite surprising given her age, she attended to the sleeping girl, stripping off her clothes and applying various poultices to various parts of her body even as she dripped some sort of portion from a large spoon into the girl's open mouth.

"Now go outside," she ordered Isaac.

He lingered outside a while, fretting about his dear friend, sister-cousin, however it was he thought of her. Here at the back of the cabins few people passed by and he could barely hear the shouts let alone the murmurings of the plantation folk going about their taking of the evening meal. Now and then a burst of noise or a burst of music reached his ears, but mostly it was quiet, quiet enough so that he could listen to the voice inside him that wondered about this life, this world, the fate of the girl inside the cabin, what little hope he might have for the future, his aging father's condition—he had some sort of illness that kept him out of the fields and most of the time flat on his back in his cabin—the faint memory he had of his mother, poor woman.

He pulled himself back from those thoughts, focused his mind, as he was doing more and more as he became more and more adept at the tasks associated with rice farming, on the state of the crop, at the prospect of good weather, thinking then of what powers made weather, wondering whether it was God—as the master would have it, steeped as he was in the lore of his religion—or the gods of old Africa, whom many in the cabins still spoke of and spoke to, or the Jesus he had heard about when he spoke with slaves from other plantations. Now this Jesus, who was some sort of son of Moses, the Jews' hero, was supposed to be the Son of God, and Isaac could believe that, except that he knew too much about Okolun and the other great spirits who gathered around Yemaya and made the world a much more lively place than the way the Christians would have it. Those folks, he heard, didn't like drinking and dancing, not to mention doing the thing with each other, male and female, not that he had done that yet, but he certainly knew of it, it was all around him, part of the life of the fields and streams, the rivers, and the ocean he observed whenever he went to town. The Christians, if they had their way, would change the music, take out the drums, make only feeble moans to a God he simply did not understand, a God without flavor, without thirst, without the drive to make the world over every year the way he and his fellow slaves made the fields over, planted, cultivated, harvested, and then planted another crop. Not that the Jews were much better. Look where the Jew got Liza—with an inflated belly and a great sorrow in her big sweet young girl's heart.

The cabin door opened and the witch woman peered out.

"Bring me the water, boy," she said to Isaac. Fortunately he found some in a small wooden basin in a corner of the room. He stared as the old woman washed the younger woman.

The woman seemed to forget that he was present.

After a time, the witch woman asked Liza, "Do you want to see the outcome?" pointing to the small roll of sheets where the aborted child lay enshrouded.

"Never!" Liza said, still naked on the bedding. "Never, never!"

Isaac, too shy, even in the faint light of the cabin, to stare for very long at the naked girl, turned his eyes toward that small bundle on the floor in the corner of the hut. A tall boy, it hurt his back to lean over and peer down at it, to squint deeply into the dim light. What he saw did not seem worth the effort—a reddish-blue stump of flesh, ears slightly pointed, tiny eyes closed forever. He shook his head and pushed it out of his mind, or tried to, moving back closer to the old woman and Liza, as the woman began to sing and hum some old country song for the girl, as if the music might heal her, or at least calm her down.

So strange—he told Liza a long time afterward—how happy he felt. Just plain happy, happy, happy! Staring down at that still-born child, he wanted to take wing and fly.

The girl remained a bit feverish, and he walked her to her cabin and put her to bed. Still, he felt as though he had learned something he could not yet quite put into thoughts in his mind. But he felt nonetheless quite happy. In that same mood the next morning he went to his duties in the stables, beginning his work day—even now, after all that had happened the night before—still in darkness. He worked first on the horses, his daily duties taking him deep into the barns where such heady odors arose from the manure piles that now and then he felt somehow drunk on the fumes. As he walked from the barns to the big house his gait wavered, his arms tingled, and his head went around and around in confusion, so he might as well have been drunk.

Then it came to him. He had thought up a simple plan. Here is how he enacted it in his mind. An old Yoruba man they called Walla-Walla oversaw the business of the stables, having taken over the job after Isaac's father years ago, around the time Isaac's mother died in giving birth to him, collapsed into a daily bucket of dangerous brew. Isaac, a hard worker who always finished the day's duties before the end of the day, would easily elude his surveillance, sauntering from the stables toward the big house with a large bridle slung over his shoulder, as though he had business with it just ahead.

Once at the house, he would gain entry by the back door, where perhaps Liza herself might be working—though not today, so the plan would not work today—and yet he longed to strike out now, now, because of the immediacy of the event that brought his blood to a boil and kept him sizzling in his veins through the day—yes, then she would open the door to him, and with a pat on the shoulder he would slip past her into the dining room and the sitting room beyond where he would find the master in conversation with the missus, and he would throw down the bridle at the master's feet, pull him from his chair, and knock him to the floor. He would keep one foot on the big man's chest and study his face, and study it, as if to see if there were some resemblance. The Jewish man's eyes would cry out for mercy. Mercy! Mercy? Out would come the knife Isaac's father had given up to him long ago for trimming rope in the barn and—this seemed like justice, as much as he could imagine it, justice!—with one swift thrust he would stick the master in the throat, and gouge at him until he lost so much blood he could not survive.

And he would do the same to the missus.

And why not?

She lived with the man who fathered the child, she raised the child who grew to the man who did all of them such misery and wrong. The thought of the missus, in a white dress covered all in blood, twisted in his belly and he stood tall, breathing deeply, waiting for the nausea to pass.

He would next mount the stairs to the wing of the house where the young master's family lived, and slaughter them, like birds in a coop. He was sweating now, and licking his lips, even as the faintest wave of nausea still crawled up and down his chest and belly. But he would slaughter them, yes.

And then he would wait for the son. The hot blood pooling at his feet might cool, and the light fade at the end of the day. But he would wait. And after a while the young master would come in the door, call out to his parents in greeting, and step into the parlor. Isaac would take him around the neck with one arm and gouge out his eyes and then slit his throat and leave him for dead on the bloody floor.

Oh, what a thing it would be next! He would call all the people together, and they would celebrate, light fires and cook a meal, and dance and sing. He would take Liza in his arms and she would dance with him, and they would steal away to her cabin before too long and he would take up the water basin and wash away this blood, and take her in his arms again, this time not to dance but to make a night of love.

And in the last dark of the night he would venture out into yard and call out that it was time, and they would all, every single man, woman, and child on the plantation, steal away into the woods, and head for the Big Swamp. He could see it now, a town growing under their hands, and fields of vegetables and fruit, not an easy life, making their own cloth and clothes, raising their own bulls and cows and horses. But it would be their life, their own life, and it would be precious, because it was first watered with blood.

Oh, Isaac, poor Isaac!

"Boy!"

Old Walla-Walla, in those days, before Isaac took over, still a fixture in the stable, came up behind him slapped his fist at the bridle and nearly knocked him down, so unbalanced he was in his vision of revenge, murder, and blood.

"You think the horses going to feed themselves? Back to work, boy, back to work."

He shook off the mayhem in his mind and went back to work. He worked, he mucked. Time enough went by so that Liza seemed to have forgotten much of her pain and turmoil surrounding the young master's brutality. She rose each morning and went to work in the house, looking like her pretty young self, which was what she was, and crossing paths now and then with the man, but more often again than not with his wife. No looks passed between them let alone words.

In the odorous stables, in his mind, young Isaac could not stop the boiling in his mind.

When old Walla-Walla told him one morning to hitch up the carriage and drive the young master to town he devised yet another plan. It was so firm in his mind that after he had finished getting the carriage ready he went back among the cabins to where his old father lay, drunk already since dawn.

"What are you doing?" his father said with a moan and a groan.

"I'm going to town," he told the older man, to look at him, a broader-faced and slightly darker version of himself.

"Why you tell me, son? Something special? You go to town always, but you never come all the way here from the barns to tell me."

It was true, Isaac scarcely ever visited his father. He did not like to see a man crushed by life, a man always drunk on some kind of home brew or other, from waking up to going to sleep. He had not worked ever since Isaac could remember. And yet the master never bothered him. This gave Isaac too much to think about, so he did not think much about it at all.

"What is in your mind?" The old man looked up at him from a pallet low on the cabin floor.

Young Isaac took a deep breath. And then spoke.

"Mama. How I miss her. And this girl, Liza, how I like her. And these white people and Hebrews, I hate them. The Christians, too. I hate them. You have lived your whole life already, father, but I am only half—"

"Less than that, I hope," his father broke in to say.

"—if you say so, but I do not want to live it—"

"Like me?"

Isaac turned away, unable to look his father in the eye.

"Yes."

"You want to live like this? Good, tell yourself that. Because you ain't got no choice, anyway."

"I do," his son broke in.

"What's your choice?" his father said. "Going to sleep just after sun-down or going to sleep before the moon goes down?"

"Daddy, what are you talking about?"

His father rolled over on his side and talked to the wall.

"You got a choice, wall? Lean one way on a Sunday, lean another way on a Monday?"

As if the fantasy he had created for himself of slaughtering the entire family had never entered his mind, Isaac said, as slaves often did, "It ain't so bad here, Daddy. It ain't so bad. I hear of whippings other place, and a lot worse."

"Boy," his father said, "worse has been here. You just sort of missed it by a little."

"What are you talking about?"

The older man reached for a cup of his liquor and took a swallow.

"I loved your mother, Isaac," he said.

"Daddy, why are you talking about that now?"

"I loved her I don't know you ever can know…"

"Daddy?"

Young Isaac backed away as his father turned over on his belly and began to snore. All during the ride into town he thought of that, rather than stopping the carriage and dragging the young master out and beating him to death in the woods.

But after the ride he thought of it again, and brooded.

In My Margins

Mysteries and Family Secrets

Oh, Isaac, what you did not know will when you learn of it kill you!

Run, hurry, hide! But you are a brave young fellow and so you won't do that, will you?

Storics

And then death seemed to gather all about Isaac, like a cloud, like a cloak. He carried the scheme around with him in his mind, and though it faded out when he worked at day's end he found it haunting him again, the revenge plot against the master's son, the master's son who would one day, sooner, no doubt, than later, become master himself, the revenge against the entire family itself before this happened.

It did not help that as he now reckoned his own father was fading so quickly. In the cabin after sunset he would sit with the older man and gaze into his eyes, and he swore he could see a light flickering, as if his soul were like some candle about to gutter out in the wind.

"Daddy," he said, "tell me about when you came here."

"Why you want to know about that?"

The older man shifted on the pallet as though caught up in a dream, except that he was wide awake.

"I just want to know."

"Doesn't do you good to know. Back in the old country my father might have been a king. What good that do you here, slave as you are?"

"Was he a king? I did not know that."

"No, no, son. I was joking. He was…a slave," the older man said. "The story he told me, hunters took me from him, but living with him I was not free there either. I will be free soon."

"What do you say?"

"I am going to be free."

The darkness settled around them, flowing from outside in, as though it were a liquid to be poured, a substance that flowed, on which the lightest objects might float. An ailing angry man, his angry son, the pair of them surrounded by the dark that grew deeper and deeper, it made a picture you scarcely ever see, real life among our people, an aspect of the pose and emotion of all manner of people since our ancestors—everyone's ancestors!—first came down out of the trees to walk about and forage, oh, never to return to those heights.

After his father fell asleep Isaac left the cabin and wandered over to visit Liza.

The dark had settled over the quarters so deeply and indelibly it seemed impossible that light would ever return. It surprised him to find Liza in her own small cabin, illuminated by a steady-burning fire, holding a book in her hands.

"What you doing?" he said.

She looked up at him, inclined her head toward the fire.

"Reading."

He knew books, there was a room in the big house full of them, though he had never touched one, let alone opened one. Ever since the doctor began teaching Liza, and it began when she was a little girl, there was always one book or another lying around. He just had never felt the desire to pick one up and start reading. Though he usually liked it when she read to him.

"What's that one?" he said, pointing to the volume that lay open on the floor of her cabin.

"A good story about a good boy living with bad people. Would you like to hear it?"

Isaac shrugged, held up his hands. *(When did the shrug first appear as part of human behavior? Did an animal shrug? Or was it something that happened on the ground, walking away from that exploding volcano? Or much later? When?)*

She picked up the book and turned to the front of it. She moved her lips, she sounded, mostly correctly, these words *(and it took her a much longer time to do this than it would take you or me, much longer)*:

"*'Although I am not disposed to maintain that the being born in a workhouse, is in itself the most fortunate and enviable circumstance that can possibly befall a human being, I do mean to say that in this particular instance, it was the best thing for Oliver Twist that could by possibility have occurred...'*"

"What is that, what is that?" Isaac paced back and forth in the small cabin, unable to settle down and listen.

"'The fact is, that there was considerable difficulty in inducing Oliver to take upon himself the office of respiration,- a troublesome practice'"—Liza went on reading, with all sorts of troublesome pronunciation and emphases, but read she did nevertheless *"'but one which custom has rendered necessary to our easy existence; and for some time he lay gasping on a little flock mattress, rather unequally poised between this world and the next: the balance being decidedly in favour of the latter. Now, if, during this brief period, Oliver had been surrounded by careful grandmothers, anxious aunts, experienced nurses, and doctors of profound wisdom, he would most inevitably and indubitably have been killed in no time. There being nobody by, however, but a pauper old woman, who was rendered rather misty by an unwonted allowance of beer; and a parish surgeon who did such matters by contract; Oliver and Nature fought out the point between them. The result was, that, after a few struggles, Oliver breathed, sneezed, and proceeded to advertise to the inmates of the workhouse the fact of a new burden having been imposed upon the parish, by setting up as loud a cry as could reasonably have been expected from a male infant who had not been possessed of that very useful appendage, a voice, for a much longer space of time than three minutes and a quarter...'"*

"Who is Nature? What is pauper? Workhouse like a plantation?"

Liza answered his questions as best she could and then continued reading for awhile. When she had finished she shut the book and held it to her chest.

"What is that?" Isaac said again.

Liza opened the book and looked to the small type across from the title page.

"That was London, that is what it was. That was London."

"How do I know?" Isaac said. "London, what? I never been there and neither have you. So how you know?"

"The words make it happen."

Isaac, seeming perplexed at first, now took a different tack.

"How you know how to do that? What do you do? You stealing something to do that? Why you keep on doing it?"

Liza took a deep breath and allowed herself a smile.

"Because it makes me free."

Isaac might as well have been wearing chains the way he clanked around in his mixture of anger and resentment. His father was sinking. And whenever he saw the master, his urge to slaughter him and the entire family rose up in his gorge and fire spread through his chest up into his throat.

One day Old Walla-Walla caught him lashing at one of the horses and grabbed his arm.

"What do you think are you doing?" the old man said, holding him in a crushing trap of arms.

Isaac went limp.

He did not know. He was scarcely aware that he had been mistreating the animal. He had just picked up the whip and went at him, in blind fury, in the rush of terrible rage. Damn, damn, damn! Only after the old man stopped him did he hear the animal squealing, hoarsely, in pain. It took hours for them to calm the beast down and treat its wounds.

On another occasion, after a day of watching Liza at some distance at work in and around the house, he turned up at her cabin and found her reading again.

"Hello, Isaac," she said without looking up.

"More books?"

"Yes."

"This one good?"

Now she looked at him.

"I am not sure. It is very hard for me to understand."

"Read to me," he said, lowering himself onto the pallet next to her.

She gave him a half-smile, and began to read.

Every one loved Elizabeth. The passionate and almost reverential attachment with which all regarded her became, while I shared it, my pride and my delight.

"This about love," Isaac said.

Liza nodded, and kept on reading.

On the evening previous to her being brought to my home, my mother had said playfully—"I have a pretty present for my Victor—to-morrow he shall have it." And when, on the morrow, she presented Elizabeth to me as her promised gift, I, with childish seriousness, interpreted her words literally, and looked upon Elizabeth as mine—mine to protect, love, and cherish. All praises bestowed on her, I received as made to a possession of my own. We called each other familiarly by the name of cousin. No word, no expression could body forth the kind of relation in which she stood to me—my more than sister, since till death she was to be mine only...

"I thought this was about love, but this about the slaves," Isaac said.

"I suppose so," Liza said. "Or perhaps not."

"The big folks know you take these from the house?"

Isaac tried to show his concern by touching her on the arm, but she pushed his hand away.

"The doctor gives me books," she said. "I told you that."

"Doctor, he ain't been around," Isaac said. "Some folks say he sick."

Now Liza looked interested.

"Where did you hear that?"

"Nowhere in particular," Isaac said. "I just heard it."

"What kind of sick?"

Liza set the book down, spine up—*Frankenstein* was the name on it—and reached over for Isaac.

"Heart trouble, what I heard," Isaac said.

"Cousin," she said, "when—?"

"What you call me?"

"Cousin. Like in the book, Isaac. It is a close name, something of affection."

"Affection? Hungh!" He snorted like a horse. "This reading playing some tricks on you, Liza. Times, I do not know what you are talking about."

Liza tried to ignore his discomfort.

"Tell me about the doctor, what else you heard?"

"Nothing."

"Nothing?"

"I will ask folk but for now I hear only nothing more."

He settled in next to her on the pallet, boyish, despite his bulk.

"Read to me?"

"All right."

She picked up the book and tried her way through another chapter, while Isaac, though tired from the day's labors, remained awake and alert.

How can I describe my emotions at this catastrophe, or how delineate the wretch whom with such infinite pains and care I had endeavoured to form? His limbs were in proportion, and I had selected his features as beautiful. Beautiful!—Great God! His yellow skin scarcely covered the work of muscles and arteries beneath; his hair was of a lustrous black, and flowing; his teeth of a pearly whiteness; but these luxuriances only formed a more horrid contrast with his watery eyes, that seemed almost of the same color as the dun white sockets in which they were set, his shrivelled complexion and straight black lips...

She explained this to him as she read, and he gave it his best attention.

"Aiiee, this monster got yellow skin and black lips. I do not want to meet him in the woods in the dark."

"Do not walk there and you will not meet him."

"How come no one ever told me about him before this?"

"It is a secret."

"Our doctor make him?'

"No, Doctor Frankenstein made him."

"He live in Charleston?"

"He lives in this story."

"What are you talking about? I don't know what you're talking about."

"What I just said."

She gave him a playful shove, which turned out to be harder than she had intended, and he went rolling over onto the dirt floor.

"Were you listening?"

"I was listening."

He brushed himself off and crawled back onto the pallet.

"Keep on reading." He snorted again like a horse. "Monsters! I ain't afraid! Here they got black skin and yellow lips...So what's afraid of that?"

In My Margins

Isaac

*H*urry! Run! Hide!

Isaac's New Plan

*I*saac meandered.

First he went to the barn and checked on the horses, and then he took a stroll out under the trees, gazing up into a sky as clear of clouds and so beautifully ultramarine that it might have been an ocean itself.

Ocean, ocean—could he have deep water on his mind?

Half the day passed before he returned to his father's cabin, which shows that a man enslaved can sometimes find ways to waste time if he has been enslaved long enough. The woods, the creek, the fields, the creek again. Beside the waters he sat down and rested his back against a tree, listening to the quiet rush of the stream.

And yes, he dreamed. But of what, on awaking, he could not recall. It grew quite hot and he took off his shirt and marveled at how the drops of water pooled on his chest. Now he imagined more wildly while awake than he had while sleeping.

What if his skin turned pale and he stood up, a white man in rags, shirtless, and decided that he would wander to town.

Take his time. Dawdle. No one to shout at him about returning to work.

In town, he would check in at the shipping office.

A ship to England where all those authors lived?

Yes, he would pay with his white money and shop quickly at some of the nearby stores and return with a wardrobe adequate for his journey.

And then board.

And sail!

Away, away across the ocean, the waves rolling beneath the ship, the ship moving in a direct line across the heaving water toward London.

But why not return to the old country?

No, no, too many slavers there still. He heard the stories.

The stories.

He lay there beside the creek, eyes closed now, listening to vagrant murmurs from the current and the leaves above his head.

Thoughts of his father drifted through his mind.

And how did he himself compare to this man?

He had now reached this age, and he had nothing, no wife, no child. Only the work to which he was bound by (invisible but nonetheless strong strong) manacles. Some friends, a slender thread tying him to Liza. Animals he liked. Now and then a woman.

At least his father had a son.

Father worked himself into drunken lassitude.

He himself, thinking of running, running, but where?

Anywhere.

If he could only…

If he could…

Put these Jews and Christians all behind him and ascend into the sky with the great gods who would grow wings on him if he dared to try…

Wings…flying into the ultramarine ocean of sky, sky of ocean not far away. Over to London, perhaps even to Africa! Dozing, musing. He slept.

And awoke, the sun now much lower in the sky. And such a certain stillness in the air that made it difficult for him to imagine that anything else was going on anywhere else on the plantation, in the county, in town, in the ocean or sky, in the entire world as he knew it.

Except that he probably should move along toward pretending to work. It set a bad example when an overseer oversaw as little as he did. Nevertheless, the Jews did not seem to care. Except for the young master, who seemed happy with nobody, nobody seemed unhappy with him. With a yawn and a sigh he picked himself up and headed back toward the cabins, seeing no one, passing no one.

Now the sky was turning darker than the earlier blue, giving him unaccountable thoughts about his own color and how he might, or the gods might, change it, lighten him or darken him, however they would have it.

The sun does that to white folks.

Dark-tinged Langerhans, for instance.

Oh, Okolun, may you burn that Langerhans to a dark crisp that he might know the pain of enslavement!

He was enjoying this thought when the old witch woman met him at the door of his father's cabin.

"What you doing here?" he said. "Where's my Daddy?"

"*Went away*," the old woman said, her voice deepening as she, oh, yes, oh, yes, spoke through herself in his father's voice. The power of it knocked him backward into the yard.

"What?"

He dusted himself off and returned to the door.

"Daddy?"

"*Gone*," the voice said. "*Gone with your Mama!*"

"Gone what?"

He pushed in through the narrow space and saw no one but the old crone.

"Gone where?"

"*Gone, I'm gone. Come in here! A last word for you. Poor woman couldn't hep herself. Master took it from her. These years, I hide it from you.*"

"What, Daddy? What are you saying about my Mama and the master?"

"*Sorry, my boy. So sorry. One night, a dark night, he come to the cabins. Found her sitting on the step. Where was I? Out dancing to the drum way off in the forest. I come home, everthing changed. Here you come. That's why she drowned herself after she birthed you. All these years…*"

Isaac grabbed the woman by the throat. His first thought was to wring her neck like a chicken, but he could feel this pulse in his hand, racing, powerful. Even if he wanted to, he might not be able to do it.

"*She not me,*" said his father. "*I'm gone. She here. I'm gone with your mama.*"

In spite of himself, Isaac shoved the woman and sent her flying back against the far wall and ran out of the cabin.

A week went by before they found his father's body in the creek, partly eaten by swamp animals, right there near the tree under which he had dozed and dreamed.

Isaac started walking in a circle, then running, running, running around.

Chapter Sixty-nine

Permission

*W*ho brought the news? The news just traveled, person to person to person, in this instance from the lips of someone from a neighboring plantation who met someone from the cabins out there in the fields, who told Precious Sally, who told Liza—that the doctor lay quite ill in his house in Charleston, and she, who had felt the suffered clasp of slavery every day in her young life now felt it in the most subtle ways, because she wanted nothing more than to go to town and visit her mentor except that there was no way for her to do this.

Except there was one way.

And did she know she could go through with it? The fact that she thought of it and kept it in mind and almost immediately put her plan into action suggests that she knew what she had to do, she knew what would probably occur, and she had prepared herself for that.

Did this mean that she had become a new woman or that everything in the past that had pushed her to this point was now about to begin blossoming? When it happened she had little idea, if any, of how much would transpire in the aftermath. In all of our lives we live in unknowing fashion, acting without thinking about consequences, until one day we stop to consider the consequences before we act, and it seems as though our life has become so strange it might be someone else's life.

This slave child, daughter of slaves who were children of slaves who in their turn had been slaves, never to see the light or even contemplate the possibility of seeing the world by that longed-for illumination of freedom, how much did she know beyond the immediate plan of action? How much did she fret about what that plan might bring about? What do we know? Do I know, do you? Some doctors and geniuses think they can predict human behavior. I think at best, if we are lucky, that we might with great struggle possibly with some accuracy describe it.

Though sometimes even the actors cannot recall what took place in elaborate and significant detail.

This way, that way. It seems that everyone had a plan in those days. For example, Liza recalled putting *her* plan into motion by waiting in the big house at the end of her day, waiting for her father to arrive.

He might have been traveling, she didn't know, and perhaps his return to the plantation took place some days after she first considered what she might do in order to get to town to visit the doctor. In memory hours, days such as this melt together.

Came the hour when he did arrive at the house, whether from the rice ponds or from some journey of further reach we do not know, and she was waiting for him.

Though she did try not to show this, her anticipation and her hope, her worry, and her desire. What good might that have done? She waited for him with a calmness she had never noticed before in herself, as calm as waters some days before a winter storm, as calm as sky before the end of daylight. Such were the ways she tried to describe her state of mind to herself as she waited for this man who had ruined her and yet had kept her alive. The harm he had done her she could not calculate, but aware of his power she understood just how much she had to placate him. As simple and at the same time as complex had been her ties to the gods—the ties she sometimes felt resonating in her limbs and chest and belly—her links to this man seemed both tame and wild.

She despised him, she had to admit to herself, and yet when she heard his footsteps on the front steps and then the sound of the front door opening her chest went taut and she could scarcely take a breath yet she needed to breathe more desperately than ever before in her life. Caught between sucking in air and holding her breath—she took a stance few others could imagine holding until they themselves, unlucky folk, might one day find themselves caught in the same way.

"You, girl," he said when he stepped into the parlor, "what are you doing here? Your work better be long done. Is there something wrong with you?"

"Not with me, sir," she said. (Not with me, *father*, she wanted to say, but he had forbidden such form of address ever since she could remember.)

"With whom, then?" he said. "My missus alright?"

"Yes, sir," she said. "But sir?"

He frowned at her, his hands busy at his sides.

"What is it?"

"Sir, the doctor has a sickness…"

"Yes, I heard he was ill."

He looked this way and that, as though trying to find something in the room.

"I would like…"

Now he focused on her again.

"You would like what, girl?"

She found a breath and sucked in hard, and then spoke, suddenly, forthrightly.

"I would like to visit him."

Her father's eyes sparked, and he made his mouth into an odd shape.

"You would like to visit him."

"I would, sir, yes, please."

"Visit," her father repeated.

"Yes, sir."

"Follow me."

Without another word, he led her from the parlor to the kitchen and into the pantry behind it where Old Dou had kept a pallet on which now and then she would nap between large chores. Liza had inherited the chores, and the pallet, though now she was not so happy about the latter. Everything she feared might happen in this encounter began to take place.

"Take off your clothes," her father said.

She knew it, she knew, but still she hesitated.

"Did you hear what I said, girl?"

Without another word and certainly without looking at him, she removed her apron—easy—and then her dress, and the small cloth tied to cover her lower parts—so difficult she thought she might cry, or cry out. (But then her plan would evaporate and she would be left with nothing but her miserable indentured self.) In a moment she was standing naked before him, as if he were the doctor himself.

Without warning he slapped her in the face and she went reeling against the pantry wall, scattering boxes and bottles and bowls as she staggered.

"You put that man above me?"

"No, sir."

She did not dare touch a hand to where her face burned and ached.

"Does he own you?"

"No, sir." Now her breath seemed to fail her, and then started up again.

"Who owns you?"

"You do, sir."

"Who made you live?"

"You did, sir."

"Without me, you would be nothing, do you understand that?"

"Yes, sir."

"You would not be a thought, you would not be a breath, not a wisp of air or the smallest part of bone."

"Yes, sir."

"Lie down," he said.

Liza had prepared herself, and pictured a dark rice pond into which she stepped carefully, and then, turning her face to the darkening sky, stretched out on her back and let herself float downward beneath the surface until the frothy water covered her face and breasts and thighs, and still she sank, deeper and deeper.

Liza heard distant noises floating above her where she floated beneath the surface of the water.

And splashing about, and pain down there, below, in her own deepest parts.

She opened her eyes to find her father kneeling next to her, working three fingers of one hand inside her while he held his loose naked member, loosened from his trousers, in his other hand and worked even harder.

For a moment she held off the pain, picturing three horizontal lines engraved on an otherwise smooth stone. She reminded herself of the story that followed from it, the star above Timbuktu, the flight across the desert, the years in the forest. *Yemaya*, she said in a whisper in her mind, *Yemaya-ay! I am yours, the way my unborn mother was yours when you rode the ocean together in the death ship. Come to me or I can come to you…Yemaya, dear…*Finally she could hold back the pain no longer.

"Stop," she said in a whisper. "You're hurting me…"

"Oh, my little African honey girl," he said in a sing-song childlike voice, "sweety-weety, I don't mean to hurt you, little African honey girl, tweety-sweety, I don't…"

But he didn't stop, and it kept on causing her pain even as he howled in frustration—the master howling like a dog!—and pulled away from her.

"Get dressed," he said.

She pulled her clothing on while he stood and pushed himself back into his trousers, of a sudden pulling her close and wiping himself on her dress.

Her instinct was to draw away from him, but she stood there, intent on getting her way no matter what. And the worst had already taken place.

"Go back to the cabins," he said.

"You promised," she said, leaning against the door frame of the pantry.

Finally, with a slight nod of his head, he spoke to her as he might speak to a dog, "Very well. Tell Isaac to drive you to town. You may stay only an hour. Do you know how to tell time?"

She knew she risked everything to say what she said next in the tone in which she said it, but she said it anyway.

"You never taught me, father."

He shook his head. If smoke might ever appear from a human skull, it might have puffed out of his nostrils just then.

"One hour," he said. "Now go."

She bowed her head.

"Thank you."

"*One* hour."

"Yes…master," she said, waiting until he turned and left the pantry so that she might push her face against the wall and weep a while, feeling as though her head might explode. It hurt when she walked out of the room herself, but she did not care. She walked faster. Outside she ran.

Chapter Seventy

A Grain of Rice

*E*ver since the last encounter with her father her thoughts and feelings had become terribly confused, she noticed that her appetite waxed and waned, and some mornings before sunrise she felt a longing to sleep perhaps forever and on other mornings long before the moon had set she jumped up from her pallet, ready for the day that was still hours away.

Now and then Isaac came by to comfort her, especially after sundown when he could decide what he wanted to do on his own.

"What he do to you, Liza? What he do?"

His questions became more than insistent, they reverberated in her mind and made her already wandering imaginings worse than confused.

Isaac meanwhile swung pendulum-like between resignation and rage. And on one particular visit not long after the awful event, he swung further than ever before.

"I kill him," he said, raising his arms as if grasping a declaration of his deed to come.

And Liza held him in her arms and said she did not want that.

"He is my father," she said.

"I will cut him," Isaac said. "I will drag him behind my horse."

"He is my *father*. What do we do? What do I do? What do you do? I don't know what to do!"

Isaac suddenly shoved her aside.

"I will kill him!" he shouted, standing tall in his rage.

"And they will tear you apart," Liza said.

"Ah, ah, ah, ah!"

The boy charged the wall of the cabin and began banging his head against it.

"Stop!" Liza shouted at him. "Stop now!"

Isaac pulled away from the wall for a moment, blood having sprung from his skull.

"The man owns me, I am his creature, I am his animal! They owned my mama, they owned my papa!"

With a dramatic flourish, he turned back to the wall and resumed banging his skull against it, until exhausted and bloody about the face and neck he stumbled backward and then, regaining his balance, rushed out the door.

"Isaac!"

Liza followed him, terrified that he would race up to the big house and commit mayhem on her father. But he ran directly toward the rice ponds and from there, as far as she could see in the early morning light, into the woods beyond.

Slowly she returned in the direction of the cabins, but when she had almost reached her own, where she and dear Old Dou—long gone, gone now!—had lived through her childhood, she stopped, and here, one might say, at this point, where she felt helpless, hopeless, and on the verge of the sort of illness that had driven Isaac to such useless rage, the goddess touched her gently on the shoulder, and gave her a gentle push in the direction of a certain cabin other than her own. She stumbled toward it, in a daze, in a dream.

"Back again?"

The old witch woman greeted her at the door, in apron and heavy gown, as though she already knew she was coming and had dressed for a visitor. She took one look at the girl and told her to lie down. The cabin smelled of old sweat and dried blood, of animal stink, and the reek of certain natural compounds that must have come from the rice-ponds.

"Look at this," the old woman said as she held up a ball of herb and bone, in fact, twirled it, over Liza's head.

Liza stared at the thing, feeling her breath coming hard even as she lay back without exertion. For a moment she thought Old Dou had returned to help her, to save her. How she wished she could return to her infancy, when the old woman tended to her, hugged her to her great blooming chest. It was something she either remembered, or dreamed, that feeling of early life safe beyond the bonds of slavery, and she couldn't say which.

"Breathe deeply," the old woman said.

Liza willed herself back into the present moment. She felt her breath lapping in her lungs like waves from far offshore. Dots and wavering lines danced before her eyes. She heard the woman strike a match, and the phosphorous odor rose into her nose with a blooming stench that nearly pushed her head back against the wall.

She felt as though she had passed into another world, and the flesh on her neck rippled as the old woman took her hand, as if to keep her from floating away.

"Do you feel the change?" the old woman asked her.

"What change is that, mother?" Liza said.

"You know, I know, we all know. Do you feel it?"

"In my...?"

"Of course, this is what I talk about."

Liza hesitated, then told her the truth.

"I'm afraid."

"Because of it."

"Yes."

"We can do something. No creature from that wanton bastard ever wants to be born, not now, not in the future."

"I did not choose it," Liza said. "I did not choose to be born."

"None of us do, my child. Whether we come into slavery or freedom, we do not choose it."

"What can we do, Mother?"

She reached into the pocket of her apron and came up with a single grain of rice.

"Put this on your tongue, dear," she said.

Liza, without hesitating, took the tiny offering and placed it on her tongue.

"Now you go," the old woman said.

Liza swallowed, thinking to herself, this old woman, like Old Dou, is she making health or making wisdom, or are these one and the same? And even as she was thinking this, she felt her body, which moments seemed as though it might float away, taking on weight, great weight, and with only the lightest touch of the old woman at her shoulder, she lay down on the floor of the cabin and closed her eyes.

And sank beneath the floor, through the sandy soil beneath, and down through the sand into the tunnels of sea-water that washed in with the tide not all that far from where the cabins and plantation stood. She knew, she knew, it was a dream, but it seemed so real, or was the dream the real thing and all else that seemed so real, the pain and sorrow of her life so far, and all the travail that brought her to be born here after the long journey from Africa, was that the dream?

Down into the waters beneath the waters, where handsome Okolun suddenly leered at her through the bubbling current and reached out his hand to her, and she grabbed it, clenched it tightly—or did matters somehow turn around and he clenched *her* hand?—and sailed behind him as he rushed through the water with the powerful churning of a shark.

She took a wild ride, water streaming down her throat and curlicuing through her body and pushing from her anus, propelling her forward with the velocity of the god who rushed alongside.

"Daughter?" the god spoke in her mind even as he sailed, with an oddly calm expression on his face, lips closed, eyes straight ahead.

"Yes, Father?"

"I am your real father, yes."

"Yes, you are."

"That man who attacked your mother and now has attacked you, what is he? A belch in the belly of a god with a sense of humor. Can you laugh about it, is the question?"

"All these questions."

"But can you, can you laugh? I went all the way home to Africa and have only just skipped back to see you, to see if you can laugh." The god Himself giggled and made bubbles in the water. "Oh, I do hop and skip all about the world, all about the stars…It is a merry life, this infinity I inhabit…"

Liza wasn't listening carefully, but struggled with the possibility of laughter in the face of her pain, wrestled with it, soared along beneath the water torturing herself with it, and nothing came, nothing, except the difficult question and the water rushing through her, light all around and then dark all around, and then light again, and her belly rustled and a tickle rose in her chest, a tickle rose, and the grain of rice in her lower parts turned over and doubled in size, some miracle in nature and finally, "Yes," she said. "Yes," she said. "Yes, I can laugh, I can laugh!"

"Then I will tell you a joke," the god said.

"Tell me," she said.

"There is a man coming…"

"What?"

"A man…"

"Who?"

"This is for you to find."

"What about him?"

"Oh, seek him out and you will know."

"Seek him out?"

"You will come close, but do not be indifferent. Take a step toward him, and all will change for you."

Liza turned her head aside, preferring to stare down into the dark water rather than gaze in that moment at the smug face of the god.

"No," she said, "I don't want to take a step toward a man. I do not want a man. I have had one man and that is one man too many. I will keep myself from men, because such creatures will destroy my life and make my children miserable down to several generations."

It was the god's turn to turn away.

"You are so difficult!" he said. "You make me, girl, so exasperated! Where is your hope, child? Where is your love of the future? Where is your love of yourself?"

"Sleeping," Liza said. "Fast asleep."

"Nah," said Okolun, "nah, nah."

"Oh, yes! Fast asleep!"

"Slow asleep is what you are. But you had better wake up, girl. Because your chance is coming, coming down the sea-road, and you don't want to pass it up because it may not come again."

"You say 'nah'? I say it now back to you, nah, nah..."

"Oh, you are such a trouble!"

Liza heard herself scream out underwater—"Because I have known trouble, because I have lived trouble before I was born and when I was born and now in my young life!"

"Still yours to take," the god said.

Suddenly he released her hand, and she immediately fell behind him in the rushing stream of his watery power.

"You are on your own now, girl, so wake up! Wake up! Yours to take up!"

Before she could reply Liza felt herself both slowing down and sinking at the same time. The god became only a dark blur in the water some distance ahead of her, and now some distance below her, and now was rising to meet her.

She opened her eyes, soaked through to her skin, the old woman hovering over her.

"Is it done?" the woman said in her creaking croak of a voice. "I think it is done."

And then she croaked something, one last thing.

"This," she said, "you forgot this."

And she extended her hand, clenched, and opened her hand, and there was the stone, missing for some years, which had squirted out of her womb in a dream.

Voices in My Ear

Yemaya Exults

We are coming so close, she is coming so close!

The Doctor Attends to Himself

He was a creature of habit, and had to be, but was any single morning typical of the way his days moved along? The doctor didn't think so. You would notice if you were observing him that he rose before dawn and in nightshirt and slippers, with a cup of tea at his desk side, spent an hour or so reading and making entries in his notebooks by lamplight before the early sun made it just as easy to read and write in natural light, though by then his hour was usually up. He had done this before he had married, all the while during his marriage, and continued it after his beloved wife had gone to her rest. Even that one hour out of twenty-four of peaceful contemplation of the words of philosophers and historians and some poets made even the worst day that followed something he could endure.

Homer's Achilles fought bravely for all time against the Trojans. The doctor was reading his story as he did each year since college, touching his wedding ring and with some difficulty, because his digits appeared to have swollen a bit, turning it slowly around and around on his finger. His heart raced as he closed his eyes and imagined the battlefield, the plain of Troy, and eventually his heart slowed a bit and he reached for his notebook and made an entry, and then set that book down.

Homer, this season, he thought to himself. And next would come Shakespeare again. Oh, he had plans, he had plans. Thinking ahead he pictured *Hamlet*, filled with ghosts and wisps and woes and worries, and swords. And then, a comedy. He would read *Midsummer Night's*, or *All's Well*. But all was not well, he knew that, and he only hoped that he might read at least one more play before going to that undiscovered country so well put forward in the other play.

Oh, that this too solid flesh…

To be or not…

Once more into the breach…

As it turned out, that year he finished all he had planned to read and still remained alive on this earth, and so he took up the late plays, first *A Winter's Tale* and then *Pericles*, marveling at the sweetness and fluency of the older Shakespeare.

And still he remained!

And so he went back to *The Tempest*, of his early education.

And then, as the seasons turned, Homer's time came around again.

That was the volume on his lap on one of those early mornings, birdsong in the air even before the light made its way up out of the sea and across the fields and ponds to his house on the outskirts of the city as he was making an entry in his notebook—"…in the course of human freedom…" the fragment read—and his pen must have fallen from his fingers as caught in the ripple of pain in his chest he grasped himself to himself, and all the possibility of morning light fell away.

A knock at the door returned him to this world.

He mustered all his strength and called for the visitor to enter.

"What a surprise! Come sit…"

The doctor patted the place on the sofa next to where he sat, and Liza, after hesitating a moment, placed herself next to him. She felt awkward, no doubt, in her plain dress, dust on her bare legs, the faintest whiff of horse still clinging to her because of the ride on the bench of the carriage.

"How have you been, my dear?" He cleared his throat, and found his normal voice.

"Been fine," Liza said.

"No trouble out there…" He dipped his head vaguely in the direction of the plantation. But here, in his house, he might easily have been gesturing toward the river to the north, or to the sand dune islands that bordered on the ocean. This close to the water the breeze sometimes blew in off the water, sometimes it blew out from the farmland west of the city. The doctor had begun to savor these small incidents of life, the daily round of street noises and gulls calling, those visiting breezes, and surprise visitors such as this.

"I am sorry I have not visited…"

"Pay no mind, sir," Liza said.

"I miss making my rounds…"

"Yes, sir…"

"So many years on my feet, bending toward my patients, trying to comfort them through all the worst…these past few months I have missed it terribly…"

"We have missed you, sir," Liza said.

"And all's well? I know I am repeating myself."

Liza did not hesitate.

"Yes, sir, all is well."

"You have no problems?"

"No, sir."

What could she say that he did not know? What good would it have done to have said anything at all? This peaceful room, the breezes blowing through it, the serenity of the moment.

"Would you like some tea?"

"I will make it, sir," Liza said.

"Would you? It is some ordeal now for me to get up. I have a woman who cooks for me and such. She is out at the market at this moment."

"I will be happy to, sir," Liza said.

While she prepared the tea, he talked much more openly than he had ever done before about his life, about the countryside he loved, about the city he enjoyed, walking along the Battery in the early morning and again at the end of the day, the whisper of the wavelets against the embankment, the sounds of the rivers converging in the ocean harbor, gulls overhead, always gulls, music and light from the nearby houses, and he had done some things, good things, he hoped, and made life a little better for those for whom it might have been otherwise.

Why some men turn their lives into the duty of making kindnesses for others and why some turn toward making other people squirm and even suffer there is no answer, is there? Who could say? Who knew, who knew?

He asked her about her reading. He gave her some new books.

Just before she left for her ride back to the plantation, he took her hands in his—it was the strangest thing that had ever happened to her—force she knew, anger she knew, worry she knew, pain she knew, but never this before, never this—and stared deeply into her eyes.

Just before she went out the door, he said, "I wish you a good future, Liza."

Chapter Seventy-three

A Meeting

$\mathcal{T}$he air in the kitchen that morning roiled thick with the odor of frying meat and baking breads while Precious Sally prepared my breakfast in silence. I ate in silence. Until the hour when Jonathan and I made our departure from The Oaks in the carriage, rolling along the leafy trail that led to the main road, I did not speak a word aloud.

Finally, I could not help myself.

"Explain to me again, Cousin, just what are we going to hear?" My mind was filled almost entirely with thoughts of Liza. Politics was not something to which I wanted to give any thought.

"Here is the essence," Jonathan had said to me as we rode to town. "You'll recall my brother-in-law, Joseph Salvador, who sits in the legislature?"

"Yes, I remember him. Tall, red-haired? With a nose that looks as though it's been flattened by a spoon?"

"I hadn't thought of it that way. But yes. He has invited us to this gathering, to which he has gained entry by virtue of his service in the legislature."

"And they are discussing what?"

"The perils of nullification, the possibilities of secession."

"Nullification?"

"The state of South Carolina rejected some years ago the principle that the federal government might set tariffs for all the states. It was hurting our merchants and farmers."

"And secession?"

"A more drastic proposal. If Henry Clay had not persuaded Congress to pass a bill keeping tariffs low, it might have found more backing."

"I am thinking," I said, "that if New York City seceded from the Union, we might form our own sovereign island. And make our own navy of the river barges that go back and forth to Albany, capital of another country."

"It is amusing to think of these matters, yes, Cousin, if you are not from South Carolina. Here it is deadly serious."

"Money is always a serious matter," I said.

"Oh, yes, and add to that a matter even more serious, and you have a palimpsest of trouble."

"A palimpsest?"

"One matter laid upon another."

The day was hot, dust rose in columns toward the branches of the leafy oaks, and we stopped speaking for a while.

After a time my cousin inclined his head toward me and said, "You are very quiet, Cousin Nate. Are you feeling poorly?"

"Just fine, Cuz," I said, taking a deep breath, so that I did not allow myself to spew out everything that I wanted to say.

"Quite hot today," he said, wiping his brow with the back of his hand. "Makes you almost wish you were a nigger, does it not? You'd be used to this heat, having lived your life in Africa. Or having a father who lived there."

"Your slaves," I said, "most of them I think were born here, of parents who were born here."

"Yes, but back of every one of them, you find an African."

I paused to ponder that, musing about all of the mysterious Africans standing in long rows behind my Liza. I knew where I came from, and I wondered, wondered about her. All my wondering rose up with the billowing towers of dust.

In town the streets as usual bustled with commerce and society. We quickly made for the garden of a house on Water Street where we settled in to listen to a number of men in black coats and stiff white shirts giving reasons of a very serious sort as to why South Carolina should not only ignore the tariffs imposed on it by the federal government—"even at these lower rates, thanks to the Clay bill?"—"Yes, because we are fighting for a principle here."—but should seriously consider a proposal for secession.

My cousin's brother-in-law, Joseph Salvador, the red-haired Jew from Charleston, stood in the thick of it.

"If we are to live as real men," he said, "then we can only be governed by a union of free men." He pointed to a man across the veranda from him. "I am a real man. And you are a real man."

"Indeed," the man said, touching a finger to his collar. "But what do you mean by 'real'?"

"Free," said Joseph Salvador. "A real man is a free man."

Another man spoke up. "But are we now free?"

"Not until we govern ourselves," said Joseph Salvador. "To give power to a federal government that is made up of no one makes no sense to me. Real men are states' men. And a government with no state is not a real government."

"Especially a government that may one day tell us we cannot hold slaves," the same man Joseph Salvador had addressed now spoke up.

"A government whose very fortress sits at the entrance to our harbor," said another man.

My cousin leaned toward me and said in a whisper, "He is the head of our bank."

Tariffs, money, slaves, the conversation continued for a while, leaving my head both swirling with matter-of-fact thoughts and oddly disposed to dreaming. Liza, yes, she was on my mind. A slave. And might she one day be freed by federal fiat? Become a real person? Her eyes, her mouth, her hair. None of these men would wish it so. Was she real, or only a dream person? The way she touched me. Her fingers on me. Her beating heart. The perfume of her steaming breasts and loins. The flavor of her color, the vinegary smoothness of her flesh to my tongue. The anti-federals wanted to keep her a slave, the federals wanted to free her. And so where did I stand?

The meeting—and my daydreaming—went on for hours. After it adjourned Joseph Salvador joined us in the yeasty warm half-light at a local tavern.

"And what did you think, Mr. New York?" he said to me while we tore apart two roast birds and drank tankards of vinegary ale.

"Of the meeting?"

"Of course, of course, the meeting."

I chewed, swallowed, washed the food down with ale, dabbed at my lips with my coat sleeve.

"It put forward an interesting perspective."

"Merely interesting? It shines a light on a path, I believe. And if we follow it, both terrible and wonderful things may occur."

"Secession, you mean?"

"That, yes."

"We are all—" and I had never thought about this before but the thought came naturally—"one family, all of us in the various states, and so secession seems wrong to me. Rather like a son declaring he is no longer part of a family."

Now my cousin spoke up.

"Your example is flawed, Nathaniel," he said. "The states are not children. If it is a family, it is a family made up all of fathers."

"Brothers, perhaps?"

"If you will."

"If half of the brothers withdraw to make their own family, what happens to the others?"

Joseph Salvador made an answer, but I was withdrawing at that moment back into those thoughts of Liza, enhanced, no doubt, by my draughts of ale. Her eyes, one the color of dawn, the other the color of trees.

"The truth!" my cousin said, jarring me from my reverie by pounding his fist onto the table.

"Don't push the man," Joseph Salvador said. "He is new to our ways."

"No, I want him to tell us the truth," my cousin said.

"The truth?" I looked up from my ale, wondering about the nature of the question.

"If you could live here like us," Joseph Salvador said, "you would, would you not? Away from your cold climate, at ease on a plantation, or, urban fellow that you are, enjoying yourself in this city."

"And," my cousin put in, "You would find yourself a pleasant wife, perhaps Anna, or another of Rebecca's many appealing relatives and friends. And you would open a branch of your father's, my uncle's, import business. You would raise a family. And you would have the power and the choice to keep your private life interesting, if you understand what I mean."

"Do I know?" I said.

"Perhaps you do."

Jonathan laughed a laugh so hard he spit bubbles of ale across the table.

"Pardon, pardon," he said, "I am not usually this less-than-fastidious."

"I ask you, Cousin, what do you have in mind?"

"In mind? In mind? The long history of our people, darkened by slavery in Egypt, long in bondage there until our savior Moses led us out of the land of captivity."

"A long procession through the ages," Joseph Salvador added, "up to where we sit now, with Jews like myself in the state legislature."

"That is not what my cousin was saying."

Jonathan feigned innocence.

"And what might I have been saying except what I said?"

"You were speaking about our freedom, and thinking about certain aspects of your own private life here."

"Or perhaps I was thinking about *your* private life here? Might there be a certain dark woman who figures in that?"

"What, dear Cousin, might you know about that?"

"Know? So there is something to know?"

"It is time to go," I said, pushing back from the table so brusquely that I nearly overturned it.

"Oh, yes, Cuz, because we have one more meeting."

"Another?" Now I was not merely angry with my cousin but mystified. I would have been even more mystified, not less, if I had been aware that I was approaching a cross-roads in my life, knowing only that I had a deep sensation that great change was in the works.

Jonathan gave Joseph Salvador a conspiratorial glance.

"Jonathan," I said in protest, "has your wife tried to put me in that company of her cousin Anna again?"

"Anna?" Salvador shook his head. "No, no, don't fear the fires of social obligation. This is something quite outside the bounds of etiquette."

"What then?" I said.

The pair of them ignored my question.

Our meeting had gone from morning, through mid-afternoon, and now the sun, as we stepped out onto the brick walk before the house, was swinging westward toward the end of the day.

"Will there be some food and drink at this mystery rendezvous?" I inquired.

"Plenty for the belly and the spirit," my cousin said.

Salvador gave a shake of this thick red mane and bid me climb aboard the carriage.

The ride to the fine house at the edge of the Battery took no time at all. Liveried servants ushered us inside. My cousin and his brother-in-law made conversation about this and that with a slave woman as dark as night and shoulders as broad as a man's. She served us tea in the parlor. Yours truly still fumed, but not so much that he could not admire the fine portraits on the wall and the deep, cushiony carpets, some with abstract weaves, others depicting certain scenes from our history, such as the signing of the Declaration of Independence and the burning of Washington.

Music from a spinet drifted down from the floor above.

"And where are the other conspirators?" I asked of my cousin.

"They will be here momentarily," he said.

Sure enough, within moments we heard voices in the hall, and a quintet of beautifully dressed slave girls walked lightly into the room.

"Is this the meeting?" I said, standing up.

My cousin shook his head at what he took to be my impossible attitude. I certainly did feel impossible and stupidly surprised.

"Can you ever rest your busy mind, Cousin?"

"Sorry," I said with a shake of my head, "this is not what I had in my mind at all. I am not passing any judgments on you, Cousin. This is just not…" I stood up. "If you will excuse me, I am going to take a stroll."

His manner quite cold my cousin said, "Meet us here in two hours, or walk back to The Oaks."

"Very well," I said and left the room.

A servant let me out of the house just as a trio of stringed instruments sounded in the hall. I walked down the steps and fairly well loped across the park to the ocean-side.

What a marvelous way to clear my head! The sea was calm, or seemed so at least in the fading light. Out beyond the squat shape of Fort Sumter on the horizon the sky appeared to be striped with multi-layered clouds, some pink, some peach, some darker, like fog. But even as I watched the cloud-shapes shifted and the colors turned to lavender and then to red, the darker turning light, the lighter turning dark as Nature made her paintings on the sky. If I could have stood here forever, fixing my attention on the works made in air, I would have chosen to do that, fixed in time, certainly, but in the knowledge that however difficult might be the choice I had to make I would not now or ever have to make it.

Chapter Seventy-four

A Death

An hour later I stood once again in front of that house on the edge of the Battery. Within moments of my arrival, both my cousin and Joseph Salvador emerged from the front door and even before I could speak the clatter of horse and carriage sounded behind me.

Joseph Salvador, avoiding my eyes, waved a farewell to my cousin, who joined me at the carriage. We rode back to The Oaks, which took not an inconsiderable amount of time, in darkness and silence. Only as we neared the end of our journey did he say anything at all, and this began as small talk about tariffs and nullification and secession.

"Father will be interested to know what transpired," he said.

"Shall we tell him everything?" I said.

"Don't be such a moralistic oaf," my cousin said. "Do you believe that he is a paragon of virtue himself? Good God, Nathaniel, when you finally see the truth of things I expect it will come as such a blast of light that you might nearly go blind."

"And will I ever see the truth?"

"Cousin, I really do not know."

"I know enough about you, sir, that I find it, I must say, truly uncomfortable to ride with you like this."

"Is that so?" Jonathan turned to me and over the sound of the moving carriage and lay a hand on my arm. "Just how much do you know? Enough to worry about any partnerships we might make? Or enough to challenge me to a duel?"

I clenched my fists, having never been spoken to like this before in my life by one of my own kin. But I forbore, saying nothing. We rode in silence under the great starry vault of the sky. It was a moonless night, and

though the stars glittered everywhere above us, in some places seeming to
be as thick as dust, the moisture in the air kept us from a perfect sight of the
heavens. Things blurred, things faded. But that was the way we saw such
matter in this world. And I thought to myself, what if there were a way for
us, me and Liza, to grow wings and fly up into that space, and hurry away
to some star where we might be alone and together and happier and easier
than we are? And then I said to myself, I will book us passage on that ship
to New York, the two of us, and we will sail away, if not fly.

At last, the great dark tunnel of trees lay just ahead. We rode along,
beneath the shadowy wood, darkened by the darkness.

Then we saw at a great distance at the end of the low road the house all
aglow, candles in every window.

"What is it?" I asked my cousin. "Another meeting? It looks as though
they might even be having a party!"

When we made our way inside the house, we found the front parlor
filled with weeping slaves and wailing Jews. Rebecca sat in a chair near
the door, moving her head from side to side, crying out, "He's gone! He's
gone!" while my aunt lay unmoving on the couch, Precious Sally was
kneeling next to her, dabbing at her face with wet cloths.

"Oh, my aunt," I said, rushing to her side.

She coughed, let out a whimper, cleared her throat.

"It happened so suddenly. He went up to take a nap, and awoke a short
while later with a small fever. He said he was tired, and went back to sleep.
I looked in on him while he was sleeping, and he was soaking such a sweat
I didn't know what to do. After a while I asked Sally to make a poultice."

Tears flowed from her eyes and it took her a few moments to regain
her composure.

"She went out back and did not return for a long time. When she did,
she wore a terribly long face. 'There's another man, Jason, sick out back in
the cabins,' she said. 'The Master is sick upstairs,' I told her. 'You must pay
attention to him.' 'The man in the cabins, he seen the Visitor,' she said.
'Please, Sally,' I told her, 'don't you start a panic. Please go up to lay the
poultice on the master.'

"She went up, and after a while she came part way down the stairs, the
saddest look on her face. 'You better come up, missus,' she said to me. I
could not move. I asked Rebecca to go in my stead."

Rebecca spoke up from her chair.

"I went back upstairs and found him lying there, a feeble smile on his face. His head appeared huge to me, his skin pale and taut across the bone beneath.

"'Has the rice come in?' he said.

"'Yes, my beloved uncle,' I said, 'the rice has come in.'

"'I am glad,' he said, closing his eyes. Next he whispered something so quietly I could not hear. I leaned my ear close to his lips.

"'Free them,' he said. His last words before he lay still, so quiet and peaceful. I tried to wake him."

Her voice rose into the higher registers. "I could not! I tried, but I could not!"

From outside the house the voices of field hands drifted up—

> *Working all day*
> *And part of the night,*
> *And up before the morning light,*
> *When will Jehovah hear my cry*
> *And set a poor soul free?*

They stood huddled in a corner of the veranda, shaking their heads, singing under their breath, and Isaac stood with them, singing, talking. I look around for Liza, but did not see her. My heart beat back and forth from calm to hectic, calm to hectic. All the while the slaves kept singing.

> *When will Jehovah hear my cry*
> *And set a poor soul free?*

Jonathan had gone up the stairs, and now he came down.

"Well, now, folks," he announced, and he appeared to be looking directly at me, "I have seen my father, and he has passed away." More weeping and wailing from all gathered here. Jonathan waited until the noise subsided somewhat and then said, "I suppose this means that The Oaks is now mine."

I felt as though I had taken a blow to the face.

"I must see him," I said and turning from my cousin—his hard jaw gleaming red in the light of the fire, I mounted the stairs, footsteps following after me. I turned with a start to see young Abraham at my heels.

"Abe," I said, "you must not go in now. The sick room is not a good place for you to visit."

He shook his head, and tears rolling down his cheeks he clambered past me up the stairs.

"Do not touch the...do not touch him," I called after him as with fallen shoulders he stepped into the room where his grandfather lay.

Leaving them both to the dark, I wandered along the hall and entered my own room. It was dark inside, and a few traces of Liza's perfumes and odors lingered in the air. I closed that door and drifted back down the hall. From the sick room came the sound of a young boy sobbing hoarsely, as for the first time in his life. From the parlor the sounds of mourning grew louder and louder.

"Cousin," Jonathan called up the stairwell. "Come down, it is time, and I have some things to say." It was odd how strong his voice sounded, given the loss he had just suffered. "Come down!"

The candles fluttered as a breeze stirred in the otherwise quiet hall. At the bottom of the stairs moved the shapes and shadows of the mourners and the slaves. I shook my head, my limbs, though, froze me in place, and my heart settled almost to a stand-still, either in calm or in fear.

A floorboard creaked behind me.

"Abe?" I turned around, staring into the dark.

A hand came up and touched me at the small of my back, and I turned yet again, my blood chilled with fright.

"Nate," Liza said, "it is time. Come with me!"

Chapter Seventy-five

The Other Way

*L*iza clearly knew her way down the damp dark narrow back staircase, leading me by the hand as we descended into the room behind the kitchen and stepped to the rear door of the house.

Promise stood there quietly waiting along with my cousin's usual mount. "How—?"

Isaac stepped out of the shadows and offered me the reins.

"Up you go, massa," he said, giving me a hand up and then hoisting Liza onto the back of Jonathan's horse.

Now the animals jittered about in the dark.

"What are we doing?" I asked.

"Running," Liza said. She sounded a bit out of breath as she spoke, but it could have been the snorting and clattering of the horse.

I felt as though struck by a bolt of lightning.

She led, I followed, as we took the dark trail behind the barns and on into the woods. In a moment the house, for all of its lights, was swallowed up in the gloom of the trees.

"We must turn back," I said, feeling as though I had just come out of a dream. "I cannot leave them in the midst of their mourning just for…" I stopped speaking, unsure of what I could say.

"I can't leave them neither," she said. "'In the midst of their mourning.' But it is my mourning, too."

"You liked the old master, did you not?"

"Yes," she said, "I did. I liked him."

"No matter that he owned you?"

"He did own me, and then again he did not."

We talked, but we did not stop. Perhaps it was an illusion created by the dark but it seemed like no time had passed before we came to the fork in the road and ducked under the trees to take the trail to the brickyard.

"Wait here," Liza said as we arrived at the clearing. She dismounted and I watched her shadowy figure enter the small brickmaking shed.

Promise moved about in a small circle, sniffing and snorting, swatting his tail. I knew the creek was nearby. I could hear creatures splashing about in the water.

"Liza?" I called out, just as she reappeared in the clearing, a sack over her shoulder and a shadowy companion at her shadowy side.

"You know this boy, I think," she said.

I peered down at the young fellow, who was, because of his skin color, almost invisible in the dark.

"You!" I said.

It was the slave boy from Perth Amboy, who traveled with the mean-spirited man, and ran away.

"Have you been hiding all this while in the brickyard?"

The boy touched his hand to his forehead in a sort of salute and moved with Liza to the horse. In a moment she had remounted, and he swung up onto the animal behind her.

"Are you ready?" Liza said.

"Am I ready? We have to go back to the house. I must go back. And you, too. All will be forgiven. If you go back now there will be nothing *to* forgive."

"Perhaps in another life."

I still did not understand, or did not want to.

"Liza, my uncle—"

"He's dead," she said, "and there will be nothing but trouble."

"No, no," I said. "Jonathan is the heir. I will buy you from him. I will take you north."

"If he sells me," she said. "it won't be to you. He will sell me at the auction block in the town."

"I can bid for you there."

Such a sound of disgust mingled with horror burst from her throat that even in the dark I could measure the intensity of her response.

"I will not allow you ever to *bid* on me!"

"I will do whatever I must do."

"You will not have the opportunity, I tell you now. He will sell me down river or kill me first."

The horses pawed at the ground, snuffled and snorted, anxious to move somewhere, anywhere.

"Why?" I said, "Why?" and I despised myself for the horse-like whine I could hear in my speech.

In a voice I had never heard her use before, it was so drained of spirit, so ghostly, she said, "He will see the will and he will sell me."

"The will? My uncle's will? How do you know this? How do you know about my uncle's will?"

"He left it in his desk. One day I found it there. I read it. Thus the dangers of teaching your inquisitive slaves to read."

Again, the horses asked us, *Can we please move now? Now?*

"There was a surprise," she said. "The way we live here, there is nothing anymore to surprise us and then along comes a surprise."

"And what was that?"

"He had another child," Liza said.

"By some other wife? Did he keep a family down in the Islands?"

"No, no," she said.

"Oh, no, not him!" I could not hide my pain and dismay at learning this. "He, my dear uncle, also went down to the cabins?"

"He did, indeed," Liza said.

"I do not know the laws of the state in this matter," I said. "Could it be possible for him to leave property to a child born of a slave?"

"I don't know the law," she said. "But in the will he recognized the child as his own."

"And who is this child?"

Please, said my horse. *Now, I truly need to move now.*

"Easy, Promise," I said. "Easy."

"The child did not know. He is a man now and suffers to know. None of *us* knew, not until I read the pages. When your cousin hears the news he will be very very angry. He will sell the man down river, or somehow arrange for the patrollers to take him into their custody."

"Who is this man? Do I know him?"

"You know him." Liza sighed, and bent to pat her own insistent horse while the Amboy slave slipped his arms around her waist and held to her.

"Who?"

I thought of all the Africans I had met here, I thought of the African men, toiling their lives away in the heat and dust and flowing and ebbing waters.

And then it occurred to me.

"Oh, Liza! It is Isaac! My uncle is his father! He is a cousin to me and half-brother to Jonathan!"

"Whatever Jonathan is to any of us. Now we must start moving. He will have probably already discovered we are gone, and it will be all Isaac can do to distract him from our trail."

"Our trail? And just where are we going?"

"With this boy in tow? Where do you think? We are going away. Or I am. You, of course, are *free* to stay."

Liza gave her horse a kick, and he set to moving, and so Promise moved, and all of us moved into the dark.

—————————————•

Chapter Seventy-six

Moving into the Dark

$\mathcal{W}$e began our journey by heading back toward the main road. It was a risk, but the choice lay between abandoning the horses and making off through the woods on foot, or taking our chances on meeting trouble on the road and keeping our superior means of travel.

"They may be waiting for us at the house!" I called to Liza over the noise of our animals.

"If Jonathan has gone after us, he is already on his way to town," Liza called back to me.

"How do you know?"

"Isaac will have told him we have gone that way, and he will be leading him there. Jonathan will remember that you went to town to visit the shipping office."

"Should not Isaac be running as we are?"

"He will not run," Liza said. "He is too proud."

Oh, I said to myself, *and I have no pride, and so I am running.* But another voice came to me and said, *Yes, you are running, running with this woman to love and freedom!*

Suddenly we broke into the clearing and looked back and saw the house still all ablaze with lights. I pictured my aunt and Rebecca gathered about my uncle's body in the upper room, or huddled together for succor in the parlor, their ears inclined toward the sound of our passage.

Oh, Uncle, I called out to him in my mind, *I am stealing what was not yours to keep! And what is not mine to take!*

Perhaps my uncle replied to me from the world of the dead, but our horses made too much noise for me to hear anything but the beating of their hooves against the hard dirt of the road.

Pounding away they were as we raced down the tunnel of trees to the main road—and headed northwest instead of southeast.

"Do you have a plan?" I called to Liza as we hurried along. She didn't turn to look at me, but the slave boy did, his young face showing no emotion as we moved under the dark trees on a part of the road I had never traveled.

"Lord," I said to all and no one, "I wish I had my pistol!"

She did not reply, but the boy turned his head and gave me a knowing nod.

What did he know? Who was he, he still almost a child, who had boarded that ship in New Jersey and traveled with the wickedest man I had ever met, and then escaped, hiding at the brickyard at The Oaks all these weeks, harbored, of course, by the other slaves?

If he had truly escaped.

Long minutes passed. Liza noticed the animals were beginning to tire, and so we slowed down a bit, but still moving forward along the dark road. It was late for country life, and no one was on the road, and if there were other people living out in the fields along the road they were sleeping or sitting up awake in the dark.

"Liza?"

"Hush, Nathaniel," she called back to me. "We'll have time later to talk."

"I should have—"

"Hush!"

I had spoken too soon, because I saw, as she did, a light flickering up the road far ahead, a light that danced and waxed and waned I hoped against hope it was a phantom lamp, one of those will-o'-the-wisp tricks of the darkish air, product perhaps of swamp gases and the dampness of the hour. But as we approached the light became still, and hovered at just the height it would if it were a torch or lamp held by a man on horseback.

It was in fact two lights, each held by a man on horseback.

"Whoa!" called out one of them as we slowed down on our approach, as if he were talking to his own horse.

"Liza—"

"Hush!" she cautioned me.

"Well, well, well, good evening, Mister Yankeeman," said the patroller Langerhans, holding up one of the torches. "Out kind of late, ain't you?" He turned to smile to his two assistants, who nodded back at him, smiling.

"As are you," I said.

"I'm on patrol," said the slave-catcher. "And you?"

"Me?"

"Yes, sir," he said, slurring his *esses*.

"I'm going about my uncle's business," I said.

"In the middle of the night? With a slave girl riding along? And what? Who is that darky sitting up behind her? Wouldn't be the young nigger we come out to look around for not long ago, could it?"

"He is nobody to you," Liza said.

"Liza, I'll take care of this."

Langerhans made a clucking noise in his mouth.

"Will you?"

"Stand aside," I said.

Langerhans shook his head, which gave his already rather monstrous aspect in the wavering light of the torch an even more grotesque appearance.

"I can't do that. I get paid to keep niggers from running off and if I don't my children aren't going to eat."

"She has a pass," I said.

"Really? And does that boy have a pass, too? Where're y'all riding in the middle of the night?"

"She is going to visit family," I said. "North of here."

"That's funny. All the family I ever hear about is living north, when all the family I ever know about has gone south."

"I'll show you the passes," I said, reaching into the inside of my coat.

"Slow," Langerhans said. "Show me slow."

"Of course," I said, preparing to pat my pocket as though I had lost the paper, a ghastly empty place swelling in my heart because of the absence of my pistol.

"Slow!" he said again.

In the wavering light of the torch I saw a movement at Liza's side.

Langerhans saw it too, and made a joke.

"Oh, my," he said to his men, "do you see what I see? This nigger girl's holding a pistol just big enough to take off a toe or the tip of a nose."

The men laughed as Langerhans turned in his saddle.

"But she don't even have it cocked. Might be loaded, though I doubt that, but it ain't cocked. If you're lucky enough to know it's even loaded, how you going to fire a weapon it ain't cocked, I ask you that?"

"Liza," I said, meaning for her to lower the weapon.

Instead she moved her free hand across it and we all heard the sound.

"Lordy," Langerhans said again, as though he were announcing a show, "looked what she done! She done cocked that weapon! Oh, oh, oh, ain't she smart? I mean, smart for a nigger bitch!"

"Liza," I said again, speaking but feeling unable to breathe.

"Liza," Langerhans said, mocking my voice. "He wants you to put that gun down now. Even if it ain't loaded."

Liza in silence kept that weapon level and pointed directly at Langerhans.

"Liza, you hear him?"

Langerhans sounded a bit impatient now.

"Liza," he said again.

"Liza," I said.

"Come on, you bitch—" Langerhans reached toward her.

Came a loud blast and flash of light, a man screamed, the horses jumped about, I grabbed Promise's reins. At that moment my heart felt as though it might break through my rib-cage and fly away like a terrified bird.

"Ride!" Liza called to me.

And we rode.

A second loud bang, and a flash spurred our horses even faster.

I heard a voice, a moan. It was mine, but it also echoed along behind us in the dark.

After about half an hour we slowed, then stopped, looked down the road and saw nothing, no light, nothing—and when the horses settled a bit, stopped their nickering and whinnying, we breathed in the dark, wondering, hoping, worrying, wondering.

"Are you all right?" I said.

"No," she said. "But I'm not bleeding."

The slave boy spoke up from behind me on the horse.

"I ain't breathing."

"You are if you're speaking."

"Then I'm breathing," he said.

"Hurry now," Liza said, giving her horse a start.

I rode up next to her, making up the way through the woods.

"How long have you been keeping my pistol?" I asked her.

"Long enough," Liza said.

And we started off again, two runaway slaves and a Yankee, each of us now a murderer. I carried heavy regrets, oh, yes, I carried regrets, and a mixed burden of hope and despair. Liza and I were running, and I would not see the harvest.

Chapter Seventy-seven

Darkness of the Dark

Darkness of the dark, black pitch tar-hole dead of night starless moonless abyss of nothingness nothing...The dark had a scent to it, the thick green stink of fecund plant, root and stem, bole and leaf, and the rot of still waters, and the spoor of invisible animals that swam or crawled in the pitch-black around us.

And the dark had a sound, which, when now and then when we stopped to get our bearings—or, I should say, Liza stopped us, and she figured our path a little further—and the horses quieted down, we could hear as a constant whirring of insects and an occasional chirp or squawk of bird or sigh of hunting animal, or the splash of some creature fishing in the swamp.

But it was not until we had ridden for what seemed like many hours in the pitch of night that I could distinguish darkness upon darkness and make out certain shapes and figures—trees, mainly, and more trees—against what had been a dark so empty that it took on heft and girth, and I could hear sounds buried under other sounds, and it seemed almost that I could hold my breath and appreciate the purring of ticks under the wings of sleeping birds and the liquid whispers of mother fish as they herded their fry beneath the placid liquid dark of the ditches and eddies of the swamp.

Now I could see Liza riding ahead of us and despite the first light I felt a terrible inward rush of emptiness and false bearings.

"Wait!" I called to her.

She slowed her horse and my Promise nearly collided with it.

"What is it, Nate?" she said.

"What is it? I still cannot rid my thoughts of this. You killed a man. And I am a party to it."

"You would have done it, if I had not."

I reached for the reins of her horse, but it skittered away.

"If you had not stolen my pistol, perhaps."

Liza laughed a laugh all too gay given the circumstances, as though we might be waltzing about the lawn of the big house to the music made by violins.

"How can you laugh at such a time as this? When you have killed a man and we are running?"

"When *we* have killed a man," she said. "You just agreed to that."

A terrible thought occurred to me.

"What else did you take? Did you steal money from my dying uncle?"

"I took nothing that was not mine," Liza said.

And by the early light of our new dawn together I saw her reach into the sack she had carried with her as we had made our escape from the house—in which she had kept, among other things, the pistol she had taken from my room—and extract one of the silver candlesticks, inscribed so long ago in an eastern country, and hold it up to show me, grinning a girlish grin that never would have allowed you to believe, if you had not been there when it happened, that she had shot and killed a man only hours before.

Now it was daylight, and we edged the horses into the narrow trail into the swamp, needing to find a place to hide for the long day to come.

Slavery is so simple, freedom so complicated. Here I was huddled in a damp hole beneath a towering swamp tree while the light of green day showed me my sleeping companions, Liza, her coffee-colored face unscarred by care, and the runaway boy, his features puckered into something resembling a dark wrinkled fruit.

If I could have seen myself in a glass, what would I have viewed? Shirt open, coat torn at the sleeves, hair askew, face smudged with leaves and mud, so that with darker skin I might have been mistaken for a runaway slave myself. We had been moving so quickly since we left The Oaks that it was only now that we found ourselves at rest that I began to question what I had done.

The shooting.

Running away.

Betraying my family.

Was that not what I had done?

I leaned over and reached for her hand.

She sat up, nearly fully awake.

"What? Are they here?"

"Liza," I said, "I wish to speak with you."

"They are not here?"

"We are alone," I said. "Except for the boy."

"Why wake me then? I am worn down, Nate."

"We'll have all day," I said. "I understand, we must not move by day."

"You're learning."

"I am learning," I said. "But I have not learned everything I want to know."

She shook her head, rubbed her eyes with her knuckles, and leaned back against the tree.

"What do you mean?"

"Tell me," I said.

"Do you know what you are asking?"

"No, no, I do not. I have only my suspicions."

"And what do you suspect?"

And just as I was saying what I said next I understood that until I began to say it I had not understood it all!

"You came to my bed so that I would help you run away."

Chapter Seventy-eight

Dark Tales by Light of Day

Coming to your bed," Liza said, "was not my idea at first."

Her words hit me in the chest like a fist.

"Whose idea was it?"

I reached over and took her hand, and took some deep breaths. The atmosphere of the swamp oozed damp and stink, a difficult place in which to breathe.

"Jonathan sent me to you."

"What precisely do you mean by that?"

"He ordered me to visit you."

"He did this? And you obeyed? Why on earth——?"

"Nathaniel, I *belonged* to him. He could do anything he wanted to do with me."

"And he sent you to me?"

"Yes," she broke in, "and if I could feel shame ever again I might feel it about this."

"My head is a-whirl," I said. "Is there more? Tell me everything."

"Oh, it is quite sordid. Too sordid for a New York gentleman to contemplate, I'm afraid."

"I want to know," I said, already feeling as though someone had just torn away a swathe of skin from a blistering wound on my heart. "I love you, Liza. I offered to buy you. Is that not proof of how I felt?"

Liza laughed sardonically.

"If that is proof of love, folks all over the South would be feeling it every day. I buy you, I love you. I sell you, I hate you. As a matter of fact, Nate, slaves don't find much affection in being either bought or sold."

"No, I suppose not." I spoke formally, but my heart, with its wound, now felt like a large rock in my chest, weighing me down, pulling me toward the ground.

Liza could see this on my face.

"Let's try to sleep," she said.

"You told me you would explain everything," I said.

She kept her silence for a moment.

I glanced over at the sleeping boy.

"Tell me everything."

Without taking much of a breath, she said, "I decided to seduce you so that you would help me run away."

"Please," I said. "And so you would not prostitute yourself on your father's orders. But you would do it on your own?"

"Please don't speak about it like that."

"You did not have to give yourself to me," I said. "I was, I am, in love with you. I would have done without the...the bait."

"It is not as if I didn't, and don't still, feel strongly for you," she said. "What I did—was come up to the edge, and then cross over."

"Ah, yes, the edge," I said. "But had you never thought of running away with Isaac?"

"I thought of it, but he would never run."

"Why not?"

"Not until he took his revenge. Do you forget that your uncle raped his mother and destroyed his father's life?"

I took a few long breaths, but did not, could not, respond.

"So...it was me or no one?"

"Yes."

"If you had made your predicament known I would have helped you without..."

"Seduction?"

"Yes, without that."

"You might have," Liza said. "It did not seem absolutely certain to me that you would have. You almost surely would not have run with me if it had *not* happened. I knew that if the patrollers had met me and I was alone on the road I never would have gotten past them."

"Liza," I said, " I offered to *buy* you. Is that not that proof of how I felt?"

"Yes, but you forgot you were never going to *own* me. Jonathan would not allow his father to sell me to you. The older his father became, the more power the son took on. I was his daughter. He would have killed me, I have told you, before he ever let me go."

The woods nearby, the swamp, had come alive with the sunrise, with sounds and calls alerting us to the nature of the world. Everything was bird and animal and insect, tree and water, rushing and stagnant, this was the place we lived in, and made our ways as best we could.

"My cousin is a vile, disgusting, deceitful and dishonorable man," I said. "He deserves to be horse-whipped, or worse."

"And yet he is my father," Liza said.

"And my relative, yes. A man who only days ago made clear his desire to become my business partner in a family enterprise."

Now Liza inched further away from me, but kept her lips closed as the boy from Jersey awoke and looked around.

"Is there anything more?" I said.

"Even more," she said.

"What might that possibly be?"

The sun had risen to a true extent, and I imagined beneath it the rolling ocean that had carried ship after ship from African shores to our own, here near Charleston, and to other southern ports where this national horror and the deep bloodstain upon our nation first began. It was clear to me now in a way that no legislative debates or newspaper reports or even, as perhaps would happen, the narratives of future historians might tell of it, that how it bent bodies to the pleasure and finances of the owners was nothing, nothing, compared to the way it bent souls.

"Yes. When I came back that second night—"

"At his orders."

"No. I acted out of my own free will."

"And are you acting now?"

"As in a play? I have heard of plays, Nathaniel, but I have never seen one."

"You should see one," I said. "They are good stories, performed upon a stage for all the audience to see. Consider my story. Stealing away my cousin who literally, in a most unromantic fashion, belongs to another man, this slave, also my cousin, with whom I have committed incest—oh, it would make a good play, I think."

Quick as some lithe snake that snaps around and takes its poor unthinking prey, without a second's delay, Liza slapped me in the face.

"It was my only chance," she said while I held a hand to my stinging cheek.

"And am I nothing but a stepping-stone to you," I said.

"At first, yes," she said, touching a hand to my cheek.

I drew back, disturbed, yes, even disgusted.

"You are nothing but a temptress," I said. "Eve, tempting me to crime."

"You enjoyed the temptation."

"Yes, worse yet, I enjoyed the crime."

"Will you still help me now?"

"I don't know that I have a choice."

"You can leave us here and return to The Oaks."

"If I knew the way."

"I can point you in the right direction."

"Yes, as you pointed me toward my crime. With your directions, I would probably lose myself fairly quickly in these bogs and be eaten by alligators."

"You are sweet enough meat for them," Liza said.

"Don't be so scandalous as to joke about all this. We are in terrible danger."

"I am, the boy is, not you."

"I am aiding and abetting."

"Your cousin will not take such offense if you return now. Say that I kidnapped you at gunpoint."

"With my own pistol that you stole from me?"

"It is a good story. It might make a good play."

I ignored her attempt at humor.

"He will see through it," I said. "He sent you to me. He knows what must have happened. And so he will know that you turned me against him and the rest of the family."

"A family of slaveholders," Liza said.

"If they are to be condemned, then the entire South is to be condemned."

"And should it not be?"

"The wives? The children?"

"Wives hold slaves along with their husbands."

"What of the children?"

"Innocent, until they reach their majority."

"Liza…" I sighed.

"Yes, Nate?"

She had inched so close to me by then her warm acid night-breath bathed my face in the foul truth of its scent, a perfect match for the foul taste in my own mouth. Though I had questions for her, her proximity made it impossible for me to ask. I encircled her in my arms and held her close. She trembled, as tough as she seemed.

One kiss—our awful breaths combining—and then another. And then we fell back, exhausted, like two halves of some broken animal, against the tree.

"Our last gasp," I said, "our pathetic last gasp of freedom. They will be sending dogs after us. And there is a lot of the South that lies between us and the North. Liza, I am afraid that I know the city, not the woods. I will not be much help to you in this from now on."

"Nate," she said after a while, "I have a plan."

She began to speak. Towards the end of her describing it to me my eyes wandered over to the edge of a stand of ferny trees to see the slave boy hunkered down there, as they say in these parts, awake and alert. I wondered how long he had been watching.

"Jersey Boy," I called over to him.

"Yes, sir," he said.

"When Liza has finished explaining her plan to me, will you tell us your own story? We have a long day today and tomorrow and tomorrow. I hope you will tell us."

Chapter Seventy-nine

The Jersey Boy's Tale

I was born free," the boy said, while the light of the morning sun drifted down through the pines. "Up there in Perth Amboy. In a little shack behind a big house on Water Street. Early as I can remember in my life, I used to lie there listening to the waves slapping against the rocks below, and I would dream of ships and the flow of water. From the top turret of the big house, where I climbed some time after I grew a little you could see over Staten Island right out past the bay into the ocean, the great ocean where ships from all parts of the world came sailing.

"My Ma, free-born herself, she worked in the kitchen of the big house. Most days and nights I'd sit in a corner of the kitchen, enjoying the smells of the food, and Ma or the wash girl who did the dishes, offering me a morsel now and then. Fish. Meat. Carrots. Corn. All the fresh flavors, and sometimes dessert, cake with rum. I'd be sitting in my corner while Ma was rushing about serving the folks in the dining room and I could hear the noisy music of their talking and smell the rosy stink of the cigars the men were lighting up and puffing on. That rum would take my thoughts and melt them down and I'd flow away, dreaming of my Pa and sailing ships and the way the gulls swooped across the beach and dove toward the rocks to crack open oyster shells they'd picked off the beach.

"I liked it there on the sand and sneaked down as often as I could to run along the water line and pick up shells and stones.

"'One, two, lucky stone!'

"I'd throw one hard out over the water, sometimes getting it to skip real good.

"'One, two, lucky stone!'

"Once I thought, hey, what if I could ride a stone out over the water, and just keep skipping till I got someplace else?

"'One, two, lucky stone!'

"There was some other boys, free boys like me, but born to slave mothers who got bought or somehow otherwise came up from the South to New Jersey. We ran together on the sand, ran like these horses we rode away on, dashed up to the waves and back again, and I can still taste that salt in my mouth, deep salty, not like this stinging taste of the water in this swamp.

"Sometimes we built castles in the sand. Once we made a jail and put the little sand crabs inside, saying these are the prisoners. Another boy said the crabs was our slaves. Why, we could keep them, but we couldn't make them do nothing. They wouldn't build nothing. They just tried to dig their way out of the jail. Not good slaves.

"I was thinking, give them a chance, give the slaves a chance. I was thinking, slaves got a Ma, slaves feel hurt, slaves want to be free, look at them dig.

"But because that was all they did, one of the boys says, 'Let's drown 'em,' and he took water in his hands and poured it over the crabs. But they liked it, they swam around, and all of them was digging in the wet sand, disappearing into it.

"'Slaves, they get away,' the boy is shouting. And the others are calling out, 'Yay, catch them slaves!' 'Catch them!'

"I went to make to catch them, but used my hand to smash open the wall of the jail.

"And they got away! They got away!

"I would walk back up the hill feeling happy for the crabs! They got away!

"All the time we played there on that beach, it was a wonderment, that's how my Ma called it, when I told her what we did.

"I wish I could have told my Pa. But I never did know him. Ma told me every now and then he was a tall handsome man from Spain who worked on the repair of ship's sails right down near the ferry slip. I remember seeing him once only, late at night, when I was a little boy, when he came to the shack smelling of tar and whiskey and cigar smoke, and Ma went out with him and I began to cry.

"'Hush now,' she said, poking her face back into my part of the shack. 'Hush, you hear. That's your father, and you don't want to make him unhappy.'

"No, I didn't want to do that. Never.

"So when the lady of the house, Mrs. Christian, came out to the kitchen one day and took me up and into her room, saying, 'Charles (that's my name), do you know how to read?' I said 'No, ma'am.'

"I wasn't much for that, because something told it was a lot of work. But she said if I learned it would make my Ma and Pa happy so I said I would try.

"She learned me my letters, and how to read on the Bible. 'And Moses went and spake these words unto all Israel...' See, I remember what I read. 'And he said unto them, I am an hundred and twenty years old this day; I can no more go out and come in; also the Lord hath said unto me, Thou shalt not go over this Jordan...' And if you think that is all I know, what about, 'Amaziah was twenty-and-five years old when he began to reign, and he reigned twenty-and-nine years in Jerusalem. And his mother's name was Jehoaddan of Jerusalem...' or 'And in the second year of the reign of Nebuchadnezzar, Nebuchadnezzar dreamed dreams, wherewith his spirit was troubled, and his sleep brake from him...'

"You heard enough? What about, 'The sin of Judah is written with a pen of iron, and with the point of a diamond: it is graven upon the table of their heart, and upon the horns of your altars...'

"If I knew what the 'horns of the altars' was...

"Yay, so I could read, and sometimes now at her parties Mrs. Christian asked me to come out and read to the guests.

"And that is how I know who among her guests was mean and who was friendly, the tugging at my ears, the pinching.

"A lot of time went past. I know it, because when I started thinking about who I was and where I was I only came up to a low ink mark on the back of the kitchen door and when this bad thing happened to me I was a number of marks taller. And that took time.

"The bad thing?

"It was the man with the loud voice and the white hair and the wild eyes, dressed like a rich man, though he had a smell about him, something like the beach where the fish stank but worse. I don't know anybody else smelled it, except me. Now he came to the Christian house, traveling, he was, in from some place such as a city in the north or a city just to the west, wherever he was from, I don't know, I never heard him say a word about where he come from, his city, his Ma and Pa, almost as if he came from nowhere, and that was where he was going, except he made a stop along the way to the house.

"I suppose he had been there before, because he knew my name, and he knew the Christians. It happened I was in the kitchen, helping my Ma carry out a tray, when he saw me, and next thing I know he was pinching my cheek and saying how much I looked like a little nephew of his.

"'He is dark like you, perhaps not as dark, but dark enough. And his eyes are aslant like yours, rather like a Musulman's.'

"I didn't know what to say, so I said nothing.

"'Have you ever seen a Musulman?' he asked me.

"I didn't know what he was talking about.

"'You are a smarty boy. I heard you read.'"

"'Yes, sir,' I said.

"'You are a gift to the world.'

"Yes, sir."

"'And a great boon to the household here. Do you have a mother?'

"'She works in the kitchen, sir.'

"'Big black woman?'

"'Yes, sir.'

"'You both are a boon to the Christians.' His eyes narrowed and he took a big breath, breathing that smell on me when he breathed out. 'I have a packet for the Christians,' he said, 'out in my carriage. Can you come help me lift it, boy?'

"'Yes, sir,' I said, because what did I know?

"I told Ma and she didn't pay attention because she was working with the meal so hard, and I followed the man down the steps out front and down to the street and he told me we had to go in his carriage to the pier where the packet was on a boat.

"Some of my friends were walking up from the beach, white boys, born free as free, lucky ones.

"'Hey, Charles!' 'Charles, what you doing?' They called out to me.

"'Tell them you are helping me,' the man said.

"I was a good lad.

"'I'm doing some help!' I called back to my friends.

"'Git a penny for it!' one of them shouted as the man pushed me up onto the carriage seat.

"I loved riding high up above the street, and loved watching the houses

pass by, and seeing the ships come up over the top of the hill and then we
rode down to the water and we climbed down.

"'Do you like ships?' the man said to me.

"'Oh, I do,' I said.

"'We'll fetch that packet now,' he said.

"I went along, riding with him up to the piers, and next thing that happens is we are climbing aboard the ship where we met you, sir, and going
down into his cabin, where he tells me to wait.

"I didn't know what to do except do what he asked. I was no slave, but
I was a polite boy, because Ma raised me that way.

"So I waited, leaning against a wall of the cabin, sitting on the bed,
standing up, looking out the porthole, seeing the bay. The boat was rolling
from side to side, and I wondered why, some waves come in from the far
part of the bay, I figured, because I had seen the bay in storms a lot since I
first remembered running on the beach. When the land started moving, I
shook my head, couldn't figure it.

"We cleared the tip of Staten Island before I understood what was happening, and by then it was too late, there was nothing I could do."

(At this point in the boy's story I shivered with a round of chills, recalling, as the sun moved around the sky, how tired I was and physically drawn
by the events of the night before.)

"I was sitting on the bunk with my head in my hands crying when the
man came back to the cabin. He carried a sack with tack and fruit and sat
down next to me and handed me the sack.

"'Where the bee sups,' he said.

"'Thank you, sir,' I said, taking a piece of tack from the sack and chew-
ing on it.

"After a few minutes, the man jumps up and says, 'Come to me, you
little black gumbo,' he said, 'I'll give you comfort.'

"I went on crying.

"'Yes, yes, weep your tears,' he said, 'weep your little nigger tears,
crocodile tears, jungle tears, and I will feed you candy.'

"I didn't know what he was talking about, maybe he didn't know either.
But he came over and sat next to me and put his arms around me—and
threw me on my back on the bed.

"I gave him a fight, same way I'd give a fight to some big boy in town who
jumped on me from behind, trying to hurt me. But this was something I never

knew, what he did, pulling my trousers down and stripping off my under-clothes, throwing me on my back again when I tried to push up, push away.

"'Gumbo, Sambo,' he said, whistling, gurgling through his teeth like some kind of animal in the woods.

"He kept pushing against me just when he leaned over and snuck his head down there, and he tried to eat me up, and his biting hurt and I screamed, and he pushed his hand over my mouth and kept on eating, except he didn't chew me and swallow me, he just chewed, and he didn't stop until I was choking, and coughed up nasty yellow slug in his hand.

"'You!' He made a sound like a man has taken a long drink of water.

"Over and over again that night—it happened again and again. Once I pushed him away and he slapped me. After that he did whatever he wanted, like a child discovers he can get free sugar candy whenever he wants. Next morning I didn't feel so good, in my heart, in my everything. And it wasn't just me, it was the ocean. I ran on the sand, I dug my holes in the sand, I dug for those crabs, but I had never been on the water before, so I didn't know if it was the rolling ship or what he was doing to me that was making me feel so bad.

"I suppose it was both, water and awful man, and his breath smelled like nothing I had ever smelled before, until I went out here into the swamps.

(I was truly shaking by then, shaking and shaking, the story producing in me a fever such as I had never known. And the light had faded and it would soon be time to move.)

"We got off the boat in Charleston and he took me to his rooms in a hotel, and he made me serve him like a slave. He had these meetings to tend to and he always took me with him. Sometimes the other men there stared at me, stared at him, but he didn't pay no mind, except when now and then he would grab me by the back of my neck and pull me up so that I had to stand on my toes, and he'd say, in a big voice, 'The question is property, gentleman, property, property. Can a tree think? Can a horse pray? Does a nigger have a soul? I ask you that, I ask you...'

"Every day it was like that, every night he attacked me, treating me like a dog. There was a time or two when I could have run off but I couldn't get my feet to move, and where could I get my feet to go? I didn't know anybody where I was, didn't even know where I was until later. He just kept me with him, like his pet dog.

"Now, through all this, I saw lots of slave people on the street, and one day when I was alone in the room in the hotel I leaned down and called to a strong-looking man, 'Hey, hello?'

"And he looked around, looked up, saw me waving to him, begging him with my hands and eyes, but he kept on walking.

"Darn, it near broke my soul to see him walk away without helping me. But a little while later, when the man was still out at one of those meetings, came a knock at the door, and it was a hotel maid, and behind her stood the black man I called to on the street.

"'I'se knowed sumpin' is wrong,' the woman said to him, and he nodded, and they talked to me and I told him I was a free boy and the man had stolen me away from New Jersey.

"'Darlin',' the woman said, 'we got to help you.'

"She sounded so much like my Ma, it made me cry.

"'Darlin', you going to be all right.'

"They asked me about the man, and I told them he left the room every morning, and so they told me they would come back the next day.

"The next morning, after waiting for the bad man to leave on his business, quick as lightning they stole me out of that room, and took me downstairs, and they wrapped me up in cloth and put me in the cart with all sorts of tarps and ropes, me burrowed underneath, and they rode me somewhere to where I could smell the water. I could hear the talking, I could hear shouts and I could hear dogs bark and I could whistles and bells. We stopped and they took me out of the cart and onto the boat, and my heart felt so good, I am going back to Amboy! I felt like I could nearly fly there like a bird I felt so light and uplifted!

"The boat went up the river to the creek and took me to the brickyard at the plantation, and there the niggers hid me for all this time, and even when I didn't even know it turned out I was waiting for Liza and you to come for me."

Shadows filled the spaces between the trees and we were up and moving, even as the trees themselves began to fade into the general dark.

"We are going to do that," I said.

"Oh, I pray you, sir, please, because I do so want to get home. My Ma will be thinking long ago I was dead, and I feel that way, I've been so much put upon. But in my heart—"

I was listening to him and his pathetic tale, but I was staring at Liza, this woman who had brought my life to such a strange and unexpected turn.

She was staring back at me.

"What is it?" I asked her.

"I am glad you have run away with me, Nate," she said.

"You do feel some affection for me then? You did not merely plan to seduce me and enlist me in this plan of yours?"

"I feel more than affection," she said.

"Really?" I said.

"Really," she said, watching as the boy curled up against the tree to take the last of the day's rest.

Within a moment he was sleeping. "Nate?"

"Yes, Liza?"

"There is something more," she said.

"And what is that something, Liza?" I said.

"I am carrying our child."

Chapter Eighty

Swamp Vision

All that second night I walked while carrying the thoughts about that child in my mind, and it both weighed me down and kept me buoyant, blotting my fears of possible interception and capture—who knew what slave hunters or horsemen waited on the fringes of the marsh? However, by the next morning I felt strange and awful, a living playground of chills and then after a while what felt to me like heat rising on a sun-bright day in autumn.

Frogs croaked, birds splashed into the swamp to fish for them. Snakes wound their way through the tree branches. In the distance birds called to each other, singing about fish and snakes.

"You must try to rest," Liza said.

"How can I rest when you—?"

"Hush, you," she said, taking me like a child in her arms. "You must sleep."

"And you?"

"I'll try," she said. "Yet when I close my eyes I begin to hear sounds—"

"Splashing, as if horses are tramping through the swamp?"

"Yes."

"Voices, that turn out to be swamp birds?"

"Yes, I heard them."

"You sleep and I will keep watch," I said. "And then you can keep watch and I will sleep."

"Let's turn that around, Nate," Liza said. "You sleep first. Then me."

"You must have your rest. You are…" I could scarcely think the word let alone say it.

She shook her head and laughed lightly in her throat.

"It is as strange to me as it is to you, Nate."

I pushed my head against her breast.

"I never knew my mother beyond my seven or so years," I said. "But she was a good mother, she was. I have the hope that you will be, too."

"And yet I worry about this child," she said. "I have talked to the other women about it. We, you and I, being cousins…"

"I have heard stories," I said. "There is a danger. But not as great a danger as if we had not ever met."

She pressed me in her arms and touched her lips to the top of my head, holding me as though I myself were her as yet unborn child.

"You are sweet to say that, Nate."

"Your sweetness lingers on my lips as I say it."

And as I spoke a sudden convulsion of coldness and heat overtook me, and I said, with teeth chattering, "I love you, Liza. I want never for us to part."

"Hush, now," she said, "we'll save all that for when we're free."

"I was once a free man, but now I am your slave."

"Tish," she said, "tish, tish."

"Sometimes the brute truth sounds harsh and brittle. But this truth is soft and sweet and full of music."

"Yankee words," she said. "Trying to knock me off my guard."

"Words I say to the woman who will become my wife. Words I say to the woman who carries my child."

Liza bowed her head as if in prayer. I would have spoken but another wave of chills passed over me again, and I did not know if I was sick with fatigue or if the thought of marriage gave me fright—or wild hopefulness!

"You will marry me, will you not?" I said.

"Hush, now," she said, whispering a lullaby in my ear as I sank further into her arms, closing my eyes and attempting to keep myself awake with thoughts of the child within her womb. When next I opened my eyes Liza was asleep, slumped against the tree, her arms wrapped around herself in an even more gentle version of the posture in which she had held me. Charles slept, curled up at her feet.

The swamp too had settled into a delicious, yet ominous, stillness. Even the bright daylight, turned a shade of deep green by its reflection against so many green plants and trees, seemed to retract into itself, as though it were trying to become in broad daylight as close to dark of night as it could. But even as it grew darker, its odor became broader and stronger, so that even its fetid stink began to have a stench all of its own on top of its odiferous self.

I settled myself, listening intently for any signal or sign that we might have hunters on our trail.

Nothing.

And nothing.

And nothing.

Until I heard a faint clacking, as though some bird were peck-peck-pecking on a tall tree nearby.

(A-hah! I felt like such a fool when I realized it was the noise of my own teeth!)

All the rest of nature settled down as I quieted myself once more.

And caught my eye on a nub of dark plant floating in the pool of water mid-distant between our tree and the far clump of plants that made up an island, like a stepping stone, in the marsh. I studied this small mark upon the placid inlet, bore my eyes down on it.

With a flip of a lid that startled me back into the shivers, it opened an eye on me.

And then another.

It floated toward me, rising a little as it moved, so that soon I could see the knotted hair, the broad and spectral brow, the woman as brown as Liza, hair spiked like star-shine, her breasts ascendant as she rose out of the water.

Charles! I cried out, but my throat went dry and so I could say nothing. *Liza!*

As if I had called *her* name, whatever she or it might be, she floated, her breasts buoyant and rising, her glance falling directly on me.

What could I do but shield my eyes and cry out, *Run, Liza, run!*

Forgive me, but I was afraid and fascinated all at once, hypnotized and mystified by this apparition of the swamp—for surely she was a hallucination, and I was losing my mind. Did I wake or sleep?

Nate! I heard the woman calling to me. *Goodbye, Nate! I'm running!*

Chapter Eighty-one

Smoke in the Air

I awoke to white light turning into golden light streaming in through the windows, and hovering over me, with as it seemed to my senses, a slight odor of smoke adhering to her, a dark figure, herself all dressed in white, and she turned, and I saw her face.

"Precious Sally," I said.

"You back!" She raised her hands as if at a political rally or prayer meeting. "Thank the God Jehovah! He's back!"

But of course if she was standing there I was back at The Oaks. I strained to speak, and my voice sounded to my own ears like a noise filtered through a long hollow log. "How did I get here?" Every joint of me ached and my head felt as though it were on fire.

Precious Sally leaned over me, dabbing at my forehead with a damp cloth.

"You arrived on that horse," she said. "Somebody slung you over the horse like a dead animal. When I saw first you, you was out, like in a deep, deep sleep, I almost thought you was already dead."

Gathering what little strength I had, I sat up quickly, but immediately fell back onto the bed.

"Where is Liza?"

Again Precious shook her head, and leaned close to me, so that I could drink deeply of her by-now-familiar breath.

"Gone," she said. "You know she run off. You run off after her, didn't you? Hoping to catch her, right? That's what I told Mr. Jonathan. Isaac told him, too. Said he saw her take the horse and run, and then you come running, and you took off after her, you and that boy who just come up out of nowhere. The nights go by. And then you come back, tied onto the back of the horse. You're shivering and burning. Shouting and seeing things. Please, Mister Nathaniel, I know you got touched by the Visitor, but you got to get out of bed now and makes things all right! There's a lot of more trouble here at The Oaks. Master Jonathan took off after Liza, dragging Isaac with him. He had a gun, oh, gods, a big old gun. He supposed to be here to watch over the massa but now the men come from town and put him in his grave. I don't know, what kind of son that is, goes chasing off into the swamp for a missing girl when he supposed to be watching over his father! It's more than a day gone by. And the Visitor still here, it took our poor Jack while you was sleeping, and half a dozen men from the cabins, they gone. Now the missus is sick in her room. Miss Rebecca, she went to town with the burial men, hoping she wait out the Visitor there."

I listened and listened to her catalog of doom, while my heart leaped out into the terrible forever, sick with regret because Liza was on the run without me. It made me even more sick than I was to think of that, but then how if she had not left me behind could she run far enough and fast enough to escape the patrols?

"Precious Sally," I said, upright again and holding steadier than a moment before, "has my cousin read his father's will?"

"The what, suh?" she said.

The what, I said to myself, *the what, indeed!*

"I am going to try and evict myself from this bed," I said. "Precious Sally, can you meanwhile go down to the barns and see if Isaac has returned?"

"Yes, massa Nate," she said.

"Thank you," I said, and lay back, listening to her feet, the sound of her walking along the hall, then descending the stairs. How was it that I had found myself back here again after all our plans for running? Oh, yes, I arrived on the horse, tied there no doubt by young Charles from New Jersey. But where had he gone? Was he off and running again? Some moments passed—or was it minutes? Certainly not an hour went by while I lay there, my mind hoping all the best for the young boy and my soul hoping to rush along at the speed of a horse to catch Liza so that I might run with her even further. My legs, however, would not move.

I lay there in that bed, even more helpless than before, despising myself for collapsing under the weight of the illness—that Visitor, as the slaves called it—unable to help Liza. I must have dreamed, because I recall a fleeting image of Liza, and of that same female creature, brown-skinned, with bountiful breasts, whom I had seen rising out of the swamp.

A commotion arose outside my window, horses whinnied, and wheels spat up stones along the drive. A strong odor of smoke and burning drifted in the window and into, as I imagined, all the halls and rooms of the house.

"Precious Sally?"

I cried out, finding the strength in my belly if not in my lungs.

Shouts down below. Heavy footsteps in the hall. Suddenly as though from a blast of wind in a sudden storm, the door burst open and in came my cousin Jonathan in torn coat and filthy trousers, swept along by the odor of smoke and burning.

"Well, hello, Cousin. I hear you are not feeling so well. While you were ailing things have moved along. I have been led off on a wild goose chase and that bitch is on the run! And there is this!" he said, holding up a sheaf of smoldering paper.

"What are you doing?" I said to him in challenge.

"What am I doing?" He waved the paper in front of me, bringing it almost within my reach, and so I could smell the stink of the whiskey upon him even stronger than the odor of the fire. "I am making the future. I will not be bound by the past. My late father, now, turns out to have been a man quite haunted by the days gone by, the days when he was a thin gentleman with a thick lust for love among the cabins." He barked out a monstrous laugh. "Like father, like son, do we say? Except that the son did not know this important fact about the father! The son believed that he was the sole heir of this already God-forsaken enterprise! But the father, the father was skulking about the cabins, making other heirs!"

Again, he waved the paper in front of me, as though he were an attorney arguing a case of law and I was the jury.

I felt all of a sudden absolutely ice-cold lucid and hauled myself upright on the bed.

"And you? You hypocrite! You dare to judge him?"

Jonathan laughed a wild and reckless *caw-caw-caw*ing of a laugh.

"Who will judge him if not me? Cousin, are you Jews in New York mere pale imitations of the Gentiles? Do you sit around and say to yourselves, 'Well, sirs, man cannot judge. Only God can judge?' Here, in this deep place of rice and water, of ocean and woods, oh, yes, here, we make our own judgments about ourselves and others. At least do we Jews!"

I swung my feet around and steadied them on the floor next to the bed.

"At least do you who call yourselves Jews," I said, amazed that I could find my balance. "Slaveholders that you are, you are much more like Pharaohs!"

"Ah, and you, pure heart, have not dabbled with a slave? Not you, no. Who is the hypocrite here? Who wanted to make a purchase of a certain young female!"

"Do not speak of her as though she were an animal, Cousin."

"You used her as such, did you not?"

I took a step toward him, intending to slap his face, but my knees buckled and I fell back toward the bed.

"You have used her in much worse fashion."

Ignoring my accusation, he countered with another. "She is a murderer, you know. I have seen the evidence."

"It was my pistol," I said.

"Are you saying that you shot Langerhans? I never would have thought you had it in you, Cousin."

"You have done so much worse," I said.

"Have I?"

"Bastard!" I reached for him and my breath came up short and the room began to spin.

I tried to regain my balance even as my cousin went about the business of completing the burning of the will.

"I will not let you get away with this," I said, "I know what that paper contains."

"Oh, and will you take me to court? On whose behalf?"

"On Isaac's," I said. "On the part of your half-brother."

He opened his hand and the remaining shreds of charred paper drifted to the floor.

"Half no more," he said.

"What do you say?"

"A sad and unfortunate accident," he said.

Now I pushed myself from the bed again and stumbled toward him, fists raised.

Deftly, he stepped aside and I went stumbling to the door, where I held myself in tenuous balance.

"What do you say?" I repeated hoarsely, turning myself around.

"Do you want to know the truth, Cousin?"

"Tell me what you did," I said.

"What I did?"

"Tell me what happened."

I could scarcely catch a breath, but I hovered there at the doorway, waiting for him to speak while the stink of smoke drifted in through the windows and, in fainter fashion, crept up the stairwell and sneaked into the hall, that insidious odor of the worst things to come.

Chapter Eighty-two

Fire

*J*onathan had known something had gone wrong that night almost immediately after he saw his son Abraham come trundling down the stairs.

"Papa, they are running," the boy said. "I saw them."

The boy's words startled him.

"They are upstairs," he said.

"I saw them go down the back stairs, sir," the boy said, a wide smile on his face, this lad who sought approbation from his otherwise-distant father.

"They are in distress," Jonathan said. "We are all in distress. Come, Abe, let us visit your grandfather together and make our farewells." At which he led the boy back up to the second floor and the room of his recently deceased father.

Which, except for the corpse, they found empty.

"I told you," Abe said, "They are running."

"So be it," Jonathan said. "The patrollers are riding tonight, as always. They will not get very far." He kneeled a while at his father's bedside, and his son followed his lead, dropping to his knees and folding his hands, but, like his father, at a discreet distance from the body and the sheets.

One can only make a wild surmise about what went through the boy's mind. His childhood lessons from the Bible taught to him by his grandfather spoke of freedom and yet he was surrounded all his young life by slaves. He read little, played games with stones and small knives, loved his horses, and in town he spent time with distant cousins who disdained the slave-holding of his family even as they invited them here and there, dinner to tea to musical nights at the synagogue. Abe—he knew nothing, he was a noisome child and a little citizen to be admired. Given the chance he would have ridden with the patrollers, enjoying the glamor of it all, chasing, catching slaves.

Jonathan had quite a lot on his own mind, almost all of it pertaining to the inheritance. The land, now his, the house, now his, the income, now his, all the slaves now his, and all the slaves that would be born in his lifetime, all all his. And the debt was now his. He had never considered himself a greedy man, and he had worked hard for this plantation and the inheritance of it, keeping watch over the overseers, keeping watch over the expenses of the business. He and his family, as he saw it, never pushed any of it toward the line where necessity passed over into excess. They had the slaves build furniture and the necessary appurtenances of persons and household, they bought what farm equipment they could not make themselves, and the food for all and the food for the slaves, and the doctor's attendance upon them, and whatever small things they required that they could not manufacture themselves. Sorry as he was to see his father go, he worried no worry out of the ordinary, at least for the few hours left in the night that passed when he had not yet read the will. That was how sure of himself and his inheritance he was. And that was how free he was of greed, that he would not feel compelled to make certain that these lands and this house all had with his father's passing come to him. The only compulsion he felt was to keep after me and press me to draw my father into the business of the plantation.

At dawn he sent Isaac with word of his father's demise to the congregants in town. He then retired to his bed, besotted, immediately drowsy with the understanding of what had happened. Birds, awake since before the first light, sang outside the window, keeping him awake for a while longer, during which moments he made a fantasy of what he would say to Liza on her return, and what he would say to me—she, the ungrateful daughter, and me, the cousin and betrayer, traitor to the family and our race. But of course he would then soften a bit toward me, needing me as he did to help shore up the accounts. Toward Liza he would be unrelenting, though he wondered what he might do if I pleaded her case. Eventually all this meandering of mind was too much for him and he sank beneath the waves of sleep.

But did he dream? Revealing certain fine aspects of his sensibility I had never known before, he explained that he had some fluttering visions in that early morning doze, and he claims he heard songs in a musical scale that he did not recognize, and he felt a certain presence, like that he had known only once before, as a boy in the Dutch Antilles when he was nearly drowned in the surf. The presence felt feminine, he said, and it came as a kind of pushing with physical muscle, a kind of urging, without a voice or even a gesture to move him along. Coming out of the dream he saw himself as the descendant of Moses, the Liberator of his People, and if he understood such a contradiction between himself and the figure out of the Old Testament, who led the Jews out of bondage and thus into a world of freedom unlimited and the beauty of living without masters, he gave no sign. The irony of better seeing himself as a Jewish Pharaoh never came to mind.

Immediately upon awakening he called for Isaac, now back from town, whom he told to notify all the slaves that the master had gone. (How little he knew of his own small dominion that he did not surmise that almost from the exhalation of his father's last breath every last slave on the plantation learned of his going.)

Stepping into the morning sun, followed by his faithful Isaac, he looked up at the cottony brilliant sky and announced "I am now the Master," and then gazed off into the trees near the border where the distant creek took in the tidal flow.

"Yessir," Isaac said, without any untoward glance or questionable fluctuation of his voice except that which normally occurred in moments such as this.

"Fetch the horses," Jonathan said.

"Yes, sir," said Isaac.

Jonathan watched as the slave turned and ran toward the barn. Just then a shiver passed through Jonathan's body, a cold so fierce and of the instant that he looked over to the trees with the thought that some minor whirlwind might have crossed the borders of the plantation as if, or so he wondered in that instant, it had come to carry away the soul of his immediately deceased father. Was it the Visitor clasping an arm around his shoulders in a confederacy of chills and illness? He brushed that worry aside, certain in his own well-being and assurance, though another thought came to him, which Isaac's presence in his sight may have engendered. He was not quite sure.

He had felt at such loose ends before, in his rage and rapist rampage in the pantry, he had felt his blood turn so hot it nearly boiled his brain. But never ever had he heard a voice in his mind say to him such as, Go back to the house and read the Will.

As if led by an invisible hand he turned and walked back in the door and went through the kitchen and up the stairs to his father's study where there he searched—it took only a minute or two—for the Will, which rested in the same place on the desk where Liza had first seen it. (He could not have known, of course, that Liza had been here before him. But almost as if he could read thoughts on the ether something caused him to go to the window, papers in hand, and look out toward the barns where Isaac was preparing the horses.) "Hurry, you nigger," he said out loud, as if his voice could carry through the wall.

Glancing down at the papers, he read along, making quiet noises in his throat, noises of assent, until his eye stopped on a name.

"You, nigger!"

He dropped the Will on the desk and without looking back retraced his route down and through the house, out the back way and walking steadily toward the barn.

He saw Isaac leading the horses to him and barked out a command.

"Fetch my gun!"

"Yes, sir," Isaac said, tying the horses to the back rail of the porch and going into the house.

In a moment he returned with Jonathan's long gun.

"Going to catch us a runaway nigger," Jonathan said as he took the weapon from Isaac. With a bit of clumsiness he held the weapon in one hand and used the other to mount the horse.

"Liza?" Isaac said.

"That is the nigger," Jonathan said. "That is the one."

They rode at a fast pace to the edge of the swamp and then slowed down. He knew full well that Liza had at least a half-day's start on him. When in the distance he saw the young Jersey boy leading a horse upon whose back I lay draped, his heart sank. He wanted no impediment to his quest.

"Take him back to The Oaks," he told the boy when they stopped and met on the faint trail into the swamp.

"Yessir," said the boy.

"Now tell me which way she went," Jonathan said.

Unprompted by the barely conscious passenger on the horse—the fever-crazed creature that I had become—the boy jagged a finger to the north.

"Up there," he said.

"North?" Through his nose Jonathan made a snorting noise like a horse.

And then almost with a kind of familial pride, he said, "I never took her for being that stupid. She is an educated girl. She knows her geography. The damned doctor taught her that." And then, almost as an afterthought prompted by paternal pride, he added, "She has read many more books than most white folks." He looked over at the boy and without a word flicked out his hand and slapped him across the mouth.

"Do not lie to me, boy," Jonathan said.

"Yessir," the boy said. Scarcely visible against the darkness of his skin, a thin line of dark red blood ran from his nose to his upper lip.

"Take my cousin back to The Oaks. Don't you be running or I'll set the patrollers on you quick as anything. Don't know why they did not catch you all in the first place, running the way you were, noisy as hell, I would guess." He said no more to the boy.

Without looking back, he goaded his mount and followed by Isaac continued along the road into the watery turf where muscly-vined trees raised their bushy heads to blot out the direct light of morning. They had not ridden more than another half mile when they saw a cluster of birds, turkey vultures jigging around and upon the bodies on the road.

"Isaac!" Jonathan shouted. "What is that?"

The slave—Jonathan's half-brother, let us say it!—rode forward and stepped just short of the bodies. The birds cocked their heads at him and returned to their work—it was steady and vigorous work—on the bodies.

"Massa Jonathan?" Isaac called out.

"Yes?"

"Shoot the gun!"

"What do you say?"

"Shoot the gun in the air!"

Jonathan obliged, bringing off a loud report and watching, along with Isaac, as the carrion birds scattered into the air with a sound like wet canvas flapping in the wind.

Isaac then dismounted and kneeled beside the bodies.

"Langerhans!" he called out to Jonathan. "It is Langerhans!"

"And the other two?"

"Patrollers, like him. I don't know their names…"

Jonathan watched him as he leaned closer, pulling apart the trio of tangled bodies. After a moment or two he stood up, holding one of the patrollers' pistols in his hand.

Jonathan urged his horse a step or two closer.

"What happened here?" he said.

Isaac shook his head.

"I don't know how she do it! Killed one or two, the other killed the other. Guess it happened in the dark, only this lamp here—" he kicked at the lamp lying nearby—"to see by."

"How do you know Liza shot them?"

"Massa Nate, he wouldn't shoot."

"Why do you say that?"

"He's a good man."

"He would not do it to help Liza run?"

Isaac stared up at him, noticing that Jonathan had raised his gun.

"Naw, I don't think so. Look, Massa Jonathan, he came back. Liza, she kept on going. Maybe she even kept her gun on him to keep him with her."

Isaac was staring at the gun.

"You think she did that?"

"Could be. I dunno."

The large birds flapped their wings, making a sound unlike anything Jonathan had ever heard before, a cross between a beating heart and wet laundry set out to dry in a strong wind.

Isaac saw that he was staring at them.

"Don't be worried about those birds," he said. "They won't come down when we're standing here."

"Good, good," Jonathan said.

"Now this little thing," Isaac said, holding up the patrollers' pistol, "it couldn't keep—"

Jonathan aimed his weapon at Isaac and pulled the trigger. His horse gave a little dance as the blast knocked Isaac off his feet. The vultures started into the air and then settled back in the tree.

"You killed those patrollers," Jonathan said, leaning over his horse. "Not Liza. She's just a runaway."

Isaac, lying on his back on top of the body of Langerhans, blinked and blinked, making small noises all the while blood bubbled up from his chest.

"Did you know that you are my brother?"

Isaac said something, but Jonathan could not make it out.

Jonathan shot him again.

In that instant his soul surged with rage upon his already murderous rage as out of the corner of his eye he saw the young black boy from New Jersey, apparently having tied me to the horse and slapped the animal into making his lazy way back to The Oaks on his own, tearing out across the fields in the direction of the swamp.

Chapter Eighty-three

A Conflagration

*J*onathan's return to The Oaks was not a happy one, he explained to me. A number of slaves had seen him ride out with Isaac, but saw no Isaac with him on his return.

He has stayed behind with the bodies, he rehearsed to himself. But he did not have to explain. There was no one to explain anything to but himself.

Or perhaps to yours truly.

Which is what he began to do when he came through the door, the smoking remains of his father's will in his hand, and the currents of smoke floating up the stairs behind him.

When he had finished he said, "Now I must go, and I suggest you do the same."

I coughed on the wafting of the rising smoke and stood up tall again, still feeling rather faint.

"Goodbye, Cousin," Jonathan said. "I am going to put this place in order and expect that I will write to you for your reply."

"Y-yes," I said, "yes," trying to understand him correctly and make a plan even as I stumbled weakly to the door.

My last glimpse of cousin Jonathan came as I reached the ground floor and saw him through the rear windows running, weapon in hand, toward the burning barn.

Precious Sally came up behind me and touched my arm.

"A horse out front for you, Massa Nate," she said.

I thanked her and went to the door.

A great commotion came from the burning barn and from the cabins beyond. Someone fired shots. Someone beat on a deep-throated drum (and where had that instrument come from, I wondered in my still-lingering delirium).

She raised a hand. "Better go now, Massa Nate."

I slipped out the door, where a young slave child, apparently under Precious Sally's orders, had brought me my old Promise and stood there holding the reins, as still as a statue amidst the rising commotion of sound from the barns. Quickly, I mounted the beast and the boy released the reins. He gave the horse a slap on the rump and I—the least experienced of horsemen—kicked my mount to turn him toward the drive that led to the road to town just as from around the corner of the big house charged a cadre of slave men waving pitchforks and scaling knives. As more slaves came running from the barns, some of these men carrying torches that burned deceptively diminished in the bright light of the morning sun, my horse, apparently frightened and distracted, broke into a gallop, carrying me directly toward the burning barns. Only a flaming length of lumber that just then peeled away from the arch above the door and fell in our path turned the animal away from its apparent goal of taking refuge in the burning building itself. It danced to the left, and then arched a step to the right. I felt the beast nearly trip and falter, as it stumbled over a sack at the side of the barn—which turned out to be the body of my cousin, blood running from slashes along his neck and face.

"Jonathan!" I called down to him.

My cousin, wretch that he was, lay there as silent and still as a stone, a blood-drenched life-sized sack of flesh.

Shots rang out behind me and I turned to see the small boy who had held my horse now standing on the back veranda, a gun—I was too far away to recognize it as Jonathan's—in hand. He fired again, into the air just as from the upper floors of the house above him a great volt of flame leaped out through the windows of what had served as my room.

Promise came suddenly to life and surged around the flaming building, carrying me into the woods, in the opposite direction from what I took to be a route for my escape.

"Halt!" I cried out. "Whoa!"

He kept on galloping, and I nearly fell as we entered the first curtain of trees sheltering the land along the creek.

More gunshots echoed behind me, and the smell of smoke lay thick about the branches past which we rushed. But when we entered the clearing at the brick house landing all seemed calm and quiet. Men worked at the ropes that kept the brick barge in place at the water's edge. One of them turned and saw me, and then another and another.

Promise came to a halt and I slid off his back, hitting the ground hard and lying there, almost as still as my late cousin back near the barn. My eyes remained open, and I watched the men, in their tatters and long hair, gathering around me, murmuring to each other. I was fully expecting to join my cousin in the darkness to which he had just repaired.

One of the men kneeled down and held me by the ankles. Another took me by the arms. Together they lifted me up and carried me slowly to the water. Unaccountably, they were in low voices singing a song I had only recently heard.

> Massa sleeps in de feather,
> Nigger sleeps on de floor…

"Please," I said in a whisper, having no quarrel with pleading for my life.

> When we'uns gits to Heaven,
> Dey'll be no slaves no mo'…

"No more," I said. "No more, no more, no more, no more…"

They raised my feverish raving corpus higher, almost to the level of their heaving chests, and just as I thought they were about to hurl me into the creek and leave me to drown they lowered me over the rail of the boat and carried me onto the deck, setting me down gently among the sacks of rice from the recent harvest.

A breeze came up, and the boat carried me to town where some of the kindlier Jews, those with professions, not human property, cared for me until I felt strong enough to depart for New York. This took about a week, and by then Rebecca, I heard, had already put away her mourning clothes and faded into the bosom of her family, preparing to give birth soon to her child. I heard this from her cousin Anna, who knew I was in town.

One morning, just before I set sail for home, she appeared on the veranda of the town house where I was staying, raven-haired, pale-cheeked, her long neck bared to the sun.

"Is there any chance you might stay longer in town?" she inquired over the tea my hostess had immediately set before us.

"I cannot," I said. "I must return to my father and make a report to him."

"Will you ever return to Charleston?"

Anna fluttered her long dark eyelashes and tilted her head toward me in an interrogatory fashion.

Slaves—men and women—had died, died every day, barns and houses went up in flames, and even as we were speaking fugitives hurried through the wilderness, hoping to find freedom on the other side of dark forests, tall mountains, flooding rivers. And attractive young girls hoped to make their dreams of romance and family come true, despite all of everything else. I had one waiting for me in New York. This much I had learned about life.

Chapter Eighty-four

The Last Rising Sun

A dreary Manhattan morning, the harbor filled with noise and rain. At the house Jacobus greeted me with a shaking of feathers, a phrase, and a squawk. My reunion with my father was not as pleasant. He wondered at my depleted physical state, at which time I unleashed on him all of my fury at the misery and murder the Southern branch of our family had brought into the world. He listened all too calmly—a trait, in the midst of my surprising (to me) rage, he pointed out was quite useful in business—and then explained that he had little idea that his brother and nephew oversaw such suffering.

"Little idea? Father, sir, they were keeping slaves. Did you expect the slaves to be cheerful about their servitude?"

"Nathaniel," he said, looking me in the eye, "I had no idea—"

"Or little?" I broke in.

"Or little," he said, "that the conditions would be such as you witnessed. I had to have you confirm this for me."

"And so I have confirmed it?" I said.

"Yes, you have," he said.

"Father, you sent me down there knowing what it was I would find?"

"I was not fully certain."

"But in the main you were."

"I was."

"Sir," I said, "do you know what you have done to my life?"

It was all I could do not to assault him, so angry I was at his apparent naïveté—and my own. It was all I could do not to burst out with the name of the woman who had changed my life. But to speak about Liza would have been to have demeaned her. I kept her private to my thoughts, even as my Father took some care to ensure my full recovery, ordering Marzy to be attentive to all of my needs, which of course our dear old retainer did always without needing any orders. She fed me well, she kept the rooms clean, with as much fine sunlight pouring in as the weather would allow, and because in an odd way it appeared as though she understood the nature of my continual sorrowful demeanor she kept a polite distance all the time she worked around me, which seemed to me to be some kind of tacit recognition that I was no longer the child she had helped to raise but instead the man I was supposed to have become.

I could not keep my concentration on any prose I might try, the picture of Liza coming between me and anything I attempted to give myself over to—Liza, Liza, Liza—during the day, and at night I raved about her to myself before I fell asleep, and for weeks after my return to the city I dreamed of her as well.

Yet I could not speak of her with anyone.

When my old teacher Halevi happened to pay me a visit—urged on, I am quite sure, by my father, to make some assessment of my mental state—I did raise the questions that had haunted me ever since my southern journey, the matter of human bondage and the practice of it by my own family. He wanted only to speak in abstractions, bringing up the question of Evil as if my cousin Jonathan found himself caught in the thrall of some higher power rather than giving in to particular temptations of body and mind. He must have reported to my father that I seemed gloomy and caught myself in some higher stages of desolation, because a day did not go by before my progenitor informed me that if I felt well enough to travel I could leave immediately on my tour.

So it happened that less than a month after my return to New York I sailed to Liverpool to begin my long-sought-after travels, which turned out to be so much less interesting than I had ever imagined, an endless series of castles, museums, coffee houses, taverns, and cathedrals, and here and there a synagogue or two. During this time away I suffered from bouts of loneliness and some regret (the latter arising whenever my thoughts turned to Liza, which they did more frequently than I would have desired, because they were so painful). I had plenty of company in a group of fellow New Yorkers who roamed the continent, but in my self-pitying state I often wanted only to be alone with my misery.

I returned from the Continent the next year to work with my father in the family business, marry my Miriam, and produce several children.

(Jacobus, poor Carib bird, died around the time of the birth of my first son.) I can only exult in that during those years I worked hard to make a good life for all and at my father's funeral, which came midway between that time and now, I felt a deep sadness at his demise but also a certain pride in that I had continued his good work at the business. With Halevi at my side I prayed for the strength to continue on in life. (Alas, poor Halevi himself had only about a year to live, having suffered a debilitating weakness in his chest from which he never recovered.)

I despise myself for revealing what follows, but then what is a manuscript about one's self without honest revelation about one's life and thoughts. While the children grew, and my father sank into a state of ill health from which he did not recover and I took more and more of a hand in the business, my mind went often to the picture of Liza, our final nights together. I sometimes imagined her somewhere in Ohio or even, God help me, in New York State, where she was living a quiet life, free at last from all servitude of any kind. But then I wondered, if she had found her freedom and must be living relatively close by, why it was she never tried to contact me. Had she given birth to our child or had it died? Why if the child had lived would she keep me from my offspring? Thus I sent myself into the kind of sulk that is all the worse because one cannot ever speak of it while life goes on around one. Had she died in that swamp? Had she been captured and reenslaved? All of such thoughts of mine became exacerbated when news of the formation of the Confederacy reached us in New York. They became further inflamed when the South fired the first shots of the war only a few miles from the shore of that self-same city of Charleston.

Miriam, no fool herself, could read it in my face the evening I came home after having joined our local Ellsworth's Zouaves.

"What has happened, Nathaniel?" she asked me.

"We are at war with the Confederacy," I said.

She stared at me, as only a woman who has borne your children can.

"And I have enlisted in a military outfit."

She was unbelieving.

"Have you no sense, sir? You are a husband and father, you are the head of the family business."

I took her by the hand—she was quite unresponsive, allowing herself to be led to the sofa in our drawing room where I sat her down, still holding her hand, and sat next to her.

"Miriam, I see this as my duty. I have volunteered to go into battle with them."

This, for a moment, remained beyond her understanding. Certainly I understood her consternation. Without knowing how all these many years I kept Liza in my mind how could she understand the decision I had made?

Suddenly she ripped her hand from mine.

"You will go to war?"

"It is my duty," I said.

The look in her eyes was both frightening and magnificent, the way some lion tamer must look while cracking a whip over his cats.

"Your duty is to—"

"I cannot," I said.

Now her speech gained in volume and intensity all at once.

"This is because your uncle and cousin behaved so horribly over a decade ago? This makes no sense to me. I know that slavery is wrong, Nathaniel, but your duty is to me and your children and the family business."

I sat there, stone-like, because I had to and because I could. I spoke of duty, but without revealing the torments of loving and losing Liza I could not make my complete case for going to war. Hundreds of men my age in New York and New England were volunteering, I was sure, for the fight against the Confederacy, men with deep philosophical and religious persuasions. How many of them had known Lizas? Few of them, I was sure. And if they did, they would volunteer all the more, twice, or five times, or fifty times, more, until they had given everything for the sake of a slave they had loved—still loved!—in this horrendous struggle between bondage and freedom.

I sat very still while Miriam unleashed a tirade against me, and I sat very still long after she had left the room.

And so I went off to war, carrying with me this manuscript, mostly complete, which I have worked to finish while on training maneuvers on the Mall at the capitol. And now, in Virginia, on this frankly terrifying evening before our first battle I have kept on with it as a means for trying to hold myself steady. Tonight I have added to and subtracted from here and there, hoping against hope that I have given the best account I could make of our life in all its flaws and pleasures. How fitting it seems to me that I should have recalled the final scene of chaos and turmoil and death at The Oaks against the dark backdrop of this encampment, with men singing quietly as once those plantation slaves had done, singing until when in the middle of the night many of us, my own tent-mates included, figured that we had better try for sleep rather than dare to meet the dawn without it.

That dawn, I feared, would be for some of us the last rising sun we would see. But no sleep came to me, and I lay as if already dead, until I picked up this pen one last time for the evening—or near morning as it is now—and as it happened to me so often over the many long years now gone since I last saw Liza I pictured her face, her eyes, her lips, tried to recall the press of her body against mine, and wondered wondered wondered where she might be if she were alive at all—but always hoping, as I hoped now that this battle morning had nearly dawned upon us, that she lived free.

And then, in the deep darkness of the night past midnight, a sign!

As I was standing outside my tent, thinking what I hoped were not last thoughts about family, about all of you my beloveds who may be reading this, someone called out to me.

"Mister Nathaniel!"

I turned to see a lanky young black man in plain blue shirt and trousers, holding up a large water bucket in his hand.

"What is this?" I said.

"I know you don't recognize me," he said.

I studied his black face, somewhat indistinct in the darkness, and even as I felt the press of the coming battle I took another moment, and that helped.

Yes!

"You!" I said. (I could not at that moment recall his name.)

"Yes, sir," he said, smiling in the lightening dark, his bucket at his side.

"You escaped," I said.

"I got away," he said.

I shook my head and took a breath.

"You saved my life," I told him.

"You helped me save mine," he said. "But other folks died that day, that's sure," he said, confirming for me what took place between Jonathan and Isaac.

"It was tragic," I said.

"Was Biblical, almost, my mother said when I got home to tell her," he said.

"Do you still live in New Jersey?"

"Well, I did, until I came down here. I've got a job up there, nothing much except it brings in food for my wife and little boy, and helps me help my mother who is still living there too. But with this war, I've been trying to enlist. They just keep handing me things like this water bucket and tell me the time is coming soon for me to join."

"The time is coming soon," I told him.

"Meanwhile, would you like a drink, sir?" he said, proffering his bucket.

"Yes, in a moment, thank you…"

I ducked back into my tent and returned with my cup so that he might pour me some water.

I drank deeply, and it tasted to me sweeter than wine, nearly ambrosial, and somehow cooler than ice.

"Will you drink?" I said.

"Oh, I drunk plenty," he said, "I drunk plenty."

The young free man and I shook hands, and he took his bucket off into the dark, leaving me to meditate on my fate.

Should I not survive the war and my dear wife Miriam reads this manuscript I hope she will forgive me. However I do fully expect to see many other sunrises, in war and in peace. As someone who knows that he stands on the right side of this struggle between freedom and slavery, I can only hope that the one God, the God of Abraham and Isaac, will protect me in battle and bless me in the aftermath of whatever terrible acts I may have to perform.

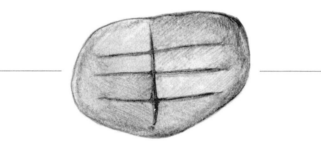

Chapter Eighty-five

Hurry, Run!

*A*nd when the sun set on that terrifying day in the swamp Liza had to make her decision about whether to remain with my ailing father or light out. So she closed her eyes and called on the goddess for guidance. When she opened them she saw glowing through the stunted pines a half-moon, with a bright star just above it, all to the west.

"Is it you, Yemaya?" she said in a whisper. "Star! Half-moon! Yemaya? Have you taken to the sky and turned it into a sea?"

At first, nothing but stillness reigned in the wake of her call. Gradually, sounds began to emerge in the darkening swamp, the last buzzings of insects, the whirr of bird wings, growls and whimperings of some animals unknown. She feared that she might hear dogs, but nothing in the rising noises of the oncoming night resembled the particular barking and howls of canines in pursuit.

She took a deep breath, sighed, glanced down at my father, who lay shivering on the sodden ground. As she raised her eyes again to the bluish-purple sky, a voice spoke to her, as if descending from the configuration of half-moon and star.

"Run!"

Or, "Come!"

Or, "Go!"

(As she recollected it, the voice remained slightly unclear, but the order remained direct. *Run, come to me, go, go!*)

"*Is* it you?" she asked. "Oh, my goddess, Yemaya! Are you still here? All these years, days, hours, I thought you had gone home to Africa!"

No voice came in response, but she knew what she had heard just before the vast silence settled over things again. She hesitated another moment, taking a deep breath, and sighing deeply. Though she had planned from the start to use my father for whatever she needed in order to make her escape, in the end she felt some affection for him, if not anywhere near the love he felt for her, the man who helped free her, a certain amount of deep and real affection. In fact, she had surprised herself with the emotion in her voice when she spoke to him about their ties even as she knew she was still using him to make her escape. The emotion rippled down her body, chest to her feet, turning them to lead and making it difficult for to take a step in any direction.

Oh, this life, she lamented to herself, where one cannot truly love without being truly free! Or be truly free without love!

Such thoughts weighed on her so heavily that she could not move.

And then she heard the dogs. Dogs! Hounds! The hounds of hell!

(Free people sometimes suffer the pangs of conscience. Slaves suffer from pursuit by vicious dogs!)

One moment the goddess leaned on the sliver of a moon and in the next stood by her side tugging at her sleeve.

"Come," she said. "Go!"

Liza hesitated only a moment more before leaving my father, supine and feverish, in the care of the young runaway boy from New Jersey and without looking back walked deeper into the swamp in what she gauged to be a westerly direction. Only after the moon disappeared altogether and the stars appeared determined to light her way did she stop to rest, but only for a short while. The swamp made for odd echoes and reverberations. Now she heard only the faintest howling of dogs, distant howling, but apparent, as if those dogs might have inhabited some of the stars directly above or to the east.

She walked and walked, her pace tempered by the need, especially in the now nearly final dark under the gnarled and obdurate branches, to keep to the narrow path that stretched into obscurity between the fetid water of the swamp and the boles of the bushes and trees. One misstep and she might slip into the water. She erred toward the trees and now and then took scratches and at least one bump on her left ear, leaning to the wood as she did.

At sunrise—misty first light steeped in residue from seeping trees—she sat down at the base of a tree and tried to sleep. Except that she could not keep her heart still, her fear of what might lie ahead driving that sweet organ to beating near-past its capacity. Winged insects as large as her hand buzzed past her. Every tiny crawling thing also conspired to keep her awake. Nevertheless, she dozed, head bobbing like a heavy flower on a drooping stem. And, with the sun as high as it would get that first day on the run alone through the swamp, she descended into deepest sleep and dreamed, yes, of what life must have been like before she was born, putting together a vision—if that was how dreams get made—out of bits and pieces of stories from the cabins and lessons from the doctor. In the dream a large white cloud settled over green forest, as though the earth itself had exhaled it and then the cloud began to sink of its own weight. *Mama,* she heard herself say, *I have come for the stone. An arm sand-colored and slender reached out toward her.*

Grrrrrrrrrrrrrrrrrrrrrrrrrrrrrrrrrrrrrrrrrrrrrrrrrrrrrrrrrrrrrrrrrrrrr—grrrrrrrrrrrrrrrrrrrrrrrrrrrrrrr rrrrrrrrrrrrrrrrrrrrrrrrrrrrrrrrrrrrrrrrrrrrrrrrrrrrrrrrrrr. Rough, rough, rough, rough!

She suddenly awoke to find herself face to face with a growling, barking alligator, wide-jawed, its pinkish-black tongue dangling between its jaws with the stiffness yet elasticity that the man's organ sometimes approximates. Its two sharp snap-drawn eyes showed her something so deadly it could almost be a smile. And here sat Yemaya on the back of the beast. Could it be true? Or had she crossed over the line into madness? What did she see in front of her? Did this goddess still exist?

As sometimes happens to us in situations of extreme distress, she found herself smiling, her back pressed against the tree, her face taut in a rictus of astonishment and fear, her bottom parts soaked from the involuntary release of lemony piss.

"Hush," said Yemaya close in her ear. "This beast, he is a distant cousin of mine, and so a distant member of your family too. Stay still." Liza complied, becoming so still that a twitching muscle in her leg felt like a clutch of leaves rippling in a wind storm.

Rough, rough! The animal roared.

She could smell its throat-stench, the stink of its scaly head. She stayed still. Still it seemed to smile. Even beyond the monstrousness of its actual being, the monster reminded her of someone! Whom could that be?

Rough!

And oh, ye, all my gods, when it came to her, she began to tremble and quake, the opposite of what the goddess had just advised, and, worse still, she reached out both hands to the open-jawed monster.

"Father!" she said. "Take me, devour me, I am nothing, I am food for the swamp, lowest of the low, a slave to everyone and everything. You have eaten me and I have eaten you, and now we are nothing, and so can begin again." [Where these words came from, she couldn't say—from her life, from her reading, from her praying, from her thinking, from the entire mix of acts and words, the million million turns and tosses of the body and mind in time?]

As if it had been waiting for her to say just this, the beast clamped shut its jaws, and Yemaya tugged it by the tail. It went sliding straightaways backwards into the viscous pond among ponds, leaving Liza to twitch and tremble for many minutes after, until the tremors of this marvelous encounter had worked themselves through and out from her body.

I will be free, she said to herself, *I will be free. I faced a beast in the swamp and I have been ravaged by the monsters of slavery and still I am here.*

She stood up and stared into the wavery haze that covered the swamp water almost to the level of her breasts.

You! She addressed every god and goddess and no one, she addressed every slave and citizen, pointing an accusatory finger at the haze, at the world beyond, above, below it, and within. *You, hear me! I...will...be...free!*

Chapter Eighty-six

Her Plan

*T*hree days later she emerged, soaked, hungry, exhausted, her legs bedecked with leeches, on the western side of the swamp where she collapsed, as it turned out, about fifty yards from an encampment of a band of renegade slaves who had made a small community in the forest.

A squint-eyed girl a year or so younger than herself and more dark than pale found her in the weeds, took charge of her, and a few days later asked her about her plan.

"Plan, honey?"

Liza shook her head.

"I plan to follow a moon and a star all the way to the end of the west."

The girl—turned out she was half Cherokee, half African—nodded.

"Half the people here came with that plan."

"Half stayed, half went?"

"That's right," the girl said.

"I'm the half that goes," Liza said.

"Do you know what's over that mountain?" the girl asked her, inclining her head toward a nearby ridge.

"Freedom," Liza said.

The girl shook her head.

"Another mountain," she said.

"And after that?"

"Another mountain."

"And after that?" And Liza answered with her, saying "Another mountain" just as the girl intoned it.

In the shade of that first mountain, darkness came early, seeping down from the side of the ridge like fog or slow heavy water held up somehow against gravity. It rained that night, and the cold entered Liza's bones. If she didn't know herself better, she would have thought she was aching from the same illness that kept my father from traveling with her. How did that half-Indian woman know how much Liza was shivering on her pallet? It remains a mystery, but before too long she had crawled under the thin blanket made of corn sacks and took Liza in her arms and held her.

"What are you doing?" Liza said.

"Keeping you warm," the woman said.

"I don't even know you," Liza said.

"I am Old Dou," the woman said, "I am the old Herb Woman. I am——"

"Mother!" Liza said, shivering and then calming herself in the woman's arms.

They touched lips. They touched noses. Power passed between them through their mouths, nostrils—and eyes.

When she awoke it was as if nothing had happened, except that she was sure she had not dreamed this, though she had. Or had not. Or had.

Moons rose and set, moons waxed and waned. Winter in the west of Carolina grew colder than winter in the east. Sporadically, snow fell.

Liza's belly grew. Heat from thinking about it kept her mind warm through the cold months. But unless, she told herself, she could keep moving she would never feel completely free.

"Still want to go west?" the Cherokee girl asked her.

"Yes," Liza said.

"Why?"

"We're not free here, we're only lucky."

Her luck held. The next stage of her westward journey began after the winter snow-melt. The half-Indian woman traveled with her. As it turned out, Liza had infected her with the longing for true freedom, not just the freedom to hide in the woods from occasional patrollers and slave-trackers. This pair climbed up over the mountains (the first range of old old American mountains, worn by many millions of years of weather from above and sinking from below). Wild turkeys strutted alongside them as they walked through glens of azaleas and listened to hawks whistling overhead. After the foothills came the flatlands, and then an ascent up limestone pathways to the top of a wildly green plateau, and then down again. It took more than a month of traveling through slave territory to reach the broad banks of the great middle river that divided the continent in half, in the last part of which, helped by friends of runaways, they rolled along hidden beneath carpets in the back of a rickety wagon. (Oh, my mother, carrying me as a seed while, like some heroic figure in a tale out of the *Thousand and One Nights*, hidden beneath those magic carpets!)

Her luck wavered again late on her last afternoon east of the Mississippi. Under the deep cover of several layers of carpets she could not smell the river. But when the wagon halted abruptly, she could hear the voices of men in disagreement, though she could not make out all the words.

"What is it?" her half-Cherokee friend said in a whisper.

"I don't know," said Liza.

And then she knew, as someone pulled the top layer of blanket away, and then the next, and she and her companion stared blinking up at a pale blue sky.

"Lookee here," said the man who pulled the cover aside.

"Two snug bugs," a companion said.

The women remained silent, not knowing who the men were, or where any of them were—except that the breeze off the river made clear their proximity to freedom.

"Leave them be," put in another voice, which Liza recognized as that of their driver.

"You leave us be, nigger-stealer," said the first man, holding up a pistol—Liza saw this by raising herself up off the wagon bed and holding on to the side railing. The driver sidled away down the embankment, as if to wait for what he believed to be the inevitable to end.

"Keep quiet," said the man with the pistol.

Liza stood up in the wagon bed.

The Cherokee woman stood up next to her, holding a pistol she had apparently kept strapped beneath her baggy clothing.

"I'll make you pay dearly..."

Liza noticed the woman's hand shook violently as she tried to keep control of her weapon.

"No, you won't."

The man with the pistol walked right up to the side of the wagon.

"Now you just hand that pistol to me and my pal and I will climb aboard and show you a little fun before we return you to your rightful owners."

He walked around to the back of the wagon and put a hand on the flatbed as if to raise himself up.

Liza snatched the pistol from her companion, took a deep breath and held it, and shot the man between the eyes.

The other man turned and ran.

"You killed him," the Cherokee woman said.

"I've done it once before."

"You have?"

"Yes, but it doesn't make it any easier," Liza said, "except I know that I can do it. He was going to have his way with us, and then sell us. What should I have done?"

Another man came running—but it was their driver.

"Get back down," he said, motioning toward the flat bed as he jumped into the seat behind the horses. "People heard that shot, they'll be coming." He turned and looked back at Liza and smiled. "Or running the other way." He clucked at the animals, and the wagon began to roll, traveling only about a quarter of a mile along the river before stopping at a small sailboat tied at a dock.

A short man with a white beard waved them aboard.

"Hurry, ladies!" he called to them.

"Goodbye, ladies," said the wagon driver, rolling away down the pier before they had even boarded the boat.

So that was how on a late afternoon that promised cold rain they crossed the rushing though meandering Mississippi, hidden on this short segment of their journey beneath a load of grain in the boat of a friendly anti-slaver. (Oh, my mother, carrying me as seed and then as burgeoning innocent fetus all these many months! Oh, mother, hiding me among grain!) The rain seeped from the sky and soaked everything under its rule, making the great broad water road of tangled currents even wetter than it already was. Her stomach heaved along with the surge of the river. If she had not been burdened by having shot the nasty man on the embankment she might have reveled in this crossing over water, because she knew it would not be the end of things, but rather a beginning. She was dreaming of this when the boatman shouted, and the Cherokee woman grabbed her hand. Liza turned to see a large shadow filled with lights churning alongside them in the near-dark.

The steamboat rushed past.

"Hold on, ladies," the boat man said, and a few moments later the wake knocked their small boat sidewise.

Ladies! Lady! I am a lady! Liza exulted to herself.

And then she threw up.

A few minutes later my mother peered out into the misty depths of Arkansas darkness. The soles of her feet touched free soil. Why go on?

The young Cherokee woman put that question to her.

"Doesn't everybody talk about an ocean to the far west of us?"

"Yes," the half-Indian woman said.

"That's why I'll keep going. To see that ocean."

The woman gave her an odd look.

"That river we just crossed ain't good enough for you?"

Liza shook her head.

"Somehow that fresh water doesn't call to me."

"And the ocean does? Why?"

"It must be the salt sea water," Liza said.

"I never seen it," the Cherokee woman said.

"Come with me and you will. The other big ocean is behind us. We can't go back."

"No, we can't," the Cherokee woman said in such a quiet way that Liza considered that she might be thinking about all this.

Liza started counting on her fingers. One, two, three…

"I have about seven more months," she said.

"Before the baby comes?"

"That's right."

"Seven moons is a long time, but it's supposed to be a big country out there," the Cherokee woman said.

"Seven moons to reach the ocean," Liza said, as though thinking out loud. "We can do it!" Death lay behind her, ahead of her all life!

Still, time was running out. In wet weather and dry, with sun, cold, wind, wind and fire, smoke and rain, it took them four months, sometimes riding, sometimes walking, to cross the plains, until eventually those majestic western mountains that seemed to rise higher and higher each day both beckoned and barred their way. One night under a sky stippled with stars she and her companion lay together in each other's arms (as was their way to keep warm) and talked about what might lay ahead for them.

"I've heard about the city," Liza said. "It sits on hills, surrounded on three sides by water."

"I want no city," the Cherokee woman said. "I want woods and streams, with here and there a clearing where I can farm."

"African people, Indians, everyone is free there," Liza said.

"You say you heard this," her companion said. "Where? In a dream?"

"I hear people talk," Liza said. "I've always listened."

A breeze blew across them and they clung all the more tightly to each other. Warmth of desire trickled through their bodies. It had happened a few times before.

"We are kind of free here," Liza said, kissing the woman on the ear.

"Free, yes, but you killed that man back in Memphis. His ghost may be following us. So you got to keep on going west as far as you can go."

"You know it's worse than that," Liza said, thinking of the dead patrollers on the dark road near The Oaks as she touched her lips to her friend's smooth cheek.

As if she could read her mind, the Cherokee woman said, "You mustn't think about those things, they can hurt the growing child."

"It's not a child yet," Liza said. "But I hope it will become one." She drew back her hand and turned slightly, so that she could touch her belly.

"It will," said the Cherokee woman. "Before you know it, it will be here."

That same desiring warmth spread out through Liza's belly and up into her chest. It was more than just wanting to love her friend this time, it was a desire for hope, too, and in its own way an unspoken prayer for the success of her journey. More than ever, so close to freedom beyond anything she had ever imagined, she wanted the small things to fall into place and make the large things possible.

"What should we do?" her companion said.

"Keep traveling," Liza said.

"What about staying here? We could build a clay-house. We could live off the buffalo."

"West," Liza said.

"I just don't know if I can go all the way," her companion said.

"I want you to—" Liza stopped in mid-speech and drew back from her friend. The other woman sat up, listening to the same thing that had distracted Liza.

A great thundering noise rumbled across the prairie. Up they stood and listened to it again.

"A storm?" Liza said.

"Could be buffalo, I have heard of them traveling and making great sounds."

Again the noise, like brakes of wagons magnified, shrieking in a hurry to stop. Or cart-drivers shrieking at their animals to start again. But it turned out to be worse than stampeding buffalo. The two women followed the echoing noise and within a few minutes stumbled into an encampment of Christ bellowers, where folks shouted their faith to the heavens.

"Jesus, Lord, I am so lonely!" the preacher called out around a blazing fire, and the dozens gathered around him shouted that same call up to the stars towards which the sparks whirled up on the wind, but fell back, falling short of heaven.

"Jesus, Lord, I am so thirsty!"

"Jesus, Lord, I am so hungry!"

"Jesus, Come down, Lord, and take me in Your arms!"

"So these are Christians?" Liza said. "I have never seen so many of them all together at prayer. They make a louder noise than the Jews, but their music is bland. The Jews are closer to the Africans, I think. I like that. They kept me as a slave, but I like the sound of them."

Even as they chanted and shouted, these Christian folk stared at the two women, the only dark faces in the crowd. One man in particular, a dried-out string-bean of a devout whose skull seemed to be trying to break through the skin on his head and face, could not take his eyes off Liza. Remembering her father all to well, she knew the look. However this man appeared to be somewhat crippled. He had suffered a terrible back injury in an attempt to cross the mountains a few years before, he told her later over a bucket of stew (and lost his wife to the cold and snow as well).

Once he spoke to her, in his own oddly grotesque way, he reminded my mother of the Charleston doctor who had given her so much help in life, and she took on the job of caring for him (in exchange, of course, for a place in his wagon).

It did not take long before the Cherokee woman began to resent this.

"That old man," she said, around the devotional fire one night, "he is coming between us."

"He's giving us a place in his wagon," Liza said.

"I don't want a place in his wagon. I want to stay here. Someday I hope to go back East and live with my people."

"I understand that," Liza said. "But I can't go back." Liza pressed the woman close and whispered to her, "I need a way west. He has the wagon."

"Use him, use me," the woman said. "You will do anything, won't you?"

Liza took a deep breath and took in the woman's words.

"Yes," she said.

The woman said nothing and turned to walk away.

"I'll miss you," Liza said.

"I'll miss you, too," the woman said.

"But one thing I will miss more?"

"What's that?"

"The life I would have led if I stopped here and turned around and headed back toward the big river."

Without a word, her once-companion walked away. It was the middle of a brightly sun-filled prairie afternoon and yet Liza could have sworn she saw a storm cloud following her friend directly above her head and she heard rumbling again, whether the storm or the ramblings of buffalo or more Christians gathered to testify to their faith, deep deep rumbling across the plain.

In dozens of wagons, the pilgrims traveled the southern route, preferring a desert crossing and less foreboding mountains to the tall peaks that stood directly to the west. In the next few weeks together the old man proved much less of a good companion. He wanted to talk about Jesus while Liza wanted only to reach the ocean where she might live freely, without ties to anyone or anything that could enslave her to one way of thinking or one way to live. The two ways of thinking seemed opposite and troubling to her. But her good samaritan had arrived at the end of his life whereas she hoped she stood on the verge of beginning again. That hope did not keep her from sinking now and then into deep despair. The further west they traveled the more difficult the old man found breathing. She sympathized with him. Up in the mountains, however more forgiving they were than the high peaks to the north, her own breath came hard and this happened to be the only time she wanted to stay put or turn back. The sky was beautiful up here, as blue-white as the underside of Carolina beach shells. Yet every breath she took seemed to catch in her chest. The burden she carried proved almost too much. She thought only of herself and her child-to-be, of the ocean she hoped to see before too long.

The animals lowed and moaned. Time unrolled to the pace of a turning wheel. A million years ago she had started out in the dank dark swamp. Back in a time before that the river rushed beneath the flat bottom of the boat she crossed on. Before that the Christians, her old man among them, bellowed on the prairie, waking the stars with their testaments of faith. She breathed hard, and time moved forward, she breathed again and time moved back, again, and time flowed out to all the horizons and time rushed like a gusher toward those recently awakened stars. At what seemed like the highest point of the high prairie over which they plodded they came to a crest from which you could look down and see, miles below, a thin strand of river. An unfamiliar voice came into her head and told her in a plain, straightforward way, that if she jumped she would sail down to meet her mother, and mother's mother, and all the mothers before her, and she would stay at peace and in serenity for all the time to come. Hawks swooped below her where she stood. Whose voice was that?

"No, no, no, no, no!"

She leaned a little closer to the edge and her gaze sank down a mile to where her very own goddess Yemaya stood breast-deep in the rushing river. It shocked her to meet the goddess so far from her home grounds.

"Shango speak to you," Yemaya said. "Don't listen. Everything I did, even saving the life of your monster father, I did so you can live near the other ocean. Don't stop now! It is always better to be born, no matter how it happens, than never to come to life! And you don't know, the child you are carrying may be the one to save everyone and everything! Back away! All of us carry such regrets, woman," the voice—almost now completely her own—said to her, "all of us. Slave or free, none of us is truly free, not in this world. And there is no next! Run! Come! Go!"

The goddess raised a hand as she raised her voice, and as if she were standing next to her Liza fell back, then fell to her knees and said to Yemaya and to the hawks floating below the edge of the cliff and to anyone else who might be listening, "My ancestors walked away from a volcano, they settled in a red city only to flee from beasts who wanted to sell their bodies, they traveled west on a river, and, captured again, sailed west on an ocean in, oh, how difficult a passage! I will keep going."

Some nights later—or was it months or was it years?—as chastely she and the old man lay together under the desert moon east of the California border, she heard him give out a loud expiration after which came silence.

First, she had to dig a grave. And when she had done this—a shallow declivity was all she could produce even with great struggle—and said a few words ("Old man, I offer you my thanks for a place in your wagon and wish you speedy transport to your heaven!") she still had a desert to cross, the dry land once a sea-bed, a hazy burning sun above! The wagon animals died next. She abandoned these bloated oxen, their tongues stiff in their mouths, and the wagon and most of her belongings, a monument to all she had done to travel this far. She proceeded first on foot and then—arriving in a small town on the edge of the desert and, with money she had taken from the dead old man's pocket, buying a horse—on horseback, north and west to San Francisco, the city she had heard described all along her way as the great and beautiful metropolis on the bay.

She sold the horse to a passing Mexican, striding up a hill, drinking in the fog. From the top of the hill—water three-quarters all around—islands—a bay—the seemingly placid ocean to the west bleeding into the low horizon. A pastel city! Half in sun, half in fast-moving fog, water and sky beyond nearly every rooftop, this dream-like metropolis caught the light and turned her around and around in joy, that she had finally reached a place where she might live as herself.

Chapter Eighty-seven

Eliza Stone (& Son)

*L*ess than a week after arriving in the city, finding a place to stay—a loft over a barn behind a large stone house on Washington Street—finding work (menial labor, to start, sweeping up in a bakery at the foot of the long hill she lived on), she went into labor. She took up the work again soon after I was born, while I slept in an ancient cradle given to her by the baker, a cradle she placed next to the ovens, and so made me a warm cache in the cool foggy San Francisco mornings in which my life began. The baker, who had come by ship all the way from New York City to pan for gold in the Sierras and found enough of the elusive metal to buy himself an oven and a storefront, fell in love with her the first time she entered the store to buy a breakfast bun for herself and me. He spoke to her—his way of making affectionate praise—of the dark (meaning African) origins of half the Italians on the lower part of the boot of his country, he recited to her parts of the *Aeneid*, a poem he had nearly memorized on his voyage from Naples to New York, and then refreshed his memory of on his voyage from New York around the Horn to San Francisco.

When he told her how worried he was about her, a mother trying to raise a newborn on her own in a city as cool and windy as San Francisco, she, while sweeping, sweeping, and washing the baking pans and helping him knead and roll the dough, told him her story in bits and pieces, saying at one point, "I was born a slave. Do you know what that means? Every day I wake up and breathe air as a free woman it remains a triumph for me!"

"It's a *triumph*? Where you learn to talk that way?"

Liza laughed at him.

"Because I was born a slave does that make me forever chained and ignorant?"

"No, no, no," he said. "I like you story. You come all the way here, you mother from Africa, you come from all the way across America, a big journey, it's like the Aeneas himself make. It's a epic, á la America!"

At the end of the work day, he took to walking her up the hill toward home, carrying me, still a rather small bundle, in his arms. People on the street often stared. At that time, with so few Africans living in the city, she was an oddity, a mahogany face among the many white folk and Chinese. She felt alone, until I arrived, but she had felt alone before. Even the worst of the things she had to do, the worst of the men she had met in her life, they were nothing compared to the great forces of mother nature, her mountains and rivers and deserts! And yet—and yet, she had to say, without these men her life would have been less than something. Our beloved ancestors, even her despicable father, the when all is said and done rather naïve but decent Nate, my father, the men she met along the way, why, all of them became stepping stones on her journey here. Even the half-Cherokee woman, of whom she thought wistfully now and then, she, too, served as yet another stepping stone. As far as what she had to do in order to reach this place, what's some degradation and humiliation compared to long years of being enslaved?

As it happened, a few months after I was born, Eliza Stone—which was the name she took when she first arrived in the city—found that at last she had put the worst behind her. Time speeded up, unusual when you have an infant to raise, but nonetheless that was what happened. The baker bought her books, he bought her newspapers, he bought me toys carved from dark wood. Eliza could tell what was coming. And on a foggy morning in winter, while the oven warmed the inside of the shop, her worst fears came true.

"Eliza," the baker said, "put down your broom."

Gently, he took the broom from her and set it upright against the counter.

"We have known each other only a short while," he said.

"Yes," she said, gazing out at the fog rolling past the bakery window.

"Yet I feel I know you."

"You have been generous to me. And I am grateful to you," Eliza said. She removed her apron and laid it on the counter.

"What are you doing?" the baker said.

"I am going," Eliza said.

"Where are you going?"

Eliza felt as though she had been sleep-walking—this was one of a thousand topics she had read about in recent months—and suddenly had awakened.

"To take my son for a walk."

"Please, please, he is sleeping in the back. We must talk, you and I, please."

She ignored him and stepped into the back room where I lay drowsing on a pallet.

"Come along," she said, and swept me into her arms and carried me up the hill into the fast-moving wall of fog. The baker followed us half-way up the hill, and then, apparently, his heart could not take it, and he slowed down, and she soon left him behind.

Marriage? No, no, no, she wanted none of that, seeing it as just another form of imprisonment. Still, she looked at me and saw traces of my father's face, and thought to herself that someday, perhaps when I had grown a lot more, we might make a trip East and look up the man who had helped her win her freedom. (In the time they had spent together she thought only of keeping her plan together, feigning whatever emotions she needed to create in order to make that plan work. Poor Nate, she had fooled him, although there had been moments, especially after she had discovered that she was carrying me, that she had come close to believing in her feigned feelings as true.)

Time blew on, like that fog. My mother sold the silver candlesticks. Just before the money from that transaction was about to run out she found a job cleaning house for a tall, pleasant woman who thought of her as a self-educated free soul from somewhere in the East with whom she often discussed, over tea, the questions of the day such as, for example, women's suffrage. Her employer believed that if it came to war between the North and the South, one of the results of a Northern victory would be universal emancipation and the delivery of the right to vote for all former slaves. Liza agreed, adding that perhaps the North might punish the South by taking the vote away from all slaveholders.

"Interesting," the other woman said. "Interesting."

They continued that discussion for quite a while, taking time off to

discuss the relation of darker-skinned people to whites—an oddity, as I may
have mentioned, in San Francisco, but not in the South and the Northeast—
and of Europeans to Africans (about which my mother had read).

They talked about politics, yes, and literature—her employer was reading *David Copperfield* at one point, and Liza was reading *Narrative of the
Life of Frederick Douglass* and *Songs of Innocence and Songs of Experience*. It
was interesting, especially when they were discussing literature, that her
employer stared at Liza in an odd but familiar way, as if she remained in
constant astonishment that a black women could recite poetry.

Especially the poetry of William Blake, of whom she had not heard until
she heard Liza recite.

"'My mother bore in the southern wild, / And I am black, but oh my
soul is white!'"

Liza's employer asked her about the south and Liza told her some stories
out of her life and the lives of her ancestors, as much as she could remember
of what she had heard, which turned out to be quite a lot.

One morning, some months into my second year (while I lay in the
care of a neighbor's daughter), the woman informed my mother that a
new private school near her home on the upslope of California Street was
hiring teachers.

"You would make a good teacher," the woman said.

"Do you truly think so?" Eliza felt tears pull up in her eyes. "I am not
at all trained. Though I had a good teacher when I was younger, a doctor,
Harvard-educated."

"Here in California we are a bit freer than in the East," the woman said.
"I see how you raise your son, I have enjoyed our discussions. I think you
will make a fine teacher of the young."

"If you think so, thank you," Liza said. "But what shall I wear? I know
I dress like a…Southern gypsy. Can I go this way?"

"I have things I can let you wear," the woman said. Later from her
closet, she pulled some blouses and skirts, and a jacket for two for a horse-
woman to wear while riding in the park.

Dressed in this fashion, Eliza went for her interview. Her fusion of
intelligence, determination, and poise won her a post there. Her classrooms
were lively, and because of her wit and passion on the subject of geography
and literature and history her students adored her. Her industry and accom-
plishments in the classroom won her an award.

Picture her on that evening.

Eliza Stone—this mahogany-skinned angel who appeared ever younger than when she had first escaped the plantation and struggled to make her way westward. And even more beautiful. Those of us born free can never know it, how finding your freedom can light a lamp in your soul and allow it to illuminate your life! At the very least this made for her stunning physical presence. In the audience that night was one of the patrons of the school, an older gentleman who had survived the last Fremont expedition and made his fortune in construction around the Bay. His young wife had died in childbirth, as had the infant, and ever since he had dedicated himself to helping students around the Bay. The light he spied in Eliza nearly blinded his soul.

This led to one of my earliest memories, which consists of blue sky, warm surf breaking across the sand at Ocean Beach, and women in bright cloth skirts swaying with hands held aloft and guitars and (what I later learned were) ukuleles accompanying the movements of their loosely jointed hips—my mother's ocean-side wedding to this tall man with streaming gray hair—much older than Eliza, he seemed already to be worn by sun and battered by wind—who paid for my schooling right up until the time I graduated from Cal.

While a preacher intoned words into the offshore winds I crawled on the sand amidst the brown legs of the swaying dancers, searching for shells and star-fish, my future as far away from me and yet as inevitable as one of the distant waves at the horizon.

To Eliza the beach meant something more than a place to play or marry and celebrate. That broad reach of sand called her back to her own mother's stories about the shores of home, the last glimpse she had of it before descending into the bowels of the slave ship—a few palms, birds skirring across the pearl-white sky, the long stretch of sand. Even in the midst of great celebration she picked at the mental scars of the awful passage over water, the loss of all things that had once belonged to her heart and soul. She could not let these memories go.

Not only did Eliza win awards *and* the love of her first husband. She accrued other honors and won other hearts. For a number of years she spoke regularly to the parents of her students, and then to groups of parents whose children she did not teach but who attended her school. Her reputation as a speaker spread through the educated class of the city, and this led to an invitation to speak at an impromptu evening that some recent immigrant from the East had put together in the hope of initiating the San Francisco equivalent of his beloved Chautauqua. Many people had recommended Eliza to him, and when she stood up before the assembly of some hundred interested folks, men and women, he understood why.

Her subject was freedom and love, things that many people, caught up as they might be in family strife and work life and the getting and spending that the poet speaks of, lost sight of and failed to grasp what these things meant in their lives, if they ever pictured them at all at the start.

"I was born a slave—" that was her usual way of beginning her talks, which, after this initial event, proliferated around the Bay for many a year— "someone owned me. How many of you were born free? How many of you claim never to have had masters?"

She had read Jean-Jacques Rousseau, she had read Emerson, she had read Homer and the Bible, the Old and New Testaments, and the Qur'an, and of our native writers she had read Hawthorne, Emerson, Walt Whitman, and the South Sea novels of Herman Melville, to whom I hope to refer briefly anon. From all these pages and stories and poems and ideas and images she made her own story come clear:

"Without love you cannot be free, without freedom you cannot love."

Her theme echoed through the minds of many hundreds, perhaps even thousands of Bay area folk who had listened.

She linked it to a second theme, something of which she also spoke a great deal.

"What do I believe? In gods and goddesses, in rivers that speak and birds that tell stories? Is that all in my own mind, projected by me, a human magic lantern, onto a blank wall? Or do I believe in inventions and inventors? Do I worship the power of the human mind over all else? Or do I believe in some power beyond it that has shaped and formed us? I was raised by Africans, enslaved by Jews, hunted by Christians—I know something of the world besides what exists in books, and everything I have lived through confirms for me the truth of what the best writers write.

"Without love you cannot be free, without freedom you cannot love..."

People kept flocking to her talks.

One day, after speaking to a large crowd at a theater in downtown San Francisco, a young woman came up to her just as she was leaving the stage and knelt before her.

"What are you doing?" Eliza said.

"Bless me," the young woman said.

Seeing her there on her knees before Eliza several other people from the audience came up and knelt as well.

"Stop this!" Eliza, terribly upset, raised her voice.

"Please," the young woman said, her eyes filled with tears. "I am a slave and I long to be free…"

"I as well," said one of the other devotees.

Eliza left them kneeling there and fled from the hall, never to give another talk again.

Years passed, like one long day of fog and sun. Now if you know our city, you know how often you can find yourself climbing a hill, and another, and another beyond it. Picture Eliza tugging me along as she goes, the toddling boy, along with her, up and up, until I could eventually hold my head up high and walk along with her, she with her cape and parasol, me (when still that young) in my buckskin knickers (because my heroic aspiration at that early age was to become a buffalo soldier, a goal I still remember clearly, though these days it brings a smile to my face).

And then came the years of braving sailing expeditions on the Bay with her husband, the man whom I came to see as my father, when she worked hard to give no sign of, as she later confessed to me, her deep aversion to the surge of tides and beat and splash of waves. Passage over water infused her with a certain dread, something she had first noticed when hidden in that boat that carried her across the Mississippi what was now some years ago. It called to mind the Atlantic crossing her mother's mother made, and her mind near drowned when weighed down by the memories and thoughts of the myriad Africans, her closest relatives and total strangers, who had come that way before. She loved to watch the ocean, but to sail?

Her dread arose on Sunday morning when her husband took her for what he called an easy sail along the north shore of the bay. At first she agreed with him about the easy part, steering out of the busy harbor around the oceangoing ships flying flags from around the world, and then skimming past the wooded islands, looking toward the gentle mountain that rose to the west, between them and the great ocean, this did soothe her, she had to admit. Her worries and nightmares of murderous passages over water flew away on the salty wind. Only when they tacked across the outgoing tide at the gateway to the ocean did her fears tighten her chest and send lightning down her limbs.

"Turn around!" she called over the wind.

"My dear," he said, turning to her as he held the wheel steady.

A pair of birds rushed past in desperate flight. Eliza heard a splash and caught a glimpse of a fish tail, and a sleek long snout and a fish tail again.

Yemaya? She wondered, could the goddess of fabled times be following them? She hoped she would keep them safe!

Her heart surged.

"So beautiful!" she called back to him.

"Dolphins rising!" her husband said. "Come, we'll follow them."

"No, no, not to the ocean, no!"

He shook his head as if at a confused child.

"You are afraid, you, and I thought you, afraid? Never…"

"Turn back," she said, reaching for his arm.

Reluctantly, he turned them around, and they sailed past rocky cliffs until again the city came into view.

"I am not afraid," she said, "it is just…the tides…"

"My dear, I know the tides," her husband said.

Still, she could not repress the dread. It became confirmed for her one Sunday about a year later when, off alone on his sailboat, tacking across the Bay through the ocean tides, a surge came up and dumped her husband and dear benefactor into the waters from which he did not emerge alive.

Several years went by after his death, and then Eliza remarried, this time to a journalist who wrote editorials for the daily newspaper. A rather rotund man with a black, dagger-like goatee who enjoyed dispensing jokey wisdom to anyone in his company, he seemed an odd choice for Eliza to have made. She stood several inches taller than him although they were a bit more equal in age than she and her first husband. And unlike the first, who enjoyed (to a fault, as it turned out) the pleasures of the Bay, this fellow enjoyed the train and the horse and wagon, and took my mother, and sometimes included me, on trips around the state, down to Los Angeles, and over to visit the redwoods and into the great woods to the east. I enjoyed his company, but what passed between us did not resonate as paternal.

Chapter Eighty-eight

Eliza Stone (& Son) (cont.)

*M*eanwhile, at a great distance to the east, the drums of war beat for years and years—and a death on the battlefield, which my mother would never know about, touched my life, though I myself would not learn about it for years and years. Of course, she now and then read a news dispatch in one local newspaper or another. The Union marched into the South and battled the army of the slaveholders, which now and then gave back as good as it got, but eventually, as she saw it, got precisely what it deserved. Even at this distance she could imagine, if she let herself, blue-coated soldiers rampaging across the landscape of plantation and swamp. The violence of war made her feel somewhat uneasy, however justified this war might seem to her. She had put great distance, both physical and temporal, between herself and the South where she had spent her first two decades of life. But now and then, long after the war had ended, she circled back and down in her thoughts to those plantation days and the angry tortures, physical and mental, of her enslavement. Even as I grew older she constantly revisited in memory those to me quite ancient days and suffered again the agonies of a life without liberty.

"I am sorry to say I am not as free as I had hoped," she told me once while we were out for a walk across the top of Russian Hill—I tried to see her as often as I could even when I was attending school on the other side of the bay, because by this time she had lost yet another husband—that editorial writer—in this case to the fault in his heart which gave out, oh, mix of love and death! while they were locked in a marital embrace— "not with the way my mind keeps going back to old days of torture and menace even in just the everyday life I tried to live. *You* are a free soul," she reminded me as we looked out at blue-white sky and the white-tufted waters of the bay, "you are free to make your life or wreck it on the rocks. The country fought a war"—ah, that war, that murderous war!—"so you could be this way. Whatever you do you are free to do it. Choose wisely, good son, choose wisely."

The next time she made almost the exact same speech to me we were sipping tea and looking out over the bay from her vantage point of our house on Macondray Lane, the house left to her by her dutiful and adoring late second husband, her newspaper man.

Some parents lose interest when their children grow older, others become more and more attentive to them and seek their company. My mother was the latter sort of mother. The older I got, the more she talked to me of her life, and what she found within it.

"Some nights when I can't sleep," she told me, "I sit here, watching the lights of ships in the bay, thinking back to the passage of my people from Africa to South Carolina, that awful journey, and nothing it seems can take me off that mark, that black place in memory. Then, as some kind of miracle, Ish, I recall Nate's face, and how in his eyes I saw the possibility of freedom. That is the gift he gave me, that young man from New York City. I wish only that I had not had to leave him behind…" (Ay, the further in time she left him behind, the more affection she believed she felt for him!) Here, she made a huge sigh, and in that expiration of breath and sound only much later could I fill in the details of desperation and love and aspiration and fear, among other emotions, that had driven her to this point in her life, where she could sit and ponder the past which had nearly destroyed her. I did not know my father, and in a visceral way, never would, so I could only listen and wonder as she continued to speak.

"I have done many things in my life that a reasonable feeling person might easily regret. Whatever I did, I did to make my freedom. I know it must seem that I have had to be a terribly hard person in order to survive. And that is true, for the most part. From anything that seemed as though it might deter me from my plan I kept my distance. But I am not so hard that now and then, as in this moment, or I wouldn't be speaking of it, that I don't think of Nate. Poor man. Rich man but poor. He was in love with me. I used him, I admit that freely. I'm sure he went on to make a good life for himself. He had all the advantages…though I do wonder precisely what he made of himself once he returned to his native New York…."

She began to cry, and I sat there, feeling chained to my chair, when after a while she wiped at her tears and gazed out at the water.

"I am sorry, Ish. Do you think I am a bad woman for keeping you from your father?" she said. "Do you think I am evil? Let me tell you, I hope that you never, well, you *could* never find yourself as I did, born into slavery, and so you will never ever understand, and blessedly so, that you would do anything—anything—to become free."

Her tears ran freely again, and it took her a while to calm herself.

She said, "I never think about *my* father, that hateful disgusting man, except that I wanted to tell you about him. I *do* think of Isaac, poor Isaac. Where is he now? Where is he?" Light and cloud passed across the waters of the Bay. She gazed out at this everyday wonder, dreaming with eyes open about who knew what. Then she said:

"Of course I think sometimes about what would have happened if I hadn't left Nate behind. As sick as he was, the dogs would have caught up with us. How the patrollers would have torn me away from him and returned me to the Pereiras. How my father would have...oh! And what Nate might have done! Oh! Yemaya, I know I did the right thing!"

She kept her eyes on the water, as if dreaming while awake. Yemaya! It had been some time since she had uttered the name of the goddess who had given her such good protection in life. *Yemaya,* she vowed, *I am sorry, I will not forget you!*

So I think it was then, when I was at a relatively late age, that the idea of finding my father, the man of whom she spoke with such affection, became something of an obsession for me.

I did not pay much attention when yet another man came into her life, this fellow a successful portrait artist originally from Holland named Jan Argus, who met her at a dinner one night and volunteered to paint her. They became quite close, though they never married, and the first portrait Jan made of her still hangs on the wall of my Manhattan apartment. (But I don't mean to get ahead of myself in recounting this story.) Jan and I became friends of sorts. He loved to hear about my interests and my studies—by that time I was attending Cal and taking courses in everything under the sun that could teach you about life on earth, early and late.

"Do your studies in the work of Darwin show you how to make sense of our story?"

"Our story?"

"The story of the world."

"We are only just beginning to talk about it," I said. "The clergymen are not happy about it."

"No, no," said Argus, "they would not be, would they? But if their god cannot withstand the discovery of some millions of years of life, why, then what kind of a god is it anyway in whom they believe? I ask you."

"And I tell you, not a very powerful god at all."

Such were the conversations one could have back then, between the end of the Civil War and the beginning of where we are now, when I was first trying to make sense of what he called "our story." Argus and I would walk and talk, and now and then he would invite me to his studio in a former barn that he rented for scarcely anything from one of his wealthy Nob Hill patrons. There I met on several occasions an astonishingly beautiful Island girl who was posing for him with or without various Hawaiian garments, a girl whom I first knew as "Holly," before we married and she introduced me to the proper pronunciation of island things.

Yes, that is how much time went by. I evolved from infant to baby to boy to young man before that morning when Eliza awoke late and as she was moving from the bed to the bath happened to step past a mirror in the master bedroom of our house and then stepped back. Something in her image caught her eye. Her rich brown face that Jan Argus had captured so beautifully in his portrait had turned suddenly ashy and she appeared to herself as a different woman.

Quickly she removed her clothes and noticed that the ashy patina covered her breasts and belly, too, as well as the tops of her thighs. She turned to see her back over her shoulder but the light would not allow her to see herself clearly from behind. She kept this view to herself and never mentioned it to Jan.

More time passed, months, years, and in bits and pieces and sometimes in longer stories she told me over many cups of tea on many afternoons, Eliza delivered to me the history of her family, and her own life, such as it had been before arriving in the Promised Land of California. I think she missed her students, and I also believe, though she never would admit to it, she missed the audiences which had once filled every seat in large theaters who had come to hear her talk.

Was this a dream or was it real? That was how Eliza put this next story into a frame.

Of a Sunday morning in August, she and Argus had been out walking on the far western edge of the city, where the cliffs overlooked the churning ocean, the beautiful, hypnotic, but deadly ocean, and he had stopped to relieve himself along the trail. She kept on walking, focusing on the large veil of fog that cloaked the sky in the direction of the Farallons. It served her as a kind of wall on which she began to project the stereopticon-like images out of her mind where thought met memory, in other words, those things never far from her everyday thoughts. That ocean—it gave her a sound show while she pictured again the ship that carried her grandmother to Carolina. Soon she imagined she heard shouts and the crack of whips and the groans and songs of all the African people, her cousins and kin, who arrived in chains and lived in chains. She heard laughter, of goddesses and gods and human beings, the crunch of thunder, the rush of water flooding the fields, the grunts and snores of men she had known, the touch of the doctor's hand, curative, the grasp of her father's brutal fingers, maniacal, spitting and caressing, kissing, fending off but not too well the inevitable thrusts of his monstrous desires, his falling away of gasp and grunt, striated breathing while she lay scarcely alive, breath turned to noxious gas, body turned to water, heart beating but not caring.

What was freedom if these visions came with it?

A fever-like shudder passed along her chest and limbs.

Did she want to go on like this, every day, every day? For this was it she pulled the trigger of that pistol, for this was it she killed not once but twice?

She walked directly up to the edge, where nothing but ice-plants and their roots held the cliff solid beneath her feet. The wind whipped about her, carrying sounds cloud and chaos she imagined soared over the Hawaiian Islands roaring all the way from Asia where she longed to go but knew she never would.

Why not?

Because of time.

What is time?

The roots that hold together the cliff on which we stand.

She held out her arms as though they were wings, and stood against the pouring wind, balanced between falling forward and falling back.

Time? Perhaps not the roots but instead the wind, the resounding wind.

She called out that name she had spoken only intermittently in these California days—"Yemaya! Oh, goddess, forgive me my thoughts about your watery abode!"

"Darling?"

Argus, her Dutchman, came up behind her and took her by the shoulders.

"Step back, my soul, so dangerous here!"

She turned and studied his face, looked into his eyes, feeling that chest-surge again, and thinking, *Who is he?* And, *Well, he is good to me.*

Oh, she had lived! So, oh, she would live a bit more!

Chapter Eighty-nine

Eliza Stone & Son (cont.)

*S*he lived long enough to see me graduated with honors from Cal, where in my studies I found new science that fed into a dream of mine that recurred around that time, a dream of our early ancestors that I had wondered about ever since my mother first told me my first stories when I was a child. In my dream an erupting volcano on the horizon of a long plain stirred inhabitants to hurry away from its billowing cloud of fire and smoke and ash. That event took place before the time of human memory, if I believed my mother (supported by some evidence about prehistoric life presented to me by some of my most radical instructors at Cal, who made it their business to try and reconstruct actual events contained within "the adult bed-time story," as one of them put it, we found in the Bible (in which the Mosaic signs from God of a cloud by day and a pillar of fire at night may well be a long-lost memory of that same volcano)). For a while that event took place weekly in my dreams. Perhaps, I had to admit, it had always been a dream of mine and I had only recently begun to wake with it as a memory.

But now something shifted in our family life soon after my commencement, as my mother ended, for whatever reason, her companionship of her Dutch painter—he moved to Los Angeles, and except for a dwindling number of post cards each year we never heard from him again—and she became a woman sure enough of herself to live alone and enjoy the solitude. These things happened, as I soon discovered when my Hawaiian Holly and I recognized that we, too, had to part ways.

Once again Eliza and I took to having many a meal together—at least once a week—during which time I began to make notes in a leather-bound volume out of which would grow my narrative, based on her facts,

about her lineage going all the way back to Timbuktu and even before,
and about her life at The Oaks, a narrative that I hoped would one day
find its way into the hands and then the hearts of whatever children I
might foster myself.

Still, I had my good high hopes for separating truth from legend, and
history from speculation—that was just my inclination both as I had been
as a student and now as a citizen of the world (which is how I saw myself
once I graduated). Long I mulled over these stories—mull, mull, mull, the
whirring of my unsatisfied mind at work—and kept her talking. Was it
possible ever to know what actually happened in my mother's life?

Her stories nourished me. Though now and then I gave back to her,
especially on one of these occasions when I read to her a poem by John
Greenleaf Whittier, which I had found in a small volume that I purchased
from a curious shop across the Bay.

"I hope you will enjoy this, Mother," I said, "what I am now going to
read to you."

"Read it, Son, and we will find out what I think."

"It's as much how you will feel as think about it, Mother," I said.

She gave me a commanding look, arching her eyebrows and leaning
back in her chair.

"Read, then."

I opened the book to the verse that had so boldly caught my best attention.

> WHERE are we going? Where are we going,
> Where are we going, Rubee?
> Lord of peoples, lord of lands,
> Look across these shining sands,
> Through the furnace of the noon,
> Through the white light of the moon.
> Strong the Ghiblee wind is blowing,
> Strange and large the world is growing!
> Speak and tell us where we are going,
> Where are we going, Rubee?

"And that is what?" my mother said. "Show me the book. Ah, it is a song,
as the poet calls it, a song sung by slaves in the desert. And the poet overheard this singing? Ah, a song from the old days. Ishmael, I have to confess,

because we have been talking about those times...even if you hadn't been asking me about them all these past few years, oh, I would have been thinking about them. Yes, I would. Yes, I would...a day does not go by that I do not think of them, those old days. And do you know, I still remember the first poem I ever read. The doctor had me learn it by heart, and it still remains in my heart. Would you like me to recite it for you?"

"I would love to hear it, Mother."

She then spoke it thusly:

> "The world is round, and like a ball
> Seems swinging in the air,
> A sky extends around it all,
> And stars are shining there.
> Water and land upon the face
> Of this round world we see,
> The land is man's safe dwelling place,
> But ships sail on the sea.
> Two mighty continents there are,
> And many islands too,
> And mountains, hills, and valleys there,
> With level plains we view.
> The oceans, like the broad blue sky,
> Extend around the sphere,
> While seas, and lakes, and rivers, lie
> Unfolded, bright, and clear.
> Around the earth on every side
> Where hills and plains are spread,
> The various tribes of men abide
> White, black, and copper red.
> And animals and plants there be
> Of various name and form,
> And in the bosom of the sea
> All sorts of fishes swarm.
> And now geography doth tell,
> Of these full many a story,
> And if you learn your lessons well,
> I'll set them all before you."

When she finished, she had tears in her eyes.

"Have I learned my lessons well? Have I? Have I?"

Eliza had two doctors, a Harvard Medical School graduate who had grown up in the Central Valley (who for her conjured up memories of her Carolina benefactor) and a Chinese herbalist who had come by boat across the Pacific only a few years before she arrived overland from the East. During a long winter and spring she suffered aches and pains but neither of them could find evidence of any serious illness. Then there came a cold afternoon in August (again) with fog and wind passing over us, as summer in our city chilled its citizens to the bone. My mother, ebullient that very same morning, felt suddenly quite exhausted and took to her bed, her vital light fluttering as if the wind from off the bay had pierced the very wall of her room, believing, or so she confessed to me, that the first sign of her decline she had somehow inexplicably detected when she looked at her ashy-tinged image in the mirror on that foggy afternoon long ago. Illness or no illness, even now her bones remained arched and triumphant, holding her face in beauty and agelessness.

Whereas in childhood she spoke to me in a strong high voice, now all of her speech had degraded to a whisper, the wisp of a whisper, in stops and starts, with many many breaths between.

"Remember how this began, with the stone," she said to me, beginning her story again from the beginning, telling me (again) of her mother, and her mother's mother, and her mother's, back to Timbuktu and so on back before then until it took that event, the exploding volcano on the African plain, to send the earliest family in our line of human beings trekking toward another home. I had tried in my studies at Cal to have imagined this event, the three of them, father, mother, and small female child, hand in hand, moving forward as the ash falls on their heads.

A million years ago? A conservative estimate, one of my advanced professors might say. No, no, no, no, much more than that. (But don't tell my pastor I said so, he might say in a joke.) But move forward they did, and so lived long enough for the young girl to find a surviving mate, and the great unfolding chain of children growing into childbearing adults—the old story about Cain leaving Eden to go into exile in the Land of Nod and there finding a mate may be an echo of the earlier eruption that evicted our first parents from their African Eden—proliferates through the ages, a novel event yet one duplicated by millions families by the time recorded history begins.

My mother asked me to find her purse and to extract from it same stone with which she began all of her stories and reveries and ta and recollections.

"You still have it?"

She nodded. *Yes.*

"I have always carried it with me," she said in a whisper.

"The original? Over all those how many hundreds of years? Hundreds? Thousands! How can that be?"

She rolled her eyes toward the ceiling, and the heavens beyond the roof.

"It may have been a thousand years," she said. "Or more. Much more."

I found it and held it in the palm of my hand.

"A miracle," I said.

She shook her head, nearly all breath and thus all words having left her.

"What now?" I said.

She gestured for me to keep it.

She nodded. Her eyes lighted up, as she saw me, and—who could know?—saw the past and the future one atop the other, in a palimpsest of time.

"Thank you, Mother," I said, taking the relic, if it *was* the same one she had told me about, the stone her ancestors had carried and given to her for safekeeping, the stone marked with signs now undecipherable that once made up a story in themselves. Had that child, perhaps, walking steadily across that volcanic plain with her parents, ash rain falling about her head and shoulders, bent for an instant and snatched that object—icon?—from the ground and passed it along, years later, to her children, and these to theirs, until one day an artisan took up a new tool and carved it into a pleasing design?

After taking a moment to study its shape and markings, I touched it to my forehead and pressed hard. It felt cool, and then warm, and then hot, as though it were passing through my skin and skull-bone into my very brain! The longer I sat there with it the pictures of Eliza and all of the words in all of the stories she had told me fell into a certain order, which in that astonishing blooming moment showed me her life and a world in all its turmoil and beauty and striving and hope and misery and worry and woe and chanting and song! Birth, love, death, rebirth! All crackled in me

ning leaping from one storm cloud to another, then like lightning
, from a storm cloud to the earth.

heard a noise outside the window, not seeing lightning but instead
ing a sea-bird gliding past. I looked back down at Eliza.

She had been watching me.

"Ishmael," she said.

"Yes, Mother?"

I kneeled beside her and kissed her on the cheek—her cooling cheek.
I drew back and saw that something fluttered in her eye, like the wing of
some bird or butterfly.

"I am not a bad person, am I?"

"No, no, no, Mother, you are not."

"I have tried to be good. Though I have done terrible things in my life…"

"You have been a fine mother to me, a wonderful mother."

"Considering…"

"Considering? Yes, considering the struggle you had to make, the
struggles. Oh, Ma…"

I kissed her again, and found that her cheek had cooled even more.

Oh, my gods, I said to myself, oh, my gods! *All* of them, because she
had taught me to be lavish with my hopes and prayers and not spend them
all on a single narrow faith.

She spoke then one last time, locking upon me that gaze of hers in
which I saw worlds within worlds within worlds.

"I never thought I would reach this moment. At last, at last, at last…I…
am…a free woman."

Chapter Ninety

A Son Appears

*B*ut I was not yet a free man, and had only a few inklings of what I might become when I saw the sign for the first time. There it was, set into the brick façade of a building on a little lane just off Wall Street, the sign I had been looking for.

PEREIRA AND SONS, IMPORT-EXPORT

I had pictured this sign in my mind ever since I boarded the train in San Francisco and headed east, the sign bearing the name that I had thought about on and off for a number of years.

How many times had I rehearsed my entrance! Touching a hand to my head and a finger to my tie, adjusting my vest, pulling my coat just so (with my other hand in my pocket feeling the smoothness and the striations of that relic of a stone, by all rational standards a legacy seemingly impossible to have been transmitted down along all these centuries, yet here it was, cool and smooth to my touch), I stepped into the office, where I would say to a welcoming receptionist that I had come to see Mr. Nathaniel Pereira.

There was no one to greet me. The large room smelled of tobacco smoke and eastern spices and the chill remnant of a morning in March and the faintest touch of tar. On the walls hung photographs of sailing ships in various harbors, one of which I recognized as our own, another which I believed was Honolulu, and others I could not recognize except for the exotic composition of the smaller boats—junks, canoes, mainly—that surrounded the larger vessels.

My eye came to rest on the photographic portrait just at the end of the row of pictures of ships.

The uniformed man, in middle-age, of medium height, posed, unsmiling, in front of a row of tents which stretched to the horizon.

My chest tightened.

"May I help you?"

The voice struck me also in a physical way, and I turned to the man, a fellow the same height and same face as the officer in the photograph, without the cast of age. But when I tried to speak I merely let out a cough.

"Sir?" the man said. "I am Emmanuel Pereira, may I be of some assistance?"

I took a step toward him, then stopped, trying to catch my breath. I had rehearsed this part also.

"Y-yes," I said, "I am happy to meet you." I paused and took another breath. And another. "I am your brother."

Emmanuel took a moment, inclining his head a tad toward me, taking in my color and my clothes, my long straight hair, the blue-green of my eyes.

"Well, well," he said at last. "I…Father had always hoped…"

"He told you about me?"

"He wrote a recollection of his life. He wrote about…your mother…"

"You use the past tense, sir. That means that he is deceased?"

Emmanuel nodded, slowly, sadly, tilting his body a little to the right.

"Yes, I am afraid that is so. A long while ago. He volunteered at the start of the war, and he died in his very first battle." A flicker of emotion passed across his face. "Our mother is likewise deceased. After a long illness."

Something weighty, like a ship's anchor, seemed to fall within me the entire length of my body.

"And mine as well." I extended him a hand. "And so, my condolences to us all…"

Emmanuel took my hand. "But, well, my…brother!"

"Ishmael," I said, taking his hand. "Ishmael Stone."

We embraced firmly, in manly fashion. My brother smelled of the salt air of the harbor and tar from the planks—clearly he was an import-export sort of fellow, and if he looked nothing like me at first, well, then, I figured, it had to be because I just had not looked long and hard enough at him. (Who knew, what after my transcontinental train trip, what I smelled like!)

"Ishmael," he said when in the next few moments we stood back from each other. "The name is Biblical."

"Yes," I said, the rest of the words tumbling from my lips, "but not what you think. My mother may have been born a slave, but she was from childhood a voracious reader, taught by a caring doctor who attended to the slaves on the plantation where she grew up. On her way west, in the part of her trip that she made by wagon—and how that happened I can tell you one day if you are interested, I can tell you all about her journey, because so much of it was extraordinary, and dangerous, and in many ways miraculous—well, but she found a copy of a book, a novel about whaling—"

"A novel about whaling?"

"Yes, and the narrator, because there is a narrator, one of the sailors on this ship that goes on a truly dangerous voyage, is named Ishmael. 'Call me Ishmael' is how the book opens. I've long since read it myself, of course."

"So, Ishmael," my brother said, "well, I must read that book too."

"It is a fine book," I said. "And a truly momentous American story."

"Reading is not my first interest," my brother said. "Business and family always stand in the way. But I always have hopes for the time for it."

"Good," I said "Good, good."

We began to talk, and he took me home with him that evening and I met the rest of the family, wife, children, step-mother. I could scarcely breathe for the sentiment I felt on meeting them and getting to know them. Whereas growing up in San Francisco where not many with my shade of skin walked the streets and so I felt constantly goggled at and pointed to, here in New York where many descendants of slaves and freemen both resided, I could only draw attention to myself by shouting in the street—which I did not do, of course—or by walking into a family gathering for the first time where someone announced that I was a long-lost brother-in-law or brother or uncle or all of these. They lavished much initial affection on me, and I tried to reciprocate as best I could, only child that I was.

Emmanuel raised a glass to me at dinner that first night.

"To my long-lost half-brother," he said. And then he stopped, took a deep breath, and said, "No, no, no, to my long-lost, and now found, brother!"

With tears in my eyes I reciprocated. And then added:

"To our father."

"To father—grandfather—all..." Family voices in celebration rang through the air.

"And to my mother," I said. "Whom I only wish you might have known."

"To your mother!" Again the voices in tribute rang through the air.

I had lived alone since my mother's death, and traveled alone, but now my singular state was fast disappearing. The next day I met two more long-lost brothers of mine, one of them a physician and the other also a partner in the family business.

They took me in, fed me, clasped my hands, kissed me on the cheeks, gave me a bed. After all of my mother's stories about life on the plantation I felt now that the Pereiras had somehow saved me from regarding family life as a pit of desolation and woe and enslavement and murder. I was, though, only beginning to learn about this side of where I came from, beginning with the end.

On a long walk along the wharves in the deep salt steep of a Sunday afternoon my brother Emmanuel described to me our father's demise.

"In the first wave of battle, apparently, at Bull Run."

I sighed, breathed in, breathed out.

"I am very sorry that I will not be able to meet him."

"I am, too," my brother said.

"The funeral must have been difficult for all," I said.

"Yes, yes."

He described to me the woe spread all around, and the weeping and wailing. And the wake that followed.

"It is, I believe," Emmanuel said, "so much worse for us Jews than for the Gentiles. They believe in an afterlife, whereas we do not." He sighed deeply and touched a hand to my shoulder. "Were you raised as a Jew or a Gentile?"

"Such as I was raised," I said, "I would have to call myself an enlightened pagan, if I am at all enlightened."

"Our father was not all that much for his religion."

"Jews believe in doing good deeds, do they not?"

"They do," my brother said.

"Our father did a great deed indeed," I said, with a wink, "in helping my mother to become free."

"Yes, yes, we have read of it."

"Have you? How?"

He then told me about our father's memoir, a copy of which he handed to me immediately upon our return to the house.

"You are named after a character in a novel," he said. "Perhaps you can tell us if this story is worth preserving beyond the immediate family circle."

I found myself extremely excited to hold my father's narrative in my hands. A large dark continent—my own history—lay before me, ready for me to explore.

After some weeks of staying at Emmanuel's I found my own apartment and went to work for the family enterprise—"as our father would have wanted it," Emmanuel said. By that time I had read the memoir once, and had begun it again, this time adding my own chapters and interpolations based on the stories my mother had told me—half-chanting sometimes, half-singing, always intense and in her heart-deep and serious way of loving the world even in its most awful and difficult moments, moments sometimes that added together to make years, always speaking what she took to be the truth. Free and educated and standing near the beginning of a grand new American century, of course I wanted see myself as part of this family and to make my way in the world. That was when it came to me, what I must do first to find an answer that would ease my curious heart.

The night before I departed, my brother and I—strangers, still, but hoping to know each other in some deeper way some day—took a walk along the piers on the East River, lost in thoughts of our father, and breathing in the stink of salt-fish, and the somehow annealing odor of tar and smoke.

At one point, we stopped under a lamp and he reached into his pocket and handed me a watch.

"This was Father's," he said, "and our grandfather's before that. I would like you to have it."

Even though I resembled a grown man, I wept a small trickle of tears as I took the gift from him, accepting the generosity of his legacy, which he now made mine. And that night as I wound the timepiece I wondered at the wonder in my heart, that so many turns and twists of feet and breath, so many passages of mind and time, so much evil and so much good had to transpire, for two brothers to be standing here in such a tableau as this, with yours truly now possessing both stone and watch.

The heart, old instrument, wonders, yes, and aches, the heart yearns, mourns, cries, but above all else the heart hopes and longs to be free, even as the ground we tread on, so unsteady where I grew up, and perhaps where you live, too, trembles beneath our feet. Oddly enough, a faint tremor rattled Manhattan—oh, the earth everywhere unstable!—the morning I boarded the ship for Africa, my hand in my pocket, stone in my hand as I began my voyage eastward, hoping that I might find the last, or, with luck, perhaps some of the first pieces of the truth of Eliza's life—truth, ah, the truth, ever-changing and yet remaining so steady, at least in the distance, that we follow it the way sailing ships follow certain stars to keep themselves on course in calm seas and stormy.

Acknowledgments

With enormous thanks to Kristin O'Shee, Shana Drehs, and, with deep gratitude, Dominique Raccah. Thanks also to Heather Moore, Nicole Lec, and Elizabeth Gutting.

About the Author

Alan Cheuse is the author of the novels *The Bohemians, The Grandmothers' Club, The Light Possessed*, and the award-winning *To Catch the Lightning*, as well as the nonfiction works *Fall Out of Heaven* and *A Trance After Breakfast*. As a book commentator, Cheuse is a regular contributor to National Public Radio's *All Things Considered*. He lives in Washington, D.C., and teaches in the writing program at George Mason University.